three
secrets

ALSO BY CLARE BOYD

Little Liar

CLARE BOYD

three secrets

bookouture

Published by Bookouture in 2018

An imprint of StoryFire Ltd.

Carmelite House
50 Victoria Embankment
London EC4Y 0DZ

www.bookouture.com

ISBN: 978-1-78681-418-0
eBook ISBN: 978-1-78681-417-3

PROLOGUE

2016

'John's coming over,' Robert said, as I was laying the table for two.

I added a third place.

How I wish I had not laid that table at all.

I sat between Robert and John, facing the tiny window. We were squashed around the three sides of the galley-kitchen table, under the tin-shade low lighting, which threw shadows down Robert's face. Gravestone shapes, the horror to come.

'I'm not ready to show you episode three,' John said.

'Just send it.'

'But it's crap.'

'You always say that, John,' I said.

'And mostly Robert agrees.' John laughed, always insecure, always handsome, with those golden flecks in his grey eyes.

Robert's foot was twitching, up and down, up and down. He was watching his handsome younger brother more than listening to him, unable to feign patience.

I should have worried more about that.

Robert suddenly pushed back his chair and slapped his hands on his knees. 'I'll find a shit-hot young writer to take your place if you're struggling.'

As the owner of Aspect Films, he could do this. I had felt uncomfortable about the power-play between them. They were brothers and they expected loyalty from one another, but sometimes I wondered if they liked each other.

Then Robert said, 'Don't look at me like that! I'm kidding! Write from the heart, John. You can't go wrong.' But the delivery had been irritable.

'What happened to inciting incidents and story arcs and Billy's character flaws?' John shot back.

'You get annoyed with me when I script-edit you.'

'True.' John sat in his thinking pose: elbow on the table, chin propped up by his thumb, fingers wrapped in a crescent moon over his mouth; smothering his words, apologetic about his worries.

'Forget Billy. That series is low-rent. Maybe there's only so much of that crap you can write. Write the love story.'

'You hated that script.'

Robert tapped his fingers in an edgy rhythm. 'You're a brilliant screenwriter. I love everything you write.'

John's lips were parted, his eyes fixed on his brother. The air between them was charged. My heartbeat had begun to speed up. I wished the window was bigger to let in some more air.

'I can't believe you're telling me this now. I was desperate to write that script but you said it would bankrupt Aspect.'

My thighs had clenched. I had never seen John hit Robert, but I feared that he might.

'I think we're all tired,' I said, feeling the strangeness of the evening come down on me. I brought Robert another cup of coffee, as he had let the first go cold.

'If you don't do what you want to do in life because you think it'll fail or because of the bloody mortgage, you're wasting your life. You're wasting the precious time we have alive,' Robert insisted, impassioned, adding, 'There are always options. *Always*. Stop thinking about the comforts. That's why we're all trapped. Don't be trapped, like me,' he said, stabbing his temple. 'Promise me?'

'Do you feel trapped?' John asked. I imagine John plays that question back in his nightmares.

Ignoring his question, Robert continued, 'Forget me and everyone else! You deserve better.'

He grabbed John's forearm and then at the same time kissed me roughly on my cheek, joining us together as an unwitting trio, swiping a tear from his nose. 'I love you guys. And Alice. You're the only three I do really love.'

I thought about Alice sleeping in her bed upstairs under pink fairy lights. I thought about Robert's parents, and how devastated they would be to hear this.

'We love you, too,' John said, cautiously, catching my eye.

'Where does Dilys think you are tonight?' Robert asked John.

John mumbled his reply. 'Research meeting with a nuclear physicist.'

Robert and I both raised our eyebrows at him.

John grinned sheepishly. 'It's plausible, isn't it? Billy needs to use an X-ray gun in episode four.'

'I've never understood why you can't just tell her you're here,' Robert said.

'She'd want to come,' John said simply, as though this explained everything.

'You know you have to leave her, don't you?'

'What?' John reeled.

'Robert?' I quizzed him with a frown, a wifely shot of disapproval. 'John, don't listen to him.'

'I want a fag.' Robert stood, patting his pockets. 'Where's my wallet?'

'Patel's will be closed now,' I reminded him.

'San will let me in.'

He kissed me goodbye.

'Your wallet's in your jacket. Don't be long, will you?' I said.
'No, no!' The front door slammed.

'He might not come back,' I had said to John.

It had been a joke.

Our eye contact had lingered for a couple of seconds too long. We had both known that Robert would stay for a smoke with Sanjeev, that he might get stoned, drink more whisky and wine, stumble back across the road sometime in the early hours. He had done this many times before.

But Robert had not made it back home that night.

He had left Sanjeev's, walked up Whitehall Park and turned left at the top of the hill towards Hornsey Lane bridge, where he had climbed up and over the metal spikes and jumped onto the A1 to his death.

CHAPTER ONE

Francesca

I prepared to move from the sofa, to turn off the television, to unpeel Alice from her spot under my arm, to seek out matching socks and untangle the four-day-old bird's nest in her hair. Robert's mother, Camilla, would expect her grandchild to be well turned out for Easter lunch. Appearances were everything to my mother-in-law. She confessed, once, to wearing red lipstick on the days she felt sad, to cheer herself up.

Today was a red lipstick kind of day. I wondered if it might help me to get through lunch. Last week, I had said I could make it, knowing it was good for Alice to see her grandparents and cousins, knowing she would enjoy the Easter egg hunt on the sprawling lawns of their West Sussex pile.

The whole Tennant clan would be there. Camilla and Patrick, and John and his wife, Dilys, and their three children. Even Uncle Ralph, who was Patrick's eccentric younger brother, would be there. All of them lived within five miles of the same village. They would be full of love; they were claustrophobic.

The remote control was in my hand, poised to turn off the cartoons. It seemed an impossible task. I kissed the top of Alice's head, swamped with love for her, and looked out at the views from the skylight: the empty, pale, shifting hues of sky and the colourless metal geometrics of rooftops. This place on this sofa in this flat was the antidote to that landscape.

The flat had once been a rich colour bomb, high above the city, small but sumptuous and sensual. Every little detail – a bone-china dish for teabags or a patchwork tea-cosy – was like a twig to a nest, carefully chosen, part of building a life with Robert, my husband, who had promised me the world, who had been so full of life. This flat was meant to be the beginning for our little family, not the end. But it seemed I had missed signs, missed secrets, missed something; and he had taken his own life. An unfathomable act, flooring me, leaving me no real understanding of why. His motive preyed on my mind, continually, allowing little else to flourish. I seemed to be searching for a murderer in his head. Some days I guessed at his rationale, blaming myself, flooded with guilt. On other days, I debunked those theories, unsatisfied, back to where I had started.

Trapped in this wretched cycle, I ducked and shuffled through this small space: a dusty relic of my previous life. Tragedy layered the palette of colours that had once represented my joy for life. The flat was stuffy and busy with sadness, as though it knew its own history, as though it hated itself as much as I hated myself. For that very reason, I needed it. This flat and I were co-dependent. The memories and the secrets that it held were a tinder box. If I moved an ornament out of place, I worried the whole building would come crashing down on my head.

I began to type a text:

Hi Camilla – So sorry, I'm not feeling so well

I deleted it. Retyping:

Hi Camilla – So sorry, Alice has come down with a sick bug

Letter by letter, I deleted it, going backwards, retreating.

I brushed Alice's hair while Scooby-Doo continued to entertain her. A knot was stubborn. I knew it was hopeless. It would have to be cut. Without Alice noticing, I found the kitchen scissors and snipped it out. The remaining tuft was obvious, and a little comical. Camilla would sniff at it. She would know I had cut a knot out; she would know I had not been brushing Alice's hair; she would think I was a bad mother, but she would not say a word.

This is why I hoped I would be safe today. The Tennants were good at keeping distasteful truths to themselves. If the worst wasn't said out loud, it didn't need to exist at all. This was how I had learnt to operate with them. Especially when it came to Robert's death. Nobody talked about it. Nobody was to blame. Nobody was accusing anybody. This was one of the few Tennant family traditions that suited me perfectly.

CHAPTER TWO

John

John could hear Dilys shouting his name. He closed the bathroom door, and turned his razor on.

A few minutes into his shave, the door burst open.

'Why the hell didn't you answer me?'

John turned off the razor. 'I didn't hear you,' he said, innocently, waggling his razor at her.

'I know you did, John.'

Everything about Dilys' face was neat and symmetrical: her straight nose and even nostrils, the balance of her almond-shaped blue eyes, her top lip that mirrored her bottom lip, her centrally parted blonde hair. But when she was angry, the pool under her eyes turned purple and uneven, her lips puckered and her under-jaw pushed out at him.

'Honestly, I didn't hear,' he insisted. He wiped his face on the towel to hide his lie. Dilys' scrutiny was penetrating.

'Don't give me that crap. I was only next door.'

'What did you need me for?'

'I can't find the bracelet your mum gave me!' she cried.

'Don't worry about it.'

'If I lost it she'd never talk to me again!'

'Mum won't notice.'

'She always notices everything.'

'Have you looked in your jewellery box?'

'Oh, yeah, I never thought of that,' Dilys retorted sarcastically, throwing her arms in the air and charging out.

As he dressed, into a smart shirt – his mother *always* noticed *everything* – and jeans, he could hear Dilys storming around, yelling at the children, throwing accusations, throwing actual things, slamming doors and shouting hysterically about the bracelet.

John had a feeling that he was lying in wait in a bunker, hoping the hurricane outside would pass, but also knowing that the door to the bedroom wasn't strong enough to keep it out.

He chose his socks and sat on the bed to put them on.

The door flew open. 'Thanks for all your help, John,' Dilys shrieked, although there were now tears in her increasingly high-pitched rage, and he felt bad, but he didn't know how to help her when she was like this. His brain went into shutdown mode.

'I don't know where it is.'

'I left it on my dressing table last night. Can you please think about whether or not you've moved it?'

'Why would I touch it, Dilys?' John bent down to put on his sock. 'It doesn't work with any of my outfits.'

His joke went down badly.

'CHRIST! I'm going to go mad! Can't you see this is important to me?' Her voice strained, desperate.

He knew it was important, but he didn't know what to suggest. He didn't have any space in his head left. A lost bracelet was the least of his problems. If he spoke, he might blow up. He bent down to put the other sock on. Then he felt a slap to the back of his head.

'Thanks for nothing, you idiot!' she screamed, and stormed out.

He rubbed his head, where her hand had hit, where other scars lay, where his shame burned.

From deep within him, he called on his strength, battling away his fear, knowing only too well how her mood could escalate. He decided to engage with her plight for the bracelet, as he probably should have done originally. She couldn't help her anger. It wasn't her fault. Not really.

Clocking through the various scenarios when he had seen her take it off, he thought of places it might be.

He pulled out her gym bag from the bottom of the wardrobe, where he had tided it away, and looked in the side pocket, immediately locating it. He took a second to admire the tiny sapphire in the delicate silver. His mother had given it to Dilys on her fortieth birthday.

He found Dilys in the kitchen. The contents of the recycling bin were strewn around her feet as she picked each discarded item out.

'Here you go.' John handed her the bracelet.

She dropped the cereal box back into the bin and took the bracelet. It hung limply in her fingers, as though the reality of it disappointed her.

'Where was it?'

'In your gym bag.'

'Oh,' she said. 'Well, I don't mean to be funny, but if you'd tidied the cupboards better, I would've been able to find it myself.'

She looked up at him with her blue eyes, as blue as the stone in the bracelet. They had a depthless quality to them; their colour was a pretty watercolour wash rather than windows to her soul.

'I'm always tidying it,' he insisted, reminding himself of the many times he had been on his knees pairing her expensive shoes to make room for his battered old trainers.

She smiled at him. 'Really?'

He clamped his jaws together, galled. Was it worth arguing with her about who tidied the most? Would it be petty to keep a logbook, charting the number of times he tidied bedrooms and cleared out the cupboards in their house? Was it worth it? He was sure he had better things to do; certain he had more important issues to worry about today. Could he rise above it, be the bigger person, drop it?

For an easier life, yes. To stay safe, yes. To shelter the children, absolutely.

'I'll have a clear out, maybe,' he said, begrudgingly accepting that they had accumulated a lot of junk they could probably do without.

'Your mum's going to go mental when you tell them the news today,' she said, re-positioning the sapphire centrally on her wrist, moving on, satisfied with his reply.

'We'd better get going or we're going to be late. And then she really will go mental.'

John was aware that Dilys had silenced him, but he could not waste energy winning a trivial argument about messy wardrobes today. His bigger worries wiped out their domestic gripes: his parents' reaction to the news about Aspect Films, for one. Francesca's desolation about the same news, another. It was going to rock the very foundations of her fragile survival mechanisms.

Thoughts of Francesca consumed him all the way to his parents' house.

'I think I'm going to tell Fran about Aspect first. On her own.'

'What's the point in that?' Dilys reached into her bag for her phone.

'It'll give her time to process it before Mum gets hysterical.'

'Fair enough,' Dilys replied, swiping up on Instagram.

'She deserves that,' John murmured, more to himself than to Dilys.

'Oh my god. You should see Polly's post. Oh my god!' Dilys cried, trying to show John a photograph he couldn't make out while he was driving, and couldn't have cared less about. 'She's such a bloody narcissist,' Dilys snorted, but she 'liked' the photograph.

'Did you just "Like" it?'

'Of course.'

'Why?'

'Polly's a friend.'

John sighed. He didn't understand his wife sometimes. He didn't understand social media. He didn't understand the world. He felt completely alone. When he felt like this, he thought of Robert, and how much he missed him, and he thought of the suppers they would have at No. 2 Cheverton Road. Robert and Francesca had been his escape from Dilys and Instagram and anxiety. Where he could air his thoughts, and be heard. Where he had come out of his own head. Where they ate good food, and argued – as they had on that final night – endlessly, about scripts and films and books. Where he had enjoyed Francesca's smile, unadulterated by sadness. How he yearned for those naive days back. How he wished he could be free of the constant gnawing guilt that was eating away at him now.

John pulled up outside Byworth End, where he had grown up. A mix of nostalgia and apprehension washed over him.

'Here goes,' he said, looking to Dilys for strength.

'Don't be wet about it, will you?' she said, placing a hand on his sleeve.

'It's not *wet* to worry about people's feelings.'

'Francesca will be totally fine,' Dilys said. 'Your parents have a great plan for her, anyway.'

'What plan?' John asked, immediately panicked.

Dilys slid out of the car, saying, 'They'll tell you later. I'm sworn to secrecy.' Before he had a chance to ask her more, she was gone; the dogs jumped and the children squealed and John was taken over by his mother's embrace.

CHAPTER THREE

Francesca

From this angle, he could have been Robert. He was crouching down, holding back the dogs from racing and jumping at the car as we drove in.

His head was covered by a cap, which hid his face and his hair, and his nape revealed the Tennant family olive skin. His broad shoulders, like Robert's, strained as he held the collars of both Labradors.

'Uncle John!' Alice yelped, opening the car door before I had pulled up the handbrake. She raced out of the car and yanked John's cap off, exposing twisted chunks of blond hair. He swept it back. I had forgotten how his beauty could make me feel. There was something about the weight of his blond eyebrows over his light grey eyes, and the worry-crease in between, that gave my heart a jump-start. This reaction to him was instinctive, and shameful. That night beat at my mind, the guilt tormenting me.

He let go of the dogs and swung Alice around as though she were as light as a feather.

My throat constricted. I imagined Robert twirling her in his arms like that. Kissing her, owning her love. Grief formed a lump in my throat. I had to get through the day without crying. The Tennant family worried about me enough. If I cried, they'd probably call an ambulance. I pressed my fingers into my eye sockets, hard, until they hurt, which felt satisfying, and then I was ready to get out of the car.

The oversized oak door swung open and Camilla opened her matriarchal arms to us.

'Francesca, Alice! Happy Easter, darlings! How was your journey?'

Her effusive shrieks of welcome echoed through the cavernous hallway. The dogs scuffled around on the large black and white tiles, circling them, kicking about the petals that had fallen from a magnificent display of peonies. Alice collapsed onto her knees to let them lick her face.

Enveloped in Camilla's hug, for a moment I luxuriated in the floral tang that hung off her permanently suntanned skin. Squeezing me tighter, she whispered in my ear, 'It's so good to see you.'

I hung our coats underneath the deer-head, dumped my keys and handbag onto the side table, and tried to feel at home. At least I no longer had sole responsibility for my life and Alice's. There were others to take care of us today. There were others whose grief was as bad as mine – or worse, if we were being competitive about it.

'*How* did you grow so *tall* since I saw you last?' Camilla gushed, kissing Alice over and over.

'The weekends get so busy,' I explained, trying to justify my absence.

We came down as often as we could. Every three or four weeks, in fact. Fewer weekends than John and Dilys and the children, of course, who lived fifteen minutes away on the other side of Letworth. My journey was a two-and-half-hour trek from North London to West Sussex. If we lived closer, I would visit more often. That was my excuse, anyway.

'Of course, darling. If you're both happy, I'm happy,' Camilla replied, standing up straighter, but still clinging to Alice, who was squashed into her middle.

John's lips twitched with a smile, but then he dropped his hands low into the pockets of his hip jogging bottoms, and hunched slightly, perhaps also braced for one of his mother's veiled admonishments. And perhaps also cross with me for not coming down often enough. I could never tell what John was thinking. He was a closed book. The worry seemed permanently etched.

John offered his hand to Alice. 'Come with me. Bea and Olive are in the pool already. Harry's playing tennis with Dilys.'

'Here, take her costume,' I said.

As we exchanged it, my hand touched his for a second, and our eyes met. I wanted to say 'sorry', for touching him, as though it had been a wrong thing to do.

It was the 'sorry' that would have been wrong.

Family gatherings, like today, when we were forced together, had become a robust buffer, where we could exist as distant relatives. I avoided being alone with him, never knowing what to say, self-conscious about what came out of my mouth, terrified of what one of us, in a bold moment, might bring up. It had been months since I had seen him last, and before that, months before that. When he had dropped by a few weeks after Robert's funeral, without Dilys, it had been uncomfortable. The bond that tied us – that ghastly, life-altering night – was loaded with thoughts and feelings that could never be aired.

John took the swimming costume from me and off they trotted through the house, hand in hand; Alice's face turned up to John, his turned down to her, ducking the occasional beam and low doorframe, smiling, chatting. Camilla and I walked silently behind them across the spongy cream carpets and Persian rugs, past the mix of bold modern art and old masters; passing small doorways and false panels, concealing sixteenth-century hidden passageways and stairways and tunnels. Many secrets were built into the fabric of this old Tudor house. Walking through it, I felt the eyes of the dead gossiping and beckoning, feeding on the drama of our unknown futures, on our fate.

Shuddering once, violently, as though a ghost had blown through me, I hurried after them, out through the boot room and into the sunshine and birdsong.

On the terrace, Camilla pulled my arm back.

'Let them go. Patrick's down there to help. I wanted to run a plan past you.'

I stopped, instantly nervous. Steeling myself, I watched John and Alice weave through the dangling poppies and daisies on the worn brick pathways of Camilla's garden. Alice's little legs were carrying her faster than they ever did in London, brushing past the balls of hydrangeas that reminded me of plastic flowery swimming caps worn by old ladies in the sea. As we watched, as I waited for Camilla to continue, John scooped Alice up under her armpits and stuck her on his shoulders. I clenched my jaw, preventing that untwisting behind my eyes; squeezing them shut, listening to the noises, promising myself I would get through this with my mascara intact.

'There's a house for sale in the village,' Camilla said. 'Number seventeen, on the green.'

I snapped my eyes open at her, to see if she was serious. 'And?'

Her strong tanned arms were crossed around her widened middle. She shook out her blonde bob. The elegant, heavy-handed black kohl that she scored under each eye every day, permanent like tattoo art, acted like an underline, grounding the inattentive mood in those deep-set blue eyes.

'It needs a bit of work, but I thought it might be a good time to make a change. The project might be good for you.'

The honeysuckle air had turned sour. Did she know I could barely leave my flat for the day, let alone live in another house all together? My heart tugged, almost out of my chest, towards London, to our flat, Robert's flat, her *son*'s flat. I could hardly breathe.

'We could contribute a little something towards the renovations,' she continued, as though talking about sharing the cost of a birthday present.

'I'd better check on Alice, she's not such a strong swimmer…'
I pointed towards the pool, and jogged off along the ancient
brick paths.

'I'll see what Valentina's doing to the lamb!' Camilla called
after me.

Wiping a layer of sweat from under my fringe, I followed the
trail of Alice's discarded leggings and T-shirt to the poolhouse,
where I found John helping her climb into her polka-dot swimming costume.

Normally, I would have taken over, but my head was spinning
with Camilla's proposition. I understood why Camilla wanted us
to move near her. Through me and Alice, a part of Robert lived
on. Through us, she could continue to care for him. I sympathised,
I really did, but I couldn't be that for her.

She didn't know me in the way she thought she did. If I lived
here, I would be closer to her grief, and to Patrick's, and to John's,
to their love for her dead son and brother. Village life involved
community spirit: dropping in for cups of tea and gossiping in
the village shop and reluctant chats in the supermarket aisles. The
Tennants would be everywhere. In North London, I could spend
my days amongst strangers, who would not remind me of that
godforsaken night.

Checking my watch, I worked out how long I would have to
stay, if at all. I could feign a headache and escape before lunch.
After Alice's swim, I would leave. Could I survive until then?

'Is Dad actually watching them?' John frowned as he snapped
the straps onto Alice's shoulders.

I followed his scowl to the other end of the pool, where Patrick lay
on one of the sun-loungers with his eyes closed. He would be watching his young granddaughters like a hawk, while pretending not to.

'Daddy!' Beatrice shrieked. Beatrice, John's youngest, was four
years old, like Alice. They were four months apart and as thick
as thieves.

'Do a dive!' Olivia ordered, always more commanding than her ten years.

John pulled off his T-shirt and bent to yank off his tracksuit bottoms. His bony broad shoulders tapered to two muscular dimples in his back. I looked away. And then back again. He sliced into the water with a perfect racing dive.

Following his tracks, Alice's feet slapped along the diving board and she belly-flopped in. Her tufted black head of hair and pale, city-life complexion bobbed about with her two blonde, olive-skinned cousins, as they said hello shyly to one another. Alice swam like a drowning puppy, her face barely above the surface, while Olivia and Beatrice showed off their flips and dives and underwater feats.

Patrick opened an eye, levered himself up from the low chair and walked over to me. In spite of being seventy-two, he was groomed like a young man: gelled-back silver hair, clipped designer stubble, black-rimmed spectacles and a white towel flicked around his tanned shoulders.

'I haven't really managed to take her swimming much lately,' I explained, a little embarrassed for her.

'London pools are rather grotty, I imagine.'

'There's a nice one near her school but I've never been much of a swimmer.'

'Robert was like a fish. We'd have to bribe him out of here with Jaffa Cakes and hot Ribena. Less so, John. He didn't have the same energy. Robert swam for the county.'

I cut Patrick a worried, sideways glance and noticed his Adam's apple push his grief down and the goosebumps ripple across his damp skin, and I squeezed his hand briefly. 'He was so lucky to have had all this,' I said, as an echo of what I had told him at Robert's wake.

Clearing his throat, Patrick said, 'There's a house for sale in the village, you know.'

I dropped his hand. My sympathies shrivelled away abruptly.

'I've just got a job as a secretary at Aspect,' I replied, tightening my jaw to prevent anything more offensive coming out.

'Yes, John mentioned that.'

'I can see Robert's awards' cabinet from my desk.'

'Robert would be very proud of you.'

'I love it,' I lied.

I was terrible at the job, with little previous experience of routine and administration. But Robert's ex-employees were forgiving of my mistakes. They knew I needed the money, and I was grateful for the distraction, and always felt closer to Robert when I was there, to where he sat, to what he believed in. He was there inside those walls still, smiling down on me, and laughing at my incompetence.

'Alice could be swimming here every afternoon if you bought that house. We know the chap who's selling it.'

Patrick's hands were behind his back again, which might have suggested thoughtfulness, but after ten years of knowing Patrick, I knew that it was a contrivance, a way to pretend to think with an air of pomposity.

I began to waffle, to drown out the house-for-sale-in-the-village issue: 'Waheed's been amazing. He's doing such a great job running the place. Robert would be so pleased…'

Patrick lowered his eyes to the flagstones, brushing a leaf away with his toe. 'I did a little research, and your flat would go for a fair bit now.'

Self-consciously, I picked at a mark on my shirt, feeling hot and pasty, and out of place amongst the groomed, tanned Tennants.

'I'm so sorry,' I mumbled, picking up my bag. 'I've got a bit of a headache. Any chance I could find myself some Nurofen or something?'

'In the cabinet in our bathroom, there should be something. I'll help you find…'

'No, no, I'll find it,' I said, slipping away from him. I could see the open French windows beyond the table on the terrace, where Camilla would be ordering Valentina, their housekeeper, around. To avoid them, I slipped in through the front door.

It was a relief to be silently moving through the upstairs of their house, away from their prying eyes. Past Robert's and John's old rooms, where their Colefax and Fowler wallpaper had been updated every few years of their childhood and their wooden toys were still displayed on the window seats. I was struck – not for the first time – by the tragic turn Robert's life had taken, by how this perfect childhood could lead to such a violent end.

Camilla and Patrick's bathroom was as large as a bedroom, with white tongue and groove panelling around the walls and an upholstered flowery chair by the window, and views across the lawn. Looking out, I imagined what it must have been like to take for granted the elegance of these grounds, and the bucolic splendour of this rambling old house. The tasteful ticker-striped roman blinds inside the diamond-lead windows acted like sleepy eyelids over the perfect scene. For Robert and John, it had simply been home. They had probably barely noticed the historic beauty of the steeply pitched gable roofs, the multiple chimney pots, and exposed wooden framework, or how lucky they were to be nestled on the edges of a bluebell wood, where they had built dens, and where Alice and her cousins now did the same.

The medicine cabinet was hidden behind the mirror above one of the two basins.

Inside, there were neat stacks of every kind of over-the-counter medicine you could possibly imagine. There were dozens of different brands of paracetamol or ibuprofen and aspirin; bottles of cough mixture and pain-relief tinctures and sachets for flu or colds or headaches… who needed a pharmacy?

I reached for the silver packet of fast-action Nurofen, wondering if I really needed to take them. The headache had been an excuse to get away from Patrick, yet I wanted to take something to help with the indistinct pain that throbbed somewhere deep inside me.

Knocking back two pills, I shoved the box back in, which unsettled the stack next to it. A box of indigestion pills fell from the shelf into the basin, followed by one small, brown pill bottle. I left the indigestion pills and picked up the brown bottle, turning it in my hand. Instantly, I recognised it. Around the edge was a dog-eared, grubby but familiar pharmacy label, with Robert's name on it, the type fading. Our GP's name, Dr T. Rose, was barely legible, and the suggested dosage rubbed out completely. What were his pills doing here?

Before I had a chance to shove everything back, I was aware of a presence behind me.

'Can I help you with something, Francesca?'

My heart lurched and I swung around, dropping the bottle on the marble floor. Camilla sucked in some air and held her breath, staring unblinkingly at the bottle that rolled back and forth at my feet.

'Sorry, I had a headache.'

Camilla came to, colour filling her cheeks again, and she darted down to pick it up.

'Robert must have left it here,' she explained, before I had a chance to ask. She zipped it away into a red washbag.

I wanted to speak. The words jumbled into a mass of disjointed, incoherent questions in my head. When I looked into her eyes, they were saying, *Don't you dare, don't you dare ask.* I felt cowed by her, spooked by her strange reaction to the bottle.

'This will probably do the trick.' She sniffed, popping out two more of the fast-action Nurofen I had just taken.

Clutching the washbag under her arm, she poured me a glass of water and watched me swallow two – more – pills.

'See you downstairs,' she said, and she turned to the right, along the corridor to her bedroom.

I wanted to run after her, to ask her why she had kept those pills and why she looked like she had seen a ghost; but the atmosphere that trailed after her was malevolent and intimidating.

I sloped downstairs. My cheeks were smarting like I'd been slapped. A punishment for being in denial perhaps; a sickening recognition of foul play. My past with Robert was twisting in and out of focus. All the unasked questions about why Robert had jumped came at me like pellets.

For the first time since his suicide, I wanted answers from the family. I wanted to pound on the secret doors in this house, and slam my fists into the false panels; to wind and duck through the hidden stairways of their inner sanctum and walk the secret passageways that they had kept so securely locked.

For too long, I had been scared of Camilla, who jangled the keys.

For too long, I had been scared of their ghosts.

CHAPTER FOUR

John

A hundred daffodils sat in a vase at the centre of the long table. Ten iron chairs, covered in pristine white cushions, tied with bows, were filled with nine Tennant family members. The spare seat was not for Robert, but for John's Uncle Ralph, who had cancelled at the last minute. This absence neither surprised nor offended the family, who had become used to making allowances for Uncle Ralph's unpredictable behaviour.

The bright, white chair remained empty. It seemed to radiate with Robert's spirit. In death, he was still with them. An unsettled presence, with unfinished business.

'Fran was telling us all about her new job at Aspect!' Patrick boomed from the head of the table, dropping his sunglasses from his head to his nose.

'It gets me out of the flat in the mornings,' Fran said, half-heartedly.

'Robert would be very proud of you, Francesca,' his mother added.

Terrified of giving something away, John nodded, vaguely, and looked down at his plate, making hard work of his chewy lamb.

'Is the lamb dry, John, darling?' Camilla sniffed, eyeing Dilys, who had been late to the table with Harry, their fourteen year old, after a game of tennis. 'I had to keep it warm in the oven for longer than expected,' she added, smoothing a wrinkle in her flawless linen tablecloth.

Dilys put her knife and fork together on her full plate. 'It *is* a bit dry, actually.'

Camilla pursed her lips, and looked to Patrick, who dutifully said, 'I prefer it *bien cuit*. I simply can't bear all that pink meat. No harm done at all. Marvellous.'

'"A little water clears us of this deed",' his mother said, quoting Lady Macbeth, with a superior smile.

There was a pause. John held his breath. He felt powerless and torn, with loyalties to both women, and scared of both.

'Isn't it such a shame that Aspect won't be able to make any more *Play for the Day* Shakespeares? They were Robert's pet project, weren't they, John?' Dilys asked, loudly, always a few decibels higher than everyone else.

John glared at his wife. She pushed her blonde hair tightly back into a ponytail. The coarse strands pulled at the skin on her forehead. She looked angular and bad tempered. When he had first met her, he had thought she was as beautiful as a film star; a little how his mother had looked in her twenties, captured in the black and white photographs of her treading the boards in Shakespearean garb as an aspiring actress.

'That's not true,' Francesca replied. 'Waheed has just started casting for *The Merchant of Venice*.'

Dilys pressed her fingertips to her lips. 'Oh, gosh, John, haven't you told them?'

John's pulse quickened. He imagined Robert looking down the table from that empty chair, reading each of their thoughts, probably roaring with laughter. *Good luck with that shit-storm, bro!*

'I was going to tell everyone...' John began, engaging with Francesca specifically, as though there were no others around them. Francesca's big brown eyes were on him, hypnotic as they blinked, a thick fan of lashes all the way round, opening her up like a book. They made him feel weak, and guilty.

'What is going on, John?' his mother asked.

He could feel the fear spread throughout the party. A twitch of Dilys' eyebrow suggested she wasn't feeling as bold as she had been a moment or two before.

'John, pray tell us why Dilys seems to think Aspect is not going to make "Merchant" this month?' his father asked, resting his elbows on the table and pushing the bridge of his glasses up.

The bone-dry hunk of meat was tough and inedible in John's mouth. He swallowed hard. 'I'm afraid Aspect is in dire straits, financially,' he said, pushing his chair back a little from the table, as if to create some kind of safe distance.

There would have been a time, once, when he might have taken a shabby pleasure in delivering news to his parents that would push the halo on his big brother's head ever so slightly askew. Not today.

'Are you just being Noddy Negative again, darling?' Camilla sighed.

'What kind of dire straits?' Francesca asked urgently.

Hundreds of hair-tips pressed up against John's shirtsleeves as he looked at her pale face. She pushed a dark chunk of hair behind one ear, which bent forward a little under the weight.

'Waheed is afraid that Aspect will go into receivership if they don't get the next series of *Billy Stupid* commissioned, which he thinks is highly unlikely since it'd be a seventh series and the ratings are abysmal.'

'Why the hell hasn't Waheed called me about this?' Patrick boomed.

Camilla flattened her hand over her heart. 'Aspect Films was *everything* to Robert.'

In spite of how insensitive it was to say so, John silently agreed. Robert's manic energy had been channelled into his film company as though it was a living, breathing being that would die without his attention. It had taken precedence over Francesca, and even Alice.

Olivia filled the stunned silence. 'Alice, did you know your daddy's television company is going to shut?' Her well-projected glee echoed across the garden.

'Olivia!' John scolded. Olivia's cheeks pinked, and she looked at Harry, who raised his eyebrows at his little sister, lifting himself out of his teenage dispassion for a rare moment of engagement.

'That's okay, Mumma,' Alice said. 'The big blue shop shuts at nine-past-thirteen and then it is open soon.'

'That's right. Just like Tesco's.' Francesca laughed, trying to reassure her little girl, pulling her onto her knee, holding her close.

'Yes, exactly, darling,' Camilla said, gathering herself with her characteristic strength. 'It's nothing to worry about. Now, come on, kids, eat up and you can start the Easter egg hunt.'

Everyone's eyes were on Francesca. John wanted to scream at Dilys, who stood up, abruptly, a plate in each hand.

Following her lead, everyone quietly cleared the table. John's three children ran off, escaping the tension. The two girls scurried in front of Harry, who sloped aimlessly around the lawn after his two little sisters as they filled the egg baskets that Valentina had given them.

Alice slid from Francesca's lap to follow the others, and John's attention returned to Francesca. Kindness radiated from those brown eyes – a tonic for anyone lucky enough to capture their gaze. She did not deserve this second aftershock, and neither did Alice. This little unit of two, for whom the whole family felt responsible since Robert's death, was in turmoil once again.

John knew that the business meant more to Francesca than financial security. It represented Robert's life, and his lasting memory. He felt he had stamped on her and kicked her out into the wilderness, again.

'At least your flat will be worth quite a bit. If you need to sell it now, I mean,' Dilys said, perhaps keen to deliver some good financial news.

John corrected her. 'He remortgaged it a few times to finance Aspect.'

Francesca nodded, her eyes wide.

'Maybe it's not such a bad idea to view that house for sale in the—' Patrick began.

Francesca shot out of her chair, knocking a glass from the table. It shattered on the flagstones.

'Oh!' Camilla cried, leaping up, staring at the mess. 'Robert gave us—'

'Don't worry,' John said quickly, shooting a dirty look at his mother. 'I'll get the dustpan and brush.'

Patrick briefly put his arm around Camilla, and then offered Francesca more wine in a new glass. She shook her head, refusing any more wine, sitting back down.

'Where the hell is Valentina?' Camilla barked.

'What house were you talking about?' John asked, when he returned outside with the broom and dustpan.

Camilla recovered instantly, and explained. 'Number seventeen, on the green, is up for sale. It needs work but the price reflects it.'

Patrick added, 'And we'd sub her if she wanted to buy it, especially now that—'

Francesca stopped their talk. 'Look, I'm really sorry, my headache has got worse. It's all come as a bit of a shock. I think I'm going to scoop Alice up and head home.'

There were the token protests, but they let her go.

As Francesca stood up from the long table, John found a way to look her in the eye. She visibly recoiled from him, as though she knew more about him now than she ever had. In a paranoid moment, he imagined that, somehow, she had figured out what he had been withholding about the night Robert had jumped. Her brown eyes closed for a long second, shutting him out, perhaps also telling him that she did not want to know.

*

When Francesca was gone, John's father took a sip of wine and said, 'She'd be a damn fool to refuse to buy that cottage.'

'It's unlike her to be so stubborn,' Camilla mused, handing Valentina an empty bowl as she cleared up around the family.

John picked up a large fragment of the broken glass, which was hidden under the table near Alice's chair, and said, through gritted teeth, 'Fran's not ready to sell that flat.'

He didn't feel he had to spell out what was so bloody obvious: leaving that flat was going to be like losing Robert all over again.

Dilys addressed him forcefully. 'Love, she doesn't have much choice now, really. She's broke.'

'It won't be that easy to sell. It's small, and up three flights.'

'You're kidding, right? On that street? In Whitehall Park? If she clears out all that junk, she'll sell it in a week.'

He gripped the broom. His knuckles whitened. 'It's not junk.'

'It'll be good for her to move down here. A fresh start,' his mother said, the oracle.

Everyone nodded and murmured their agreement.

The chips and splinters rattled as John gathered them into the dustpan. Like the glass, their sadness was fractured, split apart, unresolved. A delicate, intricate confusion existed between them all, which undercut every moment of these family days, where they pretended to be a normal family who had worked through their grief.

When he imagined Francesca's move to the village, he was hit by a rush of fear. He sensed it would somehow challenge the togetherness and functionality of his family; but his parents were more intent on marshalling their troops than noting the nuances of a potential threat.

CHAPTER FIVE

16 years ago

When Francesca had first seen John on set, her heart had galloped until she had felt sick. She didn't think she had ever found anyone so attractive before. Then again, every woman on that film set behaved idiotically around him. All of them had decided that he was wasted as a runner, that he should have been an actor. He had been talked about quite a lot. There were rumours that the up-and-coming actress with the tiny waist, who was a body-double on Unit Two, had been out on a date with him.

But then John had brought Francesca – with the wonky fringe and fingerless gloves – a cup of tea.

'Thought you might need one of these,' John said, handing her the cup.

She was bowled over, imagining that the bright key lights of the film had been turned away from the leading actress and onto them. The flecks of rain around them were illuminated like gold dust. The lightness of his grey, flecked eyes, under his blond brow, radiated pure innocence. He had an elegant, vulnerable beauty. Once she looked, it was hard for her to look away, as though she saw a neglected child who needed her attention. His diffident charm had an almost magical power to it.

'Thanks,' she said, taking the tea. Her long hair had dangled into her paint, picking up pink ends that dabbled more paint onto her shapeless, all-in-one overalls. Her fingertips were splattered, and luminous with cold in the dull light of a drizzly day. 'Haven't you got one for yourself?'

'They didn't have any left.'

'No tea on a film set? That's a first.'

He ruffled his blond hair, awkwardly, 'No plastic cups. The caterers were just getting them from the other unit, and I didn't have time to wait.'

'Did you think I'd be gone by the time you got here?'

She swept her arm over her semi-permanent setup in Hampton Court car park; a little bashful about her rickety foldaway table, miles away from the rest of the crew, inadequately sheltered by her car boot door. But she was a little proud of it, too.

A shy smile twitched at his mouth. 'You've got a good setup here.'

'Come and join me. We can share the tea.'

Together they sat on the edge of her car boot. There was a spray of drizzle on her face and goosebumps up her arms. They grinned at each other. The turpentine fumes from the bottles heightened her sense of giddiness. She handed him her tea, which he sipped and handed back.

'Why did they want you to paint them?' he asked her.

'Can't you see the difference?'

John squinted at the buckets she was repainting and shook his head. 'Nope.'

'One is "Berry Smoothie" pink and the other is "Raspberry Bellini" pink.'

'Silly me. Smoothies and bellinis. Night and day.'

Francesca laughed.

He continued: 'D'you think someone's paid to make up those names?'

'I should be paid to do that job. I'd be brilliant at it.' Francesca pointed to her brown boots. 'Dog Shit Brown.'

John pointed at his yellow sock. 'Urinal Yellow.'

Her fingers plucked at a splodge of paint on the knee of her blue overalls. 'God Damn Green.'

'Motherfucker Mauve,' John said, getting over-zealous.

Francesca dropped her smile. 'Now you're taking it a bit far,' she said, straight-faced, but she couldn't hold back her smile, then a guffaw. And then they both fell about laughing.

'Can't you just pretend you've repainted them all? Nobody'd ever notice.'

'Believe me, the art director would notice,' she said. 'And actually *I'd* notice. It's like an affliction. Someone told me once that I was "chromatically pitch perfect".' She laughed.

'Now *that's* a claim to fame.'

'Keep it under your hat.' She winked and grinned, and they locked eyes.

Francesca had never in her life wanted to kiss anyone more than she had wanted to kiss John in that moment.

But she couldn't imagine that he felt the same about her. It would be too good to be true. There was something about him that she didn't feel safe with. The shyness, the nerviness, gave her the impression that his interest in her might flit and fly away at any moment.

And, indeed, it had.

His walkie-talkie crackled. He stood away from the car and spoke into it.

'The boss wants me.' He looked apologetic.

'Bye.'

'I'll come back later.'

Francesca watched his silhouette walking away into the golden rain. His backlit form was like the sad ending to a film, as though she had known that he would never come back to her.

In the distance, at the entrance to the palace, she could see John approach Robert Tennant, the intimidating producer of the series. Robert Tennant was gesticulating at John. And then John disappeared inside.

CHAPTER SIX

Francesca

'He took sleeping pills?' Lucy asked, bending over my shoulder to peer closer at the property website on the computer screen. At her request, I had pulled up photographs of Number 17 The Green, Letworth village.

'Only when he was filming. When he was stressed.'

'And you think it's odd they were at his mum's, because…?'

'He only ever took them when he was filming,' I said, repeating my point.

Lucy pointed at the screen. 'Very pretty. All those roses.'

I stared at the photographs of the attached flint-stone cottage, on a row of four, facing a village cricket green, across from which was a pub and a small village shop; in the trees behind the pub sat an old church. The flowers in the small front garden seem to sway in the breeze and the little picture windows sparkled, but I couldn't focus on them.

I clicked out of the website, forcing Lucy to look at me.

'Honestly, she was totally horrified I'd found them.'

'Or she was pissed off you were snooping.'

'The label was really worn. I could hardly make out our doctor's name.'

'I guess it's been in that cabinet for two years, or more.'

'*Two years* after he died, she still has them. Don't you think that's strange?'

'Not really. You should see the crap I keep in mine.'

'Fine.' I sulked, turning back to the computer.

'I'm trying to understand, Fran, honestly.'

'It doesn't matter.'

'Why don't you ask John about them?'

'Maybe.'

'Are you still angry with him?'

'He was a total dick that day.'

'I think you're trying to find excuses to hate them all so that you don't have to move out of this flat.'

'It's not that. Seriously, he must have had hundreds of opportunities to tell me about Aspect, but he actually wimped out and got Dilys to do it.'

'How long has Aspect got?'

'They've given us three weeks' notice.' I sighed.

I thought about the days when Robert had started up Aspect Films as a one-man-band. A few months later an award-winning documentary director, Lynn Taylor, had joined him. Then the small team of five, including Waheed, had won a huge commission to make a new reality series, set in the Orkneys. The stylish loft space, just off Kentish Town high street, housed his vibrant team of coffee-drinking, over-educated creatives intent on changing the world through drama, and winning awards for their efforts. It had survived the industry storms, every month eking out a living for its employees, and paying the rent on our colourful flat in the eves, just.

And now both the business and the flat were water through my hands.

'If you sell this, you'll have some equity, won't you?'

'Robert remortgaged it three times. I'll be lucky if it isn't in negative equity.'

Lucy crossed one long thigh over the other and pressed her hands either side of her black, razor-sharp bob, as though squeezing thoughts out of her brain. Her top teeth bit at the side of her bottom lip.

'Can you go back to scenic painting?'

'The hours are too long. Childcare would be too expensive.'

I continued looking at her, waiting for her to do something, challenging her to find the solutions to my problems, adamant that there were none. Everything was hopeless.

Lucy clicked into the property website again.

'But the Tennants are offering to help?'

'I'm not taking a penny from them.'

'Oh, Fran. Just because of Camilla and those pills?'

'If you'd seen her face…' I trailed off.

'Have you thought she might be popping them herself?'

I considered this for a moment. 'No.'

'She could've been embarrassed that you found them.'

I pictured Camilla's expression, her mood. Had it been embarrassment? Under Lucy's scrutiny, I began to doubt my initial instincts.

I picked at the split-ends in my hair. 'You're probably right.'

'What type were they? Temazepam?'

'I can't remember, Zylatol or Xylophone or something. I've forgotten.'

Lucy snorted. 'Zopiclone?'

'That's the one.'

'My nan used to munch on those like Smarties! You're totally mad, you are!' Lucy laughed.

I shook my head, embarrassed. 'I never used to be so paranoid.'

We sat quietly for a few minutes, contemplating all the maybes, and I tried to stamp out the gnawing suspicion that there was more to that pill bottle than any of us knew. It was a hunch that I couldn't pin down with any coherence.

I began clicking into photographs of the interior of the cottage. 'It's pokey inside.'

'The idea of moving is going to be hard, I get that.'

'It's not just moving. It's moving *there*.' I stabbed at the screen. 'So close to them all. They're so bloody self-involved. I'd never be able to live my life how I wanted to live it. They'd always be putting in their two pennies' worth.'

'Just ignore all that, or tell them to piss off, in the politest possible way.'

'I'd feel guilty all the time for taking their money.'

'I really think that's dumb. They're Alice's family, and they've got pots of dosh.'

'And be indebted to those nutters all my life?'

'Maybe put it to them as an investment idea. They could lend you the deposit, and you could share the ownership, and you could pay the mortgage payments monthly, and give the deposit back when you're on your feet again. It would be less than rent, and you'd get to own a house.'

'Maybe.'

'What are your other options?'

'Not many.'

'Have you got any savings?'

'A couple of hundred from some jobs before Alice. I put it aside for Alice's university fees. I could put a deposit down on a rental somewhere and get a job.'

'Okay. Well, let's imagine you don't go for the cottage in Letworth. Let's look at some rentals.'

Gladly, I swapped places. Lucy was going to take charge. She would find a solution for me that would not involve the Tennants. She would save me.

Ever since I had met Lucy at freshers' week at Nottingham University, she had taken charge. Orienting me around campus, pulling me to the right parties, stroking my back when I was being sick after too many snakebite and blacks.

'How about this one?'

She double-clicked on a *fazenda* in Portugal.

I spluttered. 'Near Mum and Dad?'

'Just kidding!' Lucy chuckled wickedly.

'I'd move into Camilla and Patrick's bedroom before moving near them.'

'I know. I just wanted to see a little bit of a smile again,' she said, clicking into another site. 'I don't think Babs and O would want you, anyway.'

Lucy had always called my parents Babs and O. Their full names were Barbara and Owen Wrey, but when Lucy had stayed with them in Castelo Branco for two weeks in our second summer holiday of university, she'd decided that pornstar names were more appropriate. My parents were not pornstars – by any stretch of the imagination – but they lived what might be called an alternative life.

'What about Lewes? Look at this one.'

We looked at two gloomy flats in pebble-dashed terraces.

'Okay, maybe not,' Lucy said.

'What am I going to do?'

'Come on, let's just have another look at that house for sale in the village.'

Lucy grabbed the mouse to scroll through the photographs again, and then she double-clicked on one to enlarge it. 'Is that an outbuilding in the garden?'

'It's a…' I stopped. I refused to say it out loud.

'A studio space!' she cried.

'Yes,' I replied, unenthusiastically.

Lucy sat down on the arm of the sofa and sighed. When she sighed like this, I knew she was going to say something truthful about my failings.

'Babe, you've always wanted a studio space.'

I blushed, my chest full of nasty butterflies. 'Robert would never have lived in Letworth.'

Lucy cackled. 'True. If he had, he'd probably have ended up running the pub and the village shop and the cricket club.'

'And sermonise at church every week.'

'And then fall out with everyone.'

'Even God.'

We both laughed at the memories of Robert and his hyperactive energy. It had been never-ending, tireless, superhuman, even.

'Would it be *so* bad to be near his parents?'

'His mother is trouble. That's all I'm saying. And you always say I'm too naive about people.'

'I understand,' Lucy said. 'I just don't want you and Alice living in a homeless shelter, that's all.'

We laughed together, and tears threatened.

I clicked out of the property website, knowing there was little point in poring over the photographs of the cottage. Even if it had been a damp, windowless hovel with rats, I did not have a choice. I slumped back in Robert's old chair.

'I'll miss this place.'

'Tell me what you'll miss most.'

I looked at all the pretty things and all the photographs of Robert, which, deep down in my broken heart, I knew I could take with me. Like the photograph of Robert and me in Mallorca, grinning under snorkels like halfwits, as happy as any couple could be; or the photograph of Alice as a newborn, wearing a stripy babygro, flopped over Robert's shoulder.

And the memory jar. It was two feet tall with a large cork bottling its neck. Alice had to stand on a stool to plop in her memory or drawing.

Folded into one of the sunshine-yellow cards, Alice had drawn a stick figure of Robert and written a heart next to it. Already, she could barely remember her father, but I insisted we look through the photograph albums and read the memory cards every bedtime with her stories. Sometimes I reread the messages to myself, message after message, with a bottle of wine, and cried. Sometimes I stared at the jar, shooting it dirty looks. Sometimes I imagined rolling it up and out of the skylight, smashing it onto the rooftops, when Robert would be alive again, and we could go back to how life was before.

My gaze fell to my feet. 'We painted these floorboards together.'

Lucy and I scanned the worn, chipped and greying paint.

I remembered Robert and me on our hands and knees painting them bright white. As I remembered this happy moment between us, the same torturous question sliced through it, fracturing it: *Why had he wanted to leave us?*

The tips of Lucy's shoes scuffed the floorboards and nudged at my slippers, playing footsie with me.

'I'll help you pull them up so you can take them with you. Okay?'

I laughed, a tear plopping onto the paint.

'Deal?'

'Deal,' I agreed, wiping my eyes and sniffing.

'And if you live nearby, you'll be able to Miss Marple the shit out of that family and their pill bottles.'

I laughed good-naturedly at Lucy's teasing, but deep down I was not even smiling.

However much she teased, I could not shake off the deep-seated unease about Camilla. How ugly her mood had been, how illogically frightened I had felt, standing there in the bathroom, staring down at those pills at my feet. Thinking back to it was like remembering a nasty dream. It didn't make any sense, but I knew it had relevance, prescience even.

To protect myself, I had been resisting the idea of getting closer to Robert's family, scared of being infected by their stifled grief, of being suffocated by their strangled emotions. But, ironically, by remaining detached, I was stuck in a holding pattern, holding my breath, inert. In the same way that my most dysfunctional friends vociferously resisted psychoanalysis, the Tennants were avoiding their pain, plastering it over with luxury and stiff upper-lips. But Camilla's high society smile had slipped when she saw those pills, and I was going to find out why.

Living nearby would make that a whole lot easier.

CHAPTER SEVEN

16 years ago

Francesca was sitting on top of the large speakers, dangling her legs and picking at the dried paint in her hair, one eye on John at the bar. She was deliberating on the idea of going up to him. It was the wrap party. Filming was at an end. It was her last opportunity.

Her confidence waned. In the three weeks since they had shared their cup of tea, perched on the edge of her car boot, he had not once returned to her. There had been rumours that he had been moved to Unit Two, with a different crew, with the body-double with the small waist. She wondered if she had fabricated the sparks that had flown in the air between them, whether it had been wishful thinking.

Nevertheless, she held out hope, and she was keeping a keen eye on him while she waited for Waldo, one of the props painters, to get their drinks.

When Waldo returned, he had brought her red wine, and Robert Tennant.

'Those pink buckets of yours play a starring role in the flower shop scene,' Robert Tennant said.

'Oscar-worthy, I hope.'

He held his hand out. 'Robert Tennant.'

Waldo wandered off, winking at her.

She couldn't understand why the producer, *the* Robert Tennant, was even talking to her, let alone why he was aware of what she had painted.

'I'm Francesca,' she smiled, looking over his shoulder to see if she could spot John.

'What are you working on next?' he asked.

'Not sure. Karen mentioned she wanted me on something at Pinewood, I think, some kind of horror/love-story/sci-fi/thriller film.'

'Sounds interesting.'

'It sounds awful. You?'

'I've been developing a film project. I should be securing the finance for it next week.'

'What's it about?' But Francesca wasn't really interested. She had caught sight of John again. He was weaving through the crowds towards them. Her heart beat wildly in her chest.

Robert's voice broke into her thoughts again. 'Do you want me to help you jump down?'

He held out his hand. He was the kind of man she didn't feel she could say 'no' to.

'Sure.'

At eye level, she could see that Robert Tennant was handsome. Dark hair and a square jaw, with deep-set blue eyes. Over his shoulder, she saw the back of John's blond head about three feet away.

'It's about a crew of mercenaries who get lost in the Sahara.'

'How lost?'

And he began to tell Francesca about the Sahara, about his three-week recce with a crew in a Land Rover Defender, and about sleeping under the stars at night in the freezing cold. The photographs on his phone of the sand dunes distracted her from John for a few minutes.

When she looked up again, she caught sight of John by the door, talking to someone, kissing them on the cheek. Was he about to leave? She considered abandoning Robert then and there, being rude, halting their conversation, running after John to ask him out. My god! She wanted to. She wanted to be brave enough. But with one small moment of hesitancy, a little pang of insecurity, she missed her opportunity. John disappeared through the doors. The disappointment was like a stone dropping through her.

Whereas Robert seemed solid next to her, attentive and interesting, and sure of himself. She was sucked in by his energy. Everything he talked about was colourful and extraordinary.

'Do you like travelling?' Robert asked, later on in the evening.

'Love it.' It was a lie. She had always wanted to be more adventurous, but she enjoyed wearing slippers and curling up on her sofa too much.

'A friend of mine is getting married in Mumbai in three weeks. Want to come as my guest?'

The shock of his brazen forwardness made Francesca laugh. Laden with the disappointment of John's departure and soaked in her third glass of wine, the thought of going to India for the first time seemed like a great plan, and she said, 'Yes. Why not?'

CHAPTER EIGHT

John

John's phone was ringing. Before he put the last of the plates into the dishwasher, he glanced at the screen to see Francesca's name flash up. He left it on the kitchen worktop.

'Who's that?' Dilys asked, buried in her own phone at the table.

'Fran.'

'Why is she calling?'

'Mum said she needed help moving some wardrobe that the old lady left in the cottage.'

'Aren't you going to pick up?'

'I'll call her later.'

'Is she still cross?'

'Probably.'

John was trying to be happy for Francesca. But it was not going to be easy. With her imminent move to Letworth, she was to become a fully-fledged member of the Tennants, living in the heart of the village that his parents dominated. He imagined seeing her face every day of his life. The thought left him breathless. Before, in London, she had been on the periphery of the Tennant clan, never quite conventional enough for his family, never quite like them enough. He had loved that about her.

A screech echoed through the kitchen. Beatrice charged at Olivia, and slid along the curved slippery concrete floors, brandishing two fists. Blonde heads neared the black-glass kitchen table, elbows whooshed past valuable modern art on the wall behind them. All the while, Harry was threatening to throw his basketball at them both. Dilys' carefully designed, mustard and grey interior would not survive a basketball.

'Stop it!' Dilys hollered, barely raising her head from her phone. They ignored her. 'John? Could you deal with it?'

'Stop fighting, kids,' John muttered, pressing the code into his phone for his voicemail.

'John, please, I've got a business call to make.'

'On a Saturday?' John asked absently. Francesca's voice came into his ear.

> *'Hi, John. It's Fran. Your mum said you'd be able to help move the wardrobe left upstairs at the cottage. Wondering if you could meet me there next Tuesday? I need to get it out before the completion date. Let me know. Bye.'*

She sounded frosty and businesslike. If he knew anything about Francesca, his continued failure to address the Easter day issue would eventually result in a confrontation, which was the last thing he wanted. He texted her back.

> *No problem. See you next Tuesday. I'm really sorry about my clumsy delivery of the news about Aspect. Wanted to tell you before the fam. Head in sand, as usual. I blame EVERYTHING on Dilys ;)*

He knew it was lame to apologise by text, but he always found writing things down easier than saying them out loud.

Dilys barked at him: 'Who are you texting?'

'Fran. About the wardrobe.'

'Why don't you just call her?'

'I'm not in the mood.'

'That's for sure.' She clicked her tongue and slammed the door to her study.

Taken aback, he realised he had been incautious around Dilys, inattentive, distracted by Francesca. Supper had been pretty normal for a Saturday evening family meal and he had been chatty enough, or so he had thought. He had cooked them baked potatoes with melted cheese and bacon, and the children had talked about the latest films they wanted to see at the cinema. Dilys had quizzed them about school grades. He had tried to be as present as possible. But maybe Dilys was right, maybe he was preoccupied.

When he and Dilys had first met, Dilys had been charmed by his brooding, his tendency to overthink everything. He would never forget that first shot of her, weaving through the busy bar. He had wanted to do a cartoonlike glance over each shoulder, in disbelief that a woman so beautiful and sophisticated could be heading towards him. She had been wearing a three-quarter length camel cashmere coat, from which flashed her toned, tanned legs. Her conversation was sharp and opinionated, and she rarely agreed with anything he said, but she didn't probe him about 'what he was thinking about'. She didn't seem to doubt herself, nor did she seem to value the idea of feelings. This was convenient for John. He did not want anyone to press him. There was too much in his head that he wanted to protect. Instead, Dilys had taken him under the wing of her coat and led him out of the bar – and into bed, where he had laid down underneath her for an out-of-body experience. The world had stopped spinning. His worries had flown away. He had never had sex like it. Dilys had been in control from day one.

A text came through from Fran.

Dilys is so lucky to have you in her corner.

He laughed to himself. It meant she had forgiven him. Francesca never stayed angry for long.

The children rampaged around him, still fighting, but he smiled and replugged his phone into the charger.

'Okay, you three! If you give me that ball now and stop fighting, I'll shoot some hoops with you before bath time.'

Harry groaned at the prospect of more sport, and loped off.

'Come on, you two girls.'

Olivia and Beatrice charged down to John's writing shed, to which he had fixed a basketball hoop for his writer's block moments.

As he plonked balls through the hoop and into the net, and broke up more fighting, he spotted Dilys striding down the slope from the house. She rarely came to the bottom of the garden. She had his phone in her hand. His heart leapt. She looked angry.

'What the hell does this mean?' Dilys hissed, handing him his phone.

'She was being sarcastic.'

'Up to the house, girls,' Dilys ordered. 'Mummy needs a chat with Daddy.'

The girls knew when to listen to her, and up they ran, leaving the basketball to roll into the stream. His palms began sweating.

'If you read my text to her, you'd understand.'

'What's your code?'

'I'll do it.'

'*I'll* do it. What's your code?'

'1974,' he sighed, and watched her nervously while she read it. 'See?'

She threw his phone at his head. 'You did blame me!'

He rubbed his ear where the phone had clipped it. 'It was a joke. I put in that stupid little winking emoji. I wanted to apologise for both of us.'

'You screwed up, not me.' Dilys thrust her face right up to his, pointing her forefinger.

John stuck his hands in his pocket, hunching his shoulders resentfully. 'That's not true.'

And then Dilys was running, wading into the stream, collecting the dripping-wet ball, screaming at the top of her lungs, throwing the ball. He ran. It missed him, thudding into the door as he ducked inside his shed.

John watched Dilys as she stormed up the lawn, back to the house. He kicked the door, and then he shot a few more hoops to calm himself down.

Stopping for a minute, out of breath, he stared up at their 1960s, single-storey house, aptly named 'The Round House'. It had always reminded him of a strange, flying-saucer spaceship that had landed on the edge of a hillside, defunct; its uselessness allowing nature to grow around it, like some discarded Victorian china embedding itself into the ground. But it was apparently the envy of everyone who came to visit. The 'famous architect' – whom nobody had ever heard of – had built it for himself, lived in it and died in it, but John had the feeling that he had never quite left it. John certainly didn't feel he owned it.

A wail suddenly rang across the garden, all the way from the bathroom at the back. John ran.

Dilys was kneeling down at the bath, washing Beatrice's hair, but she was using the strong shampoo that stung Beatrice's eyes.

'Stop being such a baby!' she shouted.

'It's okay. I'll do it,' John said.

'Daddeeeeeee!' Beatrice cried, stretching her arms out to him with her eyes squeezed shut.

'Suit yourself,' Dilys said, standing up and handing him the shower head without making eye contact.

After the children were tucked up in bed, John wearily made his way into the kitchen, anxious about what was in the fridge for supper, fearing the lack of food would be another flashpoint for her.

He was amazed to see that Dilys had laid the table with candles and flowers, and napkins in silver rings, and a bottle of red.

'Sorry,' she said, turning to him. 'I just hate it when you blame me for stuff I didn't do.'

'I wasn't blaming you,' he insisted.

'It's okay, I know you didn't mean it, and I know I can be hard on you, sometimes,' she said, caressing the long gold necklace that dangled at the deep V of the neckline of her short, tight dress. 'It's just I love you so much and I want you to be the best person you can be.'

He was distracted by her appearance. In the candlelight, with a strand of hair falling into her eyes, she looked astonishing. He kissed her lips and held her, knowing she had been right to be angry with him, knowing he had not been honest with her, knowing that Francesca was a distraction.

'I do try to keep everyone happy,' he murmured.

John did not know how to be the person she wanted him to be.

'Try harder.' She smiled, winking at him and grabbing his crotch.

Before he had eaten a bite of the risotto she had cooked, she had hitched up her dress and climbed on top of him. Everything was forgotten. Even Francesca.

CHAPTER NINE

16 years ago

'There he is,' Robert said, tightening his grip on Francesca's hand.

They walked towards a tall figure bathed in the warm, dim glow of the pub's lighting.

'Nice to meet you,' John said, shaking her hand. 'So, you're the girl who stole my plane ticket to Mumbai.'

Francesca couldn't believe that this beautiful man, with terrible taste in paint names and an awkward shyness, whom she had guessed she would never be lucky enough to meet again, was standing there in front of her: her new boyfriend's brother.

She looked confused. 'Didn't you work on *The Anniversary*?'

'Yes!' Robert cried, slapping John on the back. 'He was my dogsbody, weren't you, bro?'

John nodded and pushed his crop of blond hair back, making no reference to their meeting, acting as though he had never before laid eyes on her, in the golden rain of the film set.

'What can I get you?'

The three of them sat down at a small table in the corner, with three pints of Guinness and a pint of prawns to share.

Francesca sat between the two men, tearing pieces off her slice of brown bread and butter. Torn in two, she listened to Robert regaling John with their stories of Waheed's wedding – of dancing to bhangra and the flow of warm orange juice and the torrential downpours – while she wanted to climb inside John's brain, get to know his every thought. The whirlwind of Mumbai, and the exhilaration of Robert's energy, was nothing compared to the thrill of seeing John again.

Throughout the evening, Robert's arm was heavy around her shoulders. She convinced herself that Robert was right for her and that John's beautiful face could deceive and beckon; that sexual attraction should not be confused with love at first sight. His exceptional, gentle handsomeness was out of reach, out of her league. His unreadable presence was too alluring to trust.

At one point, she saw John glance over at a pretty girl at the bar and she was jealous of the girl, and jealous of any girl who could win his heart, even before he had met her.

After the meal, when they said their goodbyes, John kissed Francesca on the cheek and she grabbed his hand, and squeezed it. She had wanted to tell him something through her touch: she and Robert had been seeing each other for a few weeks, they weren't married, it wasn't too late.

Later that night, Robert yanked Francesca's jeans down, and thrust himself inside her, coming quickly, holding her possessively, insistent and intractable. Afterwards, Francesca wondered if Robert had recognised John as a threat. And, in spite of how much she liked Robert, Francesca considered waking him and telling him it was over.

CHAPTER TEN

Francesca

Upstairs, in the blue bedroom of the cottage, I stood staring at the varnished monstrosity that took up half the room and sucked up all the light.

I turned the little key to look inside. The hangers clanged and a stench of mothballs made my eyes water, but today this wardrobe was my friend. It had been the perfect excuse to get John here, alone, to ask him about the pills. I wanted to find out whether John knew more than I did, from Robert, or from his mother.

The doorbell rang and I ran downstairs. The estate agent had already opened the door to John.

'Hi. I'm Alistair from South Downs Properties.'

John shook his hand.

I wiped the dust off my hands and peered over Alistair's shoulder. 'Thanks for coming.' I smiled.

'I'll let you two get on with it. I have a few calls to make down here,' Alistair said.

'Oh. Are you staying?'

'Sorry. Until completion I have to be here.'

My plan was ruined.

'No worries,' I said, hiding my irritation, thinking of a new plan. 'It's up here, John.'

John followed my lead, up the stairs. The treads creaked as we went up to the first floor.

'Do you think you might have time for a quick cuppa afterwards?'

'I have to be back at one for a call.'

'Great,' I enthused. It gave me enough time, if we hurried with the wardrobe. 'Dilys has recommended The Bakery to me before, for tea—?'

'Sure.' John pointed to the embossed shell-pattern wallpaper. 'I like what you've done to the place.'

'I think it's got potential.'

He peered around the door to the bathroom. 'Snazzy.'

'You know, I've got a view.' I climbed into the calcified pink bathtub, with my shoes and clothes still on, and lay with my head back, gazing out of the little window above the taps. I wanted him to see the potential, or get a smile out of him, at least.

'It's very small,' he said, looking away, up at the bowed ceiling, clearing his throat and darting out of the room and down the stairs.

'The wardrobe is up here!' I called down to him.

'What's the garden like?' he called up.

'It's got potential.' I laughed. But he did not respond.

I searched for him downstairs, interrupting Alistair on the phone in the sitting room, before nipping through the galley kitchen, past its orange Formica units and white Aga, and out of the back door. John was already at the bottom of the narrow strip of grass.

'You have a shed? Can I see inside?'

The bi-fold doors were stiff and I grunted when opening them. 'The old lady who lived here had a son who was an artist.'

Inside, I took a moment to again admire the walls and floor that were splattered with paint. There were some old tubes of acrylic lying in the corner and a battered, one-legged easel discarded in the other corner. The sunshine from the skylight beamed a large rectangle patch onto the wooden floor.

John was scanning the room like a prig. 'Will you have to pay rates?'

'Nope. It's got electricity but no running water.'

'You'll have to get a heater fitted. They're quite expensive.'

'Can we get on with the wardrobe?' I asked tersely, folding my arms across my chest. My fingers fiddled nervously with my watch.

'Now you're moving here, I'm warning you, Mum will force you to visit Uncle Ralph for tea. None of us escapes that fate.' He was trying to make me laugh. I did not laugh.

'You haven't said a positive word since you arrived.'

'I'm trying to be practical.' He scuffed his trainer on the floor, hitting a tube of paint, which was catapulted across the room to clatter against the back wall.

'Practical is a good way of putting it.' I tutted. We stepped out of the shed and I locked it up. 'Pissing on my bonfire is another.'

'Sorry.' We walked back up the garden, the two small back windows of the cottage eyeing us.

I shunted him with one shoulder. 'Don't worry about me so much.'

'I'm not worried.' John stuck his hands in his pockets and stole a sideways, shy glance over at me.

'Come on, let's shift that wardrobe,' I said, aware of the clock ticking.

I led him to the blue bedroom. We stood staring at the large wardrobe.

'Will it fit in your car?'

'If the seats are down, it'll be fine.' He rolled his shirt sleeves up, like an old-fashioned boxer. 'Let's do this.'

We began shouting orders at each other, this way, that way, not so fast, slow down, lower, lift it more, careful of the banisters. It was lighter than we expected but awkward to carry.

Alistair emerged from the sitting room. 'Are you guys okay there?'

'Everything's under control,' John grunted.

Alistair waved his phone at us, darting off, saying, 'I'll just take this call in the garden.'

The wardrobe began bumping down the stairs at alarming speed. I tried to keep a grip of one of its feet, but it had gained momentum.

'Hold it!' John cried.

It continued to slip out of my hot, sweaty hands and slide downwards. John lost his balance and, as he frantically tried to stay upright, the wardrobe knocked him onto his back and mounted him.

He moaned. 'Ouch.'

I began to laugh, edging around the wardrobe to get to him. 'Are you all right?'

'Not wounded, sire, but dead,' he croaked, quoting Frank Sinatra in *High Society*.

I clamped my hand over my mouth and spluttered into it. 'It could have killed you.'

'Help me get it off!'

As I yanked at it, we both burst out laughing, tears rolling down our cheeks. The wooden door of the wardrobe rattled as John's body juddered.

'Stop making me laugh!' I begged, gulping for breath, holding my stomach.

Just then the letterbox in the front door flapped open and a voice rang through it.

'Darlings! Cooo-eeeee! Hel-looooo!!'

'Mum?' John said.

Still grinning, I let her in.

'What in heaven's name is going on here?' Camilla barked. She was standing over her prone son with her hands on her hips.

'It fell on him!' I snorted, which set John off again.

'I'm not sure how funny this is. How are we going to get you out?' Camilla looked from her son's face to mine with a disapproving frown. She was so like Robert when she was cross.

I pulled my features into a sensible face, trying to stifle my laughter and kissed my mother-in-law on the cheek. 'It's not that heavy,' I sniggered, staring down at John.

John's lips were quivering, his shoulders shaking. 'It bloody well hurts!'

I was unable to fight back more laughter. 'Sorry, I've got the giggles.'

Unmoved by our mirth, Camilla dumped her handbag on the floor. 'You take that end, Francesca, and I'll pull here. John, darling, you push it this way if you can.'

The laughter was sucked out of me by his mother's distaste and good sense. I did as she said and John managed to shuffle out from under the wardrobe.

'Aren't you supposed to be the one helping Francesca with this damn thing, John?' Camilla asked, as she picked up her handbag.

'It was my fault…' I began.

'Never mind. I can't stay. I was just passing on my way to the supermarket and thought I'd check on you,' Camilla said, picking out a piece of brown wrapping tape from John's hair. I bit my lip to stop my hysterics from bubbling up again. 'Lucky I did. You're sure you can you handle it from here?'

We were like a couple of teenagers being told off by the head teacher, and I felt guilty for my display of happiness. Since Robert's death, laughter always had a sting in its tail.

'Yes, Mum,' John said, tucking in his shirt.

He was like a little boy in front of her.

When I looked at the two of them, mother and son, I thought about how little I really understood the family I had been married into for so many years. And how badly I now wanted to understand them.

*

The Bakery was empty and chilly. On the wall, an orange neon sign spelled out the aphorism: 'Life is Sweet'.

'We could sit outside—?' John suggested.

An imposing oak tree shrouded the four metal tables on the terrace with a grey shadow.

'Inside's fine.'

The chairs scraped loudly in the silence. It felt awkward between us, like before a job interview. I was the potential employer and John was the unwitting interviewee.

'Dilys always has the lime and chili poppy-seed semolina cake.'

'Sounds lovely,' I fibbed, scanning the menu for something that would not make me want to hurl. Meringue macaroons with pistachio foam or salty-caramel triple fudge quinoa cake?

A tall, pretty teenager appeared. 'What can I get you?' she asked, in a boredom-infused home counties accent.

'I'll just have a cup of tea, please.' I put the menu down, not tempted by any of the cake choices.

'Darjeeling, lapsang souchong, Earl Grey, chai or green liquorice?'

'Do you have a normal one, please?'

'We've got Assam.'

'Is that the strong one?'

'Think so.'

'Good. I'll have that, thanks,' I said, relieved.

'Two of those,' John said.

This café, and this awkwardness with John, gave me the urge to run screaming back to London and rent a bedsit with a view of the North Circular and forget about Letworth, the pills and the Tennants.

'So, are you excited about the move?' John asked.

'I didn't think I would be.'

'Why?'

'I suppose I wanted to hate the idea.'

'What changed?'

'I don't know. When I was looking around today, before you came, I was surprised… I felt…' I paused, trying to find the word to describe how liberating it had felt to seek out new possibilities, beyond the claustrophobic four walls of the flat, to have found the courage to break up my dependence on its sadness, and begin the process of finding out why Robert had taken his own life. 'I think I felt… new. Does that make sense?'

'Sure.'

'I think I've been using the flat to hide away.'

'A lot went on there,' John said, picking at a crust of food on the table, avoiding eye contact.

The silence lingered, but then the tea arrived. In square teapots, with cups with square handles.

John stared at the tea set. His expression suggested he was looking at slime in rusty tin cans.

'That's it,' he said, not as quietly as I would have liked. 'This is bloody awful. Come on,' he said, standing up. 'Follow me in the car.'

Happy to get out of that café, I followed his battered white vintage Porsche as it pootled through the lanes. It made me laugh that he was driving so slowly. Only John would drive a Porsche at 30 mph. I remembered when he had bought it with his first big pay check.

We wound through the woods in convoy until we came to a farm track that led to a tree in full, pink-blossom bloom, next to which stood a small wooden barn. Through its open doors I could see it was filled with tables covered with colourful tablecloths and flowers. It was buzzing with other people. Walking in, I could see large coffee walnut, lemon drizzle and Victoria sponge cakes sitting on stands underneath glass lids on the counter at the back. The blackboard had a list of simple food like egg baps and sausage sandwiches.

I chuckled. 'Now you're talking.'

Settling down into the worn sofa in the corner, I felt easier. I could hear the woman behind the counter cackle at something John had said as he ordered for us.

I watched the small groups of women, mostly my age, chatting at the tables around me, and I wondered if I could imagine any of them becoming my friends. There was one woman who was wearing a pair of black, Japanese-style dungarees and bright red nail polish, and I thought she looked arty and interesting.

John said hello to another woman – who looked less friendly in her black Lycra – as he dodged a few dogs and dog bowls to return with a tray.

'One slice of Victoria sponge, one slice of coffee walnut cake and a pot of tea for two,' he said, which he poured into two satisfyingly round cups and saucers.

A gust of wind blew through the barn, ruffling a chunk of hair into his eyes. He pushed it back, glancing at me, raising the hairs on my arms, reminding me of our past.

'Robert would have hated the cottage,' I said, knowing it was a dangerous thing to say. I wanted to get down to business.

'Yup.' He shrugged. He bent forward, cradling his cup without the saucer, two elbows on two knees.

'And there's the threat of tea with your nutty Uncle Ralph.'

'A rite of passage.'

'But it'll be good to be closer to the family.'

I wiped a smear of strawberry jam from my plate and licked it, letting it sweeten my tongue.

He looked me straight in the eye and said, 'Yes.'

The brief, intense eye contact caused a discomforting rise in my chest, as though he had nudged my heart upwards a little.

'Your mum will drive me mad, of course.'

'No question.'

'She doesn't see me as a charity case, does she?'

'No. She loves you.'

'I know that. I think.'

'She has a funny way of showing it.'

'She's been so brave about Robert.'

'She toughs it out.'

I paused, wondering how to say what I wanted to say. I began stirring my tea, until the grating metal of the teaspoon hurt my ears. The night of Robert's death uncurled in the back of my mind, dragging me back to my grief, sending a searing pain through my soul, but focusing my mind.

'Do you think she ever blames herself?'

His brow furrowed. 'Why should she?'

I felt my heart slow. 'Guilt is a mother's prerogative.' I backtracked, regretting coming in so strong.

His expression softened and he shrugged. 'She probably takes some responsibility for the fact that he was depressed.'

'But she never admitted he was depressed while he was alive.'

He gave me a brief, sad smile, and said, 'The Tennants don't *do* depression, remember.'

I inhaled deeply, readying myself.

'On Easter day, I was looking in your mum's medicine cabinet for some headache pills and I found a bottle of Robert's sleeping pills. His Zopiclone.'

'So?'

'Your mum was really odd when she saw me with them.'

'It was no secret he took those pills, Fran.'

'Did he ever talk to you about them?'

John poured more tea. 'Dr Baqri prescribed them, didn't he?'

I replaced my teacup in the saucer too heavily, almost breaking the delicate china. 'No. He got them from our GP.'

He looked up sharply. 'He told me Dr Baqri prescribed them.'

'Who is Dr Baqri?'

'He's been the family doctor for decades.'

'"Dr T Rose" is written on the label.'

'Strange. I'm sure I remember him telling me he was seeing Dr Baqri about his insomnia.'

'Is Dr Baqri still around?'

'Very much so. My parents still see him. He's expensive. Harley Street.' John picked up crumbs from his plate and then, after a long pause, he added, quietly: 'The toxicology reports never mentioned any drugs in his bloodstream, Fran.'

'Which is why we never questioned those pills at the time, but now I want to make sure that they were what he said they were.'

'Of course they were.'

'The label is really worn out. It was always worn out. I don't ever remember it looking new.'

'You think he was reusing the bottle?'

'I never looked inside.'

'Why would you have?'

'I want to look now.'

'I'm sure you'd see lots of little Zopiclones if you did.'

'Will you ask your mum about them for me?'

He rubbed his chin. 'I don't think that's a good idea. You know how she gets.'

'That's the problem, though, isn't it? None of us ever talks about this stuff. We're all too scared to go there.'

He hung his head, and pushed his fingers through his hair. 'Talking about it won't bring him back.'

I shook my head, disappointed in him. 'You sound just like her.'

'Mum loved my brother, more than anyone. Those pills have nothing to do with his death.'

'But I got the sense that she was hiding something, John.'

He blinked, slowly, over his grey eyes. 'Aren't we all?'

I gathered my bag, leaving my tea half-drunk, fighting back tears. 'I'd better get going.'

We peeled off to our cars, but I was trembling too hard to start up the ignition.

I watched his Porsche disappear with the urge to run after him shaking my fist. I was thrown by John's misplaced loyalty to his mother, infuriated by his family's predictable stonewalling.

I had to find another way in.

Dr Baqri's Harley Street practice seemed like a good place to start.

CHAPTER ELEVEN

16 years ago

'Film it. Come on!' Robert cried.

Francesca followed Robert around the whitewashed loft space of his new production company offices, zooming the phone down the length of his navy-blue macintosh and jeans to focus on his battered Nike trainers. Then back up again, to the back of his head, where his hair was birdnested from his restless night's sleep. He walked quickly ahead of her, energetically, his head cocked to the side, as if he were shy, which he wasn't, in the slightest.

'This will be where my beautiful young assistant will make my coffee,' he said, deadpan – she groaned and laughed from behind the camera – 'and these shelves will be where we'll put all my BAFTAs, and this desk is just perfect for *taking* you on *right now*.'

She yelped as he pulled the phone out of her hand. Her filming froze on his face – his strong jaw, his untamed eyebrows, his piercing eyes alight in the moment.

The sex had been quick and fun and filled her with confusion about ending their relationship. Everything was moving so fast. There hadn't been a moment since that strange evening at the pub with John, several months before, when it had felt right to talk to Robert about her doubts. Robert was all-encompassing. When she was with him, she couldn't see beyond him.

Today, he was showing her his new production company.

'Get dressed, you hussy. I've got a surprise for you,' Robert declared.

'Please god, no.' She hated surprises.

'It'll be fun. I promise.'

They jumped in the car and drove up through Kentish Town, through the residential streets of Waterlowe Park and up Swain's Lane, across Hornsey Bridge and down into Whitehall Park. He parked in a street called Cheverton Road.

Instead of ringing the bell at number two, he pulled out some keys and walked right in.

'What are we doing?' Francesca whispered, as they walked up the narrow staircase to the third floor in the old Victorian terrace. An old pram and a Hoover sat in the corner of the small landing, where there was a front door, which he unlocked.

The flat was a dilapidated nightmare, squashed into the eves.

In the sitting room, 'I heart Fran' was scrawled in white paint across the broken floorboards.

She laughed and he grabbed both her hands and led her to the skylight window.

'See? We can see the roof of Aspect Films from here.'

'Aspect Films?'

'That's what I'm going to call the production company.'

'And this place?'

'I've bought it. New flat. New company. New live-in lover.'

'What?'

'Will you move in with me?'

She looked around. There were holes in the plasterboard, a broken sink, filthy skylights. But she didn't hate the flat or the idea of moving in with Robert. In fact, a calm came over her. She immediately imagined her life there, a simple life: few complications, minimal stress, streamlined happiness.

She realised she would be mad to leave Robert. He loved her. He was offering her a good life. John was a figment of her imagination. An aberration. He'd had his chances, and he'd blown them. Robert was real, and he was offering her a real life.

*

With no money to do it up, Francesca had slowly added new bits of colour to their little home in the eves. Like a bird finding pretty twigs for its nest, she had found Eastern patchwork tiles in blues, ochres and greens for the kitchen, salvaged from a skip; stacked piles of pastel crockery onto the oak shelves to hide the cracks; draped the plain round table next to the sofa with a brightly printed scarf; knitted – she was in a knitting phase – a striped cushion-cover to match, in an unmatchy sort of way. From market stalls she collected a series of multicoloured glass bottles, thin, short, tall and bulbous, to line the high dormer windowsill. They refracted a jewelled light onto the walls. For the boring white bathroom she had found an aquamarine shower curtain, patterned with humming birds, and she had lugged a big green fern in an earthenware pot back from the local nursery to place by the bath.

Every day that she wasn't working, she added to her nest, while Robert worked all hours with Waheed to start up Aspect Films down the road. Every day she felt more and more at home, and more and more convinced that she had made the right decision to stay with Robert.

She firmly believed that everyone could have a good life as long as they had the right attitude to it. And Robert was going to be the one to share it with her.

CHAPTER TWELVE

John

Dilys pulled off her high heels and bent at the waist, sighing, pressing her forehead into her suit skirt. 'What a day.'

'Supper's on the table,' he said, hanging her coat up.

John was on autopilot, leading a double life. While his body carried out routine actions at home for Dilys, his brain was heavy with thoughts of Francesca and their disagreement about his mother and Robert's pills. It had triggered a nasty, low-lying, gnawing feeling in his gut that he couldn't shift.

Dilys padded into the kitchen, barely registering his presence, plonking herself at the kitchen table in front of the knife and fork John had laid for her.

'Are they all asleep?'

'The girls are. Harry's reading.'

John poured her a glass of wine, which she gulped at, throwing her head back afterwards. 'God, I needed that.'

'Bad day at work?'

'Could I have the proper fork?'

By mistake, he had laid the smaller salad fork. 'Sorry,' he said, rapidly replacing it with the one she preferred.

'Seriously, John. It's not hard to lay the bloody table properly, is it?'

John became immediately wary, double-checking the green beans were not overdone and that the dill sauce was well salted, hyper-aware that her displeasure could turn nasty. He sensed danger.

'You know that five-storey Edwardian on the corner of Bruton Square?'

'Yes,' he said, opening the oven.

The salmon steaks were burnt at the edges. He was petrified that she might see. Before he laid it in front of her, he surreptitiously picked off the burnt bits. His hands shook as he performed the task.

'Someone put an offer in two days ago and then they pulled out today after their third viewing with me this morning.'

'Why?'

She picked at her food. 'She wanted a lift installed and her planning guy said she couldn't have one.'

John guffawed, as he slid into the chair next to hers. 'Millionaires' problems.'

'*Bill*ionaires.'

'Bastards, the lot of them.'

Dilys didn't smile. She pushed her food away from her, casually, as though she was bored by it, and crossed one knee over the other.

'So, Fran moved in today?' she asked, out of the blue, reading his mind.

'Yup.'

Dilys clicked her tongue. 'I really never thought she'd do it.'

'Really?'

'I thought she'd bottle it and rent some pokey dive in Peckham, or somewhere.'

He focused on sipping his water and then said, 'Dilys…?'

'Yes, love?'

'Do you think Mum feels guilty about Robert?'

'Wouldn't you if it was Harry?'

'Don't say that.'

'It's true though, isn't it?'

'We were brought up by the same mum and I never had those issues.'

'But you've got *me*.' She squeezed his knee.

'Francesca was good with him.'

She exhaled. 'Permissive, you mean.'

'He wasn't a teenager.'

'He behaved like one.'

'I was a bit harsh with Fran today.'

'Didn't you help her with the bed?'

'The wardrobe.'

'She should be grateful.'

'She was, but at Millfords, we had an argument, sort of…'

'You went to Millfords?'

'We needed some caffeine, believe me.' He grinned, remembering how much it had hurt to laugh while he had been pinned to the floor by the wardrobe.

'Why didn't you take her to The Bakery?'

'It was full,' he lied, standing up to clear the table.

'God, she's actually going to be living in *our* village,' Dilys snorted, handing him her picked-at plate.

'You were all for it before.'

'I didn't want you bad-mouthing Letworth. You know how superior Fran can be about London.'

Dilys had often accused Francesca of being smug about the cultural superiority of London. According to Dilys, Francesca spent her whole life swanning about with actresses and film directors and songwriters, talking of books and politics, passing around joints at dinner parties. Perversely, Dilys liked the idea of adopting bohemian aspirations, which were not expressed by their expensive house and her high-powered property career and exclusive private schools for their three children. But she loved buying modern art for their architecturally interesting Round House, and enjoyed being married to a writer. John's ability to earn a good living from a creative job held a certain cachet within the mix of wealthy hedgefund managers and landowners and parochial solicitors, whom she both courted and was bored by; she slagged off their talk about their wine cellars and ski holidays, but gladly dabbled in the odd line of cocaine that they brought out on special occasions.

'Robert was the one who was superior about London. Not Fran.'

She swiped her glass from the table. 'You never agree with anything I say.' And she stormed out.

John let out a long sigh. He had tried so hard to make supper perfect for her.

*

They spent the rest of the evening in separate rooms. Dilys watched a film on her laptop and John read in the study on his lazy-boy chair, which was the only piece of his own furniture that Dilys had allowed him to keep. He liked to sit in it when she was angry with him. It was like a supportive friend. Nevertheless, when he heard Dilys go around the corridor to bed, he followed. He wanted to make things right between them. His mother had always warned him against going to sleep on bad feelings.

He stood next to her in front of the mirror of their en suite bathroom, and smiled at her reflection. Her expression remained impassive.

She applied eye-cream, apparently to lessen her eye bags. John did not see any eye bags. She smelt of coconut oil and perfumed lotion. Her legs were shiny. Her long blonde hair was centre-parted and blow-dried. John thought she looked good enough to package up and ship off to Harrods. But her reflection did not stir him. This depressed him.

As soon as he began brushing his teeth, she turned off her electric toothbrush and unrolled a flannel. She stood there with her hip sticking out, waiting for something.

'What?' He spat out his toothpaste.

She immediately ran the tap and began washing the basin.

'It's disgusting how you leave the sink filthy after you've brushed your teeth.'

'Do I?' John was genuinely baffled. She had never said anything before.

'I spend my whole bloody life cleaning up after you lot.'

Her movements were jerky and fast as she wiped. His muscles tensed. He stayed quiet and still. He recognised another shift in her mood.

'While you fiddle around on your laptop planning coffee mornings with Francesca, I'm stressed out of my head trying to earn money for this family, and the last thing I need after a long day is to tidy up your crap.'

'I'm sorry you're tired,' he said, clocking that the coffee morning with Francesca had roused her jealousy, stepping cautiously. How could he have been so careless, mentioning Millfords like that? He should have predicted her jealousy.

'Don't you dare turn this around!' she screeched, staring at him, bug-eyed, her cheeks hollowed out by the down-lighters.

'I wasn't,' he mumbled, defending himself in a rash, unthinking moment. As the words escaped, he instantly regretted them.

Dilys' face darkened, and she tightened the sharp knuckles of her hand and punched them hard into his right eye. Blobs of distorted light crowded his vision, the pain ricocheted through his skull, shaking his brain. He couldn't breathe for a moment.

'Shit,' he hissed, covering his eye, bending over his knees to stop himself from passing out, shame flushing his cheeks as though she had punched those too. '*Shit!*' he repeated, holding back his natural instinct to retaliate. He had too much strength in him to react.

Dilys dropped her fist, rubbing at it as she stalked out of the en suite. 'I'm sick of you talking down to me all the time,' she spat.

The door to their bedroom slammed.

Light-headed from shock, he lay down on their bed, cupping his hand over his throbbing socket. He fell asleep with the light on.

At some point in the middle of the night, he felt her hand pushing down on his chest, and her nakedness straddling him. In a barely conscious daze they had sex, as another small piece of his self-worth crumpled and died inside.

Afterwards, Dilys slept next to him, but John lay there awake, furious with himself for being aroused after her violence. His cowardliness shocked him, and the worming, slimy shame made him sick to his stomach.

Eventually, he became too tired to think and his eyelids drooped. But, as sleep began to envelop him, he was jolted by a shadowed vision of Robert hovering over him in the dark.

'Do you want to go on a midnight adventure?' Robert had whispered in John's ear, waking him up.

'I'm too sleepy.'

'I'm going to spy on Mummy.'

'In bed?'

'She went down to the pool. I saw with my binoculars.'

'Why is Mummy by the pool? It's dark,' John asked, rubbing his eyes.

'She always goes. I want to show you. Come on.'

'But what if Valentina catches us?'

'Stop being such a wuss.'

'I'm not a wuss.'

'Come down to the pool then.'

John had trotted after his brother, undetected through the house, his heart pounding in his skinny chest, his striped pyjama bottoms wet from the grass as they ran across the lawn.

They both stopped just before the lawn met the crazy-paving flagstones. John could see that the poolhouse light was on and he sensed that there was something very wrong about his mother being inside.

'Let's go back. I'm scared,' John whispered.

'Come on. I want to show you.'

John dithered as he watched his brother move stealthily towards the poolhouse. And then he followed his big brother.

On tiptoes, Robert was peering in through the window, stock-still, watching something that John knew he never wanted to see.

John opened his eyes into the pitch black, and twisted in the sheets, reeling from the confusion and fear that this half-dream brought. The memory was part of his deeper being, but it shocked him as if it was new. He was disoriented, petrified, but had no nightmare to refer to. *Breath.* Breathe. *Where's my breath?* In the dark, in the silence, while the world slept, his chest tightened vicelike over his heart, which was vibrating like a rocket taking off, as waves of pins and needles infected his flesh. Terror shredded his logical thought processes. He couldn't see anything but blinding spots in front of his eyes. His back was soaked with sweat. It was hard to believe that he wasn't dying. Surely this was what dying felt like. Instinctively, he reached for his phone to call an ambulance. As he scrabbled on his bedside table in panic, the phone clattered to the floor. His hands had cramped into paralysed, deformed claws. He left it. His lips had turned too numb to talk anyway.

He had been here before.

After Robert had died, they had started. The doctor said they were 'anxiety attacks'. In and out, his chest was heaving; he wouldn't get through it. In and out. In and out. *Clear the mind. Breathe.* He pictured Francesca's smile. His heartbeat slowed, he regained some form of connection between his mind and his body. He lay there, blinking in the dark, staggered by what his body – or mind – had just put him through. If that was just an anxiety attack, what was a real heart attack like? What was dying like? What had Robert been through as he had jumped? What had the expression in those deep-set blue eyes been telling him that night? Tears poured down his cheeks. How would he ever be able to forgive himself?

Very carefully he climbed out of bed. He was too scared to go back to sleep.

'Where are you going?' Dilys said, in a clear, irritated voice, as though she had not been asleep.

'Nowhere, just getting a glass of water,' he said.

He stayed awake all night, waiting for the light, trying not to think about his past, wishing that Francesca was by his side, craving her calming, understanding presence.

CHAPTER THIRTEEN

15 years ago

Francesca stopped her work on the lantern she was painting, to take a call from Robert.

'I need you to do something for me,' Robert said, sounding far away and harried.

'What time is it there?'

'Can you do something for me?'

'Are you okay?'

'Jesus. Fran. I'm fine. Can you find my sleeping pills in the bathroom cabinet and then…'

'Go home? I can't, I'm on set in Bristol.'

'SHIT!'

'You can't sleep?'

'It's so light all the fucking time. There's a fucking midnight sun, for Christ's sake.'

'Calm down, Robert.'

'I can't calm down. I'm going fucking insane here.'

'I thought you'd packed your pills.'

'They've run out.'

'Why don't you go to a doctor there and get some more?'

'I can't do that. You have to Fed Ex me some more. Today.'

'Are you serious? To Northern Alaska? You're back home in five days. Can't you find some over-the-counter herbal pills?'

'Fuck. If you won't help me, I'll sort it out myself.'

And he hung up.

She stared at her phone for ages, distracted from the lamp she was supposed to be aging. Then she called John.

'Sorry, are you busy?'

'I'm in my shed. But I could do with a break.'

'How's Billy?'

'He's just jumped off a building to save Poppy.'

'He's such a dude.'

'What's up?'

'Do you know anything about the sleeping pills Robert takes?'

'Yes. He's mentioned them.'

'They've run out and now he wants me to send them to him in Alaska.'

'Can't he get some in a pharmacy over there?'

'He said he can't. He got really angry about it. Do you think I should send them to him? I mean, is it even legal?'

'Don't even think about it. He's being an idiot.'

Francesca was relieved.

'Thanks, John. I'm glad you said that. I just wanted to check. Good luck with saving Poppy.'

CHAPTER FOURTEEN

Francesca

dpbaqri@harleystreetpractices.co.uk
RE: Robert Tennant
Dear Dr Baqri,
*Following my husband's death, I have become aware that
Robert was a patient of yours. In the light of this, I would like to
apply for his medical records. Would you please let me know
how I go about doing this? I am registered as his next of kin.
With best wishes,
Francesca Tennant*

There was something wrong about contacting Dr Baqri behind
John's back. It felt sneaky. And, strangely, it felt like a betrayal of
Robert, too.

After sending the email, the house fell too quiet. I wasn't used
to countryside-quiet. I felt very alone.

I decided to Skype my mother, whom I had been avoiding since
I'd moved. If Dr Baqri emailed back, it would flash up on my screen.

'Show me the kitchen,' Mum said, once connection had been
made.

I picked up my laptop and panned around the sitting room
of my new house, lingering on the big bunch of blue hydrangeas.

'Camilla dropped them by yesterday.'

Mum puckered her lips to take a sip from her beer bottle. 'Lovely.' And then another sip. 'Let's see the rest of the house.'

Reluctantly, I took her on a computer tour, into the kitchen, and then up to the bedrooms, and back downstairs again, running an upbeat commentary on all the changes I had made since we had moved in a week before.

Despite the time I had spent rearranging the bits and bobs on the surfaces, reconfiguring the furniture, hanging pictures, restacking Alice's large collection of puzzles on her shelves, nothing from the old flat looked right in the new space.

'Oh, Franny-pants, it looks awesome.'

My mother's screen was placed in front of her cleavage, where tanned wrinkle lines fanned out in a bloom from her top. I could see up her nose. The psychedelic print of the large scarf that was draped across the wall behind her made me dizzy.

'It's so perfect, isn't it?' I said, but I wanted to cry.

Wrong, wrong, *wrong*. Everything was wrong: the confined, low-ceilinged, damp, creaky cottage; the quietness of the village; the old ladies who stared at me; the dingy local shop with dusty greeting cards; the hairy chin of my next-door neighbour that made Alice gawp; the twee wooden 'Don't park on the grass' and 'Don't let your dog off the lead' and 'Make sure to clip your hedge with nail scissors' signs everywhere (well, not exactly as bad as the latter, but still); the twenty-minute motorway drive to the nearest town; the scuffling of field mice in the loft, and the huge spider in the bath. The list of small dislikes was endless, amounting to a great big dislike of everything about the country. The logistics of the sale and the move had been utterly exhausting, and I doubted it had been worth it.

'Your dad and I can't wait to come and stay.'

'When d'you think you can?' I asked, trying not to sound too desperate.

'Dad's coccyx is still bad, love, and money's a bit tight at the mo. But we'll get our thinking caps on, okay?'

'Sure.' I tried hard to smile. 'Managed to get hold of Emily recently?'

Mum sighed. 'One brief conversation with her in some deserted beach in San Jose. Did you see what she's done to her hair in those pictures she sent?'

My younger sister had shaved her long, dark hair off for charity. She had raised £2950 for a school in Costa Rica. I envied her. Wild and free, with a grubby backpack and dirty toes, roaming the world, doing good things for other people.

After Aspect Film's closure, I should have gone with my first instincts, bundled Alice up, packed sunscreen and escaped when I could.

'I think it suits her.'

My mother had a coughing fit. For someone who had promoted an alternative life, she did not seem to enjoy the fact that Emily had chosen a truly alternative one. She recovered herself and said, 'I'm very glad I've got one *settled* daughter, at least.'

Settled? Is that how she viewed my life, after what I had been through?

To antagonise her, I decided to praise my in-laws.

'It's been good to have the Tennants around the corner, actually. They've been really helpful. I might have felt a bit isolated otherwise.'

I was not going to tell my mother about the pill bottle.

Mum peered into the screen. 'Do you feel isolated, Franny?'

'No, I said I *might* have felt isolated, if they weren't nearby.'

'When your dad and I first left London, I thought we'd made the biggest mistake of our lives.'

'Really, Mum? I never knew.'

I related to that. When I had closed the door to the cleared-out flat for the last time, the blood had rushed from my head to my toes and I had bent over my knees to regain balance. Lucy had found me like that, and she had coaxed me away, down the stairs. The shadows from the plain trees on the pavements had danced at my feet. The strange fluttering leaves had been a focus, or a guide, to get me from the steps to the car. I drove away in a daze, my senses dulled, drugged on sadness and confusion, while Lucy chatted away from the passenger seat next to me and Alice sang happily in the backseat, unaware of what we had just done. The sounds of their voices drifted in and out, in and out, as though someone was turning the volume up and down. I assume I replied to their questions, if there had been any, but as we drove across Hornsey Bridge, Robert's voice in my head was louder than they could ever have been. He was pleading with me: '*Please don't leave me, don't leave me, don't leave me, please don't leave me.*' It was louder still as we passed Highgate Cemetery, where his body lay, or possibly now turned. He would never have wanted Alice and me to be so close to his family.

Mum said, 'I was trying so hard to put a positive spin on it but I even missed the traffic noises of London.'

I laughed. 'Me, too, a bit.'

'You'll get used to it. Just think of Alice.'

'Yes, the fresh air will be good for her. The school's lovely. And having little Bea around the corner is going to be great.'

A week before we moved, at the end of the summer term, Alice's nursery had thrown a big leaving party for her. They had pinned a painted banner across the hall saying, 'We will miss you, Alice!' and she had stared at it in awe and said, 'I'm famous, Mummy!' Every night since then, she had cried about how much she missed her old nursery and her best friend Tilly.

'It sounds perfect there, honey.'

'It is perfect,' I said, trying the idea out, but then faltered, adding pointlessly, 'I think we might have mice.'

'Call Camilla. She'll know someone.'

'I will.'

'There you go then. All right, love. I'll say goodbye. Marty and Debs are coming over for a barbeque.'

After I'd pressed 'End', I sat staring at my screen. Pointlessly, I clicked into my emails to look for a reply from Dr Baqri, knowing I would have seen a message pop up earlier if he had responded. I pressed refresh. Nothing.

The screensaver photograph of Robert and Alice kicked in. I was overfamiliar with the image: the beaming smile on her face, his big strong arms around her little tummy, brushed with sand, his handsome wide face, with the deep eye sockets and dark hair. Now he was dead, was he omnipresent? Did he know me better than he ever had when he was alive? I had a vision of the coffin, being carried by John and Patrick, and four friends in black suits, and I could smell the hot wool of my black funeral dress. The photograph in front of me, reminding me of how Robert had lived and breathed, became two-dimensional, fake almost, the back light blurring his edges, as though he had never been alive in the first place. The failure to keep the memory of his physical presence, his touch and smell, strong in my mind scared me.

I closed my laptop. It was so quiet in the house I could hear the fridge buzzing from the kitchen. Alice had conked out at seven o'clock, which was unheard of. She liked her new bedroom, at least. I had painted one wall with a colour I had used on a film set years ago. A colour I had craved, like some people might feel thirsty for a drink. The film had been a love story, and the main character's bedroom had been hot pink. The young man in the paint shop in the local market town, Wisborough, had thought I was mad when I asked him if I could mix it myself in the back room.

In bed later, I listened to the incessant scratch, scratch, scratch of the mice above me. Did they never sleep? Maybe they weren't mice at all. For all I knew, they could have been birds making a nest in the guttering. *Or rats*, I thought with a shiver. I put the pillow over my head, and finally drifted off, only to wake a few hours later dripping in sweat. I opened the window, changed my nightie and put a towel on my pillow. The scuffling above continued. I didn't like to think of their teeth and their tails. With every little scratch, their claws burrowed deeper into my thoughts, and snippets of memory came back to me. The sound of Robert opening up the pill bottle in the bathroom at our flat in London: that rattle and crack and rattle, the running of the tap – a soundtrack. When I thought back, carefully, homing in on the details of his behaviour, a clearer picture began to form of his usage of those pills. If I was honest with myself, it was not limited to filming periods only. He took them often, and sometimes in the day, before a stressful meeting, after a long lunch. As I reassessed the patterns, I recalled that this pill bottle, with its grubby label, had lurked in every scene of our past, like a sinister motif in a film noir. It was subtle but re-occurring, and it peppered our lives: in his suitcase, in his briefcase, in his bedside cabinet, in his desk drawers, in hotel bathrooms. It had been everywhere, but I had not wanted to see it. *I had not wanted to see it.*

As light began to glow through the curtains and the birds began their dawn chorus, I lay there on my back with my dry eyes wide open, waiting for my clock to show a decent time, so that I could call John, whom I had to talk to about this scratching in my head. He hadn't been listening at Millfords. I needed him to listen.

*

'What happened?' I cried, staring at John's right eye, which was purple and yellow and bloodshot.

'Dilys has a mean right hook.'

'Ha ha.' I laughed, letting him in. 'Seriously, what did you do?'

'It's nothing.'

I decided not to push for an explanation.

'Have you been using arnica cream?'

'No—?'

'It'll heal faster. I'll get you some.'

Alice came charging through the house. 'Uncle John! Come and see my new paddling pool!'

'A paddling pool? Wow! You won't want this then.' He pretended to hold back a floor puzzle he had brought her.

She pulled it from his hands and hugged it to her chest. 'Thank you!'

'More puzzles,' I said, rolling my eyes. 'We'll have to move out.'

Alice dragged him outside.

Before I nipped upstairs for the tube of arnica cream, I checked my emails, again. There was nothing from the doctor.

I joined them outside.

'Come here,' I demanded.

Poised with a blob of cream on my finger, I stood on my tiptoes. I could feel his breath on my cheek. 'Tell me if it hurts too much.'

The feel of his skin under my fingertips sent shivers down my spine. He was studying my face. Close up, I could see his flesh move over his fine cheekbones as he flinched. I wanted to smooth my hands through the golden strands twisted at his hairline to soothe him. The day we first met was coming alive again between us, as though I was seeing him as I had done back then.

With that innocent memory came always the guilt about what followed years later.

I stopped dabbing his eye. 'How the hell did you do this?'

'A branch hit me when I was on the bike.'

I screwed the cap back on the cream. 'You took up mountain biking again?'

'Uh huh.' He looked away.

'Okay, there you go, all done.'

Alice squirted him in the back with a water pistol, and he groaned and fell on the ground playing dead.

She giggled and her little body fell on top of him.

'Cup of tea? Or is it too hot for tea? I think I've got a couple of cans of iced coffee.'

'Iced coffee would be great.'

After some water-pistol games, John settled down next to me on the other stripy deck chair. I handed him a red tumbler of iced coffee with a banana-patterned straw and I leant back, listening to Alice's splashing, glad that she was distracted.

'How's your first week been?' John asked.

'I haven't been sleeping well.'

'The mice?' He sat up. 'Sorry. That's why I'm here. Want me to look at them now?'

'No, no. Have your drink first.'

'I guess it's very different to London here.'

'What the hell do you do with the kids all summer?'

'Don't worry. Dilys is compiling a list of summer clubs and activities for Alice. The tennis club still has a few spaces. And Bea is signed up for the mini-theatre club that does open-air performances. She's going to ask about a space for Alice.'

'That's very kind of her.'

He bent down and began pulling clumps of grass from the lawn, chucking handfuls to the side.

'Mum's organising a barbeque this weekend.'

'She mentioned that when she dropped round yesterday.'

'Haven't you started hiding in your shed yet?'

'I like her dropping round.'

'You won't for long.'

I tilted my head to look at him. I wondered if it was his way of admitting he had been unnecessarily defensive of his mother at Millfords.

I peered over the wooden side bar of the deckchair. 'Sorry for being so tactless about her the other day.'

'I get why everyone finds her so difficult.'

'But you love her.'

He shrugged. 'She's my mum.'

'I'm not saying that she's guilty of anything. I'm really not. It's just that her reaction to those pills sparked something off in my head. It got me thinking about them,' I said, pausing, before adding: 'Robert really relied on them, you know.'

'He told me he needed them when he was filming.'

'That's what he told us, true.'

'Would it be a problem if he had taken them more often? He did have insomnia.'

'But, John,' I said, leaning forward, 'I just don't know if it was actually Zopiclone in that bottle.'

'We've been over this.' He sighed. 'The toxicology reports…'

'Please hear me out,' I interrupted.

'Okay.'

'I'm remembering other stuff.'

'Like what?'

'Like his irritability before he took one.'

'He's always been irritable.'

'Even as a child?'

'Yup.'

'And all that toast and snacking. He had a real paunch by the end.'

'When he was a kid, he got a bit tubby sometimes.'

'And his mood swings. My god.'

'Fran. None of this is new. His mood could take over the whole household when he was a teenager. I spent my whole life trying to keep him happy and only sometimes it worked.'

'But remember Alaska?' I said, exasperated.

John took a while before he responded. 'The daylight hours would send anyone crazy.'

I leant forward and pressed my hand onto his knee, insistently, wanting him to hear me. 'You didn't hear him on the phone. He was *desperate*.'

At that moment, the back door squeaked open and we both turned around to see Camilla standing there.

She had her chest puffed out, withdrawing a gasp. I withdrew my hand. Her Labradors, Bracken and Holly, raced through, jumping up onto John.

'What in heaven's name happened to your eye, darling?'

'Mountain bike accident.'

She clicked her tongue disapprovingly. 'It's a silly sport. You look appalling.'

'Thanks,' John mumbled, scratching the dogs' necks. Alice ran over and hugged her grandmother.

'Did I leave the door open?' I asked, mildly ruffled by her sudden appearance, troubled that she saw my hand on John's leg, without context.

'I hope you don't mind, I had some keys cut from your spares on the hook.' She jangled them in the air. 'I'll put the spares back.'

'Right,' I said, gaping at John in disbelief.

'I was just walking the dogs and saw John's car, and I thought I'd drop in to tell you that I've called a pest control chap for the mice.'

'Village gossip spreads fast,' I quipped.

John looked sheepishly at me. 'There's nothing as exciting as a Tennant family emergency.'

'He's coming round at six this evening, is that okay?' she said, glaring at John. 'You can go home now, darling. Haven't you got work to do?'

'Loads.'

Camilla's lips pursed. 'Well, off you go then.'

'I'll take a look in the loft first,' he said firmly, standing up. 'There's no need for pest control.'

I grinned at him. 'I'll show you where the hatch is.'

Alice and the dogs trotted behind the three of us as we climbed the stairs.

'STAY! Bracken! Holly! STAY!' Camilla shrieked, making Alice jump.

'It's there.' I pointed to the hatch in the ceiling above my bedroom door.

The door to my room was ajar. Some of my clothes were on the floor and my duvet was rumpled to the right side of the double bed. The left side remained smooth and untouched. The left side would have been Robert's. He had always said that he liked to be near the door, to be my protector, in case anybody came in. I guessed it was more to do with claustrophobia, and the comfort of knowing he could escape if he wanted to. Perhaps Robert had spent his whole life wanting to escape.

'I think you've got a wasps' nest,' John called down.

Camilla tutted. 'John doesn't know about these things. I'll go up.'

'I'll go.'

I darted in front of her and popped up through the hatch. 'But it sounded just like little claws.'

'Come here. Listen.'

A buzzing and crackling was coming from somewhere near his toes.

We crouched down and stared at each other while we listened. The wasps were hitting the sides of their papery nest, with a spiky, scratchy energy. Their busy movements could easily have been mistaken for little animal scrapes.

'Oh, yes.' I smiled.

Our noses were inches apart. A flop of blond hair had fallen over one of his eyes. If we had kissed, it would have been like a dream; an isolated moment suspended in time. I wondered if he felt the charge between us, the bond.

'John, can I tell you something? But you have to swear not to tell your mum,' I whispered.

'What?'

'I've emailed Dr Baqri.'

He stood up and hit his head on a beam. 'What the hell?'

'Found anything?' Camilla barked up through the hatch.

Under my breath, I hurriedly explained, 'I need to put my mind at rest. I need to know for sure that he wasn't taking anything else as well, and hiding it from us.'

'Dr Baqri is totally legit, Fran.' John rubbed his head, and moved to the top of the ladder. 'You might as well cancel Paul, Mum,' he said, climbing back down to his mother. 'It's definitely a wasps' nest. I'll bring round some foam for the nest.'

'That won't be necessary, John,' Camilla said. 'I'll call Paul to tell him to bring some of his special foam.'

John winked at me. 'Special foam?' he sniggered.

I couldn't hold back a giggle.

'Oh god. Give me strength, you two!' Camilla chided. 'It's a strong chemical that zapped all four of the nests in our guttering this year.'

John became serious again. 'I'm sure we've got some of that in the garage. Somewhere.'

'Don't worry. Us girls have got it, haven't we, Francesca?' she said.

I nodded slowly, and shrugged at John doubtfully. 'Yes?'

'John, darling, will you take me home? I can't be bothered to walk back.'

John kissed my cheek.

I didn't want him to leave, but my email to Dr Baqri burned in my conscience. With all of my heart, I hoped that Robert's medical records would not offer up any nasty surprises. After today, I did not want the information to ruin John and me. It was clear that he was sceptical of my theories about Robert's pill habit. Perhaps he was right to be. Perhaps it shouldn't matter what was inside that bottle. In simple terms, John and Camilla, and the rest of the family, were alive, and Robert had chosen to die. The Tennants might be interfering, but they were here for me: dropping around with useful bits and bobs, and checking my loft for pests. It was important to remember that I was lucky to have them.

CHAPTER FIFTEEN

13 years ago

'You're going out again?' Francesca said, sitting up from her horizontal position on the sofa. It was Friday night, but she was hungover from the night before. She assumed that Robert was, too. The previous night, they had been at a screening, and then a party, into the early hours.

'Gary wants to meet me at Soho House to talk about the horror project.'

'*Gary?* That'll be a late one.'

'So?'

'I'm just saying, you've been out drinking every night this week.'

'Don't nag me.'

'I'm not nagging you, Robert.'

'I never thought you'd turn into a nag.'

Francesca's mouth hung open. There was nothing she could say to that. She could not win an argument when he was in these edgy moods. He was right. She was wrong. The status quo never changed.

'Have fun, then,' she mumbled, turning on the television.

At about ten o'clock that evening, Francesca crawled into bed with a banging headache.

At 2.38 a.m., she awoke to the sound of a text:

Staying at Gary's tonight. See you tomorrow morning. Love you x

She fell back onto her pillow. *How bloody predictable*, she thought.

By lunchtime on Saturday, Francesca received another text:

Gary's got tickets to the Arsenal game. Back later x

And then later on, another:

stayiing in hackney tonight. see you tomorro. Levo yoou

Now, she was angry with him. He wouldn't return her calls.

*

In the face of Robert's lost weekend, Francesca had met Lucy for brunch.

They ate avocado on rye toast, surrounded by pink meringues on stands and glass counters filled with rainbow-coloured macaroons.

'He has the longest leash of any boyfriend I know.'

'I don't believe in keeping men on leashes.'

'There are limits to how much freedom they should have.'

'I don't want to be a nag. He's too strong-willed. He'd run a mile.'

'What if he's still like this when you have kids and stuff?'

'Kids?' Francesca cried.

'Not yet, but you live together, and he'll probably propose soon.'

'I'll think about that when it happens.'

'Do you love him?'

The fairytale setting had been too fluffy for Lucy's stark question.

'Yes, of course I love him.' Francesca replied, irritated, but as she said it, she wasn't sure if this was true any more. She had been swept up into loving him, but he was hard to love sometimes.

'Have you talked to John about it?'

'John's in baby world.' Francesca screwed up her face in distaste. 'He's so shattered he can hardly speak. Dilys makes him do *everything*, while she has manicures and massages.'

'Is she that bad?'

'She's okay, I suppose. She's so bloody beautiful. And her body has just snapped back into shape after Harry.'

Francesca regretted the bitterness in her tone. With a wry smile, Lucy said, 'I think you need a meringue.'

She plonked one huge pink mound in front of Francesca. 'You have to talk to Robert about this binge drinking.'

'I'll do it today when he gets back.'

One bite of the meringue made her feel sick.

'Today. Promise?'

'Promise. Today.'

Today turned out to be tomorrow, Monday morning, at 5 a.m.

He stumbled in, still drunk and reeking so badly she left him in bed. She slept on the sofa. When he finally woke up, she was suitably angry to spark off the conversation she had been dreading.

'Do you think it was okay? Disappearing off for a whole weekend, like that, on some random bender?' she yelled.

'No.'

'I'm worried about you! Your health. Your liver. Your mental health? I mean, how can you work effectively when you're so hungover all the time?'

'I know. Sorry.'

'I was furious with you.'

'Was?' he said, shuffling on his knees across the sitting room floor and leaning his head onto her lap.

'I *am* furious.'

'Sorry. I'm really sorry. It won't happen again.'

'That's what you said last time.'

'Honestly. This time it's true. I didn't even have a very good time.'

Of course, it had been easier to forgive him. He was sorry. He said he would never do it again. What more could she do?

The following day, he had obsessively researched and booked a last-minute, special-deal holiday for them both to an ice hotel in Norway to see the Northern Lights.

After he booked it, his mood crashed. Over a period of days, he was in an unusually low-energy funk. He ate too much toast, and avoided all his calls, including many from Waheed and John. In the three years they had been together, she had never seen him so miserable. She felt guilty, and worried that she had been too hard on him about his weekend with Gary.

John had called his mobile six times. On the seventh, she picked up.

'He's not feeling too well.'

'Flu?'

'No. I mean… he's a bit low.'

There was a long silence.

'He's been depressed before.' John's voice was hesitant.

'Depressed?'

'I'm meeting Waheed at Aspect tomorrow. Want me to come over afterwards?' John said.

'It might cheer him up.'

John turned up the following evening, laden with ingredients for a fish stew. He cooked for the three of them. Robert had been morose and uncommunicative.

Before John left, he spoke to Francesca on the landing outside the front door, which they pulled to.

'We thought these phases had ended,' he said. 'Since he met you.'

'Who's "we"?'

'The family.'

'How long do these "phases" last?'

'Usually for a few weeks. After a film has finished.'

'That's normal, isn't it? I can get low after films.'

'Sure. It's normal.'

'But?'

'No buts.'

'No buts?' Francesca slapped her hip, like Beyoncé, and snickered, feeling a need to release the tension of the evening.

'Sophisticated,' he chuckled.

And there was that glimmer in his tired eyes, the one she had seen when they first met, which they had not once acknowledged. Francesca was relieved that she had never mentioned it. They had become friends, settled with their position as almost family.

CHAPTER SIXTEEN

John

John left Francesca's house smiling to himself, with only a pang of amused irritation at the thought of Paul, with his big, stupid muscles and special foam.

As he drove his unusually quiet mother back to Byworth End, John thought about Francesca's email to Dr Baqri. He worried she was obsessing about nothing, filled with conspiracy theories, looking for conclusive answers to a nebulous thing. They could never talk to Robert again – which would be the only sure way of finding out why he had jumped. And Francesca had not known Robert as a child, in the way that he and his parents had. He had always been difficult, years before his mind could have been altered by medication. Moreover, John did not want her raking up the past. He was finding it difficult enough to move on as it was.

'How's Harry getting along with his GCSE choices?' his mother asked, pressing open the car window.

'He can't decide between German and Spanish.'

'He should do both, of course.'

'But he wants to take art and drama.'

'He can do *art* in his spare time. And *drama* isn't a real subject.'

But John didn't like how serious life had become for his son. 'It seems like yesterday that he was playing with his Transformers.'

'I thought the school was letting him take some of his subjects early.'

'I'm worried it will put him under too much pressure.'

'Nonsense.'

'That's what Dilys said.'

'She wants the absolute best for him, for all three of them. That's why she pushes them. She is a *wonderful* mother,' Camilla said.

'In spite of being Welsh?' John joked, reminding his mother of her usual rhetoric, to try to make light of what she was implying, challenging her to laugh at herself.

She did not laugh. She closed the window again. 'All three children are very happy. They are so very lucky to have the life they have. They are exceptional children. *Exceptional.*'

'You don't have to tell me that.'

Before they turned right into Byworth End, his mother clicked on the indicator for him. He tightened his fingers around the wheel and pulled up outside the gates.

'One nine four six,' she said.

'I do know the code,' he said, stabbing it into the security system.

They waited for the gates to open onto the long driveway, whose grassy banks were lined with evenly planted rows of silver birch. When the trees had been seedlings, he and Robert had woven in and out of them on their bikes, using them as an obstacle course.

'Do you remember meeting Ian and Penelope Fraser at your dad's seventieth?'

He recalled a stuffy gentleman in a cravat and chinos, and his timid wife who had fiddled incessantly with her coral necklace. This could have described most of the people at his father's seventieth, but the Frasers had been notable for their grown-up son, who had sloped around in black drainpipe jeans, smoking cigarettes and combing his long fingernails through his greasy blue-black hair.

'Umm, I think so. They brought their son, didn't they?'

His mother nodded, her chin bunching as she spoke. 'Their son, Jasper, was a shining star at Marlborough. In all the teams, head of house, hundreds of "A" stars. He was headed for Oxford. But then Ian had an affair and Penelope found out about it, and you know what happened?'

'No,' he said, driving a little too fast over the sleepers.

'Jasper began failing everything at school. He became a total dropout. Did you *see* the state of him at our party?'

'He looked a bit grungy. He had a band. They were about to play a gig in Camden.'

'This was a boy destined for *Oxford*!' Camilla repeated, slapping her hand on the dashboard. 'But his father couldn't keep his little pecker in his trousers!'

'A charming tale, Mother.'

She sniffed. 'Just making conversation.'

And pigs might fly, he thought. He swung the car around in front of the house, slammed on the breaks and waited, sullenly, for his mother to get out of the car.

'Thanks, darling. See you at the weekend,' she said lightly, letting the dogs out.

John watched her hold her chin high as she walked in front of the car. He wanted to run her over.

CHAPTER SEVENTEEN

Francesca

'You're Paul?' I asked. He did not look like Pest Control. I was reminded of John's joke about his special foam, and almost burst out laughing.

'I've come to sort out your wasp problem.'

'Sorry. Yes. Come in.'

He seemed too tall and solid to be in my tiny house. It was like squeezing Superman into a dolls' house.

'Would you like a cup of tea?'

'I'll have a look at the nest first, if that's all right?'

'Of course. Sorry.'

Once I had shown him where it was, I left him to it, and fiddled around in the kitchen trying to remember how to make tea, feeling a little flustered. Alice was playing with her mini china tea-set in her room. By the time he came down from the loft, I had at least managed to boil the kettle.

'All sorted,' he said, putting his tool bag on to the floor, adding, 'Don't let your little one outside for a few hours.'

'Did you meet Alice?'

'She left me a cup of tea on the ladder, and a puzzle to do.' He grinned.

'A better host than I am then. How do you take it?'

'Milk, two sugars, thanks. So, you moved last week?'

'This week. Monday.'

'From London?'

'Yup.' I sighed.

'I grew up in Ladbroke Grove, before it got trendy.'

'You're a Londoner?'

'Through and through.'

'What made you move down here?'

'My wife's from around here.'

'Do you have kids?'

'Two daughters. They live with her now.'

'Oh. Sorry.' I stirred in his sugar and decided to try sugar in my tea for a change.

'Don't be. I think I'm a better dad now than I was when we were together.'

'Really?'

'I make more effort. Before, I used to take it all for granted.'

'I know what you mean,' I said, absently, still stirring.

'I'm so sorry you lost your husband. I can't imagine what you went through.'

I studied his face. He had pointy cheekbones and crinkles around his eyes, as though he smiled too much in the sunshine. His sandy brown hair was receding, but his strong features made up for it. I handed him his mug.

'Did you ever meet Robert?'

'Once or twice, at Byworth End. He was a real force of life, from what I gathered. A proper gob on him, that one. I liked him.'

'Yes.' I laughed, grateful that he did not talk about him awkwardly, as though his life had been sad before he had died. 'I bet he hovered around and asked hundreds of questions about what you were doing.' I took a sip of my tea. The sweetness made my teeth tingle.

'Honestly, once, when he was down visiting Mrs Tennant, I was fixing the drains at Byworth End, and he wanted to understand the whole drainage system of the house. Honestly, he could've sat an exam in plumbing by the end of day. And he made me four cups of tea. I was wired when I got home.'

'You're a plumber, too?'

'Nah. I just picked up some basic stuff from Dad.' He laughed. 'I'm a fireman.'

'A fireman. Wow.'

I imagined him stalking out of a burning building holding a child in his arms, muscles bulging under his smouldering clothes.

'Most of it's rescuing cats and waiting out shifts.'

'Yes, but you do have to go into burning buildings sometimes.'

He shrugged. 'Everyone has their shit to deal with,' he said simply.

It felt good to talk to someone I didn't know, to experience a different perspective, free of the Tennants' complex, overprivileged dramas. I pictured John's shy, neurotic handsomeness, and felt weighed down by it. With Paul, I felt a desire to reinvent myself.

'Sometimes I worry about Alice. She's experienced too much heartache at such a young age. I feel guilty about it all the time.'

'*You* feel guilty?'

The emphasis on 'you' unsettled me. 'I want to be both parents, and I can never be.'

'It's all about the Plan B.'

'What do you mean?'

'I read this book once, when my wife left me, which talked about accepting Plan B when Plan A doesn't seem to be panning out.'

I liked the idea of Plan B.

'Do you think Plan B will ever feel anything other than a compromise?'

'Don't know. But you won't know unless you try.'

'How's your Plan B going?'

He grinned. 'It's a work in progress.'

'I like that.' I smiled back, then shyly looked to the ground.

'Right. I'll be off. I'll leave my card just in case you have any other things that need sorting.'

'Thanks, Paul. I really appreciate it.' I followed him to the door.

On the doorstep, he turned back briefly, and said, 'If you fancy a drink in the pub any time, let me know. No strings. It's just, I know what it's like to be on your own suddenly. I was lonely after Katie left me.'

I didn't know what to say. If I had spoken, I would have burst into tears.

He walked off, waving behind him. I realised I hadn't paid him. 'Oh, wait, sorry, I've got your cash.'

'Nah. Owe me a drink. See you soon, Francesca.'

And he jumped into his pickup truck. I watched him drive away, around the green, his red taillights sparkling in the dusky evening.

As soon as he had gone, the anxiety about Robert's medical records rushed back into my mind. How could I possibly make a Plan B, when I hadn't yet let go of Plan A? The task ahead of me, and what I might uncover about Robert's suicide, clashed with my desire to live freely, to find hope beyond death. I wanted to put it all back in the box, and rewind myself back to London.

CHAPTER EIGHTEEN

12 years ago

'How long is this speech going to be?'

Francesca reached for the stack of pages that lay on Robert's desk.

'Don't read it,' Robert snapped, slamming his hand down on the mess of words.

'Why don't you have a break?'

'I've got to get it done.'

'You've got three weeks.'

'It's not enough time.'

'It's only meant to be a few short words about how much you love me,' she teased.

'I want to put some stuff in about Mum and Dad, and John.'

'It's not a memoir.'

'I need to get it all down and then I can edit it.'

'I'll leave you to it.'

'Don't watch television in here, please. It's distracting.'

'Sure.'

She kissed his head, found a book and snuggled up in bed, vaguely worried about him. A wedding speech should not have been causing him this much angst.

Before going to sleep, she checked on him. His eyes were wild and his handwriting barely legible. The written pages had accumulated, as had those in the wastepaper bin at his feet.

She brought him a cup of herbal tea, to calm him. To see him like this tormented her.

'I can't say it how I want to say it.'

'Maybe write less. Start again.'

'Start again? Are you mad?'

'Or ask John?'

'John?' he spat.

'He's a writer.'

'On a crap kids' show,' he snorted, flicking a bottle of his sleeping pills across his desk. It clattered against a paperweight, sounding empty. Francesca assumed he had taken one, and wondered whether this was the reason his focus was cloudy.

'Sorry, I'm just trying to help.'

He put his head in his hands. 'I need to get it down. What's in my head.'

Francesca retreated, deciding it was best to leave him.

When she woke up the next morning, she saw that he was not lying beside her. A light shone from under the door of their bathroom.

Blurry eyed, she peered around the door.

He was sitting slumped on the edge of the bath. There was an open box of paracetamol on the basin opposite him.

'Are you okay?'

He slurred his words. 'Feeling a bit sick.'

'Have you been sick?'

'Headache,' he replied, looking up at her. His face was clammy and deathly pale.

She picked up the packet of painkillers. 'Have you taken one?'

'A few,' he snorted, and then he slid off the bath and sank onto his knees in front of the toilet and wretched.

Her breathing slowed, her hearing sharpened, her vision tunnelled.

'When did you take them?'

He spat bile into the toilet bowl and rasped, 'Hour ago, half hour, two hours… Dunno.'

As she picked up the box of paracetamol, her movements were measured and careful. She counted each empty pocket. At twenty-six, she awoke to the reality of what he had done.

'We have to get you to the hospital.'

'Nooo,' he mumbled.

In a state of absolute calm, Francesca methodically dressed him and herself, and drove him the five minutes to the Whittington A&E department.

There was no five-hour wait for Robert: they were rushed straight through as soon as she described how many pills he had taken. She waved the empty box at the doctors. The curtain was pulled. A nurse bustled her away to a waiting area. A gastric lavage was performed.

After the procedure he slept, and then he and Francesca talked. He was groggy but raw and honest.

'I was writing about growing up at Byworth End and how happy we'd been and then I hated what I'd written. It was false, and I started all over again. All this horrible crap about Mum came out. I mean, I can't say all that crap, can I?'

'What horrible crap?'

'You know what she's like.'

She nodded. She did indeed.

'So, I started again and again and AGAIN. Like a vicious cycle. It was sending me completely fucking mad.'

'And so, you took paracetamol to…?'

He interrupted, 'I didn't want to die, Fran.'

Tears rolled down her cheeks. 'We're getting married in three weeks.'

He crushed her fingers. 'I just wanted to stop my thoughts. I couldn't stop my thoughts.'

'Do you still want to marry me?' she asked tearfully.

There had been a delay. He had looked up to the ceiling. In that pause, she held her breath and wished for him to release her from their bond. They had been together for four years and Francesca was only thirty years old and she suddenly felt stifled by the prospect of a whole life of him. She could not cope with the constant ups and downs, with the disquiet.

'You're my rock. I'd be a mess without you, Frannie. I love you more than life itself.'

The latter was a bleak and appropriate cliché. A threat, perhaps. And she accepted it.

She had a feeling that she was on a speeding train that was going too fast to jump from. She couldn't leave him. He was unstable. He was a wreck. It would kill him.

CHAPTER NINETEEN

John

'The receptionist at the clinic said he'd call me sometime this afternoon,' Francesca said.

'Let's try and enjoy the day, until then.'

The strip of green sea hung in front of them. John's ankles were crossed on the pebbles, next to Francesca's crossed ankles. Their feet were too near to the lapping shoreline. His skin tingled after a bracing swim. A blue, yellow and red striped windbreak was in a semi-circle around them. John had almost thrown his arm out of the socket hammering in the stakes. In the distance, the wind was blowing the children's hair horizontally from their heads, but John and Francesca were sheltered; warm in their fleeces, the newspapers strewn at their feet, hot tea in paper cups in their hands.

'We should move our stuff back,' she said, pulling her knees up.

'We probably have about twenty minutes before we're gonners.' John yawned, trying to ignore how tense she was. It had been an effort to persuade her to come, and now he was beginning to wish he hadn't bothered. All afternoon, Fran had been guarded and uncommunicative. There was a physical unease between them. She wasn't holding eye contact.

She began gathering their towels, her fringe blown flat back, a scowl on her pretty features.

'Don't worry! Let the sea take us!' he cried over the wind, trying to bring out her smile.

She stopped, sighing as she stood straight, rubbing her temples as she looked out to the horizon.

Then a mobile phone rang from her bag.

She scrabbled in her bag to answer it as though her life depended on it.

'Is it the clinic?' John asked.

'Yes.'

As he watched her walk up the shingle, speaking intensely into her phone, he began to worry.

When she returned, her mood had changed, as though a plug had been pulled. She did not look relieved, but her face looked wide open with shock.

'What did he say?'

She exhaled and held her hair down. 'They don't have Robert's medical records.'

'Why not?'

'Apparently, Robert stopped being a patient of his in 1990.'

Taken aback, John said, 'He was only sixteen then.'

'Yes,' she replied, throwing a pebble into the sea.

'I was sure Robert told me he saw Dr Baqri about his insomnia.'

'I've been concocting conspiracy theories, John. Just forget about it,' she mumbled, chucking a big rock into the water. It clonked on the surface and disappeared, leaving a hole in the murky foam.

But he could not forget about it now. The more John thought about it, the more certain he became about the conversation he had shared with Robert about Dr Baqri.

It had been summer time. They had been sitting on the decking at Byworth End. Robert had been spirited, and they had both been quite drunk. John had passed comment on how well rested he looked. It had prompted a conversation about his insomnia, and how much more energy he had after a recent period of good sleep. 'Thanks to Dr Baqri,' he had said, very specifically, winking at his mother. She had just come out to place a large jug of Pimm's in front of them, and scolded them for dwelling on depressing subjects on such a pretty day.

But why had Robert lied to him?

*

John let himself in through the front door of Byworth End, safe in the knowledge that his mother was at her Pilates class and that his father was clay pigeon shooting.

He could hear Valentina hoovering in the sitting room. He snuck past her and crept upstairs to his parents' bathroom.

Inside the medicine cabinet, he looked around for the pill bottle and then he remembered Francesca telling him that his mother had put it in a red washbag. He hurried into his parents' bedroom.

Instantly, he became overwhelmed by the smell of his mother's perfume.

By her bedside there was a little dish filled with her gold rings and long necklaces; laid on the bed was a white kaftan. In a rush, he was a little boy by the pool again.

A crack of light appeared through the opening door of the poolhouse.

Their beautiful mother had appeared. Backlit by the bulb behind her, the shape of her body was visible through the diaphanous cotton of her kaftan, fluttering so close to Robert's face. His small figure was crouched underneath the cobwebbed window, in the shadows to her right.

John took a step back, further under the conifer tree, shivering, teeth chattering, watching, worried his breathing was too loud. He wanted to run back to bed and snuggle under his duvet, but he couldn't leave Robert now.

A surge of guilt and shame blocked out more. He sat on the bed. His breathing became erratic. A new, burning curiosity about these pills, about everything that his mother might have been hiding from him, remotivated his search.

Finally, he found the red washbag tucked away at the back of her sock drawer.

Just as Francesca had said, the little brown pill bottle was inside. He unscrewed the white cap and shook out some oblong white pills. The pharmaceutical make of the pills was carved across each tablet, but it did not correlate with the name on the label of the bottle.

Francesca had been right.

Valentina's vacuum cleaner fell silent downstairs. He held his breath. It then started up again, but louder, closer. Worried he would be caught snooping, he closed the pill bottle, grabbed a pair of his father's golf shoes – his alibi – and dashed downstairs to Valentina.

Valentina switched off the Hoover with her arthritic fingers. 'John! Ola! Handsome chicky-dee,' she cried, pinching his cheeks and pushing his hair back.

'Hi, Valentina,' he said, kissing her cheek, smelling aniseed on her breath, and olive oil in her scraped-back grey bun. Her black eyes screwed up like raisins in her lined face when she smiled at him.

'Your mumma, your papa, is out.'

'I know, I was just borrowing Dad's golf shoes.' John never played golf.

She narrowed her eyes at him. 'Si?'

'Not really,' he confessed. Then, he pulled out the pill bottle and held it up. 'Have you ever seen these before?'

'Is your Uncle Ralph's pills?'

Baffled for a second, he said, 'Not Uncle Ralph's. No. They're Robert's.'

She threw her stout arms up in the air and switched on the Hoover again. 'Oh. Si. Si. *Me desculpe*. Si. Si. They Robert's.'

'Why does Mum still have them? Do you know?' he shouted over the noise.

She waved him away. '*Não*. No.'

He went to the plug socket and pressed it off.

She waggled her finger at him. 'Naughty boy.'

John laughed. All his life, he had heard her say that to him. She had been the one to mete out the rules and punishments: to tell them off when they were rude; to slap their wrists if they waved their cutlery about; to stand over them as they struggled with their homework. In equal measure, she had doled out as much love. If he or Robert had cried, she fed them spice cookies and wiped their tears away with her apron before their parents noticed. Neither of his parents had approved of boys crying.

'You still so beautiful, chicky.' She beamed a big, gummy-toothed smile and bustled over to the socket to turn it on again. 'But I busy,' she shouted.

He shook the pill bottle at her again and she blinked furiously, shaking her head.

'Is Robert's,' she repeated emphatically, frowning. 'You put them back. Si?'

John knew her well, and noted a hint of panic in her voice. He wanted to question her further. Her frown stopped him. It was a warning to back off.

For now, he accepted that she was giving nothing away.

But he was certainly not going to put the bottle back.

CHAPTER TWENTY

12 years ago

The chilly draught from the crypt crept around Francesca's ankles. The rustling of the layers of organza on her dress were loud every time she moved. Her shoulders were bare. She felt entirely naked. Behind her, the congregation would be staring and grinning. A few tears would be shed. Camilla's sob echoed around her head. Robert's deep-set blue eyes darted around her, everywhere but on her; the vague scent of whisky on his breath.

She listened to the priest ramble on, while her feet ached in her satin shoes, and she wondered what she was doing standing there. It was meant to be the happiest day of her life and it was turning out to be her worst nightmare. An extravaganza of ice sculptures, expensive chairs and small-time DJs waited for them at Byworth End under the marquee on the lawn. She should have been walking on air.

Searching, searching, searching Robert's face for the love she wanted to feel, she saw the man who had taken twenty-nine paracetamol tablets three weeks before; she saw the man who said he loved her more than life itself. She was going through with the ceremony, to save face, to save them. To save him. Amen.

And there John stood, next to his brother, in a matching suit, so dangerously near to her she could have reached out to touch him. They were friends, yes, but as best man, he looked like a groom. Mentally, she reworked the ensemble of people around her, switching Robert for John, like a photographer might rearrange his subjects for a pleasing shot. In her head, it looked better. The configuration worked for her, settled her soul. But John was not holding the ring to put it on her finger, he was holding it for his brother. Robert looked too anxious for the occasion. John, too sombre.

To calm her nerves, she imagined that every woman in the congregation would also be staring longingly at John. She was just one of the crowd. He had not chosen her. Robert had.

During the first dance, she and Robert shuffled self-consciously on the uneven parquet floor, and the champagne pushed away her doubts. When she sought out John's face in the circle of other guests, she saw that he was not there. She was relieved, and she felt proud and safe in her new husband's arms.

CHAPTER TWENTY-ONE

Francesca

Hi Fran, hope the wasps are gone. Fancy a drink tonight? Paul

I'll ask Camilla if she can babysit. F x

Cool.

Hi Paul – she can. Where do you want to meet? F x
See you at the Dog and Pheasant at 8pm.

I got dressed into my black T-shirt with the glittery shoulders, and I trimmed my fringe with nail scissors. My heeled boots, which I was wearing for the first time in two years, felt brand new.

Tonight was going to be an antidote to the Tennants. A cure for the ills of my in-laws. After the dead end of Robert's non-existent Harley Street medical records, I wanted to forget about those sleeping pills. Even though John had been mistaken in Dr Baqri, he was right about one thing: I had been looking for something that wasn't there.

Ahead of me, across the moonlit expanse of grass, I was conscious that Paul was already sitting outside, a small candle bobbing in its holder on the table in front of him. I tried to walk as normally as possible towards him. But I sensed that his eyes were not the only eyes watching me. Robert seemed to be present in the blinking stars and bright moon above me, probably laughing at me hobble across the green in my heels, which sunk into the grass with every step. I imagined him wanting to catapult balls of star fire down on Paul's head.

The candle flame blew in the wind, changing the shadows over his face. I had a vision of John sitting there waiting for me instead; in another life, in another universe.

He half stood to kiss me on the cheek, and our cheekbones clashed. He smelt of aftershave, which was a little strong.

'Drink?'

'Yes, please. Whatever you're having.'

I should have gone to the bar myself, to choose and buy my own drink, show him I was an independent woman, but all my energy was caught up in surviving what felt like a betrayal of Robert's memory.

'A pint of bitter?'

I hesitated, trying to remember if I liked bitter. 'Yes, please. But a half pint.'

While I waited for him, I stared at the golden bubbles shooting upwards in his pint glass. They were trying to escape to the surface, wriggling up desperately, but then dying a death the second they reached the surface.

The door to the pub opened, letting out a burst of chatter and clinking from inside. We were the only two people outside. I realised it was chilly and I hadn't brought my jacket. But I was enjoying the peacefulness. The dark silhouetted trees, the pink stripes across the grey sky.

'Want to go inside?' he asked.

'No. It's lovely out here.'

'Yes. It is.' He exhaled as he looked across the green. When he sat down, he passed me his black denim jacket. 'Here. Wear this if you like.'

It was huge and it swamped me, and I wondered why I had bothered dressing up. I imagined he was the kind of man who didn't notice what a woman wore. And then I imagined wearing nothing, in front of him, and fear gripped me. My body was ruined by childbirth; my physical self had been weakened by grief. If he wanted to have sex with me, ever, I would have to be clothed and the light would have to be off.

'What's so funny?'

'Did I laugh?'

'Almost.'

I took a sip. 'I like this, actually.'

'Not your usual?'

'I don't know.' I didn't have a usual anything any more.

He peered at me over his pint glass with a hint of a smile and a raised eyebrow. He thought I was weird, plainly.

'Who's looking after Alice?'

'Camilla.'

He nodded. 'I imagine she spoils her rotten.'

'She adores her, yes.'

'I bet Alice loves living close to John's three.'

'She hasn't got siblings, so, you know…' I trailed off.

'Harry's a great kid.'

'He is, isn't he?'

'Terrible at cricket, poor lad.'

I chuckled. 'Why do they put him through it?'

'John only makes him play when he knows the wife's coming to watch. He lets him read mostly.'

'Really?'

'John's our star player but some days he'll sit out with Harry pretending he's too hungover to see the ball. They sit on the deckchairs, watching and chatting away. They're like a couple of old women.'

'John's a great dad. Really hands-on.'

'Doesn't his wife – sorry, what's her name?'

'Dilys.'

'Doesn't Dilys work in the City or something?'

'Property. She's an estate agent for the super-rich.'

'She must earn a proper packet to afford a house like that.'

'John is really successful, too. Not that you'd ever hear it from him.'

'Writing films?'

'TV mostly.'

'Nice guy. Very quiet. Never sure what's on his mind, though.' Paul tapped his head. I imagined his skull was formed with Neanderthal nodules underneath his tough, tanned skin. Everything about Paul looked strong. The deep grooves around his eyes, the thick veins running across his muscles.

'Let's not talk about the Tennants.'

'They do tend to dominate this village.'

'Imagine being married into them…'

He smiled, uncertainly. 'Do you find it difficult?'

'Camilla's difficult.'

'So I've heard.'

'Have you?'

He finished the last of his drink. 'The old dears around here have wagging tongues.'

'What do they say about her?'

He knocked back his empty glass, as though finishing it off, but there was nothing left. 'Not much,' he replied. 'Another one?'

'Go on. Tell me the gossip about her, Paul.'

He stood with the empty glasses in his hand. 'Honestly, nothing. They just say she's a right old busybody.'

I guffawed. 'You can say that again. You know, she actually cut her own key to my house, without asking me! Can you believe it?'

'From what I've heard, I can.' He was still standing there, with our glasses, ready to get more drinks, but I was on a roll.

'She loves micro-managing everyone's lives. I literally have no independence left. They half-own my house, they have part-ownership of Alice. I basically rely on them for everything. It's pathetic, really.'

'You need a job,' he said, over his shoulder, as he turned to go inside for more drinks.

I sat in the dark, quiet beer garden, listening to an owl's eerie call, and I contemplated the search for a job.

When he returned, I said, 'But I have no skills outside the film industry.'

'What did you used to do?'

'I was a scenic painter.'

'What does that involve?'

'Painting loads of set walls, and sometimes painting the props. I loved doing that.' To illustrate, I brought my phone out and scrolled through my photographs, showing him my before-and-after snaps: before – a fibreglass container, after – a Victorian marble butler sink, the effect done completely with paint; and then an MDF box that I had transformed into a smart antique mahogany blanket box; followed by a cheap IKEA toy that had become an old Victorian keepsake.

'So, you're an artist.'

'Sort of. And a painter and decorator, of sorts.'

'My mates at the station do a lot of that on the side. They earn a bloody fortune.'

'Well, believe me, I can turn a beautiful white room into a damp, mouldy hellhole.' I chuckled, feeling whimsical about the many period film sets that I had transformed, from whitewashed to Dickensian, and how I would lose myself in the detail of the work.

'Shabby chic?' he grinned.

'Oh my god. You have no idea how many chests of drawers I painted and sanded down for friends when that look was in.'

Midway through a sip of his pint, Paul put his glass down. 'What about asking around for work in the local furniture shops? Wisborough has a few.'

'Wisborough has that lovely paint shop, doesn't it?'

'That's right. Archie Parr's.'

'It's so rare to find someone mixing paint by hand these days. I was a bit cheeky and asked the guy working in there if I could mix some hot pink in the back room. For Alice's bedroom.'

'Was it Archie?'

'No, it was Toby or Tony, or someone. He was young.'

'Probably a student. Archie's always looking for assistants. You could ask him if he has any work coming up.'

'That's quite a good plan.'

'A good Plan B, perhaps?'

'Perhaps.'

He held up his pint glass and chinked mine. 'Cheers to Plan Bs.'

As I locked eyes with Paul, I felt a little more in control of my life again. He had reminded me to be more confident about my future, and I felt a rush of gratitude for him. At the beginning of the evening, I might have been using him as a deflection from the Tennants, but now I genuinely wanted to know more about him as a person.

'We've talked about me all night. How is your Plan B going?'

'Mine is all about the kids.'

'Show me some pictures.'

He rummaged in his pocket and brought out his phone, scrolled through and showed me a picture of a little girl, about ten years old, with waist-length black hair and a round, very pretty face; and then a skinny, white-blonde, younger girl, whose features looked exactly like Paul's.

'Beautiful. They are so different.'

'Georgie, the oldest, isn't mine, technically, but she is really, if you get my meaning. Her dad left when she was one and I met Katie shortly after, and then we had Sylvie after that.'

Paul was a gentle giant. The brawn belied the softness of him. I began to imagine what it would feel like to kiss him. A kiss didn't have to lead to sex.

'Did your feelings for Georgie change at all when you had Sylvie?'

'Nah. I love them the same amount. It's just a different kind of love. I never get it when kids talk about their stepdads being dicks to them. It's not right. Just when a kid needs more love than ever, someone else comes along to crush them.'

Paul and I talked about blended families, and about his parents' divorce, and my parents' pseudo-hippy dysfunction. None of the ruptures in his life had killed him, or so he believed. They had apparently made him stronger. He had moved on. Everybody had to move on.

I got the impression that Paul was a black and white kind of man. His life was probably full of real-life goodies and real-life baddies, with nobody wishy-washy in between. I wondered where I might fit in. Did losing my husband make me a goody?

I wanted to kiss Paul. He was different to any man I had been with before. He would run into a burning building to rescue me. For now, that was all I needed to know.

When he walked me home, I was a little tipsy and I fantasised about him picking me up in his arms and carrying to me up to my bed.

Of course, men like Paul did not sleep with widows on first dates.

We reached my doorstep. He brushed my wonkily trimmed fringe back, and whispered, 'Has there been anyone since Robert?'

I shook my head, my chest fluttering. I couldn't quite say 'no'.

He kissed me on the lips, gently, briefly, and I wondered if he could taste my lies.

*

I backed into a space in the Waitrose car park of the market town of Wisborough. As I turned to look out of my rear window, my heart skipped a beat. Alice's booster seat was empty. For a split second, distracted by my nerves and full of self-doubt, I had forgotten that I had left her with Paul and his two girls. I wondered whether I was doing the right thing.

The old-fashioned bell of the paint shop jingle-jangled as I entered.

Whilst I waited behind a customer, I had time to admire the interior, which was wood-panelled throughout. I loved it as much as the first time I had been in, when I had bought the hot pink paint for Alice's bedroom.

A thick oak countertop ran the full width of the narrow space. On the walls, there were rows and rows of black and white paint tins. The sharp, chemical smells belonged to an innocent era of my life. I wanted those smells back. I was daring myself to move on.

The old man behind the till was agonisingly slow at taking the bank card from the customer and slotting it into the machine. His age-spotted, arthritic fingers shook as he typed in the various codes. But when he looked up, to hand the card back to the smartly dressed lady in navy blue slacks, he beamed a wonky, energetic smile and doffed an imaginary flat cap. He had a small face with a large, hooked nose, and very little by way of a chin. His brown eyes were wholesome and bright in his withered, battered face.

'Goodbye, Mrs Twain. Don't forget to Whatsapp me a photograph of the finished room.'

'I'll get my granddaughter to do it.' She laughed. 'See you soon, Archie.'

Archie opened the countertop flap and carried Mrs Twain's can of paint to the door. The bell tinkled her out.

'And how can I help you, young lady?' Archie asked. Over his shirt, he was wearing a black T-shirt with 'Frieda Kahlo' in white letters across the front. It made me smile.

'Hello, Mr Parr, I'm Francesca Tennant. I've come about…'

'Ah, Francesca, yes, about a job. Do follow me.'

I followed Archie Parr through to the back room of the shop, to the mixing room. As I had remembered, it was spacious, and there was a wide, arched picture window that let in streams of sunlight. The low sill was painted in a scarlet red, and covered in sample tins and little squeezy bottles of stainers and pots of pigment powders; and syringes and teaspoons, for the delicate colour-matching alchemy. There were long, mismatched single shelves at various heights, stacked with white plastic tubs of paint. At our feet there was a collection of larger tubs. A low wooden platform, paint-splattered with every colour imaginable, sat in the middle of the room like a stage.

'Come and sit down here.' He pointed to the corner behind the door where there was a desk covered in paperwork. I sat down on the wooden school chair next to Archie and stared in awe at the dozens of colour charts above his desk.

'I collect them.' He winked, noticing my interest. He studied his collection proudly. 'This one is from the 1920s. See how tastes have changed?'

'Ivory. Cream. Grey. Pale blue,' I read, admiring the simplicity of the range. 'There aren't any burnt ochres or warm golds in that range.'

'Exactly, my dear.' He nodded, approvingly. 'Only a few years ago everyone wanted lovely lemon yellows, and now they want deep teals.'

'I bought a tin of hot pink paint from you a few weeks ago.'

'Oh, so you were the one Toby told me about! You wanted to mix it yourself, I hear?'

'Sorry about that.'

'No, no, how wonderful! We made a few extra tins of it and put it on the counter and they sold out in a week.'

'Good.' I beamed. And then I added, 'I like your T-shirt, by the way.'

'My daughter bought it for me last Christmas. I'm a feminist, you know,' he said, proudly.

'Ha! So am I.'

'In that case, Francesca, when do you think you'd be able to start?' he asked, shuffling around some papers on his desk and pulling out a form entitled 'Employment Form' that looked more like a raggedy school permissions' slip.

'Really?'

'Your CV suggests you are rather overqualified for the job in one respect, and rather underqualified for it in another. But I think I'll be able to teach you the retail end of things quite easily, and you might well be able to teach me a thing or two about hot pink?'

'I would love to.'

'You know, I don't pay well, but I absolutely encourage my assistants to take freelance painting and decorating work if you'd like to supplement your income. It's a lucrative business these days.'

'Even better, thank you.'

He held out his hand to shake mine, and he crushed my bones with the strength of his grip. 'Welcome aboard.'

After covering some of the more practical details of the job, he led me back out to the front of the shop. As he dropped the counter, I noticed a stack of Paul's business cards. Lost in thought, I picked one up and turned it between my fingers, smiling.

'Got pests, have you?' Archie asked.

I thought of Camilla.

'Something like that,' I replied cryptically, replacing the card.

He grinned, as though he too knew about the Tennants, and we shook hands again, for goodbye.

Emboldened by my successful interview with Archie Parr, hungry and inspired by the warm summer's afternoon, I wrote Paul a text:

Hi Paul – I got the job! Thanks to you. Just wondering if you would like to meet me with the girls at the pub for lunch? Fran x

As I walked along the pretty high street of Wisborough, I enjoyed the empty pavements and the fresh air. I took time to admire the geraniums and petunias and the Tudor shop fronts. The pace of life was more in keeping with my natural speed setting. This country town and I seemed to suit each other. When I thought of London, I envisaged sped-up people, fast-forwarding through life, darting and dashing, shouting and coughing. Here, I realised I was wandering, pottering, thinking better.

On the way back through the lanes to the pub, I felt relaxed, and, dare I say it, content in my new habitat. I had achieved some great things here. With no help from the Tennants, I had found myself an income and a new friend in Archie Parr, and I was meeting Paul, a potential boyfriend, for lunch. This was progress. This was a life I had never believed I would be allowed again.

CHAPTER TWENTY-TWO

John

John opened his laptop and stared at the pill bottle in front of his keyboard.

For some reason, he could not yet type in the relevant search word. Part of him did not want to know about the medication inside.

The months before Robert had committed suicide began swirling around his head. Everything about his death, and the secrets that Robert and his mother might have kept from him – not to mention his own role in Robert's demise – became a neon, pulsing question mark at the forefront of his mind.

He knocked out a couple of the pills into his hand.

Across the white tablets, the word SEROQUEL was written in capital letters.

He secured the pills back inside the bottle and logged into Twitter; procrastinating, pointlessly flicking down through tweets, which included mildly diverting petitions or *Guardian* articles about actors, or trailers of new television shows by people he vaguely knew.

Finally, he typed 'Seroquel' into his search engine.

The top hit was a blog spot called 'Seroquel Suicide'.

His stomach hit his throat.

As he read, it became quickly evident that Seroquel was not a brand of sleeping pill, but an anti-psychotic prescribed to sufferers of bipolar disorder. Which happened to be the disorder at the heart of Uncle Ralph's 'eccentricities'.

Having been previously doubtful about Francesca's conjecture, John was now riddled, teaming, shaking with his own suspicions.

He read skittishly, skipping paragraphs, rereading, scrolling down, reading the last blog entries first, and then the middle. Most of the stories were American, about lawsuits involving a slow-release brand of the same generic drug, quetiapine. One mother of four, with bipolar disorder, described her suicide attempt, which she attributed to this particular drug. All the stories of suicide were about people who had been prescribed the medication by their doctors and were taking it regularly.

The more he researched, the more he read about the conditions the drug would cure, or at least manage: the symptoms of bipolar disorder were described over and over. He read about others who suffered like Uncle Ralph, with varying degrees in the seriousness of their symptoms. It seemed Ralph's condition was at the extreme end.

Having digressed, he decided to go right back to basics. He searched 'quetiapine' on Wikipedia. This gave him a useful overview of the drug. It mentioned that it could be prescribed as a sleeping aid.

The new search came up with hundreds of personal blog posts about people who had been given Seroquel as a sleeping pill. A low dosage, under 50mg roughly, seemed to have the desired effect for most patients. They would not experience the severe drowsiness of the higher doses prescribed by practitioners for bipolar or other mental health disorders.

During Robert's low periods, John had often seen him drowsy, but never slurring his words, as some of the users of Seroquel on higher doses described. Other side effects included dizziness, cold sweats, drooling, weight gain, diabetes and constipation. Some of which Robert could have ticked. Francesca would know more.

After more searching, and many strange tangents, he stumbled across a website called 'Seroquel Addiction'.

On the opening page, irritability and insomnia were listed as indicators of addiction. John's heart began running fast. On their advice blog page, there were personal testimonies written by habitual drug users, addicted to pharmaceuticals, abusing the drugs for a high; using ingenious ways to conceal their habit, including some common hiding places: inside lipstick containers, inside gum wrappers, inside prescription bottles with another person's name on it.

John stared at the worn label of the bottle in front of him. In Robert's case, it seemed he had used a prescription bottle with his own name on it. The perfect hiding place.

He read on. Some users – or abusers – liked the mellowing, calming effect, while others decided it was only worth it if they pumped it up with some form of stimulant, like an amphetamine or cocaine, to counter the effects and level the taker out. Dozens of similar experiences were written about by desperate addicts, undeniably consistent with Francesca's description of Robert's behaviour.

What John read next left him ragged with shock. The most common way of getting hold of pharmaceuticals was either on the internet, or stealing or buying them from patients who had prescriptions.

Patients like Uncle Ralph.

Surely his brother had not been stealing medication from Uncle Ralph.

The horror of this possibility ground through his mind.

No.

John didn't want to believe it.

Perhaps Uncle Ralph took another brand of anti-psychotic.

Listed online were many different brands of the generic drug quetiapine, and many varied treatments for bipolar. Perhaps Robert had been legitimately prescribed Seroquel as a sleep aid, by a doctor other than Dr Baqri. It was a possibility. A genuine possibility. John wanted to believe this. Anything but settle on the grim, seedy image of his brother sneaking around Uncle Ralph's house, stealing pills from a sick man to feed his habit.

Anyway, he thought optimistically, nobody visited Uncle Ralph without Camilla Tennant as their chaperone. Their bi-annual afternoon tea ritual as children had been a duty akin to teeth-pulling, orchestrated and enforced by their mother for reasons associated with do-gooding or lessons in those-less-fortunate; similar to the Christmas visits to the elderly care home they had endured as teenagers. Neither John, nor Robert, had a relationship with their uncle autonomously. Over the years, Uncle Ralph had developed a fondness for John, but he had never liked Robert, which made it hard for John to believe that Robert would ever get into the house without his mother's knowledge.

For now, he pushed aside the question of how Robert might have got hold of the pills, and concluded, with a pang of misery, that his brother had been an addict.

As John let this new knowledge settle into his mind, he returned to his research with a specific focus, and a slower, more methodical pace. He went back over some of the more trusted websites, like the NHS's and others, to see if suicide might be a universally accepted risk of abuse of the drug. It was, particularly if there was sudden withdrawal. If Robert had been taking them, with or without a prescription, or inconsistently as an addict, the side effects of suicidal ideation would not have been a surprise to any GP or mental health practitioner.

It seemed to John that Francesca, with this pill bottle, had found a key to a door that he had not known was locked. For two years now, the family had been reeling from the trauma of Robert's death; in denial, too frightened to take a proper look at the reasons for his extreme mood swings, skirting around the root causes of his suicide, fearing his mother's histrionics. Now, more urgently than ever before, he hungered to find out more, to get under Robert's skin, to piece his past together. To do this, to get anywhere close to understanding the fuller picture, he needed to start with Seroquel. He needed to find out how Robert got hold of the drug, and whether or not their uncle's store of medication had been the source.

John stopped scrolling and sat back. Another unwelcome thought was unspooling itself in his head. If Francesca was right, and his mother was involved somehow, he could not risk interrogating her about the brand of Uncle Ralph's medication. His mother was too cagey, too smart for that. A better strategy would be to pay a visit to Uncle Ralph.

Getting there, without a fuss, would be a challenge. His mother would be suspicious if he suggested visiting his uncle out of the blue, for no apparent reason. But if he used Francesca, who had so far escaped an afternoon tea at Uncle Ralph's, his mother might buy it. Ironically, this meant that as his mother was the inventor and arbiter of this marking event for all those in the Tennants' inner circle – into which she had drawn Francesca close, as a reward for her move – if she refused to take Francesca round, John would know, for sure, that she was hiding something.

CHAPTER TWENTY-THREE

Francesca

The large oak tree stretched above the tennis courts, protecting the children from the heat of the sun like a benevolent grandparent. The squeak from the wooden swing in the small playground competed with the *poc-poc* of the balls hitting the rackets. Woollen fibres from the rug on which I was sitting scratched through my shorts.

I looked out for both John's Land Rover and Paul's pickup truck.

To distract myself, I tried to focus on the delicate pinpricks of wild flowers dotted across the meadow that spread down the hill in front of me. The beauty of my surroundings was restful, but when a dog barked behind me I jumped as though I had heard a gunshot.

John's text had seemed urgent. Or had it? Was I reading between the lines, as I had the habit of doing, lately? I didn't trust myself any more. I read it again:

Fran, are you around today? John

I had replied:

I'll be on the green after tennis club. F x

But I had not mentioned Paul. Why had I not mentioned him? How I regretted that now.

Paul and his girls appeared from behind me. Paul kissed me on the cheek, resting his hands heavily on my shoulders. 'Hello.'

'Hi, Francesca,' Georgie said, standing above me, staring at me with an expression on her face that suggested she thought I was strange.

I felt self-conscious of my dress. It was possibly too floral, too summery, too girly, too trying-too-hard.

'You look pretty,' Sylvie said, standing next to her sister.

'Hello, girls. Alice and the others will be finished in about ten minutes. Fancy some lemonade?'

Paul rolled out his rug, lay flat on his back and splayed his legs and arms out.

'How was last night?' I asked, pouring the girls their drinks.

'Nightmare. The whole flat was wiped out by one microwave. The lady who lived there was a nervous wreck. But alive.'

I wanted to ask more about the poor woman who had lost everything, but I was too worked up to form the relevant questions. John would be arriving any minute now, and I had not yet told Paul he was coming.

'Cup of tea?'

'Yes, please.' He propped himself up to take the flask of tea, and squinted at me through the sun.

'John's coming to join us,' I blurted out.

'Really?'

'He's picking up his kids anyway, and he asked if he could join us.'

Paul looked across the green. 'Cool.'

At that very moment, John's polished Porsche pulled up in the car park, and Paul knocked back the last of his tea.

We both watched, in silence, as John approached.

To Paul, John must have appeared privileged and rich, with his all-year tan and expensive haircut. His white T-shirt and khaki shorts were a little rumpled, but well-cut, and hung beautifully on his tall frame. I wondered whether Paul could imagine that anything in John's life was a struggle. But I saw beyond John's wealth. I noted John's self-conscious gait; his distinctive, aimless walk; the five times he put his hands in and out of his pockets; the scar on his right knee where he had fallen on rocks as a child. As he got closer, I could see how the patch of hair above his ear went against the grain, like tracks through a wheat field, where he had rubbed his head while he thought.

Paul and I stood to say hello. Paul and John shook hands, and I kissed John on one cheek.

'How are they doing?' John nodded over to the tennis courts.

We could see a line of children dressed in white with a variety of different coloured sunhats on their heads.

'Alice wouldn't let me watch. We've been skulking here.'

'Uh huh,' John replied.

'Knowing those two, they probably won't have been playing any tennis at all,' I continued.

'Why's that?' Paul asked earnestly. He had his thick arms crossed high over his chest, which was pushed out a little.

'Bea and Alice are mischief together,' I explained.

John nodded.

Paul looked from my face to John's, slowly. 'I see.'

'Let's go and get them,' I said, clapping my hands.

He and John walked together, and were polite to one another. I hoped that Paul would not try to show any affection towards me and I hoped that John was not cross with me about failing to mention Paul.

Alice came running across the courts towards the three of us, closely followed by Beatrice.

'Was it fun?' I said, kissing Alice's head as she nuzzled into me.

Beatrice flung herself at John, corks and twists of blonde hair bouncing around. 'Hi, Daddy!'

'Uncle John!' Alice cried. Letting go of me, she flew at her Uncle John, completely ignoring Paul.

I wanted to tell Alice to say hello to Paul. But if I had, I would have drawn attention to her omission and embarrassed Paul further.

The tennis coach interrupted the hugs to pull John aside for a chat. The rest of us returned to the picnic rug, where everyone was introduced to Paul's children.

'Good session?' I asked Olivia.

'I won all my games.'

She would sound precocious and smug to Paul, I imagined. I hoped he wouldn't judge her. Olivia was her own worst enemy, but she was funny and clever and charming.

'Olive is a little tennis star,' I explained to Paul. I squeezed Olivia's hand. She squeezed it back and swished her ponytail.

'Good for you,' Paul said to her, an eyebrow raised at me.

'How was it for you, Harry? Heading for Wimbledon yet?' I teased.

He scuffed his racket on the grass and peered through his hair, smiling. 'Yeah, that Champion's Cup is mine.'

Paul looked surprised. 'Another tennis star?'

'Something like that.' I laughed with Harry.

Olivia took her phone out of her skirt pocket and took a photograph of the view and then turned it on us. 'Cheese!'

Paul leant into me, and I forced out a smile.

When John arrived five minutes later, I spread out the picnic.

'Everything okay?' I asked him, as I unpacked the French bread and hummus and carrot sticks and juice boxes.

'Uh huh,' he replied, sitting down on the grass rather than on a rug, as though he was an added extra to the party.

Paul addressed John. 'I hear Olivia is a bit of a tennis star.'

'Yup.'

We waited for him to elaborate.

There was an awkward silence. I watched the children on the other rug eat and chat, and I envied their ease.

'Help yourself to some food, you two.'

I ate self-consciously, thinking of something to fill the silence.

'What a lovely day. The view is beautiful,' I said, as I cringed inside.

Paul said, 'This is the best view across the Downs to the coast.'

'Didn't you do some epic bike ride across the Downs once, John?' I asked. I remembered that Paul had a mountain bike, too.

'To Littlehampton,' he replied.

Nothing more. John's brooding presence seemed to burn into my left side.

The three of us squinted towards the hazy horizon miles away. I wished I could be there, on the edge of the world, away from this picnic, away from whatever it was that John was harbouring.

Alice and Beatrice had moved on to their second course. I watched how Alice used a plastic knife to cut tiny wedges of her tart, sharing her doll-size slices with Beatrice, while Beatrice nibbled off the strawberries and licked the cream, leaving a blob on her nose.

'I'll get the kids the football,' Paul said, and he jogged to his car.

John sat up. 'How long is he staying?'

'And finally he strings a sentence together.'

'I wanted to talk to you.'

His insistence was alarming. 'What is it?'

Paul returned too soon, slugged the ball into the middle of the green and sat down next to us. I stole a glance at John, who was slumped again, elbows on knees, staring into the distance insolently. My mind raced.

'Daddy! Play football with us. Daddy! Daddy! Daddy!' Beatrice pleaded, running and jumping onto John's lap. He groaned.

Then Olivia piped up, 'Yeah! Daddy! Daddy! Daddy! Come on!'

Adding to the chants came Georgie's and Sylvie's pleas to Paul: 'Come on, Dad! Yeah! Dad! Dad! Dad! Dad!'

Alice was gaping at them. There was a strange look in her eyes as she studied their interactions, fathers and daughters. Then she got up and walked over to John and said, 'Daddy, please will you play with us?'

I froze with shock. John's whole being woke up, as though from a sleep. He didn't miss a beat. He growled, '*Grrrrr*. How can I ever say no to you two, eh?'

With one blonde head and one dark head under his arm, John carried the two flailing, giggling four year olds, dumping them on the field, and began knocking the ball about. Paul's two girls ran after John.

'Are you okay?' Paul asked.

My head thumped. 'Did you hear that?'

'Best to ignore it for now.'

'Pretend it never happened?'

'Talk to her about it later. In a quiet moment.'

'And tell her what? That she won't ever be able to call anyone Daddy?'

'Georgie calls me Daddy.'

I swiped away an escaped tear. 'The others didn't notice, did they?'

'No.' Paul began to stroke my back, up and down, making me feel sick. I straightened my back, but he didn't take the hint.

'Go and play football,' I said. I began to pack away the half-eaten food, feeling a tear spill.

'I don't want to leave you like this.'

'I'll be fine. I just need a few minutes.'

Paul joined the others.

The scattered children darting about, the beauty of the meadow before me, the purity of the blue sky above me, all of it was meaningless as the resentment swelled inside me. I wanted to caterwaul and scratch and howl at that achingly blue sky, beyond which Robert might be. If there were a heaven, or God, would he admit through his Pearly Gates someone who had squandered his own life to punish me? Robert did not die of cancer, or in a car accident: he had jumped off a bridge, in desperation, I assume, but also in spite. He should have loved us more. Could he not have talked to me first, tried harder to battle through? There had been other ways to stay alive, even if they had been messy and complicated. Anger rushed at me like a red river of blood.

John jogged over to pick up the football, which had rolled onto the rug.

'Are you okay?' he asked. The children were calling to him to return the ball.

I glared at his silhouetted form, black against the blue sky. I blamed him for Alice's blunder.

'What did you want to talk to me about before?' I snapped.

There was a pause. 'Never mind. It's nothing. Bea was playing up and I wanted some advice.'

'She seems fine now.'

'Yes. Everything's fine.'

The rest of the picnic played out as a distant memory. I could not stay in the present, I needed to be home, to be away from everyone.

CHAPTER TWENTY-FOUR

John

John rolled up his trousers and sat on the side of the pool, dangling his legs into the glistening water to cool his feet.

He looked over at the poolhouse. The blue and white striped awning was cranked over his parents' sunbeds. A few years ago, his mother had asked the gardener to plant a cherry-blossom tree by the window and entice bougainvillea to grow across the roof. Although it would droop with cheering clusters of lilac pastels in the spring time, to complement the apple-green painted wooden slats, the foliage over the window blocked out the light inside, just as the gardener had warned it would. It was why it was never used any more. Inside, there was a folded ping-pong table and old sun-loungers, damp and musty. He hated that poolhouse. But Robert had hated it even more. As a child, he had always refused to go in there, even for a quick dash to retrieve spare goggles or sun-lounger cushions. He said there were rats. But Robert had not been scared of rats in the barn in the disused paddock, which had been much spookier.

'I'm going in now,' his mother said, snapping on her bathing cap, but she didn't move from her spot.

They watched Patrick charge up and down, knocking out lengths as he did every morning from spring onwards. As soon as the daffodils were out, his father turned the pool heating on and began this same routine until the clocks went forward, when he would turn the heating off.

John's trousers were splashed every time his father passed them.

'Are you quite sure you don't want to borrow a pair of your father's trunks?'

He noted how different his mother looked without her crowning bottle-blonde head of hair, and how the sunshine cruelly accentuated the lines that dragged downwards from the corners of her mouth.

'No, thanks. I wanted to run a plan by you.'

She removed her cap and ruffled her hair. 'Oh. Yes?'

His stomach turned over and over. He pushed his calves back and forth: his heels hitting the mosaic tiles, his toes emerging briefly into the cool air.

'I thought it might be fun to take Francesca to tea at Uncle Ralph's. Show her the house.'

His mother arched an eyebrow at him, and he wondered if she could read his mind. She changed the subject.

'I hear there was a picnic yesterday—?'

John sank a hand in the water and splashed his face. 'Yes.'

'Are Francesca and Paul an item?'

'Paul?' he asked, inanely, stalling for time.

'Yes, the handyman.' She tugged at the pink rubber of her cap and it snapped back, slapping her thigh.

'He's a fireman, Mum.'

'As *well* as a pest control man?'

'Firemen moonlight.'

'Well, either way, Olivia texted me a picture of the picnic and they looked very cosy together.'

'I'm sure it's not serious,' John said, willing it to be true.

'None of us are ready for that.'

John's chest tightened.

'We can't stop her.'

She yanked his chin around to face him – just as she used to do when he was a boy, to wipe off chocolate smears – and inspected his eye socket.

'How is it, darling? Did you go to the opticians?'

'It's completely fine.' He pulled his chin out of her grasp.

'You know, Dad was a bit upset when he heard that you were back on the bike. He'd love to go out riding with you.'

He held in an exasperated groan. 'We've been on two bike rides together in twenty years, Mum.'

'Well,' his mother said, her voice trembling a little, 'your father has just turned *seventy*-one, and there won't be many years left for you to do that kind of stuff with him, you know.'

She sniffed dramatically. Only his mother could turn someone else's injury into her own.

'Mum, about Uncle Ralph.'

She grabbed the sun lotion from the sun-lounger behind them and began rubbing cream into her face aggressively.

'What about him?'

'Tea? With Francesca?'

She clicked the lid of the cream closed. 'I'll take her.'

'I'd like to come, too.'

Her head turned very slowly towards him, eyes squinting, skin greased with lotion. Her lips almost disappeared into her mouth as she drew them into a tight line. 'Would you?'

Beads of sweat prickled across his forehead.

'I haven't seen him for ages,' he said, trying to sound casual.

'We'll go another time,' she said. 'With Dilys perhaps.'

Before he could protest – knowing Dilys would refuse to visit Uncle Ralph ever again – his mother's body slid from the side and into the water. She barely made a splash. The black shape of her remained under the surface. Her pink cap sat crumpled on the slabs of stone next to him. In all the years he had seen her swimming, he had never once seen her get her hair wet.

Holding his breath, just as she would be, he waited nervously for her to emerge.

When she came to the surface, she was at the other end of the pool, clinging to the side, spluttering and coughing. Her legs kicked into his father's oncoming stroke. Patrick stopped, and tended to her.

As he stared at them, transfixed by his mother's self-imposed distress, and unsettled by its implication, he became harassed by the repetitive noise of the pool water gulping in the filter. He wanted to block it out; his memory was rewinding.

Unaware of her two young sons' silent presence, his mother reached out into the dark, patting the floor outside the poolhouse door, searching for something. John watched Robert there, so close to her, as still as a statue, his toes inches from her fingertips.

The smell of chlorine stung John's sleepy eyes as he strained to see through the dark; his dew-damp pyjama trousers sent goosebumps up his legs.

'Where did you put it?' she cackled. At first, John thought she was talking to Robert, that it was some kind of game of theirs that John was now part of. There was a moment of relief. But then he heard the rumble of a male voice.

A wine bottle clanked onto its side on the paving. It rolled back and forth. His mother giggled some more. As she grabbed the bottle, she spotted Robert.

John shivered, breaking his trance. His father began swimming towards him, snapping him into the present.

Before his father reached him, John scrambled up and jogged away, leaving his father's voice echoing in the background.

Reaching his car, out of breath, John got in, heedless of his bare feet. As he drove past the peeling trunks of silver birch, past the silvery ghost of Robert racing him on his bike, he dialled Francesca on his car phone.

It rang and rang. He tried again.

And again.

And again.

The third time he tried, it went straight to voicemail.

CHAPTER TWENTY-FIVE

10 years ago

'John's coming round, remember?' Francesca said.

'Yup.'

Robert's hang-dog expression was becoming an irritant to Francesca. His slow blink and constant face-rubbing and excessive sleeping was driving her round the bend. He was either snappy and unpleasant, or vacant, as he chewed on endless rounds of toast and Marmite, standing by the toaster, staring into space.

Francesca wanted to fly to Alaska to retrieve Robert's personality. He had left it there somewhere.

'I've booked tickets for *Waltz With Bashir*—?'

'Great.'

'Maybe you should stop eating toast, if we're eating out. I've booked a table at Odette's.'

He carried on chewing.

When John arrived, Robert was in bed.

John went in to see him. Francesca could hear them through the door.

'Come on, mate, get dressed.'

'I'm too tired.'

'They serve a mean steak at Odette's.'

'I'm not in the mood.'

The duvet rustled. Francesca missed a few lines of their exchange.

Then John said, loudly, 'I think you should go to the doctor.'

'I'm not ill.'

'You are ill. You're depressed.'

John had finally addressed the issue head on. The euphemism 'low' to describe Robert's constant despondency was not appropriate any longer.

'Okay, John. I'll call the doctor if it will get you and Fran off my back.'

'Good. Great.'

'Can you leave me alone now?'

'We're going out. Come on. Up you get.'

'Fuck off, John.'

John had emerged from the bedroom.

'Let's go,' John said angrily.

'Without him?'

'Why waste the tickets?'

In the taxi, John was brooding and quiet.

They settled at a booth table at Odette's and John ordered a Martini. Francesca ordered a glass of wine. They both chose the moules-frites.

Francesca talked about Robert's moods: up versus down, irritable versus excitable, passionate versus disconnected.

John's mussel shell missed his bowl when he chucked it. 'I don't want to talk about Robert.'

Francesca had been embarrassed. Quietly, almost to herself, she said, 'I'll make sure he goes to the doctor.'

'He won't go.'

'You're not being helpful, John.'

'I'm sick of being helpful.'

Francesca had laughed. 'Ha. I know what you mean.'

'Let's be totally and utterly unhelpful and selfish tonight.'

They had chinked glasses and John had knocked back the rest of his Martini, and ordered two more for both of them.

In the darkened auditorium of the cinema, Francesca realised she was very drunk. It was a heavy-going film about a young Israeli soldier who had blocked out a traumatic memory of a massacre in Beirut during the Lebanese war.

At one disturbing point in the story, Francesca turned to John. She saw that his cheeks shimmered with tears. Instinctively, she squeezed his hand. He wouldn't let her go. He kept her hand in his, resting it on his knee.

For the rest of the film, Francesca had not been able to concentrate, knowing that she and John had crossed a line.

CHAPTER TWENTY-SIX

Francesca

I had not offered Camilla lunch; she had simply let herself into my house and begun making it in my kitchen an hour before we were due to see Uncle Ralph together. I was not in the mood for Camilla, or for this visit. I had been trying so hard to create some distance between me and Alice and the Tennants. But here she was; and there was John's name, flashing up on my phone all morning. No doubt he wanted to talk about the picnic, and Alice's 'Daddy' moment, which I had decided not to talk to Alice about. It had seemed cruel and petty to make a big deal of an isolated incident.

Out of the window, I watched Alice crouched down inspecting something in a flower pot. *She's happy here*, I thought.

'A quick salad would be nice before we go,' Camilla said, bending into my fridge, pulling out a bag of wilting spinach leaves. 'He was in a terribly low mood this morning when I spoke to him, but Alice will cheer him up. His puzzle collection really is terribly impressive. But you know he's been very up and down since…' And on she went about Uncle Ralph's moods.

Resentfully, I pushed around some anaemic pine nuts in a frying pan, and listened with grudging interest to the stories of Uncle Ralph's and Patrick's childhood as colonial boys in Africa, to-ing and fro-ing from Nairobi airport to Eton with tags around their necks. I thought about how sad privilege sounded.

Camilla's voice deepened as she moved on to the real misery of Uncle Ralph's bipolar disorder. Up until now, this had been a subject I had not been privy to. Uncle Ralph's euphemistically described 'eccentricity' was a family secret that even Robert had been cagey about. Finally, it seemed I had earned the privilege of Tennant insider knowledge.

'He spent every penny he had?' I asked.

'Every penny,' she exhaled heavily.

'On a yacht?'

Camilla waggled the knife at me. 'For an acquaintance whom he met at the Rotary Club twice a year.'

'And this guy accepted it?'

She nodded. 'Even though Patrick got involved and begged him not to.'

'That's terrible.'

'That's why Patrick doesn't speak to Ralph. He can't forgive him for squandering their parents' trust fund.'

'But he was ill.'

Camilla turned on the tap so hard that it sprayed her ice-blue blouse, but she failed to notice or care. She washed the knife under the gushing tap, slicing the sponge repeatedly.

'Patrick doesn't see it like that. You see, Ralph has no children, and Patrick knew his money would have gone to Robert and John if he hadn't blown it.'

I turned away from her, back to the pan.

'Robert never cared about money.'

The pine nuts were burnt black. One minute they had been white, the next black. I started on a second batch of them, thankful I'd bought a large bag.

Camilla sniffed. 'There's the house, at least. Patrick's the executor now.'

'I've heard it's beautiful.'

'You'll see for yourself today.'

'Robert never wanted to take me,' I said, glancing over my shoulder at Camilla.

She was fiddling with a pearled button on her shirt, eyeing me with a cocked eyebrow; perhaps deliberating on saying more or waiting for me to say more. 'Do you know why?'

'Do you?'

'I used to force the boys to go, too much, probably. He never mentioned it?'

'To be honest, Camilla,' I laughed, 'I've learnt more about Ralph in this last half an hour than in all the years I've known you lot.'

Haughtily, she smiled, as though she was exceptionally pleased about that fact.

'The house is terribly rundown. But he would've lost it altogether if I hadn't persuaded him to see Dr Baqri, who referred him straight away to Dr Stanton. *A psychiatrist,*' she said, lowering her voice. Then, waggling a fork in my face: 'It's worth a small fortune now, apparently. The house, I mean.'

But the mention of Dr Baqri had roused me.

'Dr Baqri? Your family doctor?'

'Yes. He's wonderful.'

'Was Robert ever a patient of his?' I asked cautiously, wondering if Robert had lied to Camilla as well as to John.

'Oh, yes. All his life.'

The oil from the pan spat at my hands.

'Is that what he told you?'

'It's what I know.'

'And he knew about his depression?'

'He was very professional and never mentioned a thing to me. But I'm sure he did his best…' She trailed off.

'Does Uncle Ralph still see Dr Baqri?'

'Alongside Dr Stanton, of course. I don't know what we'd do without him. Darling Ralph is worse than ever these days. Sometimes I'm not sure he knows I'm even there when I visit, and he's terrible at taking his pills. Once, he flushed two packets of them down the loo and insisted I fish them out again.' She made a face, and added, 'Dr Baqri thinks it might be time to think about a full-time carer.'

'Thank god Ralph has you,' I said, on autopilot.

She waved my compliment away with her red-polished nails. 'Anyone would have done the same…'

'Do you want me to check in on him while you and Patrick are away in Italy?'

'Well, I was considering cancelling our jaunt this year.'

'I would be very happy to help,' I offered, burning with an ulterior motive. With sanctioned access to Uncle Ralph, I would, in turn, have access to Dr Baqri.

'I'll see what Dr Baqri thinks.'

'No!' I cried, remembering the pine nuts. 'I've burnt them again.'

I let them slide into the bin from the hot pan for a second time.

'Let me do it,' she said, prising the pan from my hand.

I was relieved to be able to sit down. Tainted by fresh suspicions about Dr Baqri, I began to question Camilla's fixation on Ralph, curious about whether he had become some kind of unconscious replacement for Robert: if she saved Uncle Ralph, she would feel better about not saving Robert. Or whether there was more to it. With this thought in mind, I decided that I was rather keen on this visit this afternoon.

Alice ran into the kitchen.

'Can we go and see the puzzles now?'

'Yes, darling. You wait until you see Uncle Ralph's collection!'

*

We pulled up in Camilla's green Jaguar outside the tall garden walls of Uncle Ralph's house. Alice leapt out and ran up the straight pathway that led through the very centre of the over-grown garden to the red-brick frontage. The classical Georgian exterior was mottled with lichen and cracks, while the roses were crumpled buds, wilting around the sash windowsills. The restrained symmetry and elegance was charming. From the out-side, it was a fairytale house, where dreams should come true.

Alice and I waited in the hallway while Camilla checked on him in the kitchen, where she had heard plates clattering.

As we waited, a text came through on my phone.

> *Mum said you're seeing Uncle Ralph today. Find out the name of his medication. I'll explain later. Jx*

My stomach somersaulted. I was thrown off, unsure of what to think, but instantly questioning his motives. If his request had any-thing to do with Robert's pills, what had changed his mind? I had an urge to start charging around, opening drawers and upending boxes to find Ralph's medication. But I knew I had to step cautiously.

I looked around us at the sinister interior of the house, at the red wallpaper, which would have been expensive in its day, but which was now faded and peeling at the corners. The mahogany antique console was riddled with woodworm and layered with dust. One half of one wall was stacked with fifty or so tubs of washing-up tablets. A randomly placed Edwardian revolving bookshelf was half-blocking the stairs and was filled with what looked like dead cress in egg boxes.

When Camilla returned, she spoke in hushed tones. 'Just to warn you, it looks like he's rapid cycling.'

I pictured Ralph on a bicycle. 'What do you mean?'

'He's in transition from depression to mania. When I called earlier, he was refusing to get out of bed, but now he's racing around full of beans, washing up every single cup in the cupboard like Mary Poppins.'

'Should we come back another time?' I asked, pulling Alice away from the dead cress, unnerved by the house, less and less keen to snoop around.

'No, no. A sudden departure would set his paranoia off. But, be warned, he might be a little OTT today,' she said, shooting out her hand for Alice to take. 'Alice, darling, this way for the puzzles. Come and see. He has hundreds of them. But, darling, no going upstairs, okay?'

While Alice sifted through the pile of puzzle boxes, Camilla and I went through to the kitchen.

Ralph stepped away from the sink, waved his bubbly hands at us, and splashed Camilla's hair.

'Whoopsie daisy!' He laughed, wiping his hands down his multicoloured checked shirt, which stretched at the stomach and was neatly tucked into pink belted moleskin trousers. His wiry, grey hair was shaped into a boxy flat-top buzz cut, and he would have looked quite normal if it weren't for his bloodshot eyes, which were a little too far apart, and bulging. He reminded me of a splendid, colourful chameleon lizard.

'Hello! Welcome! Come in! Bienvenue! Ciao! Guten Morgen! Oh, whoops! It's the afternoon! Do we know good afternoon in German, ladies?'

'Guten Nachmittag,' Camilla said.

'Such a clever woman, such a clever woman. And never you forget it, young lady!' He pointed at me, startling me slightly. 'I don't. Ever.'

'You remember Francesca, don't you? Alice is playing with your puzzles, if that's okay?'

'Quite, quite,' Ralph said, stepping too close to me. 'Such a sad affair, such a loss. You are now the tragic damsel of the family. How much my heart broke for you.'

He grabbed me with his damp hands and I felt a lump form in my throat.

'Stop being so maudlin, Ralph. She didn't come here to cry.'

Camilla's words seem to act like a blown whistle in his ear. He dropped my hands and asked abruptly, 'Tea?'

'A cup of tea would be great, thanks.'

He then listed twenty different teas, offered several different variations of milk/soya/almond/lemon/honey/milk-with-sugar/ milk-with-honey/lemon with soya/ lemon with almond. I chose chamomile, to keep it simple. But Uncle Ralph then offered me a choice of dozens of different types of mugs.

'In the morning, I drink from this one,' he explained, brandishing a blue mug, darting back and forth from his crockery dresser to the table. 'With my mid-morning snack, I have a coffee in this one.' He showed us a white, porcelain cup and saucer. 'But with my after-lunch brew, I love this pretty one with my teapot.' It was a gold patterned tea-set with delicate flowers and bees.

For the next ten minutes, he talked us through his tea-drinking routine. By bedtime, I worked out he would clock up at least fifteen cups.

Finally, Uncle Ralph sat down, only to leap up and begin talking about the various plates he would need to wash up next.

'Might you go check on Alice?' Camilla said, arching her eyebrow at me.

'Oh, right, okay,' I said, getting the hint. It was a relief to escape for a few minutes. Watching Ralph was like waiting for an elastic band, stretched too tight, to snap.

In the dining room, thick with dust motes, I knelt down next to Alice, who had brought out a puzzle of a Goya painting of a man facing a firing squad.

'That might be a bit hard for you, sweetheart,' I said, unstacking the others in the cupboard. I brought out a Monet, which had bigger pieces and a prettier subject matter.

'I need a wee-wee,' Alice said.

I decided to be brave, and I led Alice upstairs. Ostensibly, to look for a loo. It was the perfect opportunity to have a nose around. If we were discovered, Alice would be the alibi.

There was a long corridor upstairs, decorated with brocade wallpaper and oil paintings. I opened a few doors to various spare bedrooms. At the end of the red runner carpet, I saw a door ajar, revealing black and white bathroom tiles. Having led Alice in, I looked into the room adjacent to the bathroom. It was a huge bedroom with a mahogany four-poster bed and green silk bedcovers, worn out but immaculately made. It must have been Ralph's bedroom.

Just as I heard Alice flush the loo, I noticed a collection of pill packets on top of his dresser.

Slowly, I stepped across the creaky floorboards towards them.

'What are you doing, Mummy?' Alice shouted. She bounded into the room.

'Shhhh,' I said, scooping her up in my arms.

She whispered theatrically, 'Are we playing hide and seek?'

'Yes, we're hiding from Grandma Cam-Cam,' I replied, under my breath.

I picked up one of the cardboard boxes and read 'Seroquel XL' in blue and pink lettering, with the name 'Quetiapine (as fumarate)', and '400mg tablets', partly obscured by the label, which was printed with a Harley Street pharmacy address and the recommended dosage.

I opened the box and pressed out one of the oblong white pills from the blister packet. The name 'SEROQUEL', in capitals, was engraved across the chalky medication. On the other side of the pill I read, 'XL 400'.

'Sweeties!' Alice cried.

'No, poppet,' I said, shoving them quickly back inside the box. 'Not sweeties. Definitely not.'

Having returned the box to the stack, I softly crept back out of the room, keen to remember the name 'Seroquel'.

I put Alice down and held her hand as we descended the stairs, repeating 'Seroquel' in my head over and over.

From the other side of the dining room door, I could hear Ralph hollering, 'What the hell has happened in here?'

There was a sound of boxes crashing and rattling around, and the patter of small objects – I guessed puzzle pieces – cascading onto the table.

Camilla's murmured replies sounded soothing, but they did not seem to be pacifying him.

I hovered outside the dining room door, deliberating about what to do next, wishing we could bolt. Alice nestled into my legs and then Camilla burst out of the room, closing the door behind her.

Breathlessly, she said, 'I'm terribly sorry, but I think you'd better wait for me in the car. He's a little… tired.'

'I'm so sorry about the puzzles. Alice needed the loo.'

'It's quite all right. Off you pop, girls. I'll be out in a minute,' Camilla said, shooing us to the door. The noise of Ralph's rampaging reverberated through the walls of the closed room.

I took Alice's hand and jogged away down the path.

Then he flew out of the front door, pointing down at Alice, full of menace.

'Just like your father, eh? A little rascal, are you, eh? Sneaking around my house, with your sticky little fingers!'

Alice burst into tears, and I tugged at her to run faster, jolted by Ralph's accusation. If Robert had sticky fingers, he had certainly not been thieving puzzles. Seroquel was more likely.

'Now, now, Ralph, come on. That's not true. Calm down,' Camilla soothed.

I looked back, and saw how Camilla's eyes blinked rapidly, how her jaw pulsed.

Then Uncle Ralph turned on her, pushing a finger into her face, hollering at her: 'You. *YOU!* You saw Robert stealing from me with your own eyes and you did nothing!'

I stopped at the gate, alarmed by what Ralph had just said. Could it be true that Camilla had actually witnessed Robert thieving Seroquel?

Camilla caught my eye, and a streak of fear shot through her expression.

Quickly, she re-arranged her features and chastised Uncle Ralph, 'I saw nothing of the sort.'

'You're a liar! I warned Patrick against your type. I warned him! I did!' Uncle Ralph yelled.

As Camilla struggled to persuade Ralph inside, I was transfixed by their shouting and scuffling, processing what I had just heard.

'Get Alice in the car!' Camilla barked, breaking me out of my trance.

I hurried Alice through the gate and into the Jaguar.

Behind me, I could see Camilla successfully leading a placated Ralph back inside.

With the car doors locked, we waited.

Alice lay in my lap, letting out a tearful, hiccuppy sigh every now and again. 'He's so scary, Mummy.'

'He's not very well, darling,' I said, typing, with trembling fingers, 'Seroquel' into the search engine of my phone. The cursor whirled and buffered, failing every time I refreshed.

'I don't have sticky fingers, do I, Mummy?'

'No, darling. Of course not,' I said, kissing her sugary palms.

'He's not very good at sharing, is he, Mumma?'

'I think you're right.' I laughed.

'When is Grandma Cam-Cam coming?'

'I wish she would hurry up,' I mumbled, tapping refresh again.

I was eager to get home, to get Alice away from there, to research everything there was to know about Seroquel.

It took another ten minutes for Camilla to emerge.

'Well, that was a mistake,' she huffed accusingly, starting up the engine.

Quickly, I texted John, one word: 'SEROQUEL', and put my phone away, halting my search for now.

'What did he mean by Robert having sticky fingers?' I asked, pointlessly, waiting for her lie.

She snorted. 'Oh, heaven's above, Francesca. He's as mad as a bag of frogs. Nothing he says means anything.'

Under the light of the streetlamps further into the village, I noticed a bloody scratch down her cheek. There was obviously a cost for keeping such a close eye on Ralph, for making sure he didn't give their secrets away. It must have felt like trying to press down on a basket full of writhing asps.

But, this afternoon, one had escaped.

And I dreaded telling John what I had pieced together: that his mother had witnessed Robert stealing Seroquel from his uncle. It meant that she had known her son was feeding some sort of an addiction and it meant that she had done nothing about it, over all these years.

It sent a pain through my heart, and I feared it might shatter John's.

CHAPTER TWENTY-SEVEN

Francesca

John was standing on my doorstep.

'You got my text?' I yawned as I let him in.

I was weary after two hours of researching Seroquel online; reading about other dead husbands and wives, about other dead depressives or insomniacs or addicts.

'Drink?'

'Sure.'

He was restless, shifty, moving his hands from his ear to his hair to his pockets repeatedly, like a strange ritual.

'Does Dilys know you're here?'

'We had a fight. That's why I'm late. I said I was going for a drive.'

'I don't miss those kinds of marital fights.' I smiled sadly, remembering the many times I had gone for a walk, in no particular direction, through the London streets, to get away from Robert.

He rubbed his face. 'The only advantage of having a dead husband.'

It was a strangely crude thing to say. Knowing it was unlike him, I let it pass. I handed him a glass of red wine and he cradled it as though he was freezing cold.

'Why did you want to know about Seroquel?' I asked, guessing the answer before he told me.

John cleared his throat, put down his wine and brought Robert's pill bottle out of his trouser pocket.

'When did you get your hands on that?'

'I stole it from Mum's washbag a few days ago. And look…' he said. As he opened it up, he pulled my hand out, tapping a couple of pills onto my palm. 'Seroquel. Not Zopiclone.'

I gulped back my dismay. 'I found those exact pills in Ralph's bedroom today.'

I took John through our traumatic afternoon, leaving the information about his mother until last.

'He actually accused Mum of knowing?'

'I'm afraid so.'

'That is unbelievable.' John shook his head, angry, pacing, pushing his blond hair back repeatedly. His nerves and vulnerability had vanished.

'Remember, John, he wasn't in his right mind. I might have got it muddled.'

'What did he say *exactly*?'

'That your mum saw Robert stealing from him. "With her own eyes" he said.'

'That's pretty conclusive,' he murmured.

I nodded, reluctantly agreeing.

'Why didn't she tell me?' he asked, bewilderment in his eyes.

'Maybe she was trying to protect you?'

He pulled out the pills again and turned them over in his hand. 'I read loads online about how devious addicts can be.'

'Me too. And about their mood swings, and the irritability. And weight gain is really common, too. Robert ticked all the boxes. His weekend drinking binges were pretty typical as well. We already knew he took all sorts of other crap. Coke, weed, and god knows what else.'

John exhaled heavily. 'Mum might not have known all that. Maybe she thought the Uncle Ralph thing was a one-off?'

My anger bubbled up. 'Once is enough, isn't it? Stealing antipsychotics from a sick old man is totally messed-up.'

He jammed his hands in his pockets. 'And she did fuck all about it, and now he's dead.'

My stomach turned. I shared his anger. In one way, I was vindicated. The prospect of a confrontation with Camilla should have given me a thrill, given me permission to blame her openly, wholly justified. I waited to feel the burden of guilt about Robert's death lift off my shoulders. But it wouldn't budge. If anything, I felt heavier than ever. Suddenly, I wanted John to leave.

'It's late,' I said.

He looked at his phone. 'I can't go home yet.'

'Why not?'

'Dilys will be awake.'

'Does she know you're here?'

'No.'

'You should tell her. So she doesn't worry.'

Abruptly, he put down his wine and turned his back on me. 'I can't tell her I'm here, Fran,' he said.

His head had dropped and his broad shoulders rounded. A tiny edge of tanned flesh appeared between his T-shirt and his shorts.

'There's no reason to hide it.'

He turned back round.

'Isn't there?' he retorted angrily.

The air in the room thickened. A viscose slowness plugged up my small kitchen. I imagined the world beyond us speeding along pointlessly. Robert's spirit was squeezed into what was left of the space with us, standing by me, powerless, grim. John's chest was heaving, in and out, very much alive with pumping, throbbing flesh, exerted, perhaps fearful. His light eyes underneath his fixed brow were focused, trained on me, locked into my reaction.

I didn't know how to react. Not because my thoughts were muddied, but because they were as clear as they could have ever been.

'Not any more,' I said, almost under my breath, my throat constricting, my knees about to give way.

'These pills' – he paused, brandishing the bottle, as though he had pulled a sword from its sheath – 'release us.'

'You think we're blameless now, do you?'

'It wasn't our fault. Can't you see that? He was clearly an addict. If anyone is to blame it's Mum.'

'It doesn't change anything.' Until that moment, I hadn't realised that it wouldn't.

John stepped back. A flicker of horror passed over his beautiful features, as though he were looking upon a corpse he had slain. 'I shouldn't have come.'

He picked up his car keys and retreated from me. I let him go. I clung to the wall, to stay upright, and listened to the door close, listened to his car drive away.

I was the one left standing with the bloodied sword.

I reached for his glass on the kitchen table and noticed that he had left his phone next to it. I grabbed it and ran to the door, but his car was long gone.

Over and over, I replayed our conversation, exhausted by my thoughts, but too wired to go to bed, drained by the many connotations of our discovery. While I watched a film, knowing I would not be able to sleep, his phone lay on my coffee table like a dejected remnant of him.

Half an hour into the film, it rang. The screen flashed up 'HOME' – it was John, calling from his home landline. I turned the television to mute and answered.

'You left it here, I'm afraid,' I sighed.

There was a pause.

Dilys spoke. 'Is that Francesca?'

'Oh, sorry. Hi, Dilys. I thought it would be John.'

'Why have you got John's phone?' Her Welsh accent was stronger than ever.

I spotted Alice's cardigan on the arm of the sofa. 'He dropped round Alice's cardigan.'

'At eleven at night.'

I left that unlikelihood hanging between us.

'When did he leave?'

'About forty minutes ago—?'

'He's not back home yet.'

'Oh, right,' I said. 'I wouldn't worry,' I added, unable to suggest why she shouldn't. 'When he's back, tell him I'll bring the phone tomorrow morning when I pick the kids up for tennis.'

'Sure,' she replied, and hung up without saying goodbye.

My cheeks flamed. I stared at John's screensaver photograph of Harry, Olivia and Beatrice leaning against a five-bar gate in a field, all wellies and grins and innocence. Literally, I was holding them in my hands – and the responsibility of the whole Tennant family's happiness weighed heavily on my soul.

I wanted to see Robert's suicide in simple terms, as John had: Camilla and Robert were the guilty parties, and we were exonerated. But the opposite seemed true. I couldn't seem to locate that feeling of triumph, which I presumed I should feel, which I had been chasing all these weeks.

Hate and anger and blame were scrabbling around inside me, trying to find a focal point to fix on and charge at, but it was not Camilla.

CHAPTER TWENTY-EIGHT

John

John didn't want Dilys to hear the car, so he parked in a lay-by at the corner of a field, from which he followed the stream along the public bridleway to the bottom of their garden, to his shed. He had been this route many times before when he needed a walk and a think.

The moon lit his way. The rustle of the leaves under his feet was a comforting, steadying sound. He felt as though he were a formless shadow that could merge into the darkness and melt into the ragged earth. His breath curled through the air, dispersing, inconsequential. He imagined disintegrating, his molecules rotting into the ecosystem to feed the cycle of life. Somehow, it took the edge off his fear. Fear for his mother, and what she had kept hidden about Robert all these years. Fear for Francesca, who had shoved John away; who still blamed herself, and him, in spite of everything they had recently learnt.

When he finally reached the shed, he was tired out by his thoughts. He curled up on the armchair, pulled a rug over his chilled limbs and slept.

*

He was awakened the next morning by banging. Dilys' face was scowling at him through the window. John felt stiff and disorientated as he stood up to open the door.

'I thought you were dead in some ditch.' She was tearful rather than angry. 'I've been worried sick.'

Her hands were on her hips, her voice trembling. She was in her nightdress and sheepskin boots. Her face was clear of make-up, leaving purple rings under her eyes and a sallow colour to her skin.

'I didn't want to wake you,' he explained.

'I was too worried to sleep!'

'What time is it?'

'It's eight. Fran will be here in a minute.'

His heart thumped. 'What? Why?'

'She's taking them to tennis, remember?'

'Shit.'

'She told me she'd bring your phone.'

'My phone?' He patted his pockets.

Her lips thinned. 'You left it at her place.'

'I dropped in to say hi.'

'At eleven at night?'

John did not know what to say.

'Why did you go over to Fran's so late?'

John stared at Dilys and then recognised something in her stance. An image of his mother came hurtling to his mind.

John's mother stabbed a finger at Robert, holding his skinny arm, spittle flying. 'I didn't bring you up to be a Peeping Tom.'

The profile of his brother's young face was perfect, like a silhouetted cameo portrait. He twisted from her grip and he ran.

John turned on his heel to follow his big brother, but it was too late. His mother's hands were clamped around his shoulders. She turned him around to face her.

'John? Answer me,' Dilys insisted.

'I told you why I went over there.'

'That's a lie.'

'It's not a lie.'

Her worry switched to fury.

'Stop fucking lying to me!' she screamed.

She grabbed one of Robert's bronze BAFTA awards from the shelf above him and flew at him, beginning to beat him with it.

'Answer me, you bloody idiot! Answer me! Talk to me! Tell me what you're thinking for once. You're like a fucking brick wall!' she screeched.

It was a beating he knew he deserved. He curled up into a ball and took each blow with a sick sort of pleasure. The hot welts bulged and burned under his clothes.

Then the hitting stopped suddenly.

John looked up to see Francesca and Olivia staring at them from the doorway in stunned silence.

'I'm so sorry, Olivia said you'd be…' Francesca's sentence trailed off.

Dilys dropped the award and pushed past Francesca and Olivia. 'I'm not the bad guy in all this.'

John stared down at the floor, at the bronze face of Robert's award at his feet, with its one eye closed, like a wink.

'Are you okay, Daddy?' Olivia cried.

'Yes, I'm fine,' he said, moving over to his computer, turning away from them, unable to look his daughter in the eye. 'Mummy and Daddy were just having a bit of a silly fight. Give me two minutes and I'll be up at the house.'

John heard the upbeat, insincere tone to his voice and he hated himself.

The door closed. His flesh pounded. His skin was wounded, blistering and broken; sensitive against his shirt, the material like sand in a broken cut. He listened to Francesca's reassurances become quieter and quieter as she walked Olivia back up to the house. He could not believe what they had just witnessed. He knew he had to return to the house, to face Olivia, and Francesca, to get on with the normal family routine. His whole body throbbed with shame. He wanted to crawl up the grass, on his hands and knees, and collapse at the doorstep, and wait for someone to scoop him up, put him in bed, and take care of him until he was healed. There was nobody to do this for him. He had to go on, no matter what. The children needed him to be Dad, and Dad he was going to be. So, he stood up, breathed and walked, on two feet, up to the house.

As he re-entered his home, bracing himself, his battered body felt stiff and the skin over his back was tight and hot and stinging, but he would have to hide his pain.

He could hear Beatrice chattering in the kitchen.

John called out, 'Morning!'

His three children, and Alice, were dressed in their tennis whites and sitting in a row at the breakfast bar. The sun shone through the skylight onto their shiny hair, reflecting sparks of beauty around the room.

Dilys was not in the room. In her place stood Francesca, who was pouring milk into Beatrice's and Alice's bowls. Harry was hunched over his cereal reading something on his phone.

He glanced over at Francesca, who was still holding the milk carton, looking at him, poised to speak, but not speaking. Her fringe was pushed back, and a bit stuck straight up in the air. Her skin was paler than the milk she held. Her brown eyes were wide and searching, as though she might see the bruises come up on his flesh before her eyes.

'We're going to be late for tennis.' Olivia scowled, lowering the spoon that was at her lips. Her ponytail was unusually messy.

John gave her a kiss on the top of her head. 'It's okay. You'll only miss the warm-up. Promise,' he whispered. And then louder to the others, 'Where's Mummy?'

'She's getting ready for work, Daddy,' Beatrice replied through her last mouthful of cereal. 'She's going to be *late*,' she added, gleefully, clattering her spoon back into her bowl.

'Right, you three,' John said, checking his watch, 'Auntie Fran needs to get you to tennis. Go and find your shoes and rackets. Alice, you can help Bea.'

They disappeared off to do as he said, leaving him alone with Francesca. The silence was black. His skin stretched and burned as he reached across the table to collect the spoons and bowls. She brushed past him to get the cloth, and the light scent she always wore filled his head. When he bent down to the dishwasher, he flinched with the pain.

She stopped wiping the surfaces. 'I can stay until she's gone, if you like,' she whispered.

He was mortified. She was trying to be his protector. His guardian angel. The role reversal was wrong. He was the man. He was supposed to be *her* hero.

Angrily, he stood up and slammed a cupboard door shut. 'I'm quite capable of dealing with her,' he replied. 'She doesn't hurt me. She's like an irritating fly.'

Francesca bit her lip, as though biting back a smile, which kept growing, and then she spluttered, 'Sorry,' and laughed, 'An irritating fly?'

In spite of everything, he chuckled, 'You don't like my simile?'

'It's the worst, most rubbish one I've ever heard. And you call yourself a writer.'

'I suppose you're laughing at me, are you?' Dilys snapped. John hadn't heard her come in.

The humour died. Dilys was tall in shiny black heels and a tight, pencil skirt-suit. Her lips were red and her blonde ponytail was high. John detested each and every detail of her. He had to look away.

'No, Dilys, we were not laughing at you,' Francesca replied with a forcefulness that John rarely heard in Francesca.

'I know you think you understand what you saw, but you have no idea what he's like to live with,' Dilys spat, pressing the coffee machine button down. The roar of the machine took over for a minute.

'Francesca doesn't need to be dragged into this, okay?' John said.

'Fine. I'm just saying, there are two sides to every story.'

Francesca's lashes blinked slowly and heavily across her eyes.

As Dilys knocked back her espresso, the children appeared.

'I'm late for work. I'll see you later, John.'

Harry and Beatrice said their goodbyes to their mother, but Olivia did not.

'Dad, could I have a pound, please, for the drinks machine?' Olivia asked.

'Don't I get a goodbye, Olive?' Dilys asked.

Ignoring her mother, Olivia said, 'Dad, can I have it?' She stood defiantly in front of John, expectant of her pound.

'Say goodbye to your mum, Olivia,' John coaxed, tweaking her nose.

Olivia pinked and was just about to turn, when Dilys said, 'No, it's okay. If she doesn't want to say goodbye to me then I don't want to say goodbye to her, either.' And she stormed out.

Olivia shrugged. 'Can I have that pound?'

John gave her the pound. He did not know what to say to Olivia.

'Right. We'd better get off, then. John, why don't you come over for lunch? I've got a chicken pie in the freezer.' Francesca looked at him.

Beatrice and Alice jumped up and down, 'Yeah! Yeah! Yeah!'

'Can you drop me off at Max's before?' Harry asked.

'Okay, I'll drop Harry off and we'll come over after that. Thanks.'

'Good,' Francesca said. 'Come on, you scallywags, let's get going.'

They followed her out to the car. John watched Olivia lag behind, her arms folded across the racket she held to her chest. She then ran back to him.

'I love you so much, Daddy,' she said.

'Oh, Olive,' John said, bending down to his haunches, hiding the pain in his back, holding her by the arms. 'I'm so sorry you had to see that. It must have been really horrible for you. I'm so, so sorry.'

Her bottom lip wobbled. 'Are you going to get a divorce now?'

John's heart broke. 'Mummy and Daddy are going through a bit of a difficult time at the moment, that's all. Mummy didn't mean to get cross and she's said a big sorry and given me a big cuddle, just like you and Beatrice do after your fights. It's just the same. You know how annoying Beatrice can be sometimes?'

'Yes!' Olivia cried.

'Well, it's the same for me and Mummy. Mummy gets really frustrated with me because, as you well know, I can be really, really annoying, can't I?'

Olivia smiled a little and nodded.

'See? So, you mustn't worry about us. And if you're ever upset about it again, just come to me and we can talk about it, okay? Or to Auntie Fran. She's a great listener. Otherwise it scrunches around in your tummy and you'll feel worse. Promise?'

'Okay, Daddy,' she said. 'I'd better go.'

John squeezed her tightly and kissed her repeatedly until she was begging him to stop. 'Love you, Olive.'

'Love you, Daddy!' she cried over her shoulder as she ran to the car.

John had just fed his clever, impressionable daughter a despicable lie. He had made it sound normal that his mother should hit him violently like that.

A memory floated just outside his reality, in a bubble, not real, not false; like a dream, or a nightmare, but more solid.

Her knees cracked as she sank to his level.

'What did you see, John?' she had asked him. Her breath had smelt of wine.

A man's voice rumbled from inside the poolhouse.

John had been too confused to answer her.

She slapped his face.

'You are both very wicked for getting out of bed and coming down here. If Robert tells any lies about what he saw, you'll be punished, do you understand?'

She wiped a finger under each eye to clean away the leaked make-up.

'I didn't see anything, Mummy.' He sniffed, tears falling over his burning cheek.

As she straightened to standing, her gold chain necklace had swung from her chest towards him like wrecking ball on a bulldozer, capable of knocking him off his feet.

'Good boy,' she said, sickly-sweet, the charm and beauty returning. 'Don't you worry, I won't tell Daddy what a bad, bad boy you've been when he gets back from Berlin. Now, off you pop to bed.' She had patted his bottom affectionately as he scampered away.

John scraped his fingers across his scalp, feeling a rawness across the hair follicles, as though his fingers had taken that same path before, over and over.

Anger for his mother resurfaced, as he reconsidered her duplicity. Tomorrow, she and his father would leave for Italy, for a week, for their yearly romantic jaunt through Tuscany. The perfect couple. The perfect love. How brilliantly she had played out her role as their father's loyal and loving wife, while screwing another man behind his back. How loyal and loving she had been towards Robert; her first born, her pride and joy, while her love had been laced with dirty secrets, slowly smothering him, like a pillow over his face.

All their lives, John and Robert had been lulled into the idea that it was best to toe the party line, where status and appearances were more important than the truth, where a cover-up was more acceptable than the idea of authenticity and morality and happiness. An affair was one thing – titillating, glamourous even – but a drug addled son, rumoured to have stolen from his old uncle? That was damning. It would have annihilated the image of perfection that she had worked so hard to maintain. The gossip would have spread around the village like wildfire. And everyone would have known that there had been more to their childhood than good schools, swimming pools and bluebell woods; there had been so much more.

CHAPTER TWENTY-NINE

Francesca

Rain prevented us from having lunch outside. While the children ate around the kitchen table, John and I picked at the remainders of the pie.

When the heavy rain turned to drizzle, we put on our rain coats and wellies, and walked onto the green. After a couple of circuits of the pot-holed, puddled road that circled the green, we settled on the soggy bench to watch Olivia and Beatrice teach Alice how to do cartwheels. The occasional car splashed along past us, and a dog-walker crossed the grass. Otherwise it was quiet and empty.

It was the first opportunity we'd had to talk to each other without the girls overhearing. I wanted to talk to him calmly, but I was a little shaken, still. Hours later. I didn't know whether I was angry with Dilys for her frenzied attack or with John for his acquiescence.

'What exactly did I witness this morning?'

'Seriously, Fran, it's not your problem.'

He leant his elbows onto his knees and stared at the children. The rain had dampened his hair, which he had scraped back. The eye where the bruise had been had a dark circle beneath it. I imagined the marks and bruises forming across his right arm and down the right side of his back, where Dilys' blows had landed.

'Has she done this before?'

'No. We had a row. It's over.'

'And the black eye?'

He pressed his face into his hands and stood up. 'For Christ's sake! I told you what happened.'

'No. You haven't.'

'Do *you* tell *me* everything?'

An accusation. It left me speechless.

I watched him walk away, over to the children, one hand twisting at a chunk of hair, the other in his pocket.

He said something to them, and I heard Beatrice wail.

I followed him over to see what was going on.

'Come on, it's time to get home, you two,' he was saying, wearily.

'Why?' Beatrice screamed.

'Because I say so,' he shouted back, losing his temper with uncharacteristic speed. Beatrice ran away, across the green.

'BEA! Come back here, now!' he yelled.

I could tell that he was at the end of his tether.

'John, why don't you leave them here for a play. I'll bring them back later.'

He refused to look me in the eye. 'No. Thanks. I want to get them home.'

He began striding after Beatrice.

A large, black van swung around the corner of the green from the B-road, behind John's sightline. It was going faster than it should down the lane that Beatrice was now running towards.

'JOHN!' I screamed. 'Olivia, watch Alice!'

I began to run, as did John.

The energy and momentum of Beatrice's tiny limbs was terrifying as she darted towards the lane, towards the van careering along. John was making headway, but not quickly enough. It was happening too fast.

Beatrice looked left behind her to see her daddy, and the van came at her from the right.

I heard John bellow her name. The fear in his voice reverberated through me; just as it had done two years ago on Hornsey Bridge.

The van's tyres screeched across the wet lane. Beatrice's piercing howl split the air. The van was diagonal across the road, obscuring my view of her.

As I got closer, I saw John collapsed over her. The van driver was climbing out. My head was pounding.

When I reached them, I could hear Beatrice's quiet sobs into John's chest.

'It's okay,' John was saying, 'it's okay.'

Her little body was enveloped in his arms as he kissed her forehead, over and over again.

'Is she hurt? Are you hurt?' I cried.

I knelt by them, feeling the road bite my knees.

'She tripped. It's just a graze.'

I saw that her leggings were torn on both knees and there were beads of blood forming through raw skin. Relief swamped me. I almost passed out.

The psychological echoes of Robert's death were roaring through me, and I clutched John's arm. 'Thank God.'

Was he, too, thinking about the dent in the bonnet of the red car that had hit Robert? Was he, too, thinking about Robert's internal injuries when he held Beatrice just now? Was he, too, thinking about the view down from that bridge?

The van driver was standing next to us, wheezing. He was wide, with stocky calves and forearms, both exposed in spite of the damp weather.

'I didn't see her,' he repeated.

'You were driving too fast!' I screamed at him, adrenalin rushing through my bloodstream. 'This is a twenty zone, and you must've been driving at fifty, at least!'

He backed off, holding his hands in the air. 'No harm done, all right, lady. The kid's fine.'

'You're lucky she is!' I yelled back.

The driver inspected his van where its bumper had hit a bollard as he swerved. 'The bumper's dented and there's a scratch,' he grumbled. 'You should keep a better eye on your kid.'

John stood up and pushed Beatrice into my arms, saying under his breath, 'Take her back to the others.'

'John. It's not worth it,' I warned, backing away.

But John's eyes had glazed over. He was not listening.

He stalked over to the van driver, grabbed the front of his T-shirt, and slammed him against the side of his van.

'You drive like that around this green again and I will kill you, do you understand?' John hissed right into the man's pocked face.

'All right, all right, mate, calm down. I'm sorry, all right! I had a bad day and I was late. I'm sorry, mate, really sorry,' he pleaded, sounding genuinely contrite.

John let him down. The man clambered back into his van and drove, very slowly, away. I wanted to clap and cheer.

'Naughty Daddy,' Beatrice said, looking up at me with a tear-stained grin on her face.

'Naughty Beatrice for running away from us like that,' I scolded gently. And then gave her a big kiss and squeezed her body tighter to me. 'That was a narrow escape, you little rascal. I hope you've learnt your lesson.' I scooped her up into my arms and stood, beginning to walk back to the two small figures waiting for us on the bench at the edge of the green.

Bea nodded very seriously as John fell in step with us.

'Are you okay to walk, do you think, Bea?' I said.

I put her down and she hobbled along in between John and me, sniffing loudly.

We headed over to Olivia and Alice, who were huddled together on one end of the bench.

John and I did not speak on the way back to the cottage.

Once we were inside, I cleaned and dressed Beatrice's grazes, before snuggling the three of them up under a blanket in front of a film.

John and I retreated to the kitchen. I closed the door and poured two small drams of whisky.

The surface of his drink rippled in his trembling hands. 'Thanks.'

'You certainly told him.'

'He caught me on a bad day.'

'He was going too bloody fast.'

He nodded, and then shook his head, holding eye contact with me for the first time that day. 'Beatrice was reacting to my bad mood. We'd already had a fight in the car on the way here.'

'It seems to be the theme of the day.'

'I didn't get any sleep last night.'

The conversation from last night came into the room again.

'The black eye was her, wasn't it?'

He nodded, and pressed his fingers hard into his recovered socket.

'She'd had a bad day at work.'

'How long has this been going on for?'

'A long time.'

'When did it first happen?'

'Remember Robert's first secretary at Aspect?'

'Tessa. She's Head of Documentaries at the Beeb now.'

'That's the one. Apparently, I was shagging her.'

'How the hell did she jump to that conclusion?'

'Robert and I had been at a party after a screening and Tessa had left a message on our landline by mistake – instead of Robert's mobile – to tell me that she'd ordered a cab to take us home, but it was garbled and she'd been drunk and Dilys had jumped to the wrong conclusions. She went nuts when I got home.'

'What kind of nuts?'

'She pushed me, over and over again, until I lost my balance and fell back onto the corner of the marble mantelpiece.'

I stared at him aghast. 'I remember you had stitches in the back of your head. For…'

'Falling over. Yes.'

'Into that mantelpiece in the mansion flat.'

'That's right.'

'Dilys did that?'

I reminded myself of the Edwardian marble mantelpiece in their flat in Maida Vale, and how happy they had seemed in their first home together. Dilys had fallen pregnant a few months after they had moved in. Everyone guessed the 'mistake' was Dilys' ruse to force John's hand in marriage. In spite of how smitten John was with Dilys at the time, we knew that he could have pottered through their relationship for the rest of their lives without formally committing to her. Camilla and Patrick had approved of Dilys' pushiness.

John offered me a sad smile. 'Harry was only eleven months old. He never slept back then.'

'You both looked bloody knackered all the time.'

'I was working long hours on Robert's films. And she was on her own too much, I guess.'

'It's no excuse.'

'Her attacks didn't happen as much when Valentina came to help out with Harry.'

'Her attacks? My god, John. This is insane.'

John hung his head, and his hips tipped back to lean into the worktop. I stared at his stooped form, his crumpled head of blond hair hanging between his shoulders. A broken man.

'Sorry. But seriously,' I said more gently, 'she needs to get professional help. Some counselling or something.'

'She'd never see a counsellor.'

'But she can't go on treating you like this. You have to tell her to get help or your marriage will fall apart.'

'What if all the counselling in the world couldn't change her?'

'Maybe it's some kind of post-natal depression, which has festered, and it comes out in all this anger, and she doesn't know how to control it.'

'I agree that she can't control it.'

'But if she got therapy, she'd be able to find ways to pre-empt those outbursts. Find the triggers and stuff. You could work through it together.'

'I've tried. Apart from one period, when I'd had enough and I told her I was leaving her, but then she got pregnant with Olivia.'

'I had no idea it was so bad.'

'We've had some happy times with the kids. Of course.' He looked down at the floor, scuffed his shoe on the lino, and then looked up at me. 'But the kids aren't always enough, are they?'

'People stay together because of their kids.'

It seemed important to uphold the idea. My thoughts were in turmoil. It was like a complete rewriting of everything I had believed about their marriage.

'It's a miserable way of living, believe me.'

'Oh, John, I'm so sorry. You'll find the love for each other again.'

'What if it was never there in the first place?'

My mouth hung open for a second, flummoxed. 'You guys were head over heels in love when you first met. I remember you telling me and Robert about her after your first date. I remember it so well. We were sitting in the kitchen at the flat eating cottage pie. You said you couldn't believe your luck. You said she was an extraordinary woman.'

'I used to think she was.'

I took a sip of whisky, and remembered my envy of her back then.

'I guess she played the game well,' I said.

'Just like Mum.'

'Let's face it, you married your mother.'

'I always thought I'd found someone more straightforward, someone who wouldn't stand for Mum's manipulative crap.'

'Dilys doesn't stand for it. But they clash, big time. Because they're so alike, I suppose.'

He sighed. 'I'm a Freudian cliché.'

'Textbook.'

There was a pause. He scraped his hands through his hair.

'I'm glad Mum's away right now. I'm still so bloody angry with her. I just can't believe she knew Robert was taking those pills.'

'We don't know for sure that she didn't try to get him some kind of help.'

'That would have meant telling someone her son was a drug addict.'

'She's *that* worried about appearances?'

John raised one eyebrow at me, as though to say, *What do you think?* He was right, of course. Camilla would stop at nothing to keep the Tennant family name intact.

'Are you going to talk to her about it when she gets back?'

'Yes,' he said, scratching his nose, sounding unconvincing, adding quickly, 'But what about you in all this?'

'Me?'

'How would Freud explain you?'

'I'd bore him.' I laughed.

'I mean, in terms of us?'

I wanted to thump my chest with my fist to stop the fluttering feeling that was building inside. A silky thread of ribbon was winding its way up from deep inside me. I felt a long-lost connection reforming between my heart and my mind.

'We were a mistake,' I murmured.

'Dilys was the mistake.'

'Don't go there, John.'

'Why?'

I threw both palms up at him, in a 'stop' motion. 'Actually, you know what Freud would say? He'd say you love the chase and you love the secrecy. Just like your mother and your brother,' I replied angrily, trying to keep my voice down, aware of the children next door.

'Then he'd be wrong.'

'We were a mistake!' I insisted. 'You said so yourself!'

'Because I was in love with you and I was scared!' he blurted out.

'What?'

More quietly, he repeated, 'I was in love with you. And I still am. And I always will be.' His hands flopped by his sides.

'No.' I shook my head. I had heard what I had feared most, and I had heard what I had longed for. I wanted to rubbish what he had said, to dismiss it as a flight of fancy, a fantasy notion in the midst of a troubled marriage. 'No,' I repeated. 'You loved Dilys… You said…' My voice failed, tears choking me.

His grey eyes were as clear as the wide sky above my tiny house, and they rested on me, softly drawing me into him, holding me, contradicting me, reassuring me it was not too late.

'I couldn't break my brother's heart.'

'But you did! *We* did. We broke it for ever!' I cried.

I ran from the room, upstairs to my bedroom.

I couldn't fathom the magnitude of it. Whilst John had been unavailable to me, in a true sense, I had been safe. Safe from blame, protected by my denial. But John's disclosure flooded into my system, taking me over completely. He had pushed open a door in my brain, letting air on smothered, forbidden feelings, releasing the truth. By trying to shed light on the shady areas of everyone else's lives, their secrets – Robert's pharmaceutical habit, Camilla's knowledge of his thieving – I had been blotting out my own. It had been a distraction to prod around in the Tennants' hiding places, hoping to find blame elsewhere. I did not have any right to be the accuser.

I began hyperventilating in a wave of sweat and tears and I collapsed onto the bed. My stomach boiled and tossed. With a monstrous urgency, I wanted to rewind years of my life to tweak a moment of fate, to go back in time and start again.

By letting John go, on the night of the wrap party, I had made the biggest mistake of my life. A settling for something almost right, rather than what I had known, deep down, *was* right. The combination of Robert's addiction, John's misplaced loyalty, and my insecurities had overridden our basic instincts. Our combined neuroses had won.

I had never before known what it felt like to regret, to truly regret. Regret was an emotion I dismissed as folly, believing it was a warped form of nostalgia. A regret was like a failure that festered, that you couldn't learn from, that you couldn't be philosophical about. Our missed opportunity to choose each other could not be considered a regret or a failure. That 'failure' would encompass the life I had shared with Robert, and I could never regret Robert. Could I? But my muscles seemed to be cramping with regret, with a yearning to change the past. If I had known that John had felt the same about me, if I had left Robert when I should have, Robert would still be alive. If I had not found those pills in Camilla's cabinet, if John had kept his feelings under wraps, I would not have been forced to turn the spotlight on myself, now, to hold myself accountable. Raw, ravaged guilt bobbed up in my mind like rancid trash in the sea.

Behind the cupboard doors, an arm's reach away from where I lay on my bed, I pictured the box I had stored there, carefully hidden under a tartan blanket, sitting in the dark, like a crouching animal. It contained a few of Robert's possessions, and one letter that I had wanted to forget, that I had debated on burning, that I had never wanted John to read. Should I ransack the box, tear out the letter and run down to John with it now?

I could hear orchestral music from the television drifting up the stairs, reminding me of the three girls engrossed in their film. My heartbeat raged, sucking oxygen from my brain, dizzying me, unsteadying me. They, too, had been victims of our selfishness.

No longer could John and I carry on pretending that we were innocent parties in Robert's death. Our betrayal had been fatal. Our bleeding hearts dripped with guilt. We were the cause. We were an impossibility.

We were too late.

CHAPTER THIRTY

John

'Shit. Shit. Shit,' John mouthed, under his breath, trying to pace a kitchen that couldn't accommodate more than two steps one way or the other. He was trapped. The children were next door. He couldn't leave. He'd told Francesca he loved her! What the fuck had he done?

It had taken him just a few seconds to say what he had spent sixteen years holding back.

'Shit. SHIT,' he repeated, staring into the sink, wishing he could be sick into it.

'That's two in the swear box, Daddy,' Beatrice said.

John swivelled around, rearranging his features into something palatable for his daughter. 'Everything okay?'

'My knees are ouchy.'

'Oh, darling,' he said, crouching down to her level, touched by the sight of the two clean plasters over her tiny knees, reeling from what he had just told Francesca. 'I'll kiss them better for you,' he teased, puckering his lips, knowing she would not let him go near her sore knees.

'No!' she giggled, jumping back and trying to run away, but he scooped her up, careful not to bash her knees, and gave her a big hug, blowing raspberries into her neck.

'Can I have some chocolate biscuits, Daddy?' she asked.

'Ah, so that's why you came in.'

'Alice wants one.'

John laughed. 'Right. Yes. Well, if Alice wants one, we'd better find one.'

He heard Francesca's footsteps coming down the creaky stairs.

His heart was in his mouth. He began opening cupboards, to look for biscuits, to climb inside, to be busy and distracted, like looking away before an injection. More cupboards. Open, shut. Open, shut. One after another in a comical fluster.

She was in the room. He didn't dare turn around. He stared at the Marmite pot and the honey jar, shifting them around in the cupboard, pretending a packet of biscuits might be lurking behind them.

'Daddy, you've looked in that one already,' Beatrice said.

'What are you looking for?' Francesca's voice was hoarse.

'Alice wants a chocolate biscuit,' Beatrice said.

Francesca's scent reached him and her hips budged him out of the way. That gentle nudge could have sent him crashing to the floor.

'There's a very chocolatey packet in here, I think.' There was a smile in her voice.

She was bending into the fridge, her body close enough for him to feel its heat. How he dreaded seeing her face again, but he craved it too. What would he see? What signs would she leave in her beautiful features? Had he changed them?

Still with her back turned to him, she handed Beatrice a biscuit. 'One biscuit for Alice.'

Beatrice stared at it in her hands, and hesitated before going. 'She wants three.' Beatrice said.

Francesca laughed. 'What a greedy guts!' She handed Beatrice two more biscuits.

Off Beatrice went and around Francesca twirled.

Her dark eyelashes flared around her big brown eyes, holding back a blink. The brown of her iris was a deeper hue, and the searching, reciprocated love was as warm and unfettered as it had been in his dreams. Then she blinked. The blink was like a slice of a shutter lens, triggering reality. All of a sudden, he could see the real-time ravages of what he had said. Her eyes were rimmed red and swollen. Her cheeks were pink and hot, her lips dry and sad.

'Are you all right?' he asked.

'No. I'm not all right,' she replied, brushing her fringe back, crossing her arms over her chest.

'Sorry.' He felt shamefaced.

'I'm with Paul now.'

'You're serious about him?'

She shook her head, opening her mouth as if to say no, but she did not. She said very quietly, 'Your mum would never allow it.'

'Mum can't stop us.'

She wrapped her arms around her middle. 'I meant Paul and me.'

But he knew she had not meant that.

'I'll deal with Mum.'

She stared up at him, her face pale, her lips open. The recollection of the golden flecks of rain and the smell of turpentine came flooding back to him. Sixteen years on, he was still struck by her; and tickled by the memory of their chat at the boot of her car.

'Chromatically pitch perfect.' He chuckled.

A small smile. 'I was such a show off.'

'You were funny.'

Her cheeks flashed pink. 'Berry Smoothie,' she grimaced, holding her face.

'What's the hot new colour these days?'

She pointed to his whisky. 'Arsey Brass is trending right now.'

They both grinned at each other. Her brown eyes warmed his whole being.

Nothing could touch him now. Not even his mother. It was as though he had conquered the world. He had no plans or intensions or missions; he simply wanted to enjoy the feeling of opening up to the woman he had been in love with for so long, armed with the inner knowledge that she, too, had probably been fighting the same instincts. Anything seemed possible, even in the face of the breakdown of his marriage, even in the face of a confrontation about Robert with his mother – possibly his final confrontation, if that was how she wanted it to go – when she returned from Italy.

John was determined to be with Francesca. Whatever the price. Perhaps they had already paid the price: Robert's death was their brutal punishment, a life sentence.

He conjured up the crystal-clear image of Robert's face on the bridge that night, knowing he could never explain to her why he had been there, and what he had read in his brother's eyes.

Telling her would mean losing her. It was a price that he was not willing to pay.

CHAPTER THIRTY-ONE

Francesca

The roads were winding and empty. Alice had fallen asleep. Mostly she would chatter during car journeys, and I would wish she would stop for a second to give me space for my own thoughts. Today, I was so grateful to her for the peace. Last night, she had woken up three times with nightmares about black metal monsters stamping on her head.

I had ten minutes before we reached the pub that Paul had booked for lunch. I should have cancelled. What had happened with John yesterday made me want me to cancel everything, cancel life… or cancel everything in life except John.

But that could not be.

Foolishly, naively, I had drawn him into my quest for answers, into my aggressive search for the truth – so-called – to bring his mother down, to reveal her true nature. She had caused untold damage by keeping Robert's secret about the Seroquel, but, in all honesty, my attention on Camilla had been a smoke screen.

Until the time came when I was brave enough to open the box that hid in my bedroom cupboard, to read that letter again, to air my own secrets, I did not deserve to cast aspersions, I did not deserve a future with John.

'You okay?' Paul's face was in the car window.

'Oh. Sorry.' I opened my door.

'Is she asleep?'

'She had a bad night last night.'

'You look exhausted.'

'We had a bit of a shocker yesterday.' I climbed out of the car and woke Alice up. She felt heavy as I lifted her out of her seat. Paul reached out and offered to carry her. I hesitated, but decided to pass her over.

She nuzzled into his neck and wrapped her legs around his waist.

Once we had settled at the table, Alice perked up and she ran to the playground with Georgie and Sylvie.

I told him about Beatrice's narrow escape. 'I really thought the van had hit her. It was horrible.'

'But she's okay now. Just a few grazed knees.'

I was irritated by his flippancy. He was dismissing the fear I had felt. I wanted him to understand.

'Robert was killed by a car. The doctors said he would have survived the fall if that car hadn't hit him.'

Paul's face paled. 'What a shit thing to know.'

'He jumped onto a dual carriageway, Paul,' I reminded him tetchily. 'He must have known he'd be hit by a car.'

I was taking it out on him. It was unfair of me.

'I don't know how you got through that night.'

A lump like an ice-cube formed in my throat. 'It stands as the single, most defining part of me. It's who I am now. I was changed by it completely. It's hard to explain.'

I was challenging him to understand that my life had been cut into two halves. Before and after. They were two different lives in my one being. Two different Francescas: one that he could never know, and one that sat before him now. I had been the happy wife of a successful film producer. I had become the widow of a suicidal addict. The tragedy was complex. It was tinged with violence and guilt and secrecy and shame. Could he understand? Was it too much to ask of him?

'Don't you think you'll ever get through it?'

I felt like a teacher at the beginning of a child's education, already beaten by what they would have to teach the children in the years ahead, already knowing I could never teach them what they needed to know to survive in the world. Maybe it was unfair to try to teach Paul what was in my head. Maybe it would be like the teacher breaking it to her five year olds that her lessons would never prepare them for the miseries that might come their way, however well they learnt their times-tables. It would be corrupting and pointless, especially when there was the chance they might well sail through life without a trauma like mine. If Paul was with someone else, someone less damaged, he would not have to learn about my sadness and my regret and my confused feelings for a man I could never have. It would be unfair to set out to teach him that.

'I am getting through it.'

'But you say it defines you.'

'That doesn't mean it defines me in a wholly negative way. There are things I've learnt that I would never want to unlearn.'

'Like?'

'Empathy. I see people differently now. I judge less. And, after he died, I experienced such kindness from everyone around me. Even now, it moves me.'

'I know what you mean. After my divorce, I think I felt like that. Not that I'm saying a divorce is anything like what you went through.'

'There are different sorts of traumas in life.'

'You have been very brave.'

I had heard this before. I was not brave. Brave people go into burning buildings to save lives, like Paul. Brave people swim across oceans to raise money for the sick. Brave people get up on stage and sing to hundreds of people.

'I'm not brave. I'm broken.' I smiled, worn out.

'You look very much in one piece to me.'

'I'm a Tennant,' I said, with mock pride.

I wanted to be brave – a brave person like him. All widows were brave. All firemen were brave. We were one of a kind. That's what Paul believed. By telling me I was in one piece, he was willing it; he was tacitly agreeing to leave my damaged self alone, unruffled and hidden away, possibly for ever. He had no idea how far down that self could bury itself. In a raw state, I had brought an element of her to life, just now, for him, just today. I had brought the two Francescas together, and he would be naive to believe that the whole of me could be formed as one again so readily. If he was happy with that, then maybe I should be, too. Operating on two levels was one way to live, I supposed: one level for interacting with others, and another level for my internal life. John and I had achieved that separation over the years. Mistakenly, we had merged them yesterday, and we would have to prise them apart again to stay safe.

'It's funny. From the outside, the Tennants have everything.'

'That's what Camilla desperately wants everyone to believe.'

'I never wanted to tell you before, but I heard there was this couple who lived in the village years ago, when Robert and John were young lads, and there was some kind of big falling out between them and the Tennants.'

'What about?'

'Dunno, but they left the village really suddenly, I heard. Sold up, took the kids out of school and were never seen of again.'

'Because of a fight?'

'The rumour was that Camilla was having it off with the husband. But I don't know if that's true.'

'My god. Really?' I was appalled. In spite of Camilla's controversial behaviour, I had always viewed Camilla and Patrick as an ideal partnership, perfectly balanced.

'Robert never said anything?'

'Nothing. Ever. Neither has John.'

'I guess some secrets are better kept,' Paul said, reaching for the menu.

'I guess so,' I said, wondering how much Robert or John had known about this, at once fearful of what John was capable of keeping from me, questioning how much he, too, had learnt at his mother's knee.

CHAPTER THIRTY-TWO

Six years ago

It was Saturday morning. Francesca was exhausted, and desperate to stay in her pyjamas all day and all evening. But Robert had planned another night out.

'No, please. Please can we stay in tonight?' she begged.

That week alone they had been out to four events: one art gallery opening; one launch party, whose screening they hadn't been invited to; one dinner party held by a distant and unpleasant school friend of Robert's; and one Soho House drinks party, at which they had known nobody. Not one of the evenings had been anything other than draining and stressful. And every night after they had returned home, Robert had drunk too much whisky, been aggressive, and then crashed out comatose, having popped some sleeping pills. More than that, he had refused sex. Even when she had dressed up in some naughty underwear and begged him for it.

Francesca was not sex-starved. She was ovulating. She wanted a baby. This new desire had come over her suddenly, after a Sunday lunch at Byworth End, when Dilys had talked openly about trying for their third. It had been an eye-opener for Francesca, who realised they were two babies behind.

However, Robert was not throwing his heart into the process. The drinking was affecting his sex drive and possibly Francesca's fertility, and the hangovers were definitely affecting her work. That week, the crew on set had been a bunch of sexist pigs of the old-school Pinewood ilk, pushing her to breaking point. Their banter had made her cry, when usually it would just make her cross.

Robert continued his relentless pleading. 'Please, Fran. Just tonight. This guy is only over from LA for a couple of days.'

'Why is it so important you see him?' she whined.

'Fran, he wants to finance my movie. And you'll love his wife. They're treating us to The Ivy. It'll be fun.'

Furious, but too tired to fight with him about it, she threw a coat over her pyjamas, grabbed her sketchbook and some charcoals and marched out. She strode down Swain's Lane to the Heath, and up to Parliament Hill, where she found a spot to cool off.

An hour later, Robert arrived at the bench where she was sitting. She glared at him and continued sketching. He sidled up next to her, trying to take the charcoal from her hand, tapping on the page like a child trying to get her attention.

She resented the pressure he was putting her under, not really because of the hangover, but because she hated that she was never able to stand her ground, that she had lost her free will.

Sitting there, on Hampstead Heath, in her pyjamas, she had an awakening. After five years of marriage, it had finally dawned on her that Robert's time had become more important than her own. What he needed would always take precedence over what she needed. Enough was enough. She was thirty-five. It was time.

'If I go tonight, we have to have sex every night for a week, and the same next month, and the month after that, until I am pregnant.'

'If I have to,' he teased, kissing her.

So, later on, she had dressed for The Ivy and pasted on a smile for the financier, and when they returned home, she and Robert had had sex.

When he rolled off her, she elevated her pelvis and thought of names for a little baby girl. A baby would bring them closer. A baby would make them happy. John and Dilys were happy. Tired, but happy. She and Robert could be, too.

CHAPTER THIRTY-THREE

John

John was lying back on the wicker sun-lounger in the garden drinking the best cup of coffee he had tasted in months. Steam rose from the grass at his bare feet, warmed by the September sun. A red butterfly danced around a pot of dahlias. The cushion behind him was slightly damp from the rain over the past few days, but it cooled the sore wounds across his skin.

After three days of solid writing, he had finished the final episode of series seven. Billy had won Poppy. The world had been saved. He had resolved the series. It was a sweet, tied-in-a-bow finale. There were no open ends or bittersweet hooks to set the viewers up for the next series. It was probably the last series of *Billy Stupid* that he would write. It had tumbled out of him. Just as his feelings for Francesca had done. He had opened his heart to her and he had been rolling on a high ever since. Laughing off tantrums and fights and general shenanigans from the children – and ignoring Dilys' cagey, disengaged mood – he had cherished Francesca in his mind. Even the shock about the Seroquel, and all that his mother had hidden about Robert's 'sticky fingers', was obscured, for the time being, by Francesca. She was like a shimmering jewel in a secret drawer somewhere inside him. Nobody knew she was there, nobody knew that he was thinking about her, nobody knew what had shifted between them. He planned to call her later.

And then a voice. 'Darling?'

It was his mother. His stomach flipped over.

'Mum?'

'We're back! We thought we'd surprise you.'

She appeared around the corner in a white shirt, crisp against her brown, freckled skin, followed by his father, who wore a deep tan and blue towelling T-shirt and board shorts.

He was not prepared for them. Her voice provoked an avalanche of mixed-up emotions. It dredged up his anger, pulling it out through his happiness about Francesca.

He could not find a way to greet them properly.

'I told your mother we should have called,' Patrick said, smoothing back his salt-and-pepper hair, pecking John on the cheek.

'Nonsense. You don't mind, do you?' she cried, clinging to him as though it had been years that she hadn't seen him, rather than a week.

'It's great to see you. You both look so well. Coffee?'

They settled at the end of the long teak table on the terrace. He heard about the friends they had stayed with and the swims in coves and the campaniles and churches they had visited. In the past, he would be gratified that his parents were enjoying the freedoms of their retirement, wishing he could ape that romance in his own marriage. Now, there was a gritty feeling in his throat, like a tickle, a hint of something unpleasant. He cleared it away with a small cough.

'Are you coming down with something, darling?'

So much was running through his mind. There was Francesca, of course. But it was the image of Robert pilfering anti-psychotics from their uncle's house that blanked out all else. How entangled had his mother been in his brother's habit? How much had she really known? Was now the right time to bring it up? Would there ever be a right time to bring up such a thing?

'I'm addled. I've just finished the series.'

'Good, good,' his father said, knocking back the last of his coffee, probably preparing to get going already. John felt sad about how distant his father had become since Robert's death – or maybe it was before that. He couldn't remember the last time they had shared any meaningful conversation. Maybe they had just never been close.

'Tell me about the children,' Camilla said, sitting back and settling in.

John told her a couple of anecdotes about their antics. Before, he would have enjoyed pulling at her heartstrings, and relished in the love and pride she showed towards them, but today it was forced. 'Bea and Alice are obsessed with each other,' he finished.

'Darling Alice. She's so happy with her cousins. How's Francesca? Oh, we thought of them so often, didn't we, Patrick?' She sighed. 'Especially when we were in Siena.'

'Why Siena?'

'When you and Robert were whippersnappers, we had many happy family holidays there,' Patrick replied. John could see his eyes were watering. He was nostalgic about happy family holidays – how could he have been so ignorant?

His mother said, 'Poor Alice won't ever experience family holidays like that. I felt so desperately sorry for them.'

'Francesca won't be on her own forever.'

Camilla pursed her lips and glanced over at Patrick.

'We wouldn't want her to be, obviously.'

John's chest tightened, and he tried to change course. 'She's settled well this summer.'

'Paul's a handsome chap.' Camilla shot a look at Patrick, as though she wanted his support, and then added, 'But he's so *different* to Robert.'

'And?'

'Each to their own, I suppose,' she replied. 'I mean, I don't care what he does for a living. Tinker, sailor, spy or a whatsit.'

'Tinker, tailor, soldier, spy,' Patrick mumbled.

'Oh, shut up, Pat. You know what I mean.'

'Mum,' John chastised. 'It's got nothing to do with us.'

'Well, we pay for that cottage, you know. If he moved in or anything, well, it would be everything to do with us.' She laughed, but she was plainly not amused.

'Moving in?' John cried. 'They've been an item for a month or so and now you think he's moving in with her?'

'Ah. So, they're an item!' she cried triumphantly. 'See? I told you, Patrick, didn't I?'

'Mother of God, woman, you were the one who sent the poor fellow over there to sort out the mice,' Patrick cried.

'Bees,' she snapped back.

'Wasps, actually,' John added, for good measure.

'I don't give damn if they were bearded dragons, and neither should you,' Patrick retorted, probably having had a bellyful of Camilla's griping at home.

John raised his hands in surrender. 'I certainly don't care who the hell she dates.'

'I don't give a damn, either,' Camilla cried. 'I adore Francesca and I want the very best for her.'

'We all do,' John said.

She sniffed. 'But, if Robert knew. Imagine…'

He was swamped by anger, and dragged back to the disbelief and anguish of Robert's death, as if Robert had died there and then, all over again; as if his mother had murdered him with her bare hands, right there in front of John. The yearning to see his big brother alive again hurt him physically. Fury surged up from his gut. He blamed his mother for how much he missed him. He wanted Robert to be sitting with them now, to hear his deep laugh, to see him rub his large hands together with a plan. John held in his vitriol towards his mother. It was unbearable to think that she had covered for Robert, that she had known all along about his thieving, that she had failed to get him the help he needed. Yet John was too scared to ask her the necessary – and potentially incendiary – questions about why she had kept it hidden for so long.

'Robert would want her to be happy,' John said, grinding his teeth.

Camilla cuffed her fingers around her wrist, strangulating the blood flow to her hand. She was so still, the butterfly John had seen earlier landed, wings together, on her shirt.

The butterfly darted away when she slapped her hand on the table. 'It's only been two years. *Two years*. Doesn't she have any self-respect?' She was shrill, her blue eyes ablaze with fury. 'And, quite frankly, John, you've encouraged her. It's unacceptable. *Unacceptable*. Do you hear? Grow some balls and tell her she can't… she just *can't* behave like this.'

When her mood turned like this, John's normal breathing stopped, his airways constricted. He didn't respond. Ever since he was a boy, his mother had had the ability to stun him with her sharp tongue and her contradictions.

'That's enough, Camilla,' Patrick said, standing. 'We'll be on our way, John.'

They left, arm in arm, hobbling along as though his mother was an invalid, her body leaning into his father's.

After any argument, she would be the same. If she was the one who was most obviously in the wrong, she would be the one to feel most hard-done by. Everybody was against her. Nobody understood her. Nobody cared.

John's toes felt damp and cold on the flagstones.

In a rage, he swept his mother's lipstick-marked coffee cup off the table. The cup clattered onto the flagstones without breaking.

John pressed his hands into his face, trying to make sense of his mother's outburst. The hypocrisy was mind-blowing. How did she have the ability to play the victim, when she herself was the aggressor?

Under her power, he was weak. A pathetic waste of space. He had spent his life cowering or running away.

The night by the poolhouse reared up in his mind.

'Sorry, Mummy,' John had said, running from her to the house.

Once inside, he had crept into Robert's room. 'Go away!' Robert had mumbled from under his duvet.

'But what was that man doing there?'

'GO AWAY!' he shouted.

And John had retreated, slipping back into his own bed.

He lay there, the sheets pulled over his head and his eyes squeezed tightly shut, nowhere near sleep, wishing that he had not been such a bad, bad boy.

In the morning, he realised he had wet his bed for the first time in his life.

Ashamed of himself, he had bundled the sheet and shoved it into his rucksack to take downstairs to the laundry room. As he was stuffing it into the washing machine, Valentina found him.

'You want my job, chicky?'

He jumped to attention, tongue-tied, feeling tears push behind his eyes. The damp sheet was hanging out behind him.

Valentina bustled over and scooped the yellow patch of sheet into the drum of the machine. 'We no tell,' she said, pressing her forefinger to her lips.

He wondered how many other family secrets Valentina had been keeping over the years. All their lives, he and Robert had harboured the secret of the night-visit to the poolhouse. Thankfully, Robert had never coerced him to go out into the dark with him again, but John had heard Robert sneak out regularly. Only ever when his father was away. For this reason alone, John dreaded his father's trips to Berlin. Underneath the surface, it had been a heavy knowledge that he and Robert had kept inside them. When his father was home, their mother's cheating existed in an alternate space, as a separate entity to their parents' happy marriage. While they did not talk about it, it had not ever become real. But the secret had been spreading and destroying them ever since, like a metastasising cancer. The original secret, like the first tumour, had spawned others; another generation of secrets, growing and killing the healthy cells. He imagined a tumour growing large in his own gut: his own guilty conscience. When was it going to stop? How was he going to cut it out? The opening up of the body, the first slice into the diseased organs, would surely provoke a fatal heart attack, an instant death.

Instead, John was settling for this slow, insidious destruction, daunted by the harrowing memory of that night, unable to confront those last moments with his brother.

John did not know which was a better way to go.

CHAPTER THIRTY-FOUR

Five years ago

After the scene had been wrapped up, Francesca had taken herself off to the next studio to smoke an illegal cigarette and have a cry. Not for the first time the art director had yelled at Francesca, in front of the whole crew, for splattering a couple of drops of button polish onto a bathtub in shot, by mistake.

About halfway through her cigarette, John had appeared, with a dog-eared, rolled-up *Billy Stupid* script in his hand. He had climbed up next to her, onto the scaffolding.

'Don't let the bastards get you down.'

'The bitch, you mean. No wonder those painters walked off the job.'

'You're not going to walk, are you?'

'Honestly, I might do. I only bloody accepted this shitty job because Robert begged me to.'

'You calling my creative genius "shitty"?'

'Sorry. It's not your script that's shitty. It's just I hate being on set while they're filming. It's stressful.'

'You're doing a brilliant job out there. Everyone says so. Behind your back.'

She smiled, enjoying the compliment. Robert had been excessively critical of her at home, leaving her feeling vulnerable, unseen.

'Thanks, John. Sorry for saying it was shitty.'

'Believe me, I cringe at my own lines sometimes.'

'No!' She chuckled.

Cut off from the world, in that big, cold studio, hyper from over-tiredness and the heightened tension on set, John started quoting some of his worst lines in the script in a silly voice. They creased up. Tears of laughter fell down their cheeks. Then their fingers had touched, just as they had in the cinema years before. Once their flesh had made contact, she couldn't release her hands from his. Their fingers entwined, and she explored the sensations of their contact: his skin, his knuckles, his veins, the movement of his joints; the feel of him was rare silk, impossible to stop running between her fingers.

It wasn't long before his hands moved up her arms, and to her face. He pushed her hair back and tucked it behind her ear. As he did that, Francesca lost herself. She was intoxicated by him. The flecks in his grey eyes, his blond frown, his shy smile. The importance of the rest of her life shrank to the size of a pin-prick. Her desire to kiss him became utterly irrepressible. Their lips met. If sunshine had radiated from them and beamed into the universe for the whole world to see, she would not have been surprised.

They had frantically pulled off each other's clothes. Francesca hesitated, but not for long. The scaffolding squeaked and groaned, and they laughed about the noise, and about falling off, to their deaths. She thought it would be worth it. Thoughts of Robert were not even in her head beyond a fleeting spark of guilt. Nothing would have stopped her. Nothing.

Afterwards, they dressed, gingerly. The sordid reality of what they had done came seeping into their consciences.

'That was a horrible mistake,' John said, jumping down from the scaffold. 'I love Dilys.'

Her blood ran cold. If he'd asked her to, she would have run away with him that very moment.

*

At the end of the day's shoot, John turned up at the bus stop where Francesca was waiting.

'I'm sorry.'

She didn't know whether he was saying sorry for what he had said or what they had done.

A grumbling double-decker pulled up in front of them, looming over them, waiting.

'It wasn't your fault,' she said, and she stepped onto the 107 to Archway.

In the weeks that followed, she had belittled the event, bracketed it, in disbelief that it had happened at all. And she had thrown all her energies into loving Robert.

CHAPTER THIRTY-FIVE

Francesca

It had taken Alice and me five minutes to walk to Letworth Primary. I was chatting away to her, trying to cover my own nerves on her behalf.

For the second time, I checked my phone. John had not texted back. It was only half an hour since I had sent him the photograph of Alice in her new school uniform, ready for her first day at big school. The photograph had been designed as an icebreaker. So much had been said the other day. Too much, perhaps.

When we arrived at the school gates, the playground was filled with strange faces and unfamiliar smiles.

She was ushered into the reception class line by her new teacher, and her hand wriggled out of mine. Stony-faced and pale, Alice said, 'Goodbye, Mummy,' very formally.

I sped-walked towards home, away from the other mothers walking in the same direction, trying not to cry.

Just making it over the threshold of the cottage, I burst into tears.

The summer holidays had been six of the most intense, life-changing weeks of our lives since Robert's death. In spite of how exhausting Alice had been at times, we had been a good team. Without her by my side, I didn't know what to do with myself. There was a whole week to fill before my job started with Archie Parr at the paint shop.

I stood at the kitchen window and stared down towards the bottom of the garden.

Inside my shed there were stacks of boxes and bubble-wrapped furniture. None of which I had touched since the day we had moved in.

I made some tea and checked my phone. Still no text from John. I should have been happy. It was what I had wanted. I had told him I was with Paul.

Beyond the kitchen window, my shed rested quietly at the bottom of the garden, undemanding and patient.

There was no phone signal there.

No phone signal. Exactly what I needed to get thoughts of John out of my mind.

I dressed in my blue overalls that were marked with splashes of paint like a Pollack canvas and headed down to the bottom of the garden.

Inside, I breathed in deeply. The rush of paint fumes was an inhalation of joy, taking me back to happy times, to the period of my life when I had been independent and valued and free.

The first box was filled with sketches, a few of which I lingered over, and criticised. I had never wanted to exhibit or sell my pictures, as my peers at Goldsmiths had dreamt of doing. My pictures were quiet and unfashionable. Even if they had been outstanding, I doubt I would have any desire to sell them. They were for me. They represented a very private part of me.

One of my charcoal pictures, of the view from the top of Parliament Hill on Hampstead Heath, stopped me in my tracks. It was unfinished, small and drab, the one I had started after the argument with Robert about the party he had wanted me to go to.

I stacked the drawings and sketchbooks on the shelf and then opened the next box, and the next, and then snipped bubble-wrap away from my desk. It was time to set it up again.

*

The room of the shed looked cluttered and cosy, and it belonged to me. I had transformed it into my own space, in a way that I had been unable to do in the cottage.

Big tubs of paint were sitting at my feet. With a frisson of excitement, I prised open their lids. The vividness of the azure-blue filled my whole being with light and energy. The second tub was brown, earthy and rich. I pictured mixing it with white, yellows and reds until it was the dusky beige-pink of the dried hydrangeas on the bush outside the window. I opened the next one. It was white. I imagined swirling the blue into it, adding gloops with my wooden stick, stirring it like a witch until it was the colour of the sky.

The walls around me were white. I would paint them but I would not rush. I had to find the perfect shade for this peaceful space.

As I sat staring into space, there was a knock on the door. I jumped.

'Hello?'

'It's me.'

'John?' I opened the door.

The elation I had remembered on his face a week ago was no longer there. He looked haggard. His stubble was as dark as his eye sockets.

We stood there staring at each other for a few seconds, which sent my heart pumping blood into my cheeks.

'Your phone was out of signal and I was passing.'

'How did you get in?'

'You left your front door wide open.'

'Oh.' I grinned. 'Whoops. Come in.'

He came in and tripped over a paint gun as he looked around. 'It looks great in here.'

'Almost there,' I said, surveying my room, closing up the lids of the paint tubs.

He sat on one of the empty crates. And I sat on my desk stool.

The air between us was charged.

His feet in his desert boots tapped out a rhythm and his fingers were interlocked, as though in prayer, but his forefingers were pointing up, like the slide of a handgun, and he pressed them into his lips.

'How was Alice this morning?' he asked.

'Very brave. Did you see the picture I sent?'

'Beautiful.' He smiled.

'Everything okay?'

'Sure.'

'You sure you're sure?'

'Beatrice was a bit anxious today.'

'She usually loves school, doesn't she?'

'Her new form teacher is called Miss Thorne and she said she's like a big horrible thorn in her toe.'

I laughed. 'It's hard being four and so clever.'

His forefingers slid up the centre of his face, from his lips up to his forehead, between his eyebrows, where he leant into them.

'Can I ask you something?'

'Of course.'

There was a long pause.

'Did Robert ever say anything about Mum and' – he hesitated – 'and other men?'

'No,' I said. This was not a lie. Paul had been the one to tell me the rumour of the affair and the absconding family.

He shifted uncomfortably on the box and it made a creaking sound.

'I want you to be honest with me.'

'I am being honest. What brought all this on?' I asked, slightly alarmed, wondering if I should tell him what Paul had told me.

He stared at me, not speaking, as though weighing something up.

'I remember this arsehole, Edward, calling the house a lot. Especially when Dad was away.'

'Did you know him?'

'He was a theatre director, I think. He lived in the village with his wife and they came to our parties. Mum would giggle when she was around him.'

'Do you think she was having an affair with him?'

'Hmm. Maybe.'

'Did your dad know anything?'

'I have no idea.'

'He wouldn't have stayed with her if he'd known, surely.'

'I don't know. He's so hard to read.'

'He puts up a very good front.'

'I'm starting to wonder what's behind that front.'

'You might never know.'

John stood up suddenly. 'That's exactly it. My god!' he cried, squeezing his head. 'I might never know. All this stuff that is coming up, all these memories about Mum, and that guy, and this Seroquel thing. It's driving me crazy. I don't know what to do with it all.'

He plonked himself down again and, as he did so, the lid of the box collapsed in on itself and half of him disappeared to the bottom.

We both began to laugh and I yanked him out with one arm.

'You really are a wally,' I chortled.

Suddenly, we were standing face to face, close-up… too close-up.

'And you really are beautiful,' he said, tucking my hair behind my ear.

My whole body fired up as though he had switched me on. Before I could think, he was unbuttoning the front of my overalls and kissing my skin, down, down, further down, until he was clasping me around the hips and burying his face in my middle, where

I could feel tears on his cheeks. I pulled his face to mine, and sank down next to him, kissing away his sadness. Unable to let go of each other, we frantically pushed the boxes aside and pulled the tarpaulin across the floor, hurriedly making room to lie down, as though the world might end at any minute. John's touch was too electric, too mind-blowing to question, too right to ever be able to resist. He was hungry for me one minute and gentle the next, savouring every sensation and every part of me as we undressed. His body was lean and tanned and I should have been self-conscious to be naked in front of him, but I felt like the most beautiful woman alive. I felt like his whole world. How had I lived so long without this feeling?

But then his mother's face came into my mind, and then his children's smiles.

'Stop,' I said, twisting away.

John sat up. The back of his head; his vertebrae protruding.

I pulled an old dust sheet over my body.

'We can't do this again.'

'We'll always feel guilty, won't we?'

'And so we should.' I began to dress. I felt despicable. I couldn't believe how weak I was when it came to John. I couldn't do this.

'That first time. I…'

'Let's not go there,' I interrupted.

'I was out of order.'

'We've both made so many mistakes.'

'Don't go yet, Fran,' John said, pulling me back. 'Please.'

I fell back, impotent.

We lay on our backs, staring at the ceiling, fully dressed again. John's arms were behind his head, and his ankles were crossed. I had bunched up the dust sheet as a pillow. We began to talk, about Robert mainly. As the minutes turned to hours, we took turns to run into the house and bring back cups of tea and cheese sandwiches from the kitchen, like two teenagers hiding out in a secret woodland camp.

'Sometimes I think it was a miracle that he survived as long as he did,' John said.

'That's too convenient, to think like that.'

'What do you mean?'

'It lets us off the hook.'

'But he never knew what happened between us.'

I clenched my teeth tightly together, grinding them together to stop myself from saying what I was really thinking.

'How can you be so sure?'

'He was too self-involved to notice anything.'

'Don't say that, John.'

'Sorry. But I get so angry with him,' John said, thumping the side of a cardboard box. 'I wish he hadn't died.'

As the time ticked by, the minutes edged closer and closer towards Alice's school pick-up time. The thought of collecting Alice, of having to concentrate on what she needed, and ending this, whatever it was, sent a wave of misery crashing over me.

In John's arms, another hour did not seem enough. When I considered the rest of the day without him a little part of my heart tore, and when I considered the rest of my life without him close to me like he was now, I wondered how long it would be before that tear became a ragged rip through my insides.

'You'd better go,' I declared abruptly, untangling myself from him. 'I have to pick up Alice.'

He groaned, rolled over and buried his face in the tarpaulin. 'I'd forgotten Alice's pick-up was earlier than Bea's. I thought we had another hour, at least.'

I sank back into his arms, sending away the fear of what was to come, knowing we could never do this again, deciding to enjoy the moment, eking out the final few minutes before Alice's school day ended.

We walked back through the garden with flat, spiritless steps. But then I laughed out loud, unable to contain a sudden burst of happiness, and there was something in his general demeanour, when I said goodbye, that had shifted too. He had a new confidence. I had feared he might take this back home to Dilys, to confess everything.

He left the house first. The secrecy of our afternoon pricked at my conscience, but I couldn't yet locate any regret.

On my way to Alice's school, the guilt did not haunt me in the way I expected it might. The bliss, the rapture, and the sense of other-worldliness took over all of my senses. It felt as though a smile had passed all the way through my body, warming me with its healing powers.

But it didn't last. When I returned home, unable to concentrate on Alice's happy babblings about her day, the feelings of pleasure turned to jitters.

And then I did what I had vowed I would never do again.

From the bottom right-hand corner of my wardrobe, I took out the box that contained a few of Robert's possessions. Most of his other things I had given away to the charity shop. If they held sentimental value, I had either put them in this box or given them to his family.

The box smelled of Robert, and I immediately felt heady and tearful. He came back to me in a rush of feeling. I sifted through some of my favourites, inhaling the smell of his flat cap, which he had always worn on set. After he had died, I had asked John if he wanted it, but he said he could never have brought himself to wear it. So, here it was, with the vague scent of his hair still embedded in its threads.

But I was not opening this box to be reminded of Robert; I was opening it to find a document. Buried under his Ingmar Bergman DVD collection, I pulled out a manila envelope that was stuffed with Robert's school certificates and medical documents. I pulled out one letter, still in its white windowed envelope, and laid it on my knees. I did not need to read it again. I had read it over and over before, re-assessing its authenticity until the reality had sunk in.

It was time for John to see it. I knew that I wouldn't even begin to consider a future with John until I had settled the past. Until he knew my secret. Until he knew why Robert had jumped. If he forgave me for that, then we might stand a chance.

CHAPTER THIRTY-SIX

Two years ago

Robert had left for Sanjeev's to get his cigarettes.

'He'll be gone for hours.' Francesca sighed.

'He's such a selfish prick sometimes,' John said.

Francesca wanted to divert his anger, wanted to return to their original conversation, nervous of hearing further criticism of Robert from John.

'I read your film script, too, you know,' she confessed.

'Really?' John's body language changed. He sat back, alert, putting both hands on the arms of his chair, perhaps clinging on for support, or ready to stand. 'You never told me.'

'It was brilliant. I couldn't stop crying at the end,' she admitted.

The script had been a dark, episodic, ensemble piece set in a small village, revolving around a woman whose young son walks in on her having sex with her lover. Previously sceptical that John had the skill to write from a female point of view, Francesca had been amazed by how he had climbed inside the woman's head, and, seemingly, into hers, too, even though it was not Francesca's story. After she had finished it, she regretted reading it. It had stayed with her, and she had not been able to look at John in the same way.

'You really cried?'

'I fell in love with all of them, and I couldn't bear what happened to Freya. I wanted you to rewrite the ending just for me so that I could stop feeling so sad.'

John's anger melted away from his face. He opened his mouth to speak, and then closed it again, studied some spilt grains of sugar on the table.

'Sorry, I shouldn't have said that,' she said, blushing, and she stood up from the table so suddenly that she caught her foot on the chair leg. She stumbled, the chair crashing, cold coffee spilling from Robert's cup.

The coffee seeped under her bare toes.

John leapt up and straightened the chair and she rubbed at the floor vigorously with an old, paint-spattered rag that had been drying on the radiator, scared to stop, scared to look up at him again.

'Thank you for liking it,' he said, bowing forward, taking her face in his hands, kissing her. She stood up and slipped in between his arms. The world stopped spinning. The inevitability of it. The wrongness. The rightness.

Ignoring the dangers of Robert's return, or excited by the risk, John had lifted Fran onto the countertop and pushed up her summer dress. She had clasped him with her bare thighs. The pleasure was irrepressible, and she had cried out as she felt him inside her. Just once, before muffling her excitement in John's shoulder, biting at his muscle, biting away the desire to let herself go completely.

Then, she had heard something, or someone, on the landing outside.

'Shhh,' she said, pulling away from him abruptly.

In a daze, she had gone to the door. The neighbour's cat had scampered down the stairs. But she heard panting coming from further down the stairwell: a man panting, or was it an older woman's wheeze? And then the front door to the street had banged shut.

When she returned to the kitchen, John had been gathering his coat and bag, to leave.

'Did you see anyone?' he whispered hoarsely.

'It was the cat.'

'Jesus. Thank god.'

Francesca didn't want to mention the slam of the front door to the street. She was too scared to run down to see who it had been. If it had been Robert, she wanted to let him go.

CHAPTER THIRTY-SEVEN

John

'Daddy? Ask me my spellings,' Olivia said. She was sitting curled up on the sofa next to John, her school books scattered around her and a clipboard on her lap, pen poised. Beatrice was at his feet, kneeling at the coffee table, painstakingly writing out a poem she was going to recite for a competition. Harry was at a friend's house. They were a self-sufficient unit, the four of them; Dilys was not the central component of the children's day. John was. How much difference would it make to them if he and Dilys split up? Being a single dad would not change his day-to-day life. Effectively, he was already a single dad.

Halfway through one of Beatrice's poem readings, a text from Dilys pinged through:

Bad day today. Be home early. ETA 5.30. D x

'Daddy! Stop going on your phone!' Beatrice cried.

'Sorry.' John pushed his phone away and braced himself for the disturbance to their peaceful afternoon, anticipating Dilys' bad mood. In spite of her bad day, he had the urge to tell her about Francesca right away. The secret was too big to keep inside. He couldn't lie to her any more.

That afternoon, he felt he had toppled over a cliff into Francesca's arms and plunged into the waters he had always been too frightened of swimming in.

When the children were in bed, he would tell Dilys what had happened. He did not feel scared. She could flail and scratch all she liked; she was not going to control him any longer. Ironically, it was his wife's ruthlessness that helped him to conquer much of his guilt about Francesca. Her authoritative, regulated, hard-hearted attitude to her life, to their marriage, and to him, had been counter-intuitive; pushing him into Francesca's arms, where he could be messy and destructive and reckless. A bit like Robert might have felt that night.

A call from his mother flashed up on his phone. He switched it to silent. They had not spoken since their argument.

A few minutes later, a text from her came through: *Call me please. Mum x*

Why couldn't his mother call once, leave a voicemail, and wait for a response, like normal people? Most people might be alarmed by this text. Not John. This text could mean that Valentina had burnt her toast or Mrs Ambleside's cat had died.

'Okay, Olivia. Ready for your test? Here goes – disappear… competition… correspondence… aggravate… monorail,' he read, and paused. 'Monorail?'

'Come on. I've done that one.'

'Is "monorail" one of life's essential words?'

Olivia giggled. 'It's an extremely fast train, Daddy.'

'Fair enough.' John grinned, continuing the list, enjoying his daughter's conscientiousness. She didn't question the status quo, and fair enough, it was probably simpler not to.

Dilys would be home any minute. A familiar creeping fear tingled down his back, and he had a sense of Robert's omnipresence. Even in death, he lingered in John's conscience.

He thought back to Robert's aggressive sulks, his slammed doors, his loud music. If John had not complied with Robert's wishes, there was no more fun, no more play, no more love. Perversely, John would feel guilty and responsible for the shift in atmosphere, and he would try everything to make Robert happy again. But Robert's moods could shake the foundations of the whole household. From day one, he had been a charismatic and powerful character, just like their mother.

But John was going to break the spell.

On the way home from Francesca's, with the music cranked up and the windows down, he had vowed to himself he would stand up to Dilys and overcome the hold Robert had on them.

'Look, Daddy,' Beatrice said, showing him her poem, around the edge of which she had drawn emojis and a strange half-breed of animal he couldn't recognise.

'Wow, darling, your handwriting is so neat. Well done, Bea,' he said, kissing her head.

Everything he did that afternoon, he reassessed through the prism of his desire to leave Dilys, to be with Francesca. Even when he made the children their spaghetti pesto, with no parmesan for Beatrice, who thought it smelt of sick, he imagined what it would be like to be doing the same thing with Francesca at his side, with Alice scampering around.

By the time John heard Dilys' car crunch into the driveway, at six o'clock, the girls were putting their bowls in the dishwasher.

'What can we have now?' Olivia asked.

'Fruit,' he said.

'Isn't there any yoghurt?'

'I'm afraid not.'

Because of Francesca, he had failed to go to the supermarket.

Dilys would go straight to the fridge, but she was not going to find anything more than some potatoes, a leek and some cheddar cheese.

'Helloooooo-ooo!' Dilys cried from the hallway, her high-heels click-clacking along the corridor towards them.

'Mummy?' Beatrice's little face lit up. 'Is that Mummy?' she cried, as though it couldn't possibly be real. She charged through the door, careering into her mother.

Dilys hugged Beatrice. 'Hello, love.'

'Mummy! You're home two hours and forty-five minutes early,' Olivia said, looking at her watch and jumping down to hug Dilys.

'Yes, I am,' Dilys said, kissing Olivia on the head.

'Hi,' John said stiffly. He noticed her eyes looked a little blood-shot, and her usually perfect lipstick was smudged at the corner.

Dilys clapped her hands. 'Okay, girls, Mummy's had the worst day ever, so I need cheering up. Go get your jammies on, we're having movie night. I've bought popcorn!'

The girls yelped and ran off excitedly.

'It's a school night, Dilys.'

'So what?'

'They get tired and I'm the one who has to deal with the fallout the next day.'

Dilys went over to the fridge. 'Lighten up, John,' she said. 'What's for supper?'

John thought fast. 'Baked potatoes and cheese and leek special.'

She slammed the fridge. 'I hate leeks.'

He waited for her onslaught.

She turned around and her face crumpled.

'I hate leeks,' she said, bursting into tears.

'Dilys! What's wrong?'

'Why don't you know I hate leeks?'

'What? I'm sorry. I do know!' He laughed. 'I won't ever suggest leeks again.'

'Don't laugh at me,' she said, but then she nuzzled her head into his neck and continued to cry. She smelt of Chanel perfume and coffee.

'What happened today?'

'I had a row with Sebastian and he told me I was aggressive and that I needed to learn how to keep my cool if I wanted to keep my job.'

John sighed. 'Oh.'

'I know, I know,' she said, pulling away and throwing her hands in the air. 'You think I'm aggressive, too. I know. I'm a horrible person. You don't have to rub it in.'

'I'm not going to rub it in.'

She dropped onto the kitchen stool and put her head in her hands.

'I'm a nightmare. I know I am. I don't know why you put up with me, I really don't.'

John was hearing what he had heard before, many times over, but it never failed to soften her in his eyes.

'Because you'd shout at me if I didn't?' he teased.

It would usually make her laugh. 'Don't say that!'

'It was just a joke.' He shoved his hands in his pockets.

'Sorry, sorry,' she said, beginning to cry again. 'I think I need help.'

John held his breath for a second. He had never heard her say that before. 'What kind of help?'

'When I was on the train, I searched online for some therapists.'

'Wow. That's great.' He couldn't believe what he was hearing.

'You've been telling me to go for so long, but I've been too scared. There's so much I think I need to sort through.'

John imagined her kind, gentle parents sitting in front of the television in the Welsh village Dilys grew up in, and he wondered if there was more to it – in the way that there was more to his own family – than met the eye.

'I think it's a really good idea.'

He felt utterly conflicted. On the one hand, Dilys was telling him what he had wanted to hear ever since she had pushed him into the mantelpiece. But now, he felt resentful about her sudden change. If she began to turn things around, and really make the effort to manage her anger, where did that leave him with Francesca?

'I'm so sorry, John. I'm so sorry for hurting you,' she said. She stood up and moved towards him. She looked like Olivia when she was scared. Her fingers reached out towards his eye, and he flinched. She withdrew. 'I understand why you don't trust me,' she said, sitting down again. 'I don't blame you, honestly.'

He imagined she was still in shock about Sebastian's admonishment. It was ever so slightly galling that she had ignored so many of his own pleas and complaints over the years, but when suited-and-booted Sebastian told her she had anger issues, she listened.

'I've wanted you to do this for a very long time,' John said.

She sat up slightly, and smoothed her hand down her ponytail. 'Don't worry. I'm going to find the best therapist in the country to help me.'

The sound of little feet broke their conversation and the two girls came charging back into the room.

Dilys snapped a brave smile onto her face and put a paper bag of popcorn into the microwave.

'Can we watch *Cinderella*?' Dilys asked her daughters, as though she were their sister.

'You always cry when we watch it, Mummy.'

'Happy tears!' Dilys said, tickling Olivia in the ribs. 'I'm off to get my jammies on. Get the film ready. Daddy, bring the popcorn through.'

With the lights off and the volume turned right up, they found their places on the sofa. Dilys had cleaned off her work make-up and had changed into her sweatpants, and had snuggled each child into the crook of each arm. They had a blanket pulled right up to their chins.

'This is what it's all about,' Dilys said, peering over their heads to wink at John. The girls' faces were a picture of contentedness. They were in heaven with their mummy, watching a film.

John sat awkwardly next to Beatrice, the large bowl of popcorn in his lap. His mind was screeching with conflict and guilt.

He felt a heavy feeling on his chest, as if the children were physically sitting on him. He tried to concentrate on the film, in case the girls asked him questions. At first, watching it was an effort. Slowly, he engaged with Cinderella and her plight for her Prince Kit, who wanted to be brave and kind like Cinderella. Courage and kindness. John had neither, and he would offer neither if he left Dilys when she was at the point of getting help. If he ran into Francesca's arms again, he would be weak in the face of the more challenging struggle to keep his children happy. If he destroyed their lives, he would have failed as a parent. It would be cruel. Weak and cruel. He would not be those things to them.

Fantasies of having full custody, with Francesca at his side, had been madness. Dilys would never let that happen. If he left her he would become a weekend father, like a few of his divorced friends. How could he have thought, even for a minute, that he could ever break up this unit? They loved their mummy. The three children took their parents' togetherness for granted, they took their secure home life for granted. It was the way it should be. How could he jeopardise that for his own selfish reasons?

On the surface, the rest of the evening continued as normal. How easily it had been to carry on their routines together, brushing their teeth, putting their dirty clothes into their shared laundry basket, conversing about the children or the film, reading in bed now, as though nothing earth-shattering had occurred in John's life.

Inside his head, everything had changed.

Earlier, he had not been able to fathom keeping the secret inside, and now he couldn't contemplate airing it to a soul. Francesca and Dilys were like two misfit pieces of the same puzzle that he could not slot together.

Dilys' phone rang from her bedside table.

'Hello, Camilla… How are…? Oh, dear… yes… Oh, no… Do you want to speak to him?'

John shook his head frantically, miming cutting his throat.

'Right… yes, I'll tell him… okay… yes… I'm sorry to hear that… Bye.' She pressed 'End call' on her phone and sighed.

'What's "Oh dear"?'

'Your Uncle Ralph's gone loopy. She wants you to go over there tomorrow morning.'

John groaned. 'What's he done this time?'

'Ransacked his house looking for some money he stashed, apparently.'

'He doesn't have any bloody money.'

'He's stopped taking his pills.'

'Hasn't the nurse been round?'

'Don't ask me. Why didn't your mum call you about it directly?'

'We had a fight.'

'When?'

'The day they arrived back from Italy.'

'What did you fight about?'

'She found out about Fran and Paul. Somehow, it's my fault.'

His mother had not apologised for her vicious outburst. She did not do apologies. She was self-righteous and haughty and entrenched in her matriarchal superiority.

An image of Francesca's beautiful pale skin seared into his mind. He pushed it out.

'It wasn't a secret, was it? What's wrong with them dating, anyway?' Dilys snorted.

'Paul's not an accountant or a lawyer. He wouldn't fit into their parties at Byworth End.'

'But didn't she introduce them?'

'Mum wouldn't have thought for a minute that Francesca would want to date a "handyman".' John sighed, and he got out of bed, unable to talk to Dilys about Francesca and Paul. 'I'd better call Mum back.'

Here he was again, at the mercy of the bullies in his life. This was his destiny. To suffer in silence, while they walked all over him.

*

'He is refusing to take his pills until he's found his money.'

John could see exhaustion and worry running through the lines around his mother's eyes. Behind those blue eyes, she had hidden the secret of Robert's addiction, but it had spoiled her face. A blaze of anger erupted inside him. Right there and then, he should confront her, he really should. But he didn't have the courage. Old habits die hard.

'Do you think the money is really here?' he said, instead.

'Who knows, but he wants us to search every corner of the house with him, and then he promises he will take his pills.'

Uncle Ralph shuffled hurriedly towards them from the back of the house, greeting John with a hearty, manly handshake.

'How's it going, Uncle Ralph?'

'Great, great! Realised I needed to get this place ship-shape if I'm going to find that money,' he explained, stumbling over his words. 'In here, first,' he said, taking them into the sitting room.

Every spare inch was scattered with elegant, worn detritus and expensive ornaments, in leather or cut glass or bronze.

'I see why you needed the help.'

'You'd think a burglar'd been, wouldn't you?' Camilla whispered in John's ear, and arched an eyebrow at him.

Uncle Ralph bent his head into a blanket box and began pulling out stacks of photograph albums and emptying bulging envelopes. 'I'm pretty sure it was in here, Camilla. I'm certain of it. Certain of it, in fact.'

Photographs and newspaper cuttings were fluttering to the floor. Camilla began picking them up and placing them back into the envelope.

'How much are we looking for, exactly?' John asked, in all innocence. Maybe the crazy old man did have some cash somewhere, John thought. But his mother glared at him.

'Cash! £3,000, my boy!' his uncle cried, and then his eyelids stretched back from his eyeballs. 'And I've counted every single note, you understand me? So, if any goes missing,' he said in a nasty tone, wagging his finger at John, 'I'll know who took it.'

There was an air of violence about him. John thought about Robert's 'sticky fingers'.

Camilla said, 'Darling, Ralph, you start in the dining room, and John and I will start here.'

John realised it was going to be a long day. He had the time. His editor would take a few weeks to get back to him with the changes on the script. In this downtime, the distraction of Uncle Ralph's house would be welcome.

'Let's delve in.'

John and his mother knelt down next to each other at the mouth of the blanket box and peered in.

The hope of finding £3,000 for Uncle Ralph was exciting, and the quest was in stark contrast to the hopelessness of his own situation. The methodical work was strangely satisfying. They had a bin bag for rubbish, and a ruthless attitude to anything that wasn't valuable, either historically or in monetary terms. His own dilemma turned in his brain like two rusty cogs: noisily, and going nowhere fast. He thought of Fran, and how much he loved her. He thought of the children and how much they needed Dilys, and their security.

They stopped at some of the old baby photographs of his father and Uncle Ralph in perambulators, and in bonnets and velvet collared coats, or in short trousers, and Red Indian costumes, or under a cloister's arches in their Eton uniforms.

'Look at your father! He looks so uptight,' Camilla cried affectionately, lingering on this photograph.

The search for money was paused as they continued to flick through the photographs of John's father as a young man. Various peers and relations, and old girlfriends, prompted Camilla's insightful stories of Patrick before he was John's father. The antics, the accolades, the ambition.

'Who's that?' John handed her a photograph of Patrick, in his early twenties he judged, with his arm around another man, who was as handsome and brooding as James Dean.

Camilla remained glued to this photograph. 'That was Eddie.'

John studied his mother's face, which had changed. He could detect sadness and anger in her slight frown and downturned mouth.

'Who was Eddie?'

'You knew him well. He used to live around here when you were small.'

'I don't remember an Eddie at all.'

'Really? You don't remember Edward Dillhurst? And his wife Hettie?'

Now John remembered. Edward was the man who had visited too often. He and Robert had had a crush on Edward's blonde, sex-bomb wife, Hettie.

'Oh, Hettie and Edward, yes, of course.'

Immediately, John was alert.

His laces were undone but he ran through the bluebells to the hollow tree. It was the perfect hiding place for the game of Sardines.

'Mum?' John called, hearing his mother's laughter.

His mother and a tall man were shadows in the dark of the dead tree.

'John!' Camilla breathed, bending down to scoop him up in her arms. 'Ssshh. Come and join us.' She turned towards the man, her son in her arms. 'You know Edward, don't you?'

Edward shook his hand and whispered, 'Welcome to our little secret, John.'

John looked at this tall, blond man and then at his mother and, for a split second, he wondered if this shadowy man had been the same shadow he had seen in the poolhouse that night. They might have been playing Sardines then, too, he thought.

It didn't quite fit, but he had badly wanted to believe it.

Twigs cracked in the woods near to their hiding place and John coughed loudly to give their location away. He did not want to be alone with his mother and Edward any longer.

His mother hissed in his ear: 'Be quiet, for Christ's sake.'

But the guest, a little girl called Anoushka, joined them.

His mother was irritable with John for the rest of the day and he felt guilty for being a spoilsport.

His mother shoved the photograph back into the back of the album, where John had found it loose, and then she shut away all the albums. This chest, this house, seemed to be a haven of secrets, going back generations, and he had an urge to be hidden here too, with their family secrets forever shrouded.

'They moved to Somerset.' She sniffed.

'You're not friends any more?'

His mother turned to him. 'Hettie was a nasty piece of work.'

She closed the lid of the chest and stared out into the garden. Her eyes were filling with tears. It seemed she had been in love with this Eddie. In spite of everything, he felt sorry for her.

'Yesterday is gone,' she murmured, blowing a kiss at a lone magpie that hopped across the garden.

Her red lipstick left the perfect shape of her lips on her fingertips. He thought about her lipstick on Edward Dillhurst's lips in the dark of that tree. John would be a hypocrite to judge his mother. He saw the echo of her secrecy reverberating through his own life. His mother had perhaps felt the same about Edward as he did about Francesca. For whatever reason it had ended, and nobody had found out. He imagined the alternative, being that eight-year-old boy again, and finding out that his mother was leaving his father for Edward, leaving Byworth End. It would have destroyed him. Then again, if his parents had split up, Robert's secret visits to the poolhouse would have stopped.

John's skin bristled at the thought of his brother's unnatural desire to see their mother fool around with this family friend. To return regularly was a compulsion; to harbour it must have felt heavy, distracting, as though hiding a disease that was smouldering in the pit of his stomach. The urge must have filled his confused ten-year-old head with a ghastly shame, while he suffered alone with the terrible secret.

Their mother had unwittingly handed Robert unsavoury memories – of shame and secrecy – on a silver platter, ensuring he would spend his whole life trying to find extreme ways of spitting them out, getting them out of his head, getting out of his head.

John yearned for his brother now, longed to wrap his arms around him, to bring him back to life with the magic force of his love and understanding and acceptance.

If only they had talked about it, if only they had been brave enough to confront it together. If only they had stood up to their mother. If they had, he wondered whether Robert would have been able to kick his addiction, and whether he might still be alive today.

'Do you think we'll ever find the money?' he asked, moving them both away from the pain and sadness of the past.

She snapped out of her reverie. 'Darling, we're not really looking for that bloody money. It doesn't exist.'

'What are we doing here then?'

'We're using the money as a ruse,' she whispered. 'As a way to clear the house so we can put it on the market.'

'Does Uncle Ralph know?'

'Of course he doesn't bloody know, and don't you dare mention it.'

'You can't just sell it under his feet.'

'Your dad's the estate executor, darling. The money will go on his care, and then the rest will go in trust to your three, and to Alice, when he dies. I thought I'd ask Dilys if she'd sell it privately for us.'

'That's really sad,' he said, looking up at the beautiful vaulted ceiling. But John couldn't argue with the fact that Uncle Ralph needed the help. As usual, his parents had got it all worked out.

'He'll be better off in one of those nice, posh care homes.'

'This place will be a dream for someone who wants a project.'

'Well, your dad thinks we'll get top dollar for it if we spruce it up a bit ourselves. I was hoping you'd help.'

'I've certainly got the time.' It wasn't a yes but it wasn't a no.

'That's wonderful!' she cried, adding, 'I'd thought we'd enlist Fran's help, too. I'll talk to Archie Parr. Ask him if we can steal her for a couple of weeks.'

'Why Fran?' John shot back.

'With the painting?' she said irritably. 'I need her help to choose modern colours. She's a wonder with that sort of thing.'

'Chromatically pitch perfect,' he murmured.

'What?'

'Nothing. I'll say goodbye to Uncle Ralph.'

Ralph was at the dining-room table working on an enormous puzzle. John kissed his uncle's head. 'See you tomorrow.'

Uncle Ralph looked up at him. His blink was slow. He scratched the side of his nose, where there was a small raw patch. 'See you then, John.'

There was no 'old boy' or hearty handshakes now. He was subdued and vacant.

'Will he be okay?' he asked his mother, hesitating at the door.

'He'll be at that puzzle for hours,' she said, pushing back a stack of books teetering on the edge of the hall console, nudging the other clutter. Something heavy crashed to the floor. 'Oh, good gracious, look at this!' she whispered, picking up a paperweight with gold swirls inside. 'Robert, look!' she snorted, looking up to the heavens – apparently addressing her dead son – and then back to John. 'Your uncle found this blasted thing bulging out of Robert's shorts pocket once, and he went berserk! Never forgave him. Called him Mr Sticky Fingers from then on.'

'What? So that's why…' he stopped. 'Did Robert ever come over to make it right – as an adult, I mean?'

'He wouldn't have visited Uncle Ralph for all the tea in China.'

'He never told me.'

'He made me swear not to. He was ashamed of what he'd done. With good reason.'

'Wow,' John said, thinking out loud, bowled over by this new information.

It seemed that he and Francesca had misconstrued Uncle Ralph's outburst at Alice. His uncle had been referring to the theft of a paperweight, rather than his medication. It suggested that his mother might not have been lying, that Robert might not have been to Uncle Ralph's house in his adult years, with his "sticky fingers".

'Why, "wow"?' his mother asked, eyeing him as they walked down the steps to their cars.

'Only because Robert never told me,' he said, getting into his car.

His mother blew him a kiss. 'Robert hated keeping it from you.'

'I wish he hadn't,' John said to himself, slamming the car door, hard.

CHAPTER THIRTY-EIGHT

Francesca

'Do you think you can colour-match it?' Archie Parr asked me, handing me an emerald-green porcelain dish.

Life in Archie Parr's shop was so different to being on a film set. Some might think it would be prosaic compared to the glamour of the film industry, where I had met film stars and worked as a scenic artist for big, box office hits. It was the opposite. The slow pace, the quietness of the back room, the unassuming wisdom of Archie Parr, the ebb and flow of customers, and the routine suited me so well, I wondered how I had coped in the stressful, back-stabbing world of films.

The solitude of mixing paints in Archie's back room, and the satisfaction of knowing that the contents of those black and white tins could transform someone's home, someone's world, seemed deeply in tune with who I was as a person. I had found my rhythm creatively, and my independence.

Now that Alice was back at school, now that I had convinced myself that John was retreating back into the safety of his family once again, I resolved to get on with my own life. The Tennants could stay in the background for a while. I felt weightless with the release of one particular burden: if John was retreating, it was best to keep the document safely tucked away in the brown envelope, for now.

'I can try.' I knew I could match it. The pigments for the exact tone of green were swirling around my head. 'What room is it for?'

'Mrs Pendlebury's library. She's a lawyer with four children and she likes to re-do her house every two years.'

'I'm on it. Cuppa?'

'Love one. Here's the list of other stock colours ordered.'

I began my alchemy, mixing the pigments and stainers, dripping minute amounts of colour from the syringe into the paint tub, stirring and perfecting; pouring from one tin to another, inadvertently adding more splodges and splashes to the dried splatters on the wooden platform and my trusty old overalls. While Archie Parr sat at his desk, or responded to the doorbell, chunks of time were lost.

At ten past two, with twenty minutes to go before I would go home and get ready to fetch Alice, Archie received a phone call.

'Hello, Mrs Tennant.'

I let go of the mixing stick in the vat of paint. *Which Mrs Tennant?* I thought. Dilys or Camilla?

'We're rubbing along very nicely, thank you… Ah, yes, how's he doing? I heard there was a spot of bother in the village last week… Hmm… Yes… Very good… We would be more than happy to help you out…' Then, he said, 'Oh…', and the tone of his voice had changed.

The stick was slowly sinking down into the liquid, drowning in a swamp.

I tried to pick it out. Straining to make out the words, waiting for Archie to come off the phone so that he could tell me whether it was Dilys or Camilla, or some other Mrs Tennant of no relation.

'Right… We do have a group of exceptional painters and decorators you can use… I understand… Yes… Obviously, with all due respect, Mrs Tennant, that will be a decision she will have to make for herself… All right… Yes, I'll talk to her now… Do send my best wishes to Mr Tennant. Good bye.'

'Who was that?' I asked.

'Your mother-in-law.' He chuckled. 'She's been a regular customer of mine for years.'

He was moving his smartphone back and forth from one gnarled old hand to the other. I waited for him to elaborate. He placed his phone on his desk.

'She would like to steal you from the shop for a couple of weeks.'

'Are you serious?'

'I assume you know that Ralph Tennant's house needs renovating because they're selling it—?'

'No, I didn't know,' I replied, gathering myself, trying to hide my indignation about not knowing.

'He's going to a care home, apparently.'

'I knew his health was deteriorating.'

Archie nodded. 'Yes. And Mrs Tennant would like you, personally, to choose the colour scheme and repaint his house.'

'Why didn't she call me directly?' I asked, holding up my smile to cover the rage that was ping-ponging around inside me.

'She's going to call you about it later.'

'She knew I'd say no,' I grumbled, instantly regretting how petulant and unprofessional I must have sounded.

'She'd pay you the going rate, obviously.'

'Can I ask why she didn't want one of your painter and decorators to do it?'

'Because of the sensitive nature of Ralph's health.'

'She's worried people will talk?'

The wrinkles around Archie's kind brown eyes deepened as he formed an embarrassed smile. 'I'm not sure he likes strangers.'

He doesn't like family much either, I thought.

'But what about you and the shop?'

'Ralph Tennant's house will need a lot of paint. And, judging by these accounts, we need a bit of a boost.'

Too consumed by my own fury, I had not thought of it from Archie's point of view.

'I understand. Of course. I'm sorry, I didn't think of that.'

Archie patted my back, as though he understood. 'Thank you, Francesca.'

He shuffled off into the front of the shop.

This job had been something that I had found for myself, to retain some modicum of autonomy. In fact, I had enjoyed the fact that Camilla had sneered at my decision to work here. And it was galling that she was now muscling in on it: calling Archie before she called me, manipulating me out of the job for a few weeks or more. What Camilla wanted, she got. I was the conduit for her needs; the puppet to do as she wished, for the sake of her bloodline.

As I drove to school to fetch Alice, I felt the claustrophobia of the small village, and the Tennants' eyes on me. When chatting to a few of the mothers I had met in the playground, I wondered if everything I said would somehow worm its way through the grapevine back to Byworth End.

By the time Camilla did eventually call, later that evening, I had realised I had no choice about the job on Ralph's house. I was powerless, and I hated her for it. Knowing I was beaten, I managed to sound sufficiently enthusiastic about the project.

'It sounds like a great opportunity, thank you,' I said. Had I actually thanked her?

'It's a pleasure, darling. I'm glad you're on board. It's going to be a proper family affair.'

'Oh, yes?'

'John's going to clear the rooms for you, and Dilys is going to market it for us.'

I stiffened, pressing the phone so close to my ear I could feel it burn.

'I can clear the rooms by myself.'

Camilla laughed. 'Ha! You've seen the house, Francesca.'

'But I thought John was busy finishing up his series?'

'He has already delivered it. Anyway, you'll need the help with Uncle Ralph.' Her laugh was unnervingly high-pitched.

But Uncle Ralph's temper was the least of my worries. The thought of seeing John in this context overwhelmed me. We were going to be spending hours and hours, and possibly days and days, rattling around in that house together.

'I've arranged a conflab with John and Dilys at Ralph's on Saturday morning. Can you make it?' Camilla added.

'Yes, sure,' I murmured.

Following Camilla's edict, we were coming together as a family to renovate the house that had held Robert's darkest secrets and fed his addiction. It seemed to me that we were colluding in a plot to paint over the cracks of their misdemeanours, complicit in Camilla's cover-up on behalf of the family name. Ralph was to be packed off to a nursing home, possibly officially labelled a crazy man, whose medication would be carefully managed by professionals from behind glass windows. And Robert's thieving, and his addiction, would be laid to rest for ever.

Perhaps we were all going to get away with it.

The black and white image of the document that lay flat in the corner of my wardrobe burned into my eyelids when I blinked.

Perhaps I hoped we would.

CHAPTER THIRTY-NINE

John

John stood between Francesca and Dilys, with Camilla to her right, staring up at Ralph's house. To his left, John noticed the slight tremor in Francesca's fingers. She was wearing more make-up than usual. War paint, as his mother would say.

'It's such a beautiful house,' Francesca said, gazing upwards at its faded splendour.

The four of them stared for a moment at their project.

He had to fight the entrancing draw of Francesca. He wanted to touch her, to know what she was thinking; he wanted to know whether she had been replaying their day together, as he had, over and over in his mind. All week he had resisted calling her, knowing that if he had spoken to her he would not have been able to resist going over to see her again. He wondered if he might be able to snatch a moment to talk to her alone today, to explain; to mention the paperweight.

John refocused on the house, on the broken guttering, the peeling paint on the windows, the pulled ivy and dying red roses.

Camilla said, 'Your father has carted Uncle Ralph off for a jaunt, so we've got the house to ourselves.'

John was more than a little relieved. He had spent three fraught days this week with Ralph, as he sorted through the chaos. More than once Ralph had torn open the black bin bags that John had filled, and put half of their contents back on a shelf or in a cupboard.

The respite from his fussing came in his down periods, which were too heartbreakingly sad to enjoy. It was harrowing to witness his lack of energy and the bleakness in his eyes. John would want to cry for him.

'It needs a lot of work,' Dilys said, whistling at the magnitude of the project.

Her mother-in-law sniffed. 'That's why we're here, Dilys.'

On the way in, Dilys sidled close to John, and actually held his hand. His palms sweated in her grip. He noted Francesca's eyes glimpsing their joined hands, and felt disloyal to her in holding his wife's hand. Surely Francesca knew that it was she who he held in his heart? He remembered tracing his fingers down her naked skin and he slipped his hand out from Dilys' grasp. The contact, the possession felt wrong; her touch interfered with his imaginary journey across Francesca's body, where he had experienced such bliss.

It pained him so deeply to think that he could never allow himself to touch her like that again.

After a brief tour of the downstairs, Francesca, whom John had noticed was in a brooding, snippy mood, said, 'Camilla, unless you want me to spend the next year painting this place, I'm going to need some help.'

'I understand it might seem a little daunting,' Camilla said.

Francesca folded her arms over her baggy jumper and looked up at the cornicing of the sitting room. 'This room, alone, will take me no less than a week.'

'I'll take you upstairs,' Camilla said, ignoring Francesca's protest.

'I'll see you up there, guys,' Dilys said, brandishing her measuring gun. 'I'm going to measure up.'

Upstairs, the huge spare rooms, the vast landing and corridor, the three bathrooms, and finally Ralph's master bedroom with en suite, did nothing to assuage Francesca's bad mood.

'I'm afraid there is no way I can do this on my own. For a start, every room has wallpaper to strip. The prep stage will take weeks,' Francesca said, standing opposite Camilla at the end of Ralph's ridiculously grand four-poster bed.

'John, darling, you can help Fran with the prep, can't you?'

John shrugged a 'yes, feasibly' kind of shrug, while inside he was thinking of how desperately he did not want to help with the preparation. His reluctance had nothing to do with the tedium of the job. And everything to do with the temptation of Francesca. At least if he was decluttering, he would be working in a different room from her.

'No offence, John, but I need someone who knows what they're doing,' Francesca returned.

Ouch, John thought.

His mother perched herself on the end of Ralph's bed and brushed a hand over the green brocade bedspread. 'He's always been fastidious about making his bed,' she said, forlornly.

Francesca's face softened. 'What if I found someone I really like and trust? If John and I are around most of the time, Ralph might be okay with it.'

'You've seen how bad he can be,' Camilla said.

'It's worth a try, isn't it, Mum?'

His mother sighed. 'I suppose so.'

Francesca added, 'And to speed things along, John could help us with the prepping, I suppose.'

'So generous of you,' John joked.

Francesca's pretty face twitched with a smile. She tilted her head up to the ceiling and then spun around slowly, taking in the room. She exhaled. 'I have to admit this house has a magical quality to it.'

John was mesmerised by her. A ray of sun came out from behind a cloud, straight through the window, to rest on her, as though she were the only person in the world it wanted to warm. Reflections of quivering leaves danced across her cheeks, and shots of light set her hair ablaze with subtle colours. Her beautiful soul lit up the fusty old space. Then John noticed his mother's eyes on him. He looked away, knowing he had been caught out.

But Francesca's spin had stopped before she made a full circle.

Ralph had bustled into the room, wearing a pair of bright orange ear-defenders, head down, humming to himself. Without a glance in their direction, he crossed the room to his chest of drawers.

'Everything all right, Uncle Ralph?' John asked.

'He won't be able to hear with those things on,' Camilla said.

The three of them stared at Uncle Ralph as he dumped a heap of empty aluminium blister packets in the wastepaper basket at his feet, and then opened some new boxes of Seroquel. He began popping pills from the blister packets into a brown plastic pill bottle.

Camilla approached him. 'Do you need some help, darling?'

'THE SOUND OF THESE BLASTED THINGS IS DEAF-ENING!' Uncle Ralph bellowed.

'What is he doing?' John asked.

'Bipolar sufferers can be sensitive to noise,' his mother explained stiffly, popping out the pills from another packet. 'He says the blister packets sound like the crackle of gunfire and he doesn't like to hear it every day. He says it puts him off taking them. I order him generic pots from Amazon to put them in.'

John turned to Francesca, who was gaping at Uncle Ralph's fiddly, obsessive ritual.

'It's so sad, isn't it,' he said to her, under his breath.

She shook her head. Her skin had become alarmingly pale, almost translucent.

'That's why they were so easy to steal,' she said, with a strange, distant smile forming. She then shot a question across the room: 'You put some aside for Robert, didn't you, Camilla?'

John's heart stopped.

His mother swivelled around. The two women held steely eye contact. His mother replied haughtily, without an ounce of contrition, 'I have no idea what you're talking about.'

Dreamily, a little strangely, Francesca laughed at her.

A show of disrespect of this sort would usually elicit a matri-archal sniff and a fierce comeback from his mother but, instead, she returned them seamlessly to their original discussion, using her actress-on-stage voice to overshadow Francesca's implications. 'I'd have to vet whomever it is you choose to help in the house. And then, obviously, we'd have to sit them down with Ralph.'

Francesca began absently twisting at her earring as she stared at Camilla long after she had stopped talking. 'Fine.'

John felt his breathing return to normal.

'If you drop round tomorrow with some paint samples, we can get started.'

'Whatever you say, Camilla,' Francesca said facetiously. She might as well have curtsied.

Camilla shot out her chin and strode out of the room.

Francesca did not move, but she was swaying slightly. 'I can't handle it here, John. I thought I could. But it's too much.'

John grabbed her arm, to steady her or to steady himself, he wasn't sure.

'Conspiring, are we?' Dilys was standing in the doorway, armed with her measuring gun.

Francesca nipped past John, and then Dilys, saying, 'Bye, Dilys.' Her footsteps were quick down the stairs.

The front door slammed.

'Your mum's in a stinker, too. What's going on?'

'The usual,' John replied, feeling the unusualness of it too keenly.

'John, this place is easily worth two mill, and if we do it up, we could get £2.5 million for it, no problem. The work's more superficial than I first thought.' Her needy, vulnerable side had evaporated. 'Move, will you?'

She was gleeful as she pointed her gun at the back wall, disinterested in the emotional drama. The potential value of the house had taken her off the scent. For once, John was grateful for his wife's ruthlessness.

Less gratefully, he thought of his mother's ruthlessness and her deft fingers as she popped the pills into those pots with Uncle Ralph. Had she really been capable of stealing the anti-psychotics for Robert? He clutched at the alternative possibilities, unwilling to believe his mother could go that far.

His mother was stonewalling – most expertly. He would have to speak to Valentina again. This time, he would not walk away until she had given him some truthful answers, however uncomfortable she found his questioning.

*

'Oh, no, no, no, no,' Valentina sobbed, pressing her apron to her face. 'I dread this questions all your lifes, my John. I dread them. No, no, no, no, no.'

Valentina had been reluctant to sit down on the sofa that she had plumped for his parents twice a day, every day, for forty years. Her stout, stockinged legs dangled awkwardly, ending well above the tasselled skirt of the upholstery, and her raisin eyes darted around the drawing room. She looked out of place.

'Valentina, don't cry. Please don't cry,' John said, feeling tears spiking his own eyelids. From her reaction, he gathered she was holding on to some bad memories.

'But I can never say no to you, John, and Robbie, and your little beautiful chicky-dees. You so handsome now, John. You always so handsome and quiet.' She began crying again. 'I can never say no to you,' she repeated.

'You always said "no" to us, Valentina.' John laughed, trying to lighten the atmosphere.

'Since Robbie died, I live with this terrible feelings, in here,' she said, bashing her fist at her bosom.

A chill ran down his spine.

'What do you know, Valentina? It's really important you tell me.'

'I can't, I can't,' she cried.

'For Robert's sake,' John said, quietly. 'If Mum's done something bad, you must tell me.'

'No. She not.'

'Robert's spirit won't rest until the truth is out.' It was a cheap shot. Valentina believed in spirits and the undead.

Her hand shot to the gold cross at her neck, and she kissed it. She sat up straight, proudly and defiantly, and her tears disappeared, as though sucked back into her head. 'You swear you not tell Mrs Tennant. If I not have this job, I no eat. You understand?' She bunched her fingertips at her small mouth, in an eating motion.

'I promise that I will not tell Mum.'

'I tell you because I love Robbie and I love you. And the Lord, he see me.'

'Yes, Valentina,' John said. He felt sweaty with anticipation and anxiety.

'Your mumma, she did very bad thing. And I tell her she bad when she do it. But she is so desperate, she not know what to do, and Ralph's pills are in her bag and she give them to Robbie, and oh my God!' She threw her hands up to the ceiling. 'Lord forgive me, I not stop her.'

'But why? Why did she give them to him?'

Valentina began to shake her head. 'It was a terrible night, a terrible night.'

'The night Robert died?'

'No, no. When Robbie – bless his soul – was a young man. *Dezenove anos?*'

John mentally dredged up what little he knew of Portuguese. 'Nineteen?'

'Si. So young. So, so young.'

John was confused. 'What happened when he was nineteen? He was at university then, yes?'

'Terrible night,' she repeated, then stopped.

John wanted to shake it out of her, but he remained composed. 'Tell me what happened.'

'Robbie was back for a weekend. He very tired.' Valentina pressed her fingers into the pouches under her eyes. 'He look like—'

'—death warmed up.' John finished the well-worn saying for her. His mother had endlessly accused Robert of looking like "death warmed up".

'Yes, yes! And Robbie say he's going to bed. But he not go to bed. He go to the bathroom and he get in the bath…' Valentina was overwhelmed with emotion again, and she began to cry silently into her apron. John did not dare to speak to urge her on. The mantel clock tick-tocked loudly. The smiling faces in the silver frames on the baby grand and the figures in the oil paintings seemed to have turned to Valentina to hear what she had to say next.

She whispered the words hoarsely: 'He in a dry bath, with no, no water, and he taken the scissors to him, like this.'

She cut a vertical line down her throat with her finger.

John's tongue was thick in his mouth. The shock shot around his head; a bullet that had nowhere to penetrate. Before he could absorb its full impact, he needed more information.

'He cut his throat like this?' John's hand instinctively drew a line horizontally across his throat to correct her.

'No, no, like this,' she insisted, again moving her finger down from her chin to her sternum.

'A cry for help?' John asked. Robert would have known that the vertical cut would not have killed him.

'Your mumma say he did it this way, to not die. I bandage his cut, but he is in very bad, bad way. He crying and he argue with your mumma and say wicked, wicked things, and he run down to find a knife and he shout and scream at her, and I was so, so scared. And your mumma, she so terrified, too. Oh, my. It was so, so terrible.'

'So, she gave him Ralph's pills to calm him down?'

She nodded. 'She cut the pill a little bit with the knife. Tiny, tiny. She give him. And I slept in his room next to him. Poor Robbie.'

'Where was Dad in all this?'

'Berlin. Like always, back then.' Valentina tutted.

'Did Mum take Robert to Dr Baqri the next day?'

'I tell her! Again and again. He all slurred and too sleepy. I say she need to take him to hospital. But she say 'No!' She so angry. I am scared of her, John.'

'Mum is formidable when she's angry.'

She clicked her tongue. 'She is, she is.'

The next question was hard to form, but he had to ask. 'What were the wicked things he was saying to Mum, Valentina? Was he accusing her something?'

Her lips pursed. 'I hear nothing.'

'It was about the poolhouse, wasn't it?'

'I hear nothing,' she repeated, refusing to look him in the eye. John decided he could not push her too far. What she had heard that night was obviously too shameful for her to repeat.

'Did you know that Robert carried on taking those pills, for years, right up until he died?'

Valentina nodded slowly. 'I see Mrs Tennant take them from your uncle's house when I clean there sometimes – he scare the other cleaners, you know – and I catch her filling those little bottles for Robbie. Many times. Many, many times. You know'

– she screwed up her face – 'like those horrible men on the street corner with the drugs.'

He found it hard to believe that Valentina had ever seen a drug dealer on a street corner. She had arrived when she was twenty years old, straight from rural Portugal. John had been two years old, and Robert three. All her adult life she had been sheltered by the old beams and towering oaks of Byworth End, just as he and Robert had been. Then again, could life under his mother's aegis ever be considered sheltered?

'And she couldn't go to Dr Baqri because of what she was doing?'

Valentina patted the side of her nose conspiratorially. 'She scared. Very bad. Very, very bad. She not want Dr Baqri to know this bad business.'

'This illegal business.'

Valentina put her hand together, as though in prayer. 'Si. Si.'

'Did Dad really not know about any of this?'

Valentina shrugged again. 'He busy man.'

'Too busy to miss that his eldest son had tried to commit suicide?'

Valentina straightened her apron, and plucked at a duster that was in the front pocket. 'I say to Mrs Tennant that those pills make him sicker.'

'It seems to me that it was Mum who made him sick, Valentina.'

Valentina's brow wrinkled as though in pain. 'You not blame her. She do her best. She love Robert.'

'Yes, I know,' John replied, but he did not agree. His mother's best had not been good enough. A nasty swirl of anger scooped up the acid in his stomach and pushed it up his gullet.

Leaving Valentina alone after everything she had just revealed felt wrong. She needed a priest, or a therapist, to help her cope with the aftermath of her confession – or perhaps she needed a social worker to help her deal with his mother.

When she hugged him goodbye, he smelt her usual olive oil and aniseed, and he felt as vulnerable as a small boy again. She reached up to squeeze his cheeks, just as she had done when he was a child. But he could tell that she was severely shaken. Her olive skin had turned a sickly grey.

'You take care, too, Valentina, okay?'

'Your mumma look after me well, you know that,' Valentina said, forever loyal.

His mother did not deserve Valentina's loyalty. She did not deserve any of their loyalties.

As he drove home, past the village green, he envisaged Francesca at home. He should call her, he should tell her, but he could not. Every muscle in his body was drawn tightly into his bones, holding him in one piece. His teeth ached, ground together by his locked jaw. If he let his mouth open to speak or loosened his body to express it, he feared the anger, built over decades, would blast out violently, knocking down anyone in its path. Whomever he spoke to next would get a barrage of abuse that they would not warrant.

He could not believe that his mother was capable of supplying drugs to Robert. He could not believe that his mother had hidden Robert's attempted suicide. When Robert had taken scissors to slit his throat, John had been on his gap year: gallivanting through rainforests with a backpack, stretched out on wild beaches, partying under full moons. If he had known, he would have come home.

Shaken up, John's vision of the road suddenly went fuzzy and he pulled over into a lay-by. Yelling at the top of his lungs, 'FUCK YOU MUM! FUCK YOU!', he hit his steering wheel again and again until he beeped his horn by mistake. Two wood pigeons in the trees above his car scattered into the sky. John imagined the whiter of the two as a dove flying off to find Robert.

Tears came rolling down his cheeks. He felt guilty for his outburst. He refused to process Valentina's stories about his mother. The catastrophic information floated on the top of his mind. It wouldn't sink in. She had misinterpreted it, or it was lost in translation, somehow. He couldn't bear it. It wasn't true.

CHAPTER FORTY

Francesca

The hue of dusky pink on the walls, the white dustsheets over the lumps of furniture and the fresh paint smells ordered and settled my mind. The roller's motion up and down, up and down, was a methodical strain that my mind allowed my body to do automatically, like driving a car. My little radio played quietly in the background. By tomorrow, I would be finished in this room.

John was clearing the next spare bedroom on my agenda. It was a bigger room, across the corridor. I could hear him moving about on the creaky floorboards. The odd cough, or thud, or rustling were the background sounds of my day. But I would rarely see him.

He had casually informed me about the paperweight incident, which he thought exonerated Robert; adding to that, he told me that he did not believe his mother was lying about the Seroquel either, and that she was certainly not capable of stealing from Uncle Ralph, whom she loved and cared for. This rosy outlook did not explain why his mood remained charged. He was pent up. He was not communicating. He had brought an invisible wall up around him. Simple questions would take him an age to answer. When I asked him if he was all right, he would snap at me: 'Of course, why do you ask? I'm fine.'

I had no right to demand anything from him, but he was obviously being plagued by some sort of all-consuming internal dialogue. It was infuriating to know that he was wrestling with the problem on his own, as though the round and round thoughts would somehow produce a new answer. I could see he felt alone with it. Possibly arrogantly, I knew I could help if he would only let me in. I had given up asking him if he wanted to talk, and we did not share lunch breaks or tea breaks. We communicated about the work on the house, but nothing else. Uncle Ralph would sometimes insist we both take a trip with him into the garden to collect conkers, or help him to sweep the leaves, but they were snatched moments. When Camilla visited to check on things, John would put up an excellent front. Smiling and laughing and joking. As soon as she left, a switch would be flicked, and he would retreat back to his silent world.

My phone rang, rudely interrupting my thoughts. The caller was a set painter I used to work with. She was keen to help out, happy for the work. Hesitantly, I ventured across the corridor to tell John the news, but I remained at the doorway, timid in the face of his thunderous mood. I would deliver the news and retreat.

'Who?' he asked irritably, looking up from his kneeling position, smacking his hands down his jeans, leaving smears of brown. He was surrounded by cardboard boxes and black bin-liners.

'Cassie. She was a set painter I worked with years back, and I trust her implicitly.'

'Why isn't she a set painter any more?'

'She had kids and moved to Southampton with her husband, but they've recently divorced and she needs the money.'

'And you think Uncle Ralph will like her?'

'She's very pretty.' I grinned, referencing a conversation we'd shared about Ralph's penchant for a pretty face.

A glimmer of a smile began at John's eyes, but it died before it made it to his lips.

'Make sure you get Mum to meet her.'

Irritation flickered inside me.

'Oh, yes, of course, we couldn't possibly do anything without Ma'am giving us the order,' I rejoined sarcastically.

And with that, he shot up from his kneeling position and slammed the door, leaving me out in the corridor with the oak panels inches from my nose.

I banged on the door once with my fist. 'What the hell is your problem?' I yelled.

The old door handle rattled and John flew out. 'You're my problem!' he shouted.

I took a step back. 'Shh,' I whispered, frowning furiously, pressing my forefinger to my lips. Having spent days desperate for him to come out of his funk, I was now wanting to shut him down again. 'Ralph will hear.'

He walked away, back into the bedroom, hitting the door out of his way, but he didn't close it behind him.

I followed him in and closed the door.

'John, talk to me, please,' I pleaded. 'What's going on?'

'Nothing is going on,' he said, but it was a weak redress.

I looked around at the huge room, cluttered with beautiful antiques and precious ornaments. The bed had elaborately carved wooden posts that shot up to the high ceiling.

'You're not telling me everything, are you?' I knew I was being a hypocrite. The letter came into my thoughts. There was so much I wasn't telling him.

He was standing by the window, staring out. I clambered over the mess to him, and sat on the window seat, by his side.

'I had a chat with Valentina the other day,' he confessed.

I touched the tips of his fingers with mine, and looked up at him. 'What did she say?'

His fingers withdrew from mine, and he put them in his pocket, but, finally, he spoke, as he stared out.

'She told me Mum had given Robert Seroquel.'

I let out a long, deep sigh. I was sorry to have been right. The energy drained out of me. I sat back further on the window seat, and leant back into the shutter panel on one side. He did the same, at the opposite side of the window. We were facing each other, our knees pulled up to our chests.

'Do you know why she did it?'

He looked away, and rubbed his hands through his hair. 'I'm still finding it hard to believe that she did.'

'You think Valentina would make it up?'

'What am I supposed to think?' he asked searchingly, as though I could possibly answer that question for him.

'They were caught up in something they didn't know how to stop.'

'I need to talk to Mum.'

'Don't get Valentina in trouble.'

'We wouldn't have to bring Valentina into it. You can say that Robert told you,' John said.

'Me? I can't be there.'

'I need you there, Francesca.'

My heart constricted. I wanted to throw up. 'I'm not sure, John.'

'If Dad's there, it'll be easier.'

'I'm scared of her.'

'Don't be.'

'Have you told Dilys about any of this?'

He rubbed his face. 'No.'

'How is it between you two?'

'The same,' he said. 'Torture,' he added.

I grimaced, and smiled. 'Sorry.'

His gaze was penetrating. My heart began to pound.

'It's not your fault.'

I shuffled closer until our toes were touching. Our chins were on our knees, our faces close. A mischievous grin twitched on his lips. 'Robert and I used to hide behind the curtains at Byworth End when Mum and Dad had parties,' he said, pulling the curtains closed, a puff of dust lingering in the air.

It should have conjured a happy snapshot of boyhood, but the insidious images of Camilla's damaging parenting were dominant, pushed to the forefront, usurping the good. I stared out at the elm tree that glowed gold in the low autumn sun. There were sparkles of light darting from the damp leaves, like fragments of hope. But I knew that nothing could be real until I had told John everything.

Before that thought had time to germinate, there were footsteps in the room and a rustle of bin bags. The curtains of our private world were flung open.

'What are you two kids up to, eh?' Ralph grinned, his face beaming red with glee.

I jumped up to standing. 'We were just talking.'

'Ha! None of my business! I had a feeling there was something going on between you two. I'm not totally out of it, you know.'

'Best not mention this to Mum or anyone, Uncle Ralph,' John squirmed.

'What do you take me for, John, my boy?' He slapped John on the back and winked at him. 'I was young once, too, way back when, and I wasn't averse to a bit of slap and tickle, myself, you know.'

I cringed. 'It wasn't anything like that,' I protested – like I had the right to plead innocence or take offence at anything any more. 'Look, I'd better go and pick up Alice from school.'

'I must say,' Ralph continued, as we guiltily followed him out, 'I wouldn't have expected it of you, John. Your brother, definitely, but not you.' He chuckled. 'Wonders will never cease.'

My head snapped in John's direction. What did Ralph mean? John shook his head, squeezed my hand and whispered in my ear, 'He doesn't know what he's talking about.'

Ralph had seemed lucid and together enough to me. But infidelity was the one thing I had never believed Robert capable of.

I had to shake off the thought. There was no way I could process that, not on top of everything else.

Ralph was whistling a jolly tune as we followed him down the stairs.

'I think we've made his day,' John said, under his breath.

'This is not a joke,' I snapped. Hurriedly, I collected my bag from the kitchen. I couldn't wait to get out of there.

John followed me onto the doorstep, but I did not stay to talk to him. I waved behind me and whizzed off in my car, feeling humiliated and sullied and rigid with fear. If Uncle Ralph let this slip to Camilla, it would be utterly disastrous. I wasn't ready. I might never be ready.

Inch by inch, the box that held the letter was being prised open once again.

CHAPTER FORTY-ONE

Two years ago

His chair still had his indent in it. She sat into it, into the groove of his body, his living flesh. This was where he had read his scripts. This was where he had talked through the night to colleagues in Los Angeles. This was where he had written his wedding speech.

Her black tights had a snag in them, from when she had knelt down on the tapestry cushion in the church. To pray, like a good girl. Like a good widow.

A widow's quiet tears were expected at a funeral. A widow's demure smile was acceptable during the eulogy.

For two weeks, Francesca had been surrounded by hordes of friends, almost breaking her door down with support. Her sister had returned from her never-ending travels, her parents had come back from Portugal. She had not been alone for a minute. Every day had been filled with damp cheeks and shoulders, with conversations about Robert, heartbreaking stories about his role in each of their lives, and jokes about his foibles. There were home-cooked frozen meals on her doorstep, and a steady flow of flowers with beautiful clichés pinned to the stems. She appreciated the endless texts, the 'I'm here for you, if you need me' messages, even though she knew they weren't really.

She was alone now.

The weight of his coffin seemed to come crashing down on her head, killing her poise, knocking the calm out of her.

She ripped open the drawers to his desk and began throwing his documents and scripts at the wall, one after the other. Expletives, vile and thoughtless, flew out of her. Her fingers bled from paper cuts and smeared his work. Work he had loved more than her. Fantasy worlds so much more fun than real life.

Slowly her arms weakened, and she flopped back into his chair, her feet kicking at the scripts on the floor, twitching after her outburst.

As she stared down at the mess of paper, she noticed a white windowed envelope that lay amongst the scripts.

It was addressed to 'Robert Tennant' and the seal had been opened. The stamp on the outside was from 'Whittington Hospital'. She pulled out the letter inside and read the single page of official type.

CHAPTER FORTY-TWO

John

Francesca was already there. She was sitting at one end of the large oak kitchen table, with his father and mother either side of her. Her mug was cradled tightly to her chest, as though she was ready to throw its contents in his parents' faces at the first sign of trouble.

If his mother had picked up on Francesca's nervousness, she certainly wasn't showing it.

'John, darling, hi. Tea, coffee? I was just telling Fran what a fabulous job you're both doing on Uncle Ralph's house.'

'Very impressive,' his father agreed, smoothing his hair back.

John caught Francesca's eye and their expressions froze in a split second of shared panic. He wasn't sure he was going to be able to go through with his plan to confront his mother about the pills, worrying it would let loose the more private, shameful family horrors: the poolhouse; Robert's sneaking; the dry, bloody bath he took. He was not sure any of them was strong enough for such an exposure.

'Have you seen the house, Patrick?' Francesca asked.

'I took my surveyor around last night.'

'Was Uncle Ralph okay?' John asked.

'He was more interested in that damn puzzle than he was in us.'

John was always amazed by his father's lack of interest in his own brother. He never went to see him or spoke fondly of him, or even talked of his illness. He had left all of that to Camilla. And now he was secretly selling his house behind his back. It didn't seem right. John had a flash of irritation towards both his parents. He wondered if Valentina had been wrong about his father's ignorance. Had his parents colluded?

Before broaching the subject of the pills, he prevaricated, letting by another half-hour of animated chit-chat about colour schemes, and about Cassie the painter. But he realised that if he left it any longer, Francesca was going to bolt.

Gradually, he led the conversation around to Uncle Ralph again, and to his illness.

'Mum, actually, we wanted to talk to you about what happened the other day at Uncle Ralph's.'

The 'we' was loaded. His mother wiped an imaginary something from under one heavily made-up eye, and flicked a blonde strand of hair behind her ear.

'Yes?' she said, her ice-blue eyes trained on him.

John had to look away, and he glanced over at Francesca, who looked down to her mug and took a sip from what must have been stone-cold dregs of tea.

'Look, we both know that Robert took Seroquel.'

'You must be mistaken,' she replied coolly, before shooting a dirty look at Francesca.

'Ralph's medication?' Patrick asked.

John ignored his father. 'Mum, tell us what went on.'

'He took sleeping pills, darling, that's all I know.' She smiled neatly.

'You're seriously going to keep up that crap about Zopiclone?'

'Everyone takes sleeping pills, darling,' she trilled, laughing and rolling her eyes at Patrick.

'Your brother had sleep problems,' his father stated firmly.

'It was more complicated than that, Dad.'

Francesca cleared her throat and sat up a little. 'I found a bottle labelled Zopiclone in his things when I was clearing out his room after he died, but the pills inside were Seroquel.'

'Why didn't you tell us about this sooner?' Patrick snapped, looking more concerned than he had before. Francesca's lie had been clever.

'I didn't know what they were until I saw the same ones in Ralph's house.'

'Did you give them to him, Camilla?' Francesca blurted.

'Now, listen to me, you two,' his mother hissed. 'Why would I give Robert Seroquel?'

There was a part of John that felt embarrassed for his mother. He wanted to stop her from digging the hole more deeply for herself. He wanted to back out of their plan to get the truth from her, but Francesca's mood had turned from fearful to defiant.

'Honestly, I don't know why, Camilla. You tell me.'

'I have nothing to tell *you*.' Camilla snorted.

His father spoke in a low rumble: 'How dare you make up such nonsense and scare your mother?'

'Mum,' John said, 'he has a right to know.'

His mother's eyes glazed over. 'I don't know who told you that, John, but it isn't true.'

'I know it's true because Robert told me himself,' John lied.

His father's jaw slackened. 'Camilla?'

But she did not respond. She sat there, bolt upright, holding her breath. Her cheeks reddened and she wiped the sheen away from her upper lip.

'Why are you lying to us?' Francesca asked, pleadingly.

'That's enough from you, young lady,' Patrick barked at her, pointing his finger.

John had never seen his father lose his temper like that.

Francesca flinched. She moved her chair back.

'Dad, don't get at Fran. Mum's the one you should be angry with.'

'I think I'm going to faint,' his mother said, flapping her hand in front of her face and increasing the pace of her breathing.

'Mum, please,' John begged.

His mother covered her face.

She began to cry into her hands, hanging her head, unable to look at them. A flow of sympathy rushed through him.

'He was addicted to it, wasn't he, Mum?' John asked, desperate for her to open up, desperate to share the pain with her, to hear her side of the story; to free them all from the chains of the unknown, for peace of mind.

'No,' his mother said, dropping her hands. Black stripes cut down her cheeks.

'You are telling a bare-faced lie!' Francesca cried.

His father slammed his fist on the table. 'Stop it! I won't hear it. I won't HEAR IT!'

'I'm sorry this is distressing for you to hear, Patrick,' Francesca interjected, 'but isn't it best to know the truth?'

John's father took his glasses off his face and rubbed his eyes.

'The truth, eh?' his father murmured. 'Francesca thinks we should know the truth? That's rich.'

His mother stopped hyperventilating.

'What do you mean by that?' Francesca asked quietly. John noticed that her hands were quivering.

'You mean, you can't guess?' Patrick said.

Francesca laid her palms flat on the table, poised to push herself to standing.

'I think I had better go.'

'What? No! Fran, why? What's Dad talking about?' John asked, flustered.

Refusing to look at John, Francesca stood up.

John's father continued. 'Right, yes, you can throw accusations around willy-nilly at my wife and Robert, and yet when the finger is pointing at you, my dear, you want to scarper? Is that right?'

Francesca began walking towards the kitchen door. 'I don't need to listen to this,' she said, sounding very frightened.

'Fran?' John called after her, standing up.

'Come back here, young lady! We're not done!' Patrick bellowed. Francesca stopped dead in her tracks, but she did not turn around. She bent her head low into her hands, and her shoulders began to shake.

'Sit down, son. There's something you should know.'

John sat down obediently, agog at his father's outburst, and he looked to his mother for a clue. Her frown suggested she was as ignorant as he.

His father spoke in a low, rumbling voice: 'A couple of weeks before Robert died, he came to me. He was very distressed. He'd been to the doctor about a urinary issue of some sort, and the hospital had run some general tests. The tests had turned out to be negative, except one. They had discovered that Robert had a congenital bilateral absence of the vas deferens.'

'Stop talking Latin, Patrick, and explain what the hell that means.'

Francesca swung around to face them. Tears were falling down her cheeks. 'John,' she began, leaving his name hanging in the air.

Patrick finished, 'It means that Robert was born infertile.'

John's whole body began to judder. His teeth chattered as he tried to talk, 'But how is that possible? What about Alice?'

Francesca opened her mouth to explain, but Patrick flew in with his own answer. 'Two weeks before he took his own life, he had found out that Alice could not possibly be his. Isn't that a coincidence?'

'Alice isn't Robert's?' Camilla whispered hoarsely, as though testing out the words might help them to make sense.

Francesca turned on Patrick. 'If you knew all this time, why didn't you say anything to anyone?'

'Robert made me swear I wouldn't. He said he loved you – for his sins – and, with no mention of the biological father, he guessed you wanted to stay with him. He described it as a blessing because he couldn't have his own. But I guess he couldn't find a way to live with it in the end.'

Francesca let out a strangled cry and clutched her throat.

Camilla was shaking her head. 'I'm sorry, I'm finding this hard to take in. Are you saying that Alice isn't our real grandchild?'

'Yes, darling, I'm afraid I am. I'm so sorry. I'm so sorry,' Patrick said, his eyes reddening with tears. 'I warned Robert that the real father could appear at any point, but he said he would deal with it when and if it ever arose.'

John was listening, but the words seemed to be floating up to him from a distant stage. Why wasn't Francesca denying any of it?

Francesca spoke up. 'Alice *is* your real grandchild. Can't you see it in her features?'

'I don't understand,' Camilla said.

Patrick blew out a frustrated burst of air. 'I saw the letter from the Whittington, with my own eyes, Francesca. There is no point in lying to us now.'

John feared his heart would beat its way out of his chest. 'Fran. Why are they saying these things?'

Francesca's whole face contorted into a grimace of pain. 'Alice is yours, John,' she said, and she turned from them and ran out of the house.

There was a long pause in the room.

It was unfathomable. Alice could not be his. He had stopped in time, that night, that one time. When Francesca had declared her pregnancy three months afterwards, a little part of him had wished that the baby was his, but he had known that it was a coincidence, that she had taken the morning-after pill, and his brother was sleeping with Francesca, too, of course. They had been trying for a baby. There was no way Alice was his, no way.

Suddenly, his mother shot up from her chair. 'You slept with that lying, cheating little bitch?' she hissed.

John blocked out his mother's vitriol and tore from the kitchen, catching up with Francesca outside on the driveway. He grabbed her arm before she opened her car door.

'You told me you'd taken the morning-after pill!' he shouted.

'I did!'

John dropped her arm.

'So how?'

'We were the unlucky five per cent.'

'But if Robert had zero sperm count, you must have known—'

'I didn't know! He kept it from me! I swear to God, I didn't know he was infertile until after he was dead – I swear it, John. I truly believed that Alice was Robert's, you have to believe me. They even look alike. But when I was clearing out his things, I found the letter from the doctor stuffed behind a stack of old scripts in the back of a drawer.'

The revelation was blazing in his mind, a fire that licked and flared, intoxicating his thoughts, choking his airways with black smoke. 'Two years. *Two years* you've known.'

Francesca was crying. 'Robert didn't know Alice was yours, John. Robert never knew about us. I swear it.'

John staggered back, and then Francesca's face fell. She was looking over his shoulder.

'Get out of here! Leave my son alone, you whore!' Camilla screeched, charging at Francesca. 'You murdered Robert with your lies! *MURDERER!*'

Francesca shrank back, fumbling with her keys to get into her car. Once inside, she pressed the locks down and scrabbled into gear.

John stood staring at her disappearing car. When he turned to his mother, he saw his father leading her back inside. Her sobs could be heard echoing through the trees.

Collapsing onto the doorstep, incapable of facing his mother's disgust, he was lost.

The thought of Alice's innocent little face brought tears to his eyes. He could not believe that she was his daughter. He really could not believe it. He wanted to go to her school now, to see her and to hold her in front of him, to inspect her features, to see echoes of his own in hers.

He felt the chill of the stone underneath him and a cold ache edged up his spine. Robert may have been dead, but John could feel him there with him, forcefully, as though he were alive again. But his spirit was malevolent and vengeful. Not only had John taken his brother's wife, he had now taken his daughter. Robert's dead fingers were around his throat, and he felt panicky, beginning to choke and cough.

When he heard his mother call for him, 'John? Are you still here?' in a tearful, concerned voice, he lunged from the step and stumbled to his car.

CHAPTER FORTY-THREE

Francesca

I was too stunned to cry. I clutched the steering wheel, but my reaction to the sharp bends was slow, as though I had forgotten how to turn, as though the deviation from straight ahead, into a tree, into a sign, into a ditch, was written into my code. The lanes seemed to swerve and contort around me as my car wove through an obstacle course, while inside my head, thoughts of my own treachery span.

I *was* a whore. I *was* a murderer. It was no surprise that Camilla had reacted that way. If it had been my son, I would have felt the same.

His mother had finally discovered why her son was dead. She had found me out. I had wanted to believe she was lying. I had forced John to believe it, too. I had corrupted him. I was corrupted. I was a shell of my former self. I had become as messed up as the Tennants were. Worse than them, in fact.

I had betrayed Robert, knowing how dangerous it would be, knowing what it could do to him if he found out. My love for John had been insidious, creeping under the skin of our marriage, and it had produced a child. A child that Robert could never have. Another man's child. A most heinous loss. A loss that he couldn't live with.

Drunk and high, he had smashed his body into a ragged, bloody mess, leaving the rest of us to pick up the pieces of his sorrow. He had left the fight, leaving me trapped with the legacy of my own selfishness, stained from head to toe in his blood, however many times I might try to scrub it away.

On the final bend, before emerging onto Letworth's green, I tried to swerve around a fallen branch, but I must have hit something else. The steering wheel jerked and fought with me, turning the car the wrong way. The wheels were out of control. I lurched into a hedge. Twigs cracked, the metal crunched and brakes screeched. My head flew forward and back into the headrest aggressively. In the silence that followed I sat there, the hedge pressing up against the windscreen, my heart racing, wondering what had just happened.

Aside from a slight jarring in my neck, I was unhurt, but when I tried to back out of the hedge, the car made a loud whirring sound and then died. I climbed out to see the damage. The right-hand side of the bonnet was crunched and bent, and the underside of the engine seemed to be stuck on a log.

The small prang seemed relatively uninteresting, a non-event in comparison to the morning at Byworth End. I abandoned the car and walked home, wondering what would happen to me next, but too numb to be able to think beyond putting one foot in front of another. It was like sleepwalking through a thunderstorm, waiting for the next lightning bolt to strike.

Back at my cottage, I smelt the comfort of home, and I was engulfed with sadness. We would not be able to live here much longer. All of the upheaval that Alice had been through had been for nothing. I would have to uproot her again, take her away from her cousins – her siblings – with whom she had formed real bonds, and settle her in a new home, a new school, far, far away. It was what I should have done originally.

The Tennants' promises of love and support had swayed me. I had been in denial about the long-term effects of my own decep-tion. How could I have made a life here while keeping such a terrible secret from them? Why had I convinced myself this was possible?

I dragged my fatigued body up the stairs to have a bath. I sat on the edge and ran the tap, and remembered how excited I had been to own a bathroom with a view of trees. But I did not own it. The Tennants owned it. While I lived in this cottage, they owned me, and they owned Alice.

Before the bath was full, the doorbell rang. At first, I didn't know what to do. Could I hide? Had someone seen me come in? Did it matter? Then I realised it might be John, and I ran downstairs, rebuttoning my shirt.

My hands were shaking with anticipation, hopeful that he had come over to talk, to hear my side of the story.

When I saw Paul, I wanted to slam the door, as though my disappointment was his fault.

'Hi,' he said, launching in for a kiss. I turned my head and his lips hit my cheek.

'Sorry, bad time?'

'Kind of, I was just about to…' I trailed off. 'Can I call you later?'

'Sure, it's just I was driving through and saw your car. Want me to sort it out for you?'

'Oh, no! The car!'

'Forgotten that you'd driven it into Mrs Crowley's hedge, did you?'

'Oh, dear. Of all the hedges—!'

'Of all the hedges in all the world…'

A smile began at my lips, but the dark forces of my morning overrode it.

'That's kind, but I'm calling AA.'

'I'll have a look at it and pop back in a minute.'

'No, no, Paul, don't, please, you must be busy, it's…'

As I blustered on, he plucked my car keys from the wall hook and strode across the green towards my car. Then I remembered I had left the bath running and I charged upstairs to turn it off.

I slammed the loo seat down and sat down on it. The water was lapping at the edges of the porcelain. Water was gurgling down the overflow pipe. If I climbed in, the water would slop over the floor. If I didn't, it would go cold. The colder it got, the worse it would be to plunge my arm in to pull the plug. I hated pulling the plug in cold bath water.

When Paul was at the door again, I had done nothing but sit and stare at the water level for half an hour.

'I've parked it outside. You'll need to fix the front, but it's working, at least.'

Usually, I would have been grateful, but I did not have the energy. 'Thanks. I appreciate it,' I replied flatly.

'Are you okay?'

'Fine. Just a bit tired.'

'Want me to make you a cup of tea?'

I was about to say no, but then I remembered the bath upstairs. 'Come in.'

When I followed him into my own kitchen, I admired his broad, strong shoulders, which had carried children through smoke and flames. He was a good guy, a good, honest guy, who was too good for me. Might he be able to forgive me for being weaker than him?

I insisted I make the tea. 'It's the least I can do. When you hear what I have to tell you, you're going to wish you had never knocked on my door.'

His hairline receded further when he raised his brow at me. 'Oh?' He looked vulnerable. I hated what I was about to do to him.

The story became too long. The details seemed important. I imagined him thinking 'Cut to the chase', but he didn't hurry me along. He sat patiently, listening, waiting for the punch line. In the end, I simply stopped rambling and told him what I should have told him right at the start.

'I slept with John four years ago. Alice is his.'

He didn't react immediately. 'Right,' he said calmly. 'Have you been sleeping with him while we've been seeing each other?'

Tears sprung into my eyes. I squeezed them back. I wasn't the one who should be crying. I was the aggressor here. I was the one who had cheated him of the truth. 'Once, yes.' I hung my head. 'I'm so sorry, Paul.'

I heard the chair scrape back from the table. When I looked up, he was gone. The whole cottage rattled with the force of the front door slamming.

*

'Slow down, Fran. You've had a fight with Paul? Or John?'

The sobs would not abate long enough for me to talk to Lucy. My body and mind were being tumbled over and over by the rolling power of a huge wave of self-loathing. 'I can't. I can't. I can't breathe. I don't know what to do. I'm…' I gasped, unable to get the words out. When I tried to breathe in, the air seemed to catch at my throat. My lungs were crying out for more oxygen. 'I'm… I'm losing it.'

'Stop it now,' Lucy shouted. 'You have to calm the hell down.'

The shock of her anger jolted me out of my panic long enough for me to take a big breath of air.

'Good. Okay. Now, I'm going to come and get you. Stay at home. Don't answer the door or go out or call anyone. I'll be there in an hour and a half. About three-ish. Okay? Can you cope on your own until then?'

'Yes.' Breathe. 'Yes.' Breathe. 'Yes.'

After I had ended the call, I lay my head down on the sofa cushion, pulled the blanket over my chilled body and passed out into a deep sleep.

I heard the doorbell in my dreams, ringing, ringing. A vague sense of panic washed over me, knowing that Lucy had told me not to open the door while she was gone. As I came to, I checked the time. I bolted upright. It was ten past three already. I ran to open the door.

Lucy wrapped her arms around me and I began to cry again. 'Oh, lovely. Tell me what happened.'

'I'm not lovely. I'm far from lovely,' I replied, leading her into the sitting room, where I curled up on the sofa again. Lucy sat down, lifted my head and put it onto her lap, and began stroking my hair.

'Okay, then. Tell me why you're not lovely.'

After I had told her why, she simply said, 'Wow.'

And it made me laugh.

Then she added, 'I always suspected you fancied him.'

'It's more than that, Luce. I think I've always been in love with him.'

Lucy sighed. 'Not helped by Robert treating you badly.'

'Hmm.' I couldn't be bothered to deny it, but it was a reductive way of looking at it. At least Lucy wasn't storming out or telling me I was a whore or a murderer.

'He controlled everything you did. And if he didn't like it, he used emotional blackmail to get what he wanted. Just like his mother.'

'I wanted to believe that Camilla was to blame for everything. I so wanted to believe it.'

Lucy stopped stroking my hair. 'You have to stop thinking about that woman, and think about what you're going to do next.'

Questions shot through my mind at high speed: should I try to contact John? Should I wait for him to call? How was he going to tell Dilys? Would they tell their children about their new sister? How would I tell Alice? How would I tell my parents?

'God knows.'

The pain that I was going to unlock was immeasurable. When John and I had first slept together, we had not considered our loved ones, we had not considered anything but our greedy desire. How would I ever look any of them in the eye again? Would they, too, view me as a whore and a murderer?

'You'll have to tell Alice at some point.'

'At some point. Not until I've spoken to John.'

'Why don't you come and stay with us for a few days? Just while things settle down. The boys will love having Alice.'

I threw my arms around Lucy and squeezed her as tightly as I could without suffocating her. 'Thank you. That is the best idea ever.'

'Come on then, pack a bag. Let's fetch Alice and head off before the traffic gets bad.'

Ready to run upstairs, I stopped in the doorway. 'I should talk to John first.'

'You can call him from my place.'

'I feel like I've dropped this bombshell and now I'm abandoning him.'

'A few days away won't hurt. It'll give him time for it to sink in. And, believe me, you won't want to be anywhere near Dilys when she finds out.'

My stomach lurched. Not for myself, but for John. I knew what Dilys was capable of when John had done nothing to deserve it.

CHAPTER FORTY-FOUR

John

John clicked through one photograph of Alice after another. He had dozens on his computer from the summer. Zooming in on her face, her brown eyes stared back at him. Her eyes were Francesca's. Her hair was Francesca's. The shape of her face was squarer than his own, her hairline and jaw were more like Robert's and his mother's.

He couldn't find his features in hers. Maybe he needed to pull up a photograph of himself on screen to make the comparison. Somewhere in his archives, he had a scanned photograph of himself as a child. He double-clicked on that and lined it up next to one of Alice. Finally, the resemblance became clearer. For some reason, he had a truer perspective of his features when he saw himself as a boy.

His heart swelled when he noted that Alice had the same straight nose as his, and the same hard-to-catch smile, brief but genuine, and the same sense of intensity in her eyes. When he thought of her sensitive temperament, so susceptible to the strong-willed Beatrice, it dawned on him that she might have inherited that character trait from him. How many moments had he missed over the last two years, while Francesca had kept this from him? While he had blamed himself for their betrayal? While he had avoided Francesca as much as possible? The lost day-to-day moments, the lost baby years. How many special milestones had he missed, while he was concentrating on his other three children? The weight of his love had been skewed in their favour, obviously. Now that balance had shifted, scooting Alice onto the scales with the others, weighing his heart down with so much love he thought he would never be able to stand again. How strange it was to recalibrate his feelings for her, from uncle to father, from niece to daughter. He had always loved Alice, almost as much as his own children. He had assumed all uncles felt this strongly for their siblings' children. He'd had nothing to compare it with. Alice had been his first and only niece or nephew, and she had come along only four months after Beatrice.

He wasn't the only one who was going to have to adjust to Alice's new status as his daughter. Beatrice and Harry and Olivia had gained a sister. No, they had always had a sister. A sister they hadn't known about. Anger towards Francesca for holding this back from them for so long burned inside him.

He picked up his mobile and pressed her number, pulling at his hair as he waited for her to pick up. It rang out, cheating him of the opportunity to scream at her, '*How could you have done it to me? To the kids? To* him*? Did you ever plan to tell me? Was Alice going to go through her whole life not knowing who her real father was?*'

Her lie had undermined every single intimate moment they had ever shared. He thought he had known her, been able to read everything in her eyes, believed her to be the only person he could trust. Meanwhile, she was holding back the biggest secret that could ever be kept, swept along in her blame-game. How had he got her so wrong?

When he imagined confronting Dilys tonight, confessing to her, he anticipated her justified rage and accusations of betrayal, and was frightened of how her fury would fly.

He wanted to run.

*

The children were in bed. John had opened a bottle of red wine, not for the purpose of softening Dilys, but for his own fortification. Within the half-hour that he had been waiting for her, he had downed two glasses. He had not experienced the light relief of drunkenness with those first few glasses. Perhaps Francesca's news had sobered him for the rest of time.

The sound of Dilys' car arriving on the gravel sent the wine churning in his gut. He swallowed repeatedly as he pushed Dilys' glass around on the work surface, letting the sound of glass on marble grate on his teeth.

He put the wine and two glasses on a tray, and headed to the door, grabbing two rugs from the blanket box. The kitchen was not the right place to tell her. It was their family space, their safe place. What if the children woke up and overheard? He anticipated Dilys' distress, the loss of composure, her loss of control. It would be the beginning of the end of his marriage. And, he welcomed it. Regardless of Francesca, he should have left Dilys years ago. With Alice, came the truth. It would be liberating to unchain his secrets. As he looked into the future, he captured a glimpse of freedom. He had wanted it for so long. In this respect, he would have the upper hand for once. This self-possession and certainty gave him a perverse sense of satisfaction. He was not scared of losing Dilys.

He watched as she parked her Mini Cooper in the usual space between John's vintage Porsche and their Land Rover Discovery. Dilys had chosen the cars, except his Porsche. He loved the Porsche. No wonder it was the car for the mid-lifers; he felt young and free when he drove it.

'What the hell are you doing?' she shouted across the drive, seeing him light the lantern candle next to the oak bench. He and Dilys used to smoke joints on this bench together, before they gave up. Now, dinner-party guests smoked cigarettes on it and stubbed out their butts in the soil of the potted bay tree.

'I need to talk to you.'

She stopped in her tracks, and held her tote bag in front of her like a shield. 'Can't we go inside? It's freezing out here.'

'Bea's not asleep yet and I don't want to risk her overhearing.' John's voice sounded odd to his own ear, unusually low and serious. It reminded him of Robert.

'What's happened?'

'Here, wrap yourself in this.' He offered the blanket and then poured her some wine.

'You're so weird, John,' she mumbled.

She sat down and pulled the scratchy tartan rug over the shoulders of her camel coat. Her nose was pink at the tip and John noted, unemotionally, how beautiful she looked. In the candlelight, her features were softened and the blue of her eyes was less intense.

'For a long time, neither of us has been happy,' John began, expecting her to disagree. Instead, she took a slow sip of wine.

John began to talk around the subject, about Robert's illness and his mother's affairs, but he got the impression that Dilys was neither surprised nor interested in these details. Dilys didn't like details. Perhaps she sensed he was procrastinating, terrified of uttering the words out loud, nervous about her hysteria.

'For Christ's sake, John, just cut to the chase, will you? You're doing my head in.'

John stood up and looked up to the black sky, seeking out the star formations to give him courage. It seemed easier to tell the universe somehow. 'I did a terrible thing to you and to Robert.'

'You're going to tell me you fucked Francesca, aren't you?' Dilys sighed.

John spun round to face her. She was looking up at him with a smirk in one corner of her lips. 'Well? Is this the big news?' She might as well have yawned.

'You *knew*?'

'It doesn't take a bloody genius to work it out.' She knocked back half a glass of wine, leaving two smudged Joker-like curls at the edges of her lips. 'Can I go in now?'

'No. I'm not finished.'

'Look, John,' she said, standing up and shrugging off the rug, 'I decided a long time ago to accept that you and Francesca have this special little bond, and, to be frank, it makes me want to hurl, but I'm your wife, and she will always be your brother's wife, and one dirty little fuck won't change that.'

'But it changed everything.'

Dilys blinked, a tiny moment of uncertainty. 'What? You want to run off into the sunset together now, do you?'

'Today, I found out that Alice is mine.'

The nasty smile fell away, and she wiped the wine stains from her mouth neatly and accurately. It was as though she was looking in a mirror. 'What? No, no,' she murmured, smoothing her hands over her head to her ponytail, which she tightened. The hair pulled her eyes into narrow slits.

Earlier, John had wanted to claw back some power, but the flash of pain in her face was ghastly. He hated what he had done to her. 'I'm so sorry, Dilys.'

And he waited for her outburst, for her tears or her incandescence, but she remained cool. She pulled her car keys out of her tote bag.

'A drive will clear my head,' she stated simply.

'Is that a good idea?' John trotted after her, towards the cars.

'I would like a drive, darling,' she smiled, disconnected.

John's palms started sweating as he watched her climb into her Mini Cooper.

The headlights blinded him momentarily. The exhaust fired up. The engine began to rev. His eyesight cleared of the hot-white blobs and he stepped out of the way. She was backing up, rather than coming forward out of the space.

'Careful! You're backing into the…' he began loudly, as the rear lights glowed red onto the garage doors, inches away from hitting them. Before he could shout another warning, she accelerated forward and swerved into the left side of his Porsche. The crunching sound of the collision echoed through the countryside.

He ran towards his car, 'What the hell…?'

She straightened up the Mini Cooper, into its original parking place, which he guessed meant that she had finished with the Porsche. Was she going to go for the Land Rover next, or was she going to drive away?

She did neither. The wheels skidded on the gravel and the car propelled forward towards him. He turned, but before he could run, he felt an explosion of pain in his back. He collapsed and the noise of the car's engine cut out, and then his brain.

Sometime later, he came to.

Hands were gripping his ankles, and gravel scraped his shoulders as he as pulled along.

Dizzying, unmanageable pain ricocheted through him. He wondered whether he was still alive. He was adrift, untethered to his consciousness; overlapping images of Robert's face before he jumped swelled and shifted before his eyes. Could he be on the bridge with him again? But then he became aware of savage panting at his feet, and he could just make out the blur of Dilys' beautiful face, like an angel of death, above him.

*

A paramedic asked him to stay still, asked him how much it hurt from one to ten – he groaned a ten – asked him his weight, his age, cannulated him, and administered IV Morphine and Midazolam. He heard Dilys' voice in the background, replying for him. Blue lights illuminated the trees above him and the metal door of his Porsche was by his head. He closed his eyes and gasped for breath.

'Francesca,' he murmured, in his head perhaps. 'Francesca.'

One paramedic held his head straight while the other fixed a hard collar around his neck. They rolled him on his side, slipped a spinal board underneath him, and rolled him onto his back once again. He experienced a mind-bending shock of pain, radiating through his chest and his neck and into his head. Before they wheeled him into the ambulance, Dilys squeezed his hand and told him, tearfully, that she loved him and that she would follow on to the hospital as soon as she had dropped the children off with his parents.

The children! He was grateful that they could not see him now, in such a mess, yet he was so utterly relieved to still be alive for them. The acute disorientation had made him think of death, and how close it felt, and how much he desired the kind of oblivion that death would provide, some respite from the relentlessness of this mind-bending pain.

The paramedic sat by his head and talked to him. With every bend in the road and every pothole, John moaned and cried out, trying to answer the paramedic's questions, questions that he heard through the confusion that the agony brought. His body shivered uncontrollably, and the paramedic asked him to take deep breaths as he covered him in a foil blanket.

There was a strange acceptance of his fate as reality slid about on a new axis, his vision swimming and his mind bending. He hoped that the doctors in A&E knew what they were doing, that they were good doctors, that they were not too sleep-deprived or too overworked to save him.

He had not been able to glean whether his injuries were life-threatening, He thought of how easy it would be to slip away to join Robert on the other side.

CHAPTER FORTY-FIVE

Francesca

Alice and I were hidden away safely behind Lucy's blue door in her London town house. I was drinking coffee at a vast concrete table, with a view through the bi-fold doors of a patch of fake grass, a sunken trampoline and a high-rise block of flats. Alice was playing dens upstairs with Finn and Mischa. If Robert had stayed alive, we might well have aspired to this London life. As it was now, I wished to see real grass and a forest of trees, but I was unbelievably grateful to be there. We had stayed overnight, and Lucy and Graham had insisted we stay all weekend. My mobile lay face down near my fingertips, just in case – just in case John called to talk about Alice.

'You're going to have to try to forgive yourself, somehow, Fran,' Lucy said, taking a sip of coffee from her over-sized mug. 'You're not a bad person. Robert wasn't necessarily the better half of your relationship. Or the more honest.'

'His uncle, Ralph, said a weird thing the other day.'

'Why doesn't that surprise me?' She laughed.

'It was a lucid moment, and he implied that Robert had been the type to cheat.'

The pause from Lucy was enough to make me curious.

'You think he was, too?'

'I have no idea.

'Has Graham ever said anything?' I asked her, knowing that Graham had never liked Robert.

'No. Graham never told me anything. And he would have, believe me.'

'But you think Robert was the type?'

'You're not the type and look at you.'

'True.'

'If he had, would you feel better about having cheated on him?'

I was about to deny it, but couldn't. 'Kind of,' I admitted.

'Has John ever hinted he knew anything about Robert and other women?'

'No. Never.'

'Did they hate each other, John and Robert?'

'What? No!'

'It's pretty full-on shitty to sleep with your brother's wife.'

'It's hard to explain. I know it sounds unforgivable. In isolation.'

'You think?' Lucy said, sarcastically.

I didn't care what she thought of John. It was convenient to blame John rather than me, her best friend. She didn't understand what it was like to be in thrall to someone as powerful as Robert. John had looked up to Robert, but he had been bullied by him. I was John's rebellion, perhaps.

'There was rivalry. John told me that Robert went after the girls he knew John liked. And he mostly got them.'

'Charming.'

'Robert was Camilla and Patrick's favourite. He was a go-getter, much more like them. They're always putting John down. Little digs all the time.'

'So, he and Robert had issues.'

'Major issues,' I said. 'But they got on well. The three of us had such a laugh together. They confided in each other, too. John was always there for Robert when he was depressed.'

'There for Robert? Or there for you?'

I paused before I answered. It was hard to explain to anyone else how much Robert's moods had ruled us both. Not only had they controlled Robert, they had controlled us too. We had been hauled into his drama, and responded conscientiously to his neediness and manipulation, his highs and lows. His addiction had power because we loved Robert.

'Both of us,' I said, eventually. 'The three of us were like a dysfunctional unit. We were too intertwined.'

'And it all revolved around Robert.'

'We were his carers, in a way, without knowing it.'

'I feel bad,' Lucy said, moving the single sunflower in the centre of the table to the left by two inches.

'*You* feel bad? Why?'

'I should never have persuaded you to move to that bloody village.'

'You didn't exactly have all the facts.'

'Still. You kept telling me it wasn't a good idea.'

'And I went ahead anyway. I'm the idiot.'

'You're not an idiot.'

'I called the estate agents yesterday to ask if they'd put it on the market again as soon as possible.'

'Was that a bit hasty?'

'Probably. But I need to do something.'

'Maybe it's a good thing.'

'That I've estranged Alice from the only family she has?'

'That they know the truth now.'

I poured myself some more coffee, noticing it was already ten o'clock. Lucy and I had been talking since we had woken up at seven thirty.

'Where's Graham?'

'On a run.'

'Avoiding me?'

'Of course not.'

'You chose well, there,' I said.

'He's not bad.' It was that familiar smile. The smile that women who love their husbands can muster, even after eight years of marriage and two children. I don't think I had ever smiled like that about Robert.

I stared at my phone. 'He won't call, will he?'

'He'll want to be part of Alice's life, Fran.'

'But it will be begrudgingly. He'll hate me.'

'I don't know.'

'Which means yes.'

'And if he didn't hate you?'

A smile radiated from within, and I wasn't sure it had moved onto my face, but when I saw Lucy's despairing and worried frown, I knew without seeing my reflection that the smile had come through.

'You're hopeless,' Lucy said.

And then my mobile phone rang into the silence, and I jumped off the bench. 'Oh god! I can't talk to him.'

'Answer it, you idiot!' Lucy cried.

The ring continued, loud into the chasm of their kitchen.

Lucy picked up my phone to check the caller. 'It's Paul,' she said, shoving it across the table at me.

I refused to take it. 'I can't talk to Paul.'

The phone rang out. I slid back onto the bench, trying not to look at Lucy. It lay in the exact same position as it had been in before, but now I saw it differently: before it offered hope; now I realised it was only going to provide more heartache.

We heard Graham's trainers squeak down the white painted stairs.

When he came in, I tried to plaster a smile onto my face, but there was no hiding the morose atmosphere in the room.

'Looks like you both need one of my special brunches. Fried or scrambled?'

He squeezed my shoulders affectionately. I had grown to love Graham as much as I loved Lucy. When Lucy had first introduced me to him, she had asked me to guess his job. I had wanted to say ski-bum or mountain climber, judging by his torn down jacket, baseball cap and fleece; his tan was more Mont Blanc than St Tropez. I had said, 'Car salesman' to tease her. When she had told me he was a banker, I had thought she was winding me up. Now, he looked more like a banker: the spikes of strawberry-blond hair were short, and his face was gaunt. He was a banker who should never have been a banker.

I was about to ask for scrambled eggs when my phone rang again.

I showed Lucy the screen. 'It's Paul again.'

'Maybe it's about the cottage.'

'Maybe Camilla's burnt it down.'

'Go on, you'd better get it.'

My stomach flipped over as I picked it up. 'Hi. Paul. Is everything okay?'

'Where are you?' He sounded aggressive, and I braced myself for some abuse.

'I'm staying with a friend.'

I looked over to Lucy for a friendly face. She raised her eyebrows and mouthed, 'What's happened?'

'Look,' Paul began, 'I don't really know why I should care so much, but I do. There's been an accident at the Round House and I thought you should know. I think it's John, but that's only hearsay from Will at the pub.'

Lucy's face blurred and the sounds of pots and pans behind me magnified into a violent cacophony. I pressed my finger hard into my ear to hear better, pressing so hard I wondered if I was pressing into my brain, pressing away the alarm.

'What kind of accident?'

I could hear Lucy in the background telling Graham off for making too much noise. She must have seen the blood drain from my skin.

Paul replied, 'A car accident, I think. Last night. I'm not sure. I imagine you can't call the Tennants' – he paused – 'but he's at the Royal Sussex if you want to see him.'

'Thank you, Paul. Thank you so much for letting me know.'

My thoughts tunnelled into a black hole, with a light at the end that was John, whom I had to get to. Sounds were muffled and movements were slowed. I told Lucy that John had been in an accident and that I had to drive to the hospital now, and she told me that Alice could stay with them. I called up to Alice, trying to sound casual, announcing that I had forgotten something at home, that I would be back later.

I was relieved that she had not bothered to come down the stairs to say goodbye. If she had seen my face, she might have screamed.

CHAPTER FORTY-SIX

Two years ago

Francesca had waited, guiltily, for Robert to return from Sanjeev's. She had expected him to climb into bed next to her, stinking of alcohol and cigarettes and weed, and she had dreaded it. She was petrified that Robert had heard her with John, through the door, utterly convinced now that he had. But with every passing minute, she had become more and more angry with Robert for staying at Sanjeev's for so long. He was an arsehole. He had asked for it.

These awful things had been rotating around her head when she heard banging at the door.

Expecting Robert, she was shocked to see John, sweating and panting.

'Did you miss your train?'

He spoke in short, breathy bursts. 'Robert's not at Sanjeev's. I'm worried. I've heard ambulances. Please come.'

He yanked her coat from the pegs behind the door and held it out to her, imploringly.

They charged down the stairs and ran through the London streets, up towards Hornsey Lane and along to the bridge. John seemed to know where he was going.

At the bridge, Francesca stopped running, hit by an imaginary brick wall. She watched John run on, watched him press his head into the railings to see. His face was lit up by a flashing light below.

A small Virgin Mary shrine was at her side, scooped into a hole in the bridge. Francesca imagined the statue's elegant hands cradling her head, lovingly. *Go to him, he needs you,* Mary whispered in her ear.

Francesca tripped forward, to John, whose wails and cries were like shattering splinters of glass in her brain.

Over the railings, on the A1 below, lay a dark, curled form, like an embryo in a womb, in stillness, in front of a red car. The bonnet's dent was illuminated by the constant flashing of emergency vehicles, as were the figure's clothes – a jacket and trousers that she had washed only last week. Unstuck images of Robert's naked figure came to her, on top of her, his desire, his misery, this violent death. Flash, flash, flash, the view down there, two men in big reflective coats, bending down, over him, lifting him.

Get off him! Leave him alone! Francesca screamed in her head. *You don't know him! He needs me. He needs me!*

She began running, barely upright as her torso pushed her legs forward. But as her lungs and legs burned, the sirens started up, crying out into the night.

They have taken him. They have stolen my husband.

She stumbled on the pavement, landing on her knees, and she retched into the road.

Then John's arms were around her, helping her up.

'We did this to him! We did this!' she gasped, as she forced herself to stand, wiping spit and tears from her face. 'He needs me,' she sobbed, as they ran.

CHAPTER FORTY-SEVEN

John

Dilys tucked the hospital sheet around him, poured him some water, and combed his hair. She was convincing in her show of love, and through his grogginess, he was trying to locate the feelings of hate towards her.

Flashbacks to his accident came every five or ten minutes. He revisited the moment when the car hit him the night before, when everything had changed in that split second: when he had felt the crack – as if a concrete block had been dropped onto his chest – when his arms and legs had started to burn, when he couldn't move his lower body. He had seen trees above him and felt the wetness of grass. Fear and the agony had sent him reeling to another plane.

At the hospital, hours had slipped by in a blur, in and out of a nightmare-filled sleep. His bloodstream was flooded with drugs and his mind was addled by the trauma. He had been wheeled to and from Radiology for a CT scan and then for an MRI. Doctors had come to test the sensations in his legs, ask him to move his toes, and inserted a finger into his anus, asking him to squeeze it for muscle tone. He truly believed he had used those muscles, but he was told there was no movement there: a blinding terror. They asked him to shake his arms about, make strange movements with his hands. Nurses had come to take blood, to inject steroids, and to readjust his cannula, to change his wet bed, to insert a catheter. The doctors talked of surgery, but they remained undecided, and this infuriated Dilys more than him.

'Why can't they tell us anything?' she kept repeating.

He had not been able summon enough courage, or clarity, to ask her about what had happened. He had not been able to organise the facts of the accident in his head, let alone get them out of his mouth. It had been impossible to believe she had driven the car at him deliberately. Doubt about his memory, and the stability of his own mind, and fear of Dilys' volatility, had stopped him from saying anything to her while the medics circulated.

Now, he and Dilys were alone behind the drawn curtain. For the first time.

Dilys sat down on the visitor's chair next to him.

'Are you comfortable? I wonder when we'll have the CT results back. I suppose it's—'

'There's nobody h-here…' he stuttered, low and croaky. 'Drop the loving wife act.'

Her boney face loomed large above him. 'John, don't,' she whined.

'You drove at me last night.'

'No! It was dark. And I was crying so hard, it was blurry. As soon as I saw you, I swerved away. I swear it.'

Through all his confusion a mass of guilt gathered inside him, but then he remembered the sound of the wheels swirling in the gravel, the car spitting stones at the garage doors behind it, speeding towards him. John did not remember her tears.

'Then why did you' – he paused, licking his dry lips, trying to sound less slurred – 'move me. I was in the lane when the ambulance arrived.'

'You're remembering it all wrong. You crashed the Porsche *in the lane*.'

'You're lying.'

'John. Jesus. What are you saying?' she choked, sniffing. She found a tissue packet in her bag. John tried to remember if he had ever seen her cry with snot and heaving gasps and a red face.

'Did you want me to die?'

Her mouth fell open. 'I love you, John,' she whimpered, wiping her eyes carefully under her mascara, leaning over him, her hair dangling in his face.

His brain vibrated with panic while his body lay unnaturally still, alive inside but dead on the outside, desperate to move but trapped. The pain in his chest escalated. It was excruciating, like burning currents continually pulsing through his torso. He winced and hoped the morphine hadn't run out. When the nurses came in to see him, he would ask them to check its levels. Should he press the panic button now?

There was so much to say but he was too uncomfortable, he couldn't think straight.

'I'm tired, Dilys. Please just leave me alone to sleep.'

'Do you love her?'

Through his peripheral vision, he could see her red nails twirling the plastic tubes that fed him his morphine. He stared at her fingers, wondering if he dare answer her truthfully. She dropped the tube.

'Do you, John?'

'Yes.'

'Even after she lied to you about Alice?'

A bewildering flow of mixed-up chatter hammered at his thoughts, from the past, from the present; from mouths of others, from his own, from minds of others, from his own. He felt mentally unbalanced, lost in doubt.

Dilys jammed a straw to his lips, trying to make him drink. He coughed, attempting to speak, 'I'm not allowed…' he began, choking more. 'If I have surgery…' Water dribbled down his cheek.

She clicked her tongue and sat down, out of his vision.

Tepid pools of saliva gathered around his tongue and he gagged. He was furious; a scrap of clarity returned to him briefly.

'When I get out of here…' he whispered, breaking off to swallow, continuing hoarsely, 'it's over.'

'We'll get Francesca out of your system, don't you worry.'

'No.'

No longer did he care what Francesca had or had not done, or what she was guilty of or not guilty of. He knew he wanted to be with her for the rest of his life. He was more certain about this than he had been about anything in his life.

When Dilys next spoke, it was with a strained sweetness.

'The children would be so upset if they found out that Daddy had tried to run Mummy off the road, wouldn't they?'

'What? I never…' He trailed off, his memory wavering again. Uncertainty was flickering inside him like a faltering light bulb.

'You were chasing me through the lanes in the Porsche, remember? You were drunk after all that wine.'

Her lilting Welsh sing-song was like a malicious lullaby.

Then her hands were on his chest, pressing down.

He wailed, wondering if he could die from the pain.

'Oh, sorry, is that sore? I'm so sorry.' She let go.

'What is wrong with you?' he rasped.

'I just want us to be a family.'

He moaned, pole-axed by the pain, and squeezed his fingers into his upper thigh to displace the agony radiating through his upper body. He could not feel his fingernails in his skin.

'They won't believe you.' His voice came out in a whisper. He knew his children wouldn't believe her.

'When they see the dent, and then they find out about Francesca, and Alice, I have a feeling they might believe anything I say about you. Let's face it, you're no longer the dad they thought you were.'

Her voice became distant. He wasn't sure whether it was a dream or not.

'Please don't tell them like that. Don't, Dilys,' he begged.

Ignoring him, she continued. 'And I think Harry'll be so upset to find out why his uncle jumped off that bridge.'

'No. You have no idea why.'

'He jumped when he found out about your affair with Francesca, didn't he? They would be devastated to know that, John, wouldn't they?'

'That's not true. He didn't know about Francesca. You can't say that to Harry.'

'D'you think he'll want to live with you when he knows? Do you think the courts will favour you when they know you are reckless and suicidal, like your brother? How will you look after them when you'll need twenty-four-hour care?'

'I'm their dad.' It came out as a whisper, but even if he had shouted it, the statement was inadequate.

Last night, when he had seen Harry's face for the first time after the accident, he had cried tears of love and joy. And he had not cared what kind of state his body would end up in, as long as he could see his son's face and speak to him and hear his news and feel his touch. When he had seen Olivia and Beatrice that morning, with his parents, he had felt the same rush of love and gratefulness. He was lucky to be alive, to have his children in his life. He would never take it for granted. It was all that mattered.

'You're depressed, my love. Just like your poor brother. That's why you need me to look after you.'

Confusion whirled through his mind. To order his memories, he clung to Dilys' reassuringly clear version of his accident. It played itself out in Technicolor, like the scene of a film in which he played the bad guy. But conflicting memories burnt through the reel, leaving sticky holes and garbled sound.

'I need help,' he said, possibly out loud, possibly in his head. He needed guidance from a psychologist or a friend, to talk through his accident, to pin down the real events.

'If you forget about Francesca, I'll help you.'

'I can't do that.'

'It'll be easier when she's gone.'

'Gone?'

'She's putting the house up for sale. She called the estate agent today, apparently, and they called your mum straight away.'

John wanted to scream. It felt as though the bed had straps that Dilys had tightened across his legs and chest. He would never be able to get away from her. If he went to Francesca, he would lose his children. He couldn't lose them. Nothing would make sense in his life without them. Not even Francesca.

Sacrificing Francesca was retribution for betraying his brother, and Dilys and his children. On that scaffolding, he hadn't been thinking about their feelings. He'd had a choice, and he'd made the wrong one.

'What about Alice?'

'Your father called his solicitor and explained the situation. He says you'll be able to demand visitation rights.'

After this, he closed his eyes. It was the only power he had over her, to not look at her, to not see her. She left his bedside and he heard the murmur of her talking to his parents in the ward, and he drifted off into oblivion. They had it all worked out, as usual. Everyone was in line. The plan was already in action.

What more could he do?

CHAPTER FORTY-EIGHT

Francesca

By the time I had reached the A&E admissions desk at the Royal Sussex Hospital, I was none the wiser about what had happened to John. For the whole journey there, images of his rag-dolled body slumped over his steering wheel or flung into a ditch had been flickering through my mind.

'Two Ns?'

'Yes, T.E.N.N.A.N.T. Tennant.'

'John Tennant. Here we go. He's been transferred to the Bramshott high dependency unit.'

Fear shot through me.

'High dependency? What's happened to him?'

'I can't give out patient information, I'm afraid. If you take a right at the lifts, and follow the signs, you'll find it.'

The shiny wide corridors became emptier as I walked deeper into the heart of the hospital. My terror increased with every step. I did not know what to expect.

The HDU was hushed, with families clustered around beds or murmuring behind the drawn curtains. A nurse informed me that John was in a bed at the end of the ward.

Camilla, Patrick and Dilys were in a huddle, a few beds away from where the nurse had pointed. I walked towards them, stiff with dread.

'How dare you…' Camilla hissed and started towards me, but Patrick held her arm.

Dilys crossed her arms over her cashmere sweater and stuck her pointy chest out at me. She was flanked by Camilla and Patrick.

Their wan, strained, hate-filled faces glowered at me. I wanted to turn on my heel and run from the hospital. I had never felt such acute shame.

'You can't see him,' Dilys said. 'He's got an operation scheduled in the next hour.'

'What operation? Is he okay?'

'I'm not sure you have the right…' Camilla began, only to be stopped, once again, by Patrick.

Mounting fear made me angry. 'Just tell me what happened.'

Patrick answered me. 'He was in a car accident. The Porsche span out of control just outside the house. He's fractured two vertebrae and partially damaged his spinal cord in his lower back. They'll be operating later today, but the surgeon warned there is a significant risk of long-term paralysis in his legs.'

'Paralysis?' I uttered the word as though it was in a foreign language. I needed someone to translate it for me. I could not believe they had said this word in reference to John. Beautiful, strong, healthy John.

Patrick continued, using a voice a doctor might use to tell a patient, with facts and big words, but very little emotion. 'The consultant has warned us that the operation is to fuse the vertebrae to stabilise his spine, but they cannot repair the damage to the spinal cord. They'll be monitoring his movement and loss of sensation closely to establish whether or not they believe he will regain full mobility. The next few days are crucial.'

'He will regain full mobility,' I said. Saying it would make it happen.

Dilys began to cry into Camilla's shoulder.

While the two women were distracted, I moved around them to John's curtains.

Patrick did not stop me. In letting me go, I thought that he was being kind, that he felt for me on some level.

I slipped in through the curtains.

John was flat on his back, wired to drips. The tip of his foot stuck out of the end of the sheet. His exposed toes made him look vulnerable.

He stared blankly up at the ceiling from his neck brace, and then closed his eyes. The brief glimpse of his pale, lost eyes, the prominence of his cheek bones and the dryness of his lips were enough to send a series of sharp pains into my chest.

I approached the bed. I wanted to touch his arm where the cannula was wedged, where his veins were pumped up and the flesh yellow and swollen. I wanted to lie next to him and kiss him better. My love for him could cure him.

Instead, I stood there like an idiot, staring at his deathly mask. What was I there to say? What had I expected from him? That he would see me and reach his arms out and we would cry about his injury and declare our love for one another?

'Hi,' I said.

If I moved closer, to look down at him, would he open his eyes? I would wait. If I could persuade him to look at me, it would be a start. Whatever he faced, I wanted him to know that I would be there for him.

'Your parents told me what happened.'

Silence.

I looked at the blue box attached to his drip, which would be administering intravenous morphine.

'Are you in a lot of pain?'

It was a stupid question.

'You must be frightened about this operation.'

Silence. I waited, finding the courage to say what I really wanted to say.

'I'm sorry. About everything. I'm so sorry. There was never a right time to tell you about Alice.'

More silence.

I stood there until I felt my feet throbbing. I had to think of something that would get a reaction out of him.

'When you are better, Alice will want to see you.'

His eyes snapped open. He said, 'My lawyers will be in contact to arrange visitation rights.' And he squeezed them shut again.

I clutched my middle, winded by his anger. The curtain opened behind me but I was too stunned to move. When I saw Patrick's smirk, I winced. Patrick had predicted John's rebuff and he had wished me to experience it. The Tennants had closed ranks.

I pushed passed him and ran back through the plastic corridors, my lungs burning. When I reached the car park, I dropped my head over my knees and gasped for breath as though I had run a marathon.

That was it. It was over. John was going through one of the most horrifying experiences of his life, and he did not want me with him. I should have known that his loyalties to his family would always trump his attachment to me, just as it had been with Robert. I had once wanted my freedom from the Tennants, but now I had it, I felt desolate.

CHAPTER FORTY-NINE

John

When John had seen Francesca out of the corner of his eye, flushed and breathless, he had weakened for a second, believing he could beat Dilys. Then he had remembered Dilys' cruel sing-song warnings, and the reliability of his own befuddled brain. He had closed his eyes again, knowing his rejection and his silence would wound her deeply. It had taken every ounce of willpower to leave her questions hanging in the air. Would she ever be able to understand that he had no choice? Would she ever be able to forgive him if she knew he had chosen his children over her?

*

'The nurse said the operation before yours is running late,' his father told him.

John asked for the time. He could not dwell on how frightened he was. He couldn't think of anything but Francesca, and how much he had hurt her. The future without her was as bleak as any future he could imagine. This was Robert's punishment from on high. A divine punishment.

For ever, Robert will live on, he thought. The last moments on the bridge with him should have been the end, but forever he would live under the weight of his bullying.

John's tears rolled from his eyes, down his ears and onto the hospital pillows. His chest heaved, and his face grimaced with the pain.

And his father watched, with his hands linked behind his back.

His figure, silhouetted grey against the hospital window, looked like a formal statue on a plinth in a town square, full of poise and pride, but cold and lifeless. John wondered if he might find the strength to move his left leg and kick him. No amount of willpower or rage was going to move his leg. He couldn't feel them at all. The fear of long-term paralysis was not, however, at the forefront of his mind. The morphine might have skewed his brain, dampening the horror, managing it somehow, allowing the denial.

The door opened. A nurse and a porter came bustling in. 'Right! We're ready for you.'

While the nurse placed a paper cap on his head and fussed around the tangled cords of his drip, John looked up at his pompous, righteous father, and realised that he would not care if he never saw him again.

When he saw his mother's stricken face, and felt her cool hand on his forehead – reminding him of how she would do this when he had a fever as a boy – resentment smouldered inside him.

The trolley ride to surgery was painful and it took all of his strength not to cry out. He bit his lip to counter the discomfort of the bumpy journey.

As the anaesthetist brought the mask over his face to put him out, he conjured an image of Francesca in his mind, and he went to sleep in peace.

CHAPTER FIFTY

Francesca

Francesca,

We would like to let you know that John's surgery to stabilise his vertebrae went well, but the incomplete T11–12 thoracic spinal cord injury has left him paralysed. Due to low levels of sensation and small movement, the doctors believe that, given time and intensive rehabilitation, there is a small chance he might regain the ability to walk. Needless to say, this is a very difficult time for our family, and I would ask you to respect John's wish that you stay away. When you move, please inform us of your new address, for Patrick's solicitor, who will be in touch about Alice's visits to John and the children.

Dilys

Dilys' cold delivery made me want to retch every time I read the email, which was often. She had sent it two weeks ago but, still, I could not process the news.

A telephone call from South Downs Property flashed up on my phone. I answered the call.

'Hi, Francesca, it's Alistair from South Downs. Any chance I could show someone around in an hour?'

'I'll be here,' I replied, as I would do every time he called. There had been about five or six viewings in the past couple of days.

'They're first-time buyers, currently renting in London. She's pregnant and they're keen to get settled before she has the baby.'

'Sounds good,' I enthused, trying to hide my lack of interest. I didn't care who bought the cottage: I just wanted it sold quickly, before Christmas, I hoped. That gave us about six weeks, which Alistair informed me was possible due to the high level of interest in the property, and the desirability of the village.

After a thorough tidy of the house, I answered the doorbell to Alistair and a young, fresh-faced couple. The woman was wearing a fitted waxed jacket with shiny brass buttons and her husband was wearing a checked pink shirt and a puffer gilet. I imagined they might suit the village much better than I had.

After greeting them, I told them I would leave them to it.

I could tell that Alistair did not like me being in the house when he was showing around prospective buyers. Not that I would dream of getting involved – pointing out the brand-new boiler or the spaciousness of the understair cupboard – so, as always, I headed off to my shed at the bottom of the garden, where I sat and read the newspaper on my phone.

When they knocked on the door, I pretended to draw on my easel. Alistair liked that I did this. It sold a lifestyle. Little did they know that I dropped my pencil as soon as they closed the door, and when they were gone I returned to the house to watch television.

I didn't leave the cottage unless I had to. When I did go out, twice a day, to walk Alice to and from school, I had to pass the 'For Sale' sign wired to my gatepost. It shot into the air above me like a banner of shame and failure, for all to see and gossip about.

Knowing Camilla, she would not have told a soul about the recent scandal in our family, whose reputation she guarded with such ferocity. Nonetheless, I was paranoid about everyone knowing. During the short excursions to school, I might spot someone I would normally chat to in the village and they would rush past me, busy on their phones. If they did stop, the way they would ask about John, and how Alice was, with a slightly sympathetic simper, suggested they had heard the gossip. Maybe Paul had told one person, and that person had told another, and so on.

The various people whom I had informed of our imminent move – the head mistress of Alice's school, or some of the mothers – were surprised, but not devastated. They had not had time to form attachments to me and Alice; considering we had lived in the village barely six months, we were relative strangers. Alice and I would move on and disappear from their lives as though we had never been there.

Archie Parr had been different. He had sounded genuinely upset and, for a moment, I had wondered if I could stay and push through the pain barriers, to stick it out in the village. It had been a ludicrous thought, to stay for the sake of one old man; albeit a man whose kindness and intelligence had given me my hope back, whose quiet faith in me had reminded me that I could function normally in society again.

The worst was when I saw a red Mini Cooper or a black Land Rover Discovery or a green Jaguar pass by. My heart would race and I would look at the ground. I imagined little Beatrice waving to Alice, possibly confused about why she hadn't seen her lately. Or perhaps they knew about Alice. I doubted they'd been told. She and Olivia and Harry were facing a future in which their daddy might never walk again. This was enough to cope with, and I hoped that Dilys was sensitive enough to remember this.

Certainly, I knew that I would not be seeing a white Porsche trundling through the lanes. John would not be driving for a very long time, if ever.

I thought about John constantly.

Before channel-hopping to find a black and white film or a good soap to watch, I reread the email from Dilys again, wishing to read something between the lines that would give me some more hope. It never did. The thought of John's suffering had kept me awake all night, every night. In fact, night-time sleep was no longer something I took for granted. I would nap here and there in the daytime, but that was all.

I craved John, I dreamt of him, and I couldn't bear that I was not allowed to be there for him. But Dilys' email had been blunt. The Tennants had cut me out. It was obvious they would never get over it. When you were in the Tennant family, you were in, when you were out, you were so far out you might as well be dead. Dilys' use of the phrase, 'this is a very difficult time for *our* family' riled me, as did the last sentence, 'Alice's visits to John and the children'. Why could she not have said, 'Alice's visits to see us'? Was she going to exclude herself from Alice's visits? Was she going to blame Alice for existing?

Initially, I had decided not to respond. Today, I had a strange feeling that the fresh-faced couple might buy my cottage, and I put my anger towards Dilys aside. I turned the volume down on the television to concentrate, and I began to type:

> *Dear Dilys,*
> *I am devastated for John. I would very much like the oppor-*
> *tunity to see him before I leave. Please, if you could find it*
> *in your heart, I would greatly appreciate this one kindness,*
> *even though I do not deserve it. I am profoundly sorry for all*
> *the pain I have caused you. With love, Fran x*

It had taken two episodes of a trashy soap for Dilys' response to ping back, by text:

> *I'm afraid that will not be possible.*

I had expected it. She was not going to let me see John, having finally got what she wanted: ultimate power. She was not going to let go now. I had no idea where John was, whether he would endure his rehabilitation at home or in a specialist hospital but, either way, Dilys would be micromanaging his life more than ever before. I contemplated barging past her, seeing him against the family's wishes, and then I remembered John's intractable expression. I did not have the strength to experience that rejection twice. The Tennants were not the main obstacle. John was. Nevertheless, I worried for him: how he was surviving the pain and the discomfort; whether he was being well looked-after and how well he was coping; how frightened he must be. My heart twisted at the thought of his suffering.

The slow countdown to the school run passed with me horizontal on the sofa, the blanket over me and my slippers on. When my phone rang, half an hour before I would have to force myself out of the door again, I knew it would be Alistair. I turned off the television.

'Guess what?' he said.

'The lovely couple want to put an offer in?'

'They've offered the asking price, they've nothing to sell and they're keen to complete before Christmas. Is that too soon?'

'I accept their offer.'

'Congratulations!' Alistair said.

I wondered if he had noticed that the enthusiasm about the sale was one-sided.

I trudged out of the door, collected Alice from school, and returned home, only half listening to her chatter. While the cottage pie warmed up in the Aga, I opened my laptop to search for two-bedroom flats in Hastings. There was no particular reason why I chose Hastings, other than I liked the idea that it was on the coast and that it was affordable.

An Edwardian house with sash windows and views over the rooftops to the sea was available, for the right price. I called up the estate agent and booked a viewing, knowing that I had just found my new home. I did not experience excitement or nerves or doubt. I might as well have picked it blindfolded.

After that, everything happened very fast. Official letters landed on my doormat every day, from Patrick's solicitors, from my conveyance solicitors, from South Downs Property, from my mortgage company, and on and on. I was efficient and systematic about how I ran the move.

It was a completely different experience to the upheaval of selling Cheverton Road: there was no emotional attachment to the cottage, unlike our London flat, beyond the pinch of sadness about a future here that had once promised resolution. My footsteps had not worn through the carpet, and Alice's fingerprints had not left indelible marks on the walls; the ghost of our movements would not linger in the air circulating between its walls. Our life in the cottage could be wiped away easily. Perhaps we had never really been there.

On moving day, there were some boxes in the loft that I had never unpacked. While scooting them along to the hatch, I hit my head on the beam and stopped to rub it. John's face came rushing into my mind. Who knew, maybe that one powerful memory of us together might be important enough to linger in the fabric of the house. I thought back to his tall, strong figure stooping in the space, and I imagined his damaged body now. My throat tingled, threatening tears. But I redoubled my efforts to move the boxes speedily out of the attic and into the arms of the removal men below.

Later, I let Alice post the keys through the letterbox, ready for the next owners, and I promised her a chocolate croissant in the car to distract her from what we were doing.

We waved goodbye to the house, to Letworth, to Cam-Cam and Grandpa, to John and Beatrice and Olivia and Harry, and we drove away. Alice would not have understood the permanence of those goodbyes. I had not fully allowed her to understand. Her dismay would have broken my resolve and shattered my determination to remain comfortably numb about this move.

*

It had taken us two hours to get to Hastings, to our new street.

I parked up in the pretty, tree-lined crescent street, on a hill that sloped around and down towards the sea. From here, there was a five-minute walk to the shops and a ten-minute walk to the sea-front.

The sea wind sliced through my woollen coat and the squawk of seagulls reminded me of how different life was going to be.

It was the second time I had seen our new flat, but for Alice it was the first. She had circled the packing boxes marked 'Alice', stacked in her tiny room, with manic excitement. She had no concept of all that we had left behind. I wondered whether I had truly grasped it either.

On second viewing, the flat seemed even smaller than when I had first seen it. And dirtier. I noticed the marks on the cream walls and the patches on the blue carpet.

I stood at the sash windows and looked out across the swirl of streets and terracotta rooftops, to see a tiny patch of slate sea joined to the horizon.

The sea was meant to bring healing to the sick and dispossessed. If I harnessed the entirety of its power for myself, I imagined it would do no good.

CHAPTER FIFTY-ONE

John

Beatrice and Olivia were squeezed either side of John on the bed, watching a cartoon on the television, whilst Harry described the plot twists of a science fiction novel he had been reading. Dilys was shopping in the lanes of Brighton.

As he tried to listen to Harry, John's mind drifted and his gaze wandered out of the hospital window, out to sea. He stared at the grey-brown water. He mentally zoomed down to its choppy surface and dove into the water; imagining the sound of the breaking waves, loud and certain and ceaseless. The view was comforting, peaceful. Water was comforting.

When he had first been given a shower in a shower bed, seven weeks after the operation, he had been embarrassed by his nakedness and his useless limbs. But he had closed his eyes and allowed himself to be soothed by the sensations of the warm flow over his head as the nurses washed him. Afterwards, he sensed that his skin was smiling, clean and fresh.

Two months after that first shower, he was spending three mornings a week doing hydrotherapy in a small pool, which were his favourite physiotherapy sessions. The treadmill under the water forced the movement of his withered legs, reminding him of what it felt like to walk again. He could not feel his feet on the rotation belt, and his harness pinched, but he had made progress. He was now moving without his legs getting tangled beneath him. Like a baby held up by the arms of his mother, his legs were relearning the pathways from brain to spine to legs, to trigger the instinctive motion of putting one foot in front of another.

Mostly, his life was that simple: one step after another, pared down to eating, sleeping, physiotherapy and visits from family after lunch. The drips had been taken down one by one in the early weeks, to be replaced by oral pain relief and steroids, which he would take in a little paper cup at mealtimes. He had been moved from the HDU to the Rookwood spinal injury ward, to a bed with the sea view. And, unlike many of his fellow patients, he had avoided any bad skin problems or pneumonia or any of the other complications that came with paraplegia. With the exception of one urinary infection last week, and constipation – for which he had endured the humiliation of intrusive digit manipulation from one of the nurses to stimulate his bowel movements, and a manual evacuation of his stool – he had stayed in relatively good health. The frustrating spasms in his legs were ongoing but, now, he could successfully control his bladder and bowel with carefully managed procedures, and he could move from bed to wheelchair to the toilet smoothly, which was a huge achievement. Everything he did was about incremental steps towards recovery. He was working towards independence and acceptance, while keeping his sanity in the process.

Now, after only fifteen weeks, he had become institutionalised. Having spent his previous life happy in his own company, holed up in his shed, writing freely, eating at random times, avoiding structure, he was being forced into the monotony of a well-established system. And he wasn't fighting it.

In the mornings, he no longer resented the brutally early wake-up calls from the night nurses, who would burst in through the curtains and shout good morning and drop his pills on his bed table. He had even learnt to go back to sleep until he was woken at 7.30 a.m. by the noise and chatter and the smell of coffee. He looked forward to his synthetic breakfast roll and jellied marmalade every morning, which he would eat with a black Americano while watching the BBC news.

Breakfast was the only meal that was wholly edible. The food at lunch and supper was so bad he would take photographs of it to send to Harry. Harry would send back photographs of the wholesome pies that their new housekeeper – and John's soon-to-be carer – Martha would make for them. These photos would make John laugh and reassure him that the children were being well taken care of.

He, too, was being well cared for. He had built good relationships with the friendlier nurses, particularly an Australian nurse called Becky. The short bursts of banter and human contact peppered the swathes of time that he would spend alone. He was so grateful to them for their matter-of-fact kindliness during the daily humiliations and struggles of his new state. They never showed pity. John loathed pity.

Twice a week after breakfast, Dr Rahman, the specialist consultant, would visit him. Every day his physiotherapists, either Dave or Sarah, would accompany him down to the gym or the hydropool for his repetitive, and always painful, exercises.

After lunch, he would expect visitors. If they were not due, he would feel anxious about how to fill the slow-moving hours until bedtime. Mostly, he would listen to audiobooks on his iPod. These books saved him when he thought he might lose his mind. As did his notepad, which lay on his bedside, into which he would jot down how he was feeling. It was more like a diary than work. Sometimes, he would write in it to quell the panic that would rise in him when he experienced desperate urges to get up and run from the hospital. He wondered if he would refer to these desperate scribbles in the future: once a writer, always a writer, and trauma was an opportunity for copy. But specific projects and deadlines were a distant memory, and his work on *Billy Stupid* had been handed over to another writer for the final edits months ago.

He had different goals now.

To walk again.

His sleep was riddled with dreams of walking. Those light-filled, dream-state steps – barefoot across grass, or the energised pumping of his legs in a sprint down a street – would be devastating to wake up from; when he remembered where he was and what had happened. In those dark, frightening moments, staring into the shadowy hospital room, he would relive the utter shock and desolation of hearing the diagnosis from the doctor in the HDU. He would replay the strange body language of Dr Alba, who had looked down at his own feet before telling John that his chances of walking again were 'slim to none'. When these memories came to him, in the dead of night, John would feel alone in the world, and too scared to go back to sleep. At those times, he missed Francesca more than ever, and he missed home. The only way he could drop off again would be to listen to his books.

'Dad? Do you think that ending is a cheat, or what?' Harry asked, reminding John of where he was.

'Such a cheat,' John nodded, realising he had not registered a word of his son's enthusiastic ramblings about the science fiction novel.

Harry looked wounded and sad.

'Sorry. Please tell me again.'

Harry gave a monotone, lacklustre précis of the plot. A precious moment to connect with Harry had passed John by and he regretted zoning out; he cursed the medication that muddied his concentration.

'How's Mum?'

'Okay.' Harry shrugged.

'What did she need from the shops?'

'Not sure.'

'Martha still treating you well?'

Harry smiled. 'She's really nice.'

'That pavlova looked good enough for "Bake Off",' John said, remembering one of Harry's photographs.

'And she's awesome at maths,' Harry said.

Olivia chimed in: 'She is, Dad. Much better than you.'

John laughed. 'I'm brilliant at maths.'

'No, you're not!' Beatrice giggled.

'Okay, ask me a question then.'

'What's five plus a thousand hundred?' Beatrice asked earnestly.

'Umm, let me see, that's so easy, that'd be five gazillion trillion.'

Beatrice looked over to Olivia, for confirmation that this was correct.

Olivia grinned. 'There's no such number.'

John noted that Olivia had not shouted at Beatrice for her made-up number. He wondered how they were getting on, and yearned to be at home to break up their fighting. The two hours per day he would spend with them in this hospital was a phony situation. He felt disassociated from their daily struggles. It left a gaping hole in his life. In these two hours, he was desperate to reconnect. He lived for it.

He wanted to know whether Beatrice's fickle best friend was playing with her at breaktimes; whether Olivia's dance teacher had played Chopin, which she loved, or jazz, which she hated; whether Harry was still sitting next to the lovely Isobel on the school bus. All these questions he would know by being there in their daily lives, all of the little details adding up to the bigger picture of their happiness or unhappiness. None of which they could answer in retrospect. Beatrice could never relay details of her week to order. If he brought up jazz with Olivia, she would become anxious and it would ruin her mood.

And Harry would be too bashful to tell him about Isobel in front of the girls.

Instead, John would pay lip service to his past role as their day-to-day carer by asking them if they were eating their greens or closing their drawers or picking up their wet towels. But he wasn't the one standing over them to make sure they did. In fact, he might never be able to stand over them ever again, or tell them off about the petty rubbish that used to bother him. He could not imagine caring about wet towels or closed drawers ever again. He couldn't imagine caring about anything beyond existing.

For now, for another month, he was closeted in the routines of patient life. Nurses were there for him at the push of a button, meals were cooked for him, physiotherapy was only a few corridors away. The need to self-motivate had been taken away from him. Often, he would try to picture life in the outside world again, but it was such an exhausting prospect, part of him wished he could stay in limbo, in this hospital, forever.

He had heard inspirational stories about paraplegics winning Olympic medals or climbing mountains, but he decided that he was not made of such strong stuff.

When he considered his future, he fantasised about disappearing completely. He could find himself an adapted flat somewhere far from home and live life as a loner. The battle towards some form of compromised normality at the Round House seemed pointless. His past stamping ground would be a reminder of everything he had lost.

'Mum will be back any minute,' he reminded them.

'Uh.' Beatrice sighed heavily. 'I don't want to leave you, Daddy.'

Olivia climbed off the bed and sat on Harry's knee.

'What are you up to tomorrow?' John asked.

Harry groaned. 'We're going to Rupert and Susie's for lunch.'

John did not particularly like Rupert or Susie.

'I feel for you lot. Thank god I don't have to go to.'

There were some advantages to his situation. He decided that he would never go to Rupert and Susie's for lunch ever again. The thought was liberating. But it was fleeting. What worth did any kind of freedom have when he would not be free to see Francesca and Alice? He did not know where they had moved to, or how they were. His parents had refused to begin the process of negotiating access to Alice until he was home and well enough. Harry, Olivia and Beatrice still did not know they had a new sibling.

'Anna is such a brat,' Harry said, referring to Rupert and Susie's one child, who was Beatrice's age.

'Yeah, she so is, Dad,' Beatrice cried, jumping off the bed, wiggling her bottom and sticking her nose in the air. 'She walks like this.'

Everyone laughed. Beatrice got over-excited and pulled down her jeans and blew a raspberry.

'Okay, that's enough, young lady,' John said, but as he said it, he noticed a large, dark bruise on her thigh. 'How did you do that, Bea?'

Beatrice pulled her jeans up quickly. 'Don't know.'

John looked to Harry and Olivia, but neither of them could look him in the eye.

'Tell me, please.'

'She didn't do it by purpose,' Beatrice said.

Nervy pains shot down John's spine. 'Who didn't do it by purpose?'

Olivia spoke up. 'Bea was screaming her head off, as usual, and Mum got cross and pulled her out of the bath, but then Bea wriggled and she slipped out of Mum's hands and onto the side. I saw everything.'

John had to lean his head back on the bed and lower his bed a little to get rid of the dizziness. 'Has Mum been cross a lot?'

Harry said, 'Yes.'

In unison, Olivia and Beatrice said, 'No.'

'The girls are scared of saying anything,' Harry added.

'You can always tell your dad anything, you know that.'

'She made us swear not to tell you, Daddy,' Olivia said.

'Not to tell me what, Olive?' John asked.

Harry explained. 'How much she shouts. She finds the weekends really stressful.'

'She shouts, like, ALL the time, and cries a lot,' Olivia said, leaning back into Harry, whose arms tightened around her. Beatrice snuggled into her big brother's neck. The three of them seemed closer than ever, and as much as he should have been comforted, he sensed that the closeness was born out of need.

'I try to make sure you're good, don't I?' Harry said, tickling Beatrice's ribs.

'That's not your job,' John replied.

He lay there, engulfed by rage, heady with it. And as his mind teemed with ways he could try to protect them remotely, Dilys appeared through the door in a flourish of January sale shopping bags.

'I've got presents for everyone!' she cried.

The two girls rushed to the bags and unlaced the ribbons and delved into the tissue-paper to gasp at sparkly clothes and colourful stationery.

John glanced over at Harry, who raised his eyebrows at him. John managed to whisper, 'I'll be home in four weeks. Hang on in there,' John said.

Harry nodded, tears gathering in his eyes.

'What did you get Daddy?' Beatrice asked her mother, a new dress stretched over her jumper and jeans.

Dilys' blue eyes rested on John. 'Well, poor Daddy can't wear anything in here, can he?'

'He doesn't go around naked, Mum,' Harry snapped.

'Don't be so rude, Harry,' Dilys shot back. 'He's become so rude, John, it's unbelievable. I wouldn't have dared talk back to my parents when I was his age.'

'It's okay. I don't need presents,' John said, trying to calm the situation.

He knew then that Dilys did not see him as he was before. In her eyes, he was a disabled person who did not need nice clothes. He was not the John she married, he was a paraplegic.

Three days later, he got a package in the post. Harry had sent him a new pair of Nike jogging bottoms and a white T-shirt. The note said: 'Miss you, Dad. Love, Harry x'

For the next four weeks, John worked harder in his physio-therapy sessions than he had ever thought possible. He might not be able to win medals or climb mountains, but he was determined to become the dad he had been before his accident. His children needed him, and he was not going to let them down.

CHAPTER FIFTY-TWO

Francesca

'Scooter or bike?'

'Scooter.'

'Theo's taking his bike.'

'Okay. Bike.'

'Got your gloves?'

Alice pulled out her Hello Kitty mittens from her pocket.

'And hat?'

'Don't want to wear my hat.'

'You have to. We're going to the beach. It's windy and freezing.'

'No.' Alice threw the hat at the front door. There had been many little outbursts and temper tantrums since we had moved. She had settled in well at the local school, and made friends, like Theo, but at home she was taking out her anger on me. I didn't blame her for it. She had been through so much.

As I reached down for her hat, a bundle of letters fluttered through the letterbox onto my head, making Alice laugh.

Laughing too, I flicked through them absent-mindedly.

One was a cream envelope with a water-mark. The elegant writing was in black fountain pen. The company stamp was too light to read. I turned it over to open it, forgetting that we were already late for meeting Theo and his mother, Jo, a new friend.

'Let's go, Mummy!

'One minute,' I replied hoarsely, choked with fear.

Without opening it, I knew the letter was from Patrick Tennant's solicitor. I had been expecting it, but I had hoped that it would never come. It was like a blast of freezing air in my face. The contents of this letter could hold the horrors of legal battles and demands for shared custody. In the hospital, after his accident, John had talked about visitation rights, which I would encourage, but I knew what the Tennants were capable of and the power they liked to wield.

'Come on!' Alice tugged at my coat. 'Mummy!'

'Stop it, Alice,' I snapped. 'This is important.'

'What is it?'

Alice leapt up to try to grab it from me.

'Please, Alice.'

Infuriated by her pestering, I thrust it into the zipped pocket of my handbag, away from her, and out of my sight.

As we hurried through the streets to the café on the promenade, in the icy March wind, I noticed I had a fluttery stomach every time I thought of the letter's portent.

The letter did not only contain my fears, it held the promise of seeing John.

Theo and Alice were biking on the promenade, up and down, past the tall windows of the café, inside which Jo and I were sitting.

The letter was in my handbag at my feet. It was pregnant with change; it threatened both a fight, and it offered hope. I was finding it hard to concentrate on Jo, whom I liked very much. She was talking about the renovations to their B&B, 'Sea House', which she and her husband, Doug, had set up. She was easy company. We saw each other regularly and I had a feeling we were becoming good friends. Obviously, nobody could replace

Lucy, who continued to be a pillar of strength for me, but Lucy seemed faraway in London. A local friend, like Jo, was a blessing. Yet, I hadn't been brave enough to tell her about the mess of my life. Of course, she knew that Robert had died, but that was it. If I told her the rest, I risked scaring her off.

'I found some old typewriters at Ardingly that I thought would look great on the shelves, but Doug went mental. He told me I was a hoarder.'

'Were they expensive?'

'No! A fiver each. And they're beautiful.'

'Very "Lifestyle", next to all your clothbound books.'

'You see? I knew you'd get it. And we do get writers and creative types sometimes.'

'The sea view, I guess.' I looked out at the angry sea and thought of John. 'Robert's brother is a writer,' I added.

'Would I have heard of him?'

'Doubt it. John Tennant. He's written kids' TV for years. He's talented, though.'

I stirred my coffee, thinking about his film script, and wondered if he would ever work on it again.

'Send him down to Sea House!'

'I don't talk to him any more.'

'Oh. I'm sorry.'

I didn't know whether it was the letter at my feet or the sea air, or Jo's friendly face, but I wanted to talk about John. Months had gone by since his accident, and I pined for him. Having imagined that the physical separation would become easier with time, I found that my isolation had only increased my want. Our separation began to feel more like penance than good sense.

I checked that Alice and Theo were still busy on the beach choosing pebbles for their bucket.

'I wish I did see him. We were good friends.'

'What happened?'

I could have told her about the accident, but I didn't want her to imagine him as a tragedy. I wanted her to hear about him as the man I loved.

'I kept something from him. And he hasn't been able to forgive me.'

'That sounds complicated,' she said.

'Very.' I smiled.

'You want to talk about it?'

'Not yet.'

I gulped back the dregs of my cold coffee and thought about the letter.

'I'm just going to the loo,' I said, taking my bag with me.

Safely locked away in the cubicle, I brought out the letter and ripped it open.

Skimming through to the bottom, I read rapidly, impatient to get all the information into my brain as quickly as possible. In stuffy legal jargon, it explained that John wanted to see Alice as soon as possible, on a mutually agreed upon date. Furthermore, they wanted her to stay with Camilla and Patrick for two nights, once a month, at Byworth End. They described it as a familiar base, taking into consideration John's new circumstances.

Before going on to read the last paragraph, I stopped and clutched the letter to my chest, exhaling, briefly letting some wisps of relief and excitement seep in. One weekend a month was doable, and it would mean I would be seeing John very soon. My heart sang.

There was a bang to my cubicle door and I jumped.

'Mummy! I need a wee-wee!'

'One second, darling!' I replied, looking again at the letter to finish the last paragraph.

It was this last paragraph that delivered the punch.

'However, as a condition to the above, John would like to communicate his wish that the biological paternity of Alice

*remain undisclosed to save further distress and confusion
to the family, particularly in the light of his accident. He
understands that we cannot force you to do so, but he would
like to appeal to your good nature, hoping that his wish is
respected. Any attempt to undermine this will add more
burden to a very challenging situation at home.'*

'Mummeeeeee! I can't hold it in!'

Alice's yelling outside the door was a background echo. I stood
with the letter in my hand, unable to move.

'I'm desperate!' she squealed.

I opened the cubicle. Alice was hopping around, pressing her
hand into her skirt to stop the flow.

'Sorry, darling. In you go.'

The hopping stopped abruptly.

'Come on, then,' I said, gesturing to the cubicle.

'Sorry, Mummy,' she said, hanging her head.

A pool of wetness was gathering at her feet and a tear ran down
her cheek.

'Oh, darling, I'm so sorry. It's my fault. Don't you worry. We'll
clean you up.'

As I mopped the accident with a wad of tissues, and washed
her legs with hand-soap, and tucked away her pants and tights
into a pocket of my handbag, I thought about the letter.

We had become the Tennants' dirty little secret, we were
the skeleton in their closet. While we skulked around in a
shame-ridden life, away from them, we could be forgotten
about, wheeled out occasionally to salve their consciences. Our
occasional appearance in the village would reassure the gossips
that Robert's widow and child were well, that we were still part of
the respected Tennant family, that their dead son's memory could
never be disgraced. Any unsavoury rumours could be quashed as
an untruth, a fabrication by a scorned ex-boyfriend. In Camilla's

eyes, it didn't matter what the truth was, it was the keeping up of appearances that mattered. She had created fake news, alternative facts. John had washed his hands of us, too. Two days a month as Alice's uncle was all he wanted.

'What about my pants?'

'You can go commando!'

She giggled. 'My bum-bum is cold.'

I grabbed her into my arms and rubbed her bottom. 'It's going to be very draughty indeed.' I laughed and I took her hand and led her back into the restaurant.

'All good?' Jo whispered, once the children were settled at the table, chatting and drawing with crayons.

I mouthed, 'Alice had an accident', and Jo nodded knowingly. She mouthed back, 'Need some pants?'

I shook my head.

I decided that Alice and I didn't need anything from anyone any more.

CHAPTER FIFTY-THREE

John

'Alice and Auntie Francesca are coming today!' Beatrice had jumped onto his bed, her blonde curls bouncing around.

'That's right, Buzzy Bea!'

'And 'member we're staying for a sleepover at Grandma Cam-Cam's?'

'Yes, I remember,' he reassured her. How could he have forgotten?

He pressed the button on his electric bed, wincing as his stiff hip joints screamed at him. Not that he minded the pain so much this morning. The thought of seeing Francesca and Alice at lunch today at Byworth End for the first time since his accident was enough to cure him completely.

'Have you packed your rucksack yet?'

'Yes!'

'Remembered Teddy?'

'Yes!'

'Had breakfast?'

'Shreddies!'

'Good. Is Mummy up?'

He imagined Dilys stretched out in their king-size bed wearing her silk eye-mask. She had commandeered their old bedroom for herself, while he now slept in the cramped, featureless spare room.

There was enough room for his wheelchair to turn, between the single bed and chest of drawers, but that was about it.

Beatrice brought his bed-table over her little legs and reached into the drawer for her colouring book and crayons. 'She's in the gym,' she answered, colouring in a rabbit's ear.

Dilys had converted his writing shed into a small work-out space, with floor-to-ceiling windows, kitted out with physiotherapy equipment specific to his needs and gym equipment for hers. She used it almost more than he did. In spite of the symbolism of the shed's changed purpose, he had to admit, grudgingly, that it had turned out to be a blessing.

Every day, during his two-hour exercise routine with Jenny, his physiotherapist, he stared out across their garden and over the fields, naming trees and spotting birds and noting the little changes that promised spring's approach. The view was therapy in itself. The state of the art sound system helped, too. Jennifer, who had an earring in her nose and pink hair, had the same taste in music to him, or pretended to, at least. They played The Jam a lot. And some Morrissey when he was feeling low, when she would allow him to wallow in self-pity. The threat of depression seemed so close, hovering behind him; if he turned around, he feared he would see a dark mass ready to engulf him. The counsellors in the rehabilitation centre had warned that it might come. *Not yet*, John thought, *not yet.* He had too much to work towards to let depression get in his way.

'I'm going to make breakfast for you, Daddy.'

'Yum. Please may I have a bowl of Shreddies, with lots of sugar? And a glass of orange juice. Get Olivia to help with the pouring.'

'Okay!'

She scampered off.

The self-motivation that he required to get out of bed in the mornings did not come naturally to him. The arduous monotony of his day-to-day routine was about functioning and survival and uncertain recovery. At times, the challenges verged on insurmount-able. Each day was a test of his stamina. Nothing was easy, nothing was taken for granted, nothing came automatically to him. In time, he had been told, the simple tasks would become simple again, but after four months, he was nowhere near to mastering it.

Today, however, was not about survival; it was about love and hope. It was about Francesca and Alice.

Before getting dressed, John used a hand mirror and torch to check his backside and the back of his thighs and calves for bedsores. Bedsores could lead to infections, which could lead to septicaemia, which could lead to death. He had to check for them every day.

Then, he made his bed, which he would do every single morning, religiously. He had learned how to make it with precision and neatness, unheard of before the accident.

His shower was next. It was a military operation. He made sure everything was in its right place before lifting and scooting across from his wheelchair, over the top of the children's bath – the en suite was too small for wheelchair access – to the special stool. The care he took to avoid slipping or scolding himself, or failing to dry himself properly, was a life and death business, and took huge amounts of concentration.

He then wheeled himself back into his room and reached for his clothes in the low chest of drawers, balanced them on his lap and slid back onto the bed to dress. A few weeks ago, Harry – his new sartorial advisor – had bought him a pair of jeans and a crew-neck cashmere sweater in navy blue, and insisted that John let a hairdresser come round to trim his wild hair.

As he pulled his jeans straight, his socks rolled onto the floor, a little out of his reach under the bed. He wanted to yell out with frustration. Instead, he breathed in and out, gritted his teeth and got back into the wheelchair, positioned it carefully, and used his grabber to retrieve them. Back on the bed, he used his special method to lift his wasted legs into his trousers and socks, but he was still slow and clumsy with them. They spasmed and quivered. He tried to ignore it, but it slowed him down.

Finally, after an hour and half he was dressed. He felt like a superhero.

When John had left the rehabilitation hospital, he had been intimidated by the prospect of surviving a day on his own. The world outside had been like the Wild West. During the car journey he had been hit by the colours and noises and speed, and felt angry that he was no longer part of the throng of people he saw walking and running about, living out their normal days, taking for granted their two working legs. At home, for the first time, he noticed how the floors in the Round House were wonky and sloping and littered with obstacles. The rooms had seemed large and cold and hazardous. He had craved to be back in the warm wards and to sleep in his well-equipped hospital room with the knowledgeable nurses at hand.

Dilys screeched with laughter as he came down the ramp into the kitchen.

'You've got your jumper on the wrong way round!'

He braked and looked down. So he did. He flushed. The three children were silent.

'Come here, I'll do it.'

'It's okay, I'm quite capable.'

Humiliated, he wheeled himself out of the kitchen again. He was tired of asking people to help him. The sense of his slowly developing autonomy was vitally important to him, for freedom and dignity, both of which were thwarted frequently. If he fell off the bed or failed to successfully transition from chair to the toilet, Martha, their housekeeper, and his carer, would pick him up with a big, strong grunt and remind him she'd seen it all before. But the humiliation and frustration would leave him in a state of abject misery. He missed Martha at the weekends. He had grown very attached to her. Everything about her was practical and unfussy. John imagined that she had been like a cosy grandmother all her life, with her brown curled bob, and her tucked-in lilac outfits.

'Better?' he said, whizzing into the kitchen and twirling his chair around. It was a trick he had recently learnt.

Harry, Olivia and Beatrice clapped and laughed. 'Very handsome, Daddy!'

'Go and get in the car, you three,' Dilys barked, putting on her second high heel.

John watched her muscular calf flex as she pointed her toe. He felt sick at the sight of it. In fact, John had developed a hatred for Dilys that was so strong he worried it would eat him alive. He hated her with a feverish obsession. Everything she did and everything she said grated on his nerves: the lilting tones of her accent; her fast-paced, efficient manner; her high-pitched laugh; her obsessive neatness; her vanity dressed up as health-consciousness and self-discipline. He could barely look her in the eye. Either she didn't notice or didn't care. Probably the latter. This made him hate her more. She seemed to be enjoying the control that John's disability had given her. No longer did she have to pretend to be anything she wasn't. He imagined she viewed him as her fourth, unwanted child, for whom she was obliged to provide basic care, when it was needed – but not love. This was fine by him.

He was going to get better, and he was going to leave her.

'Let's go,' he said, trying to pull his jacket off the peg in the hallway with his grabber, while balancing the apple crumble that Martha had made for lunch on his lap.

Dilys stood staring at his attempts, and then laughed. 'That thing isn't very efficient.'

John dropped his arm. His muscles were jangling with the effort. 'Could you get it for me?'

'It's not surprising you don't have the energy.'

'My upper body is probably stronger than yours.'

'Not physically. I mean, *mentally*,' she said, emphasising the word 'mentally' as though it was a shameful word.

'I'm fine, really.'

'You don't know what you're like to live with.' She sighed, crossing her arms over her chest. 'Your negativity is *suffocating*.'

He replayed his moods, and felt a stab of guilt. Had he become an emotional burden to the family, as well as a physical one? He needed to get out of these four walls, to see others, to gain perspective, to be with his whole family.

'Could you pass me my coat?'

'You won't need it.'

'It's freezing out there.'

'You won't be going out.'

'What?' He laughed.

'Bless. You actually thought I'd let you see her, didn't you?' She took the apple crumble dish out of his lap.

'I wasn't waiting for your permission.'

She guffawed, looking at his legs. 'No?'

'She's my daughter, Dilys.' John undid his brake and began wheeling himself to the front door. Dilys stopped his movement forward with the point of her shoe.

'I wasn't talking about Alice,' she said, shoving his chair away with her foot.

The chair spun around. Frantically, he wheeled himself towards the door again. Just before he reached the ramp in the doorway, Dilys stepped in front of him and outside, and she slammed the door in his face.

He yanked desperately at the handle to pull it open again, almost coming off his chair. There was a click of her keys in the bottom lock, which double-locked the door. Her footsteps crunched across the gravel. He slammed his fists into the door, shouting, and then wheeled himself through the kitchen to the back door. It was locked, and the key that hung from the hook was gone. She had thought ahead.

His phone.

He raced round to his bedside. It was gone. Surely, this could not be happening. She could not have been that calculating. Then he reminded himself of what she was capable, and why he was in a wheelchair. Of course she could be that calculating.

He had a scream pent up inside him that he wasn't ready to let loose yet, not until he had exhausted all options.

The landline.

He headed to the sitting room, where the receiver usually sat on its station behind the propped open door. It was gone.

Lastly, he checked for his laptop. Also gone.

Then he remembered the children's desktop computer in the den. Surely she would not have packed that away.

When he saw it, he punched the air. She had forgotten this. He could email his parents or FaceTime Harry.

The family password blocked him. He tried many codes, including 'youfuckingbitch2018' but, finally, his repeated attempts disabled the computer entirely.

He had the same problem with Harry's laptop, which had been lying next to the family computer.

John wheeled himself around the house, round and round, in utter disbelief, thinking, thinking of ways he could get out, until his arm muscles were so weak he could barely move them.

He stopped, finally, at the locked sliding windows in the kitchen, his arms flopped in his lap. There was no way to get out or to get help. He was caged. A lame animal.

He looked out to his beautiful garden. The daffodils were bending and shrivelling already. He watched the cottonwool clouds scudding across the blue sky and thought of their journey around the earth, and he thought of how small and irrelevant he was by comparison. The roof of his shed – now the gym – was just visible. He missed his commute down the lawn after the school run; sauntering along, thinking of the next scene of his script, carrying a mug for his coffee and his notebook. Since he had arrived home, the notebook had been stacked under a pile of books on his bedside table. Its journey to and from his shed was no longer part of his routine. Its purpose was redundant. Just as he was. He might as well have been shoved under a pile of books and left there.

He looked at his watch. It was one o'clock. Francesca and Alice would be arriving at Byworth End any minute now. The opportunity to set eyes on Francesca's face and to hold Alice as his daughter was gone. He wondered why Dilys cared that he saw her. Sexually, the doctors confirmed that he was fully functioning, but Francesca would not possibly find him attractive now. The threat of an affair was gone.

Until today, John had underestimated Dilys' jealousy. Was it jealousy? Or was it possessiveness? Or a fear of failure? Divorce would be a failure in Dilys' eyes. Dilys did not do failure. Or perhaps it was her psychotic competitiveness. If he chose another woman, Dilys would be the loser and Francesca the winner. It didn't matter that Dilys didn't love him; it didn't matter that he didn't love her. It didn't matter. None of it mattered except the need to feed her narcissism. He was a pawn that she moved around for her own gain. How he fared in the game was not her concern. When she had driven her car at him, had she wanted him dead? Was his death preferable to the humiliation of divorce? Thoughts of his accident made him feel anxious, and a prickly sweat broke out across his back.

His eyelids were slumping. With his shaky, weak arms, he wheeled himself to his bedroom, where he wanted to sleep, and maybe never wake up. All his gargantuan efforts in physiotherapy, every single day, to gain a small twitch in his little toe or a tiny movement in a thigh muscle, or some sensation on a small patch of his calf, which had been previously numb, seemed pathetic to him now. Dilys – everyone – must be laughing at him. *Poor John, he thinks he can walk again, poor, poor John.* He imagined Robert, up there, all seeing, all knowing, looking at him and telling him he had got what he deserved. And he agreed with him.

Slowly, he passed Beatrice's room, and then Olivia's, and then Harry's door. He stopped abruptly. He had forgotten about Harry's iPad, which had used to be his. It had all of his contact details stored on it.

The doorway into Harry's room was tight for the wheelchair, but he managed it, grazing his knuckles in the process. Thankfully, there were only a few clothes on the floor in a puddle by his chest of drawers. Otherwise, there was a clear path to his desk. The iPad was in his desk drawer, lying in wait for him.

His fingers trembled as he typed in the four-digit code. The home screen flashed open. Triumphantly, he pressed Harry's mobile phone number and waited, feeling nervous, worrying about how he would ask his son for help, deciding it would be best to ask to speak to his parents directly.

When he saw Harry's face on the screen, he wanted to cry.

'Harry! Oh, hi! Thank god. I managed to FaceTime from your iPad! Can you believe it?'

Harry looked surly. 'You can do that from your phone, you know, Dad.'

'Can I talk to Grandma?'

'We're just starting lunch.'

'How are Fran and Alice?'

'They're good. What's up? Are you feeling better?'

'Much better. Hand me over to your grandma.'

'Grandma!' he shouted, walking into a noisier room, where he could hear Alice's voice. His chest expanded.

'Grandma, Dad's calling.'

The device was transferred from Harry to Camilla.

'Why are you FaceTiming, darling? Are you okay? Shout hello to Uncle John, Alice!'

Alice called out, 'Hello, Uncle John!' and John's insides melted. He wanted to see her, but he couldn't see anything except the ceiling.

'Mum, can I talk to you in private?' he asked.

Dilys piped up. 'Do you want me to talk to him?'

'No, no. It's quite all right. I'm quite capable of talking to my own son, thank you, Dilys.'

John wanted to hug his mother, who was now walking Harry's phone into another room. Judging by the beams, it was the sitting room. He heard her grunt as she sat down, and then she positioned the phone facing her string of pearls.

'How are you, darling?' she asked in her 'sweet' voice, usually reserved for the children. Before he had a chance to answer, she said, 'It's okay, Dilys explained. There is no need to worry about today. You can see Francesca and Alice tomorrow.'

Exasperated, he said, 'No, Mum, I'm fine. Really. I wanted to come today. Dilys got the wrong end of the stick and she left without me.'

How could he possibly explain that Dilys had locked him in? She would never believe it.

Her chest heaved. 'Yes. Dilys did say she had to.'

'What do you mean "had to"?'

'She said you were being unreasonable.'

'By wanting to wear a coat?'

'What? Nothing about a coat, darling. She was worried about the car journey.'

'What are you talking about?'

'Well, you know, your accident, darling, she was very worried, you know, with the children in the car, well… I'm sure you would never do such a thing, but…' She sniffed.

'Are you serious? She thinks I'd pull at the steering wheel or something? In some mad attempt to kill us all?' John laughed.

'Well, you've been through so much. We wouldn't blame you if you were depressed.'

'I'm not depressed, Mum! I know everyone would assume I was, but I'm not! I'm perfectly okay!' John shouted.

'Stop shouting. The children will hear.'

He took a deep breath and calmed himself down. 'I'm not depressed,' he repeated quietly. He wanted to add, *I'm not Robert.*

'Dilys says you keep repeating this.'

'Repeating it? I've never had to say it before, not once, and if you were living with me, it would be obvious I'm not depressed. Ask Martha. Ask Harry.'

'Harry wouldn't notice such a thing. And Martha is paid to be polite.'

'Of course he would notice!' John felt desperate. 'Go on, ask him! Ask him how excited I was to come today! Ask him about the haircut he booked for me. Ask him, go on.'

'I'm not going to ask him. Calm down. You don't sound yourself at all. Now I see what Dilys means.'

'Mum. Please. *Please*,' he begged, clenching his jaw, forcing the frustration down. 'Just jump in the car and come and fetch me. And ask Dilys for the front door keys. She locked me in. By mistake, I'm sure,' he added.

'Valentina has just served lunch. We're about to sit down. I'm sorry, John, but I have to think of the children. They've been very disrupted lately and I want this to be a lovely, normal family lunch. They'll still be here tomorrow, so have a good night's sleep and get yourself better for then. I'd better go, darling. You get some sleep.'

The view of her neck moved to the floor, and John could hear the rustle of her trousers as she walked. 'Harry, darling? Harry, how do you turn this blasted thing off?'

John called out, 'Mum! *Mum!* Harry?'

Then the line went dead.

'Mum!' he cried, staring at the blank screen. 'Francesca…' John sobbed.

CHAPTER FIFTY-FOUR

Francesca

'Crumble, Francesca?' Dilys asked, dangling a large spoonful over my head.

'Yes, please.'

Dilys slopped it into my bowl, and a piece of burning-hot apple flicked onto my cheek and flecked my jumper.

'Whoops!' Dilys said, trying to mop me up with my napkin.

Of course, Dilys had got what she wanted and she was lording it over me.

Her smugness did not bother me as much as John's absence.

I had not been able to get over my fury about his no-show. I was devastated that he had not made every effort humanly possible to make it here to see Alice. Perhaps it was heartless to judge him, but I could not quite settle on a good enough excuse for him. John had been the only reason I had agreed that Alice could stay for the weekend, the only reason I had agreed to the monthly visits. For weeks I had craved to see his face, to touch his hand, to hear his story. I had even brushed my hair, and scrubbed my fingernails and worn clean jeans, ridding myself for once of the paint in my hair and on my clothes and skin. I was permanently splattered with 'Dove Grey' since Jo had given me some work painting and decorating four rooms at Sea House.

John had been the reason I had motivated myself to find work. John was the reason I got out of bed in the mornings. John filled my thoughts all day, every day. I reckoned that if he was managing to cope, after everything he had been through, then I certainly could.

My face ached with my smile. I was play-acting my way through the hearty traditions of Byworth End and I hated myself for it. We were sitting around their kitchen table, behaving as though nothing had happened. In a warped way, I should have felt at home. There were shady lies that bound us together, their ties stronger than normality, more effective than functionality. But I wondered how much longer I could sit there with them playing happy families. Tomorrow, after breakfast, I would be able to make my escape, but it seemed like a very long way away.

'This is delicious, Dilys,' Patrick mumbled through a mouthful, having already tucked in.

'How did you make it, *Mum*?' Harry piped up, with a strange aggression in his tone. His teenage nonchalance had disappeared, as if he'd had to grow up overnight since John's accident. He seemed wound up like a spring.

'One of Mum's recipes from the valley,' Dilys sang. 'I can make it with my eyes closed.'

'Wonderful,' Camilla agreed, taking a small bite.

Her enthusiasm for Dilys' cooking was a hint that this horrible lunch was anything other than normal. In the past, I would have expected Camilla to stir it up with a competitive remark. I almost willed it. But the conversation remained upbeat and jolly.

'Mummy! Can I have your phone?' Beatrice yelled across the table.

At this point, Dilys was deeply involved in a property conversation with Patrick and absent-mindedly replied, 'Yes, it's in my bag.'

Beatrice ran to the kitchen island and dragged Dilys' huge red tote bag across the floor. Bits and bobs began to fall out. Two phones slipped out of the side pocket.

'Stop it, chicky-dee,' Valentina huffed. 'It's all coming out.'

Beatrice grabbed one of the phones, huge in her little hands.

'This is Daddy's phone!' she cried, dropping it back into the bag and picking up the other phone. She trotted off to Alice with it.

Both Valentina and I stared down at the phone. No one else had noticed. The phone was switched off but it was definitely John's. I recognised its brown leather cover. By the puzzled look on Valentina's face, I imagined she, too, was thinking the same: what was Dilys doing with John's phone? If he was at home without a mobile, was he safe? He had called Harry earlier via FaceTime, which suggested he was safe, but when I thought back to the tone of his voice when he had asked Camilla to talk to him in private, I began to worry. There was something about that phone being in her bag that was not right.

Valentina was not in a position to ask Dilys. But was I? Even less so than Valentina.

Quietly, I said to Valentina, 'She must have put it in there by mistake, thinking it was hers.' I put it back in the bag.

Valentina offered an upside-down smile. She said hurriedly, under her breath, 'I no see John these days. We put the rolly-ramps, and do the toilet seat, *voce entende?* Si, si, but he never come.' And she bustled off.

When Dilys came up behind me, I jumped and dropped the bag's handles. 'Sorry! Beatrice dropped all your stuff out and we were just putting it back.'

'Beatrice!' Dilys bellowed. 'Come here!'

The whole family fell silent. Beatrice's little face blanched as she looked up at her mother.

'I've *told* you to keep out of my bag.'

'But you said…' Beatrice began.

'Don't answer me back,' Dilys hissed, in a vicious tone, and she sat back down again next to Patrick, who pushed his chair a little away from her. He was sitting up straight, seemingly as perturbed by Dilys' nasty outburst as I had been.

Unnerved, and unable to plaster the smile back onto my face again, I slipped out of the room, my phone in my pocket.

Once I was safely locked away in the downstairs loo, I tapped into FaceTime and tried to call John. The call failed.

I looked around me. The walls were papered in a floral meadow pattern. Hanging in wooden, artfully mismatched frames were dozens of childhood photographs of John and Robert. Grinning, grazed knees, muddy faces. And Camilla on stage, looking tragic in Shakespearean costumes. The pictures seemed to close in on me. The suffocating atmosphere of this house, with its low beams and small windows, smothered any of its beauty and luxury. Robert's and John's childhoods here – with their parents' false bonhomie and rigid traditions and repressed feelings – must have been a nightmare. I could not wait to get out tomorrow; and, in the light of John's absence, I had a strange feeling that I might never come back here again.

When I returned to the kitchen, they were chatting about a plan for tomorrow morning.

'Can we go swimming, Grandma Cam-Cam?' Alice asked.

'The heating has been off all winter and it's still freezing out there.'

'We could put it on now and it'll be warm for tomorrow?' Patrick suggested.

Camilla looked out of the window, and said whimsically, 'We're late heating it this year. The daffodils are on their way out already.'

'Please, Grandma Cam-Cam. It would be such fun,' Olivia said primly.

'If we must. As long as I don't have to get in with you.'

'Daddy can go in with us!' Beatrice cried.

There was a stiff silence in the room. I caught Dilys' eye, and waited for her to explain to her daughter that John would not be able to swim. But her face had frozen solid.

Olivia jumped down from the table, trotted over to her little sister and put her arm around her. Softly, she explained, 'Daddy can't swim any more, Buzzy Bea. But it's okay, I'm big enough to swim with you.'

Tears came to my eyes.

I looked over at Camilla, who was fixated on her two grandchildren. The extra-heavy eyeliner blackened her sagging under-eyes. Her face was ravaged, in spite of her red lips. How much effort she had made to try to hide its cracks, and how little she had got away with. On the surface, yes, she was free, she was functioning, she was upholding the family traditions, maintaining the beautiful family pile, and the family reputation, beyond Byworth End's walls; but I hoped that her inner life was a hellish turmoil, seething with regret and self-hatred.

'Maybe your daddy can be the judge for a diving competition?' I suggested, wanting to bring John into the plans somehow.

'He'll give me ten stars for mine!' Beatrice cried.

'I'll probably come last.' Alice giggled.

'I always win,' Olivia said.

Dilys came to life again, and spoke up. 'Well, let's not get our hopes up about Daddy coming tomorrow.'

'You don't think he'll be better by then?' I asked her, with a sharp twinge of suspicion.

She sucked her teeth and stretched her lips back. 'Well, he was very poorly today.'

'I'm sure he'll be fine,' Camilla barked, clearing some plates away.

'I'll look after him tonight and make sure he gets to bed early,' Dilys said. 'In fact, I should probably get back to him quite soon.'

There was a false note in her show of sympathy. She was trying too hard to play the loving wife. The insincerity slid through every word.

Considering her violent history and my discovery of his phone in her handbag, I decided that I would try to get hold of John that evening, just to make sure that Dilys was looking after him as she should.

CHAPTER FIFTY-FIVE

John

When John woke up, he saw that Dilys had still not returned his wheelchair to his bedside. Without his chair, he had not been able to self-catheterise the night before. He was now lying in his own urine, which he could not feel on his legs, but could feel up his back. Hot shame and fear engulfed him, just as it had when Valentina had caught him as a boy, stuffing the sheet into the washing machine.

Worse now. He was a grown man. Worse still, it was Sunday. Martha would not be there to clean it up and fuss about bedsores and insist she inspect his backside with her professional lack of embarrassment. Instead, he would have to call for Dilys, who would tell him off and humiliate him. He would disgust her.

But he could not delay getting help. It was too dangerous. If his skin broke, it could get infected and he could be back in the hospital.

'Dilys!' he cried. 'Dilys! *Dilys!*'

The thick oak doors must have stopped the sound of his voice from travelling.

He lay there staring at the ceiling, feeling the agonising ache in his stiff joints, exacerbated by his acute stress.

Why isn't there any noise outside the door? he thought. He listened, barely breathing in case he missed a child's chatter or footstep. They might have been instructed to leave him alone, to let him sleep. All three of his children had shown so much attention and sensitivity and nervousness around him, so they would be doing just as Mummy said, and leaving him to rest. He wished Beatrice would return to her naughty self and barge into his room, ignoring Dilys' orders. Before his accident, she would ignore John's orders all the time, much to his frustration. Now, all three of them were as good as gold for Dilys. He didn't like it. It was unnatural. They were scared of her, jumpy around her, waiting for her mood to turn, on a knife-edge. He remembered his mother being similar. Her moods had made homelife stressful. John had always felt like an irritant to his mother. He was too dreamy, too slow, too disorganised, too whiney.

'Harry!' he yelled.

There was absolute silence in the house.

After another ten minutes of calling out, it finally dawned on him that Dilys had purposefully left him there to fester in his own warm piss. Had they gone to Byworth End without him again? Cursing himself for sleeping late, he slammed his fist into the wall and wailed into the chasm of his empty house, until he was hoarse and torpid.

Eventually, John sat up, groaning with the ache. The journey from the bed to the door was about twelve feet. Would he be able to fall out of bed safely? He knew he could bum-shuffle to the door, but he had no idea where Dilys had put his wheelchair and his panic alarm. His upper body wasn't strong enough to carry the dead weight of his legs around too far. But he had to try. He had no choice. If he stayed in this wet bed all day, his skin would rub and rash and break, like a child's skin in a wet nappy.

Having managed to roll off the bed, he shuffled over to the chest. From the floor, he couldn't reach the drawer where his clean trousers had been neatly folded by Martha. He pulled off his pyjama bottoms, knowing he could not risk staying in damp clothes, but he kept on his mostly dry pyjama top for warmth.

As he dragged himself across the rough carpet of his bedroom to the corridor, his nakedness, his wasted legs, the smell of urine on his skin, his ungainly movement, shocked him. He stopped, confronted by the full impact of his own uselessness. He had never known it was possible to feel humiliated while nobody was there to see him. His gut roiled at the thought of this state he found himself in, and he experienced a vivid flashback of the accident.

It was unbelievable that it had come to this; that this had happened to him.

His arm and stomach muscles were violently quivering with cold, with the effort, with the sheer hell of the futile search for his wheelchair. The chair was not in the main bedroom, or in any of the other rooms. He began to imagine that Dilys might have parked it outside. If it was outside, wouldn't the children have seen it? He looked out of the sitting-room window from his position on the floor by the sofa. The glass was sprinkled with rain droplets and he felt a strong draught coming through the floorboards. He could not contemplate the ghastly thought that his wheelchair – his lifeline – was wet, or blown away.

He had to struggle on. His priority was to find it. He had to find the iPad again, to call Harry, although he suspected Dilys might have thought of that already. Somehow, he was going to make it to Byworth End to see Francesca and Alice. *Somehow.* But, when he reached Harry's drawer, it was empty. The iPad was gone.

He pulled himself through to the kitchen, down the rutted ramp, which scraped his skin, and slid onto the stone tiles. He lay back for a second, allowing the warmth of the underfloor heating to soothe his tired limbs. Overwhelmed with fatigue, the idea of engaging his muscles to move again seemed too much. All of his energy seemed to drain from him. He lay his head on the floor and rested, just for a second.

*

He must have fallen asleep or passed out, for he woke to the sound of banging on the window.

A muffled, 'John? John! Oh my god! JOHN!'

He looked up.

The silhouette of a figure in a rainhood and heavy boots was looming at the window.

At first, he was too disorientated to recognise her.

He could see a strand of long, fizzy blonde hair flick from her hood as she placed a phone to her ear. It was Cassie, Francesca's friend, who had been working on Uncle Ralph's house.

'Cassie!' he cried, trying to pull himself up to sitting, forgetting the state he was in. After the effort of earlier, his limbs were too weak to push himself up. He flopped down, suddenly mortified by the indignity of his position, half-naked on his kitchen floor in a piss-stained pyjama top. But he was not in a position to tell her to come back later at a more convenient time. This thought made him smile, or maybe it was the presence of a kind human being that made him smile.

He watched her talk into her phone with urgent hand gestures.

The howling wind and rain blew her hood off.

She banged on the window. He forced out a weak grin and shrugged, to show her he was all right, even though he wasn't. Her anxious grimace turned into a beaming smile.

'Do you have keys?' she yelled.

'Dilys has probably double-locked it,' he returned hoarsely.

'What?'

He shook his head. He didn't have the energy to shout again.

'I'll be back!' she cried. 'Hang on in there!'

After she walked away, he managed to edge his way around to the cooker, on which a line of linen tea-towels hung. He pulled one down and laid it across himself and waited, feeling a mix of relief, wretchedness and excitement.

*

The wait seemed interminable. John's legs were locked in a series of spasms, almost continually.

Finally, he heard footsteps on the paving outside, and a male voice. He wondered if Cassie had called the fire brigade, which would heap a pile of fresh humiliation on top of what he was already braced for.

From where he was, by the cooker, he couldn't see the window. A male voice. 'John?'

'I'm here!' He began to edge round.

'Stay away from the window, okay, mate?'

John backed away again.

A quick, efficient smash of the window came next. Within minutes, a tall, handsome Paul, with all his muscles, was standing above John. A flash of historic jealousy sliced into his heart.

'How did you know?' John looked up at a hovering Cassie. He tugged the tea-towel a little more neatly over his groin, which he noticed had a flower blooming from its middle, sending a wave of heat to his cheeks.

'Tea-towels are so last year, mate.' Paul grinned.

'I see you got dressed up for us,' Cassie added, in her husky Manchester accent.

'Why were you here?' he asked again.

'Fran called from Byworth End. She was worried, and asked me to check on you.'

'Francesca called you?' He was overwhelmed, baffled, elated.

'Come on, let's get you on the chair. Cassie, avert your eyes.' Paul crouched down and put John over his shoulder in a fireman's lift. The tea-towel fell off, exposing John's backside for all the world to see. 'Where's your wheelchair, mate?' Paul grunted, placing him on a chair at the kitchen table and handing him the fallen tea-towel.

'I think Dilys left it outside.'

Paul frowned at him. 'Why?'

'It's a long story,' John replied.

'I'll find it,' Cassie said.

Within minutes, Cassie wheeled his chair down the ramp into the kitchen and placed it by his side. He smiled shyly at her, admiring the mass of blonde hair that took over her tiny features, feeling as though he had shared something with her that morning that made them instant friends.

'Where was it?' John asked, patting his chair, feeling that it was dry.

John remembered a time when he had hated his wheelchair, hated the thought of being in one, but now it was like an old friend. He wanted to kiss and hug it.

'It was just out there, under a cover.'

At least she kept it dry for me, John thought bitterly.

He checked the brake was on and heaved himself along and onto the chair, managing to keep the tea-towel on his middle. 'I'll just go get something on. Help yourselves to a cup of something.'

When he returned, both of them were sitting at the table, cradling mugs, talking in low tones. They stopped talking when they saw him come in.

Cassie leapt up. 'Tea?'

He looked at the wall clock. It was ten-thirty. If they were quick, he would catch them.

'No. Thank you. Could one of you please get me over to Byworth End?'

''Course,' Cassie said.

'I'll stay and fix this up.' Paul nodded at the broken glass. 'Got some gaffer tape and an old cardboard box?'

'In the garage by the cars,' John replied. 'Thanks, Paul. Thanks, both of you. I'm so sorry.'

'You have nothing to be sorry for!' Cassie cried, throwing her arms up.

He had heard Dilys talk about Cassie's work on Ralph's house as 'passable'. Knowing Dilys' disdain for anyone or anything associated with Francesca, it had been high praise indeed, and he could see why Cassie had earned it.

Paul helped John into Cassie's car, folded his wheelchair into the boot, and said goodbye.

As John and Cassie drove, they were silent. John clutched the sides of his seat, feeling as though her 30 mph was 100 mph.

They passed by Letworth's green. A flash of him running, running, running – like the dreams he had regularly – towards Beatrice as the van had approached. He had taken the strength of his legs for granted. Who would run for her like that, now?

They drove past Francesca's old white cottage door, and he envisaged Alice standing in the doorway.

His heart raced when he imagined holding her in his arms. His love for Francesca, and their shared selves, were wrapped up in Alice, like a perfect, surprise gift. He was itching to get to Byworth End. He prayed to anyone who was listening to keep him safe, just until he could see them both again. That was all he wanted.

And, perhaps, he wanted to see the look on Dilys' face when he arrived.

CHAPTER FIFTY-SIX

Francesca

I cradled my phone. Finally, Cassie's text came through:

He's safe. We'll be there in ten minutes. Cassie x

I wanted to yelp with joy, but I held it back, watching Dilys frolic about with the children in the pool, in the drizzle, swamped by Camilla's swimsuit, which was baggy on her boney bottom and padded unnaturally around her chest. Knowing Dilys had a vain streak, I imagined she loathed wearing it, which made me smile to myself. I enjoyed the prospect of seeing her jolly smirk drop from her face when John arrived.

Camilla and Patrick surveyed Dilys and the four children from their sun-loungers, which were pushed back underneath the stripy canopy that Valentina had cranked out from the poolhouse roof.

From where I sat, at the other end of the pool, sheltering under the big tree, I could see them both grinning like fools at Dilys' galling exhibition of good mothering.

I fixated on Harry, who was swimming in a leisurely pace up and down the pool, marking time with each length, and I willed John and Cassie to appear.

Huddled in my coat, my heartbeat was loud in my hood. I clapped conscientiously when Alice belly-flopped, and forced out a laugh when Beatrice performed her comical backwards jumps. Inside, I was full of apprehension: for John, for me. I had wondered if his paralysis would change how I felt about him somehow. It was an uncomfortable thought. I was ashamed of it.

And then I saw Cassie's wild hair, and stern expression, bob up from the slope as she pushed John in his wheelchair.

I caught my breath. In that instant, I knew his disability could not possibly change my feelings for him. That face of his was the same; the one that I had fallen in love with on the film set all those years ago. Albeit pale and a little thin, he was the same John. My heart constricted. His ordeal today must have been humiliating and traumatic. And now he would have to face Dilys.

As I walked the length of the pool towards him, ours eyes locked. We shared an unmistakable moment of mutual pleasure. His beauty sent my pulse racing. It was both thrilling and comforting to see him, if it was possible to experience both at the same time.

Cassie parked him under the window to the poolhouse, away from the rain. Camilla and Patrick shot up off their chairs.

'Darling! You made it! How wonderful!' his mother cried, kissing him on the cheek a little tentatively. Next, his father gave him a half-hearted slap on the shoulder and a limp handshake.

John looked to me. 'Hello you,' he said.

I bent down to kiss him and he wrapped his arms around me, holding on to me for long enough to provoke a sniff from Camilla and a throat-clearing from Patrick.

'Good to see you,' I said, pulling away.

We stood in an awkward semi-circle around him.

Camilla turned her frown towards Cassie. 'What are you doing here, Cassandra? Is Ralph okay?'

'Not sure. I don't work at the house on Sundays.'

'Oh, right, yes, of course.' She sniffed. 'Right, well, maybe you could go and help Valentina to get some hot chocolate on the go for the children?' she said.

Cassie glared at her. 'I'll probably get going home, actually. Now John's okay.'

I offered to walk Cassie to the car, mortified by how Camilla had treated her.

'That woman!' she seethed. 'I'm not her bloody servant!'

'I'm so sorry for dragging you into all this,' I said.

Cassie stopped dead and turned to me. 'Go back. Make sure John's okay.'

'Thanks. For everything.'

'Keep me in the loop. I'm here if you need anything.'

I gave her a big hug, and returned to the pool.

Camilla was clapping and shouting at the children. 'Come on! Time to get out, you lot! You rascals have had quite enough fun for one day.'

I stood next to John. Patrick was on his other side, waffling about the weather.

My heart picked up a fierce beat as I watched Dilys swimming towards us, in slow breaststroke, away from the kids in the shallow end, a fixed smile on her face.

As she climbed out, I stood closer to John.

Like a monster from the deep, she dripped and shivered, slimy and bedraggled.

'Oh, John. How did you—? I'm really not sure it's a good idea you're here,' she said carefully, and quickly wrapped herself in a blue towel.

The younger children spotted John. One by one, they hopped out of the pool and showered him with wet hugs and kisses.

'Go and get your towels, children,' Camilla ordered. 'Off you go, into the house. Valentina's inside. You can have hot chocolate by the Aga.'

They scampered off.

'I was having more fun than they were,' Dilys smarmed, twisting another towel so tightly on her head her eyes slanted.

Camilla flashed her an approving smile. 'You deserve a hot chocolate, too, Dilys.'

A gust of wet wind blew through the five of us, and the raindrops pounded heavily on the striped awning above us, which sagged, while the lilac petals of the bougainvillea drooped.

'Thanks, but I don't think we should stay. Come on, John. I think it's best we get you home again, don't you?'

She moved around to the back of his chair and took the handles. I froze, not sure of what to do.

'Get the hell off my chair,' John said, pressing down on the brake.

Camilla gasped and shot a hand to Patrick's arm.

Dilys raised an eyebrow at Camilla. 'You see what I mean?'

Camilla bunched her chin, and bent down to John. In a sickly voice, she said, 'John, darling, it's best you get home.'

'I think John would like to stay,' I said firmly.

Ignoring me, Dilys undid the brake, and began to turn the chair. John twisted around and grabbed her leg. Dilys screamed and jumped back, as though he had stabbed her with a ten-inch knife. The towel on her head fell to the ground.

'John! That's enough!' Camilla scolded.

Noticing that John was unbalanced, I steadied his upper body and grabbed both handles of his chair, marking my allegiance.

Camilla and Patrick stood melded together as a unit to our left, with their calves pressed back into a sun-lounger, the striped light of the awning shadowing their faces; and there was Dilys, hovering near the end of that same sun-lounger, where the awning didn't stretch. She was drenched and exposed, and the grey light flattened her features.

She gulped back some pretend tears. 'Can you believe he's behaving like this? Day in and day out, it's the same!'

'That's not true,' I said, gripping the handles as though John's life depended on it.

'I don't think you're aware of the full story, Francesca,' Camilla said.

'I am very aware of the full story,' I replied.

'Whatever he's said, Fran, it's a lie,' Dilys whimpered. 'He's deluded. Utterly deluded.'

'Cassie told me that you hid his wheelchair from him overnight,' I said.

'I'm scared of him at night! He comes into my room and starts shouting abuse, and I feel very threatened.'

John threw his head back in laughter.

Dilys cocked her head at him sympathetically. 'You see? He's not himself at all.'

His parents stared at him, no doubt believing that he was not. A speck of doubt floated through my own mind. Nobody would blame him if he showed signs of strain.

'I'm not going home,' John said, pulling himself together suddenly. 'I'd like to stay here for a few days, Mum, if that's okay? Paul can bring my things here.'

Camilla patted his shoulder, and looked at Patrick doubtfully. 'I'll get Valentina to make up the sofa-bed in Dad's study, darling. Will that work?'

'Yes, that would be great,' John said, and he began wheeling himself around.

'It might not be such a bad idea if you had a few days away from the kids,' Dilys said, picking up her towel and stepping under the awning.

John swivelled the chair around. 'The kids will be staying here with me.'

'That's too much for your parents,' Dilys said.

'We'd love to have them,' Camilla said.

'I don't think it is a good idea,' Dilys insisted. 'You don't know his schedule.'

'We'll learn it.'

'But you can't leave him alone with them for one second,' Dilys added, a little desperately.

'We'll watch them,' Camilla said.

'Don't worry.' John laughed again, the same hollow ring to it obvious to all. 'They don't need watching around me, Mum.'

'No, of course not, darling,' she replied, casting an anxious eye at Patrick again.

'I'm afraid they do need watching, Camilla, that's why I have to take them home now,' Dilys said, with a fake apologetic tone.

'If you take them, I'll call the police,' John said.

Dilys snorted. 'They're my kids.'

'Come, now. There's no need for any police,' Patrick interjected.

'There will be, if she takes them.'

Camilla tutted. 'John, really.'

'Dilys locked me in the house for twenty-four hours without my chair, leaving me without a phone or food or drink. You think that is acceptable, do you? You think your grandchildren should be around someone who is capable of that?'

'I think there must have been some kind of misunderstanding,' Camilla said, looking rapidly from Dilys to John, and back to Dilys.

The gooseflesh on Dilys' face had pushed up tiny white hairs across her cheeks, and her head of blonde hair was rag-tailed in ugly clumps, undermining her physical beauty. She was almost unrecognisable.

'Of course, why would you believe me?' John scoffed. 'I'm not myself at all!' Wildly, he shook his hands in the air, looking a little unhinged.

'Don't be like that, John,' Camilla said.

'Camilla,' I said, focusing on the facts. 'Both Paul and Cassie had to break into the house to help John.'

'She left me lying in my own piss!'

Dilys picked up the wet towel at her feet, and stood tall in front of John. 'You're mad. I would never do that to a cripple.'

Patrick stepped in front of Dilys. 'Don't speak to my son like that.'

She backed off. Her lips juddered and turned blue as she stared at us from the edge of the pool.

'So, you're going to gang up on me, now, are you?'

'It's nothing like that, Dilys,' Camilla said.

Dilys moved backwards, until her heels were almost hanging off the flagstone surround to the pool. 'You fucking Tennants,' she hissed.

'Excuse me, young lady?' Camilla spluttered, staring at her aghast.

Dilys began to laugh. 'Once an outsider, always an outsider, right, Fran?'

'Nonsense. We've loved you like our own,' Camilla said, saving me from replying, sounding genuinely hurt.

'Like your own?' Dilys sneered. 'Jesus. Fuck me. Spare me that nightmare, won't you?'

'How dare you? After all we've done for you!' Camilla cried.

'What have you done exactly? Brought me into your fucked-up family and fucked with my head, just as you did with Robert's?'

'Robert's depression was not our fault.'

'Yeah, that's right, you tell yourself that, you tell yourself it had nothing to do with the fact you fucked the next-door neighbour in the poolhouse!' Dilys stabbed a finger at the door behind them.

Camilla gasped and pressed her fingertips over her lips.

Patrick left her side and began pacing, back and forth, in small steps up and down the length of the sun-lounger in front of his wife, brushing his hand over his hair, again and again. And then he stopped, next to her once more, and spoke up calmly, regally almost. 'Camilla had a short-lived affair with Edward Dillhurst, one of our neighbours, many years ago. She told me all about it and we got through it. It has nothing to do with Robert's death.'

'But you know that Robert stood there in his cute little stripy jammies and watched them at it?' Dilys asked, wide-eyed.

'What do you mean, watched?' I cried.

'That's preposterous!' Patrick shouted.

Camilla sat down heavily on the low lounger behind her.

'Robert said he rather enjoyed it, actually.' Dilys laughed cruelly. 'Until now, I'd wondered if he'd said it to shock me but, judging by Camilla's face, I'd say it was true.'

'How do you know about this?' John asked her, under this breath.

'When your brother drank too much, he talked about a lot of things,' Dilys said.

Shut up, I thought. *Shut up, shut up, shut up.*

Camilla wiped the tears that had begun streaming down her face. 'I caught Robert and John snooping around one night. One night only. That's all. He saw nothing. Neither of you saw anything – you swore it, John, you swore that your brother didn't see anything,' she rasped.

'I was eight years old, Mum, and I was scared.'

'You really saw us?' she cried, reeling from him.

'Robert saw much more than I did,' John confessed. 'He came down many times and looked through that window at you both.'

Camilla threw a fist into her belly. Her cry was muffled by the rain beating down above us.

'No,' I said, under my breath. 'No.'

I let go of the chair and turned to the poolhouse behind me. The dark, cobwebbed window sat inert and full of horrors. I remembered the description of this very window in John's film script. His powerful story had been based on a memory. It explained why Robert had hated it so much.

'If Robert knew, he would have said something to me…' Patrick said, his craggy, handsome face suddenly sunken and wizened.

Dilys sat slumped over on the end of the same sun-lounger that Camilla sat on. Large droplets from the edge of the canopy fell onto the curve of her bare back, and ran in rivulets across her shoulders.

'Dad. There's something you don't know. The night Robert tried to talk to Mum about it, he attempted suicide for the first time.'

Patrick stared at John, then Camilla, as though his whole world had caved in. 'Camilla?'

'He used scissors to cut his throat, this way,' she whispered hoarsely, pressing her finger downwards on her throat, pressing it into her clavicle. 'It was a cry for help, more than anything. It wasn't deep enough to scar, even.'

'But he was hysterical, wasn't he? So much so, you had to sedate him with Seroquel,' John added.

Camilla buried her face in her hands and spoke through her fingers. 'He kept asking me to get him more and more. Those first few pills seemed harmless, and they worked, they really seemed to help his anxiety, but then it escalated and I was trapped in it with him. He kept trying to stop, like after that trip to Alaska, but he said it was too hard and he said he needed more pills to feel better. He was insatiable. I didn't know what to do. He said he would kill himself if I didn't get them for him. I had to do it! I had to!' she cried, snapping her head up to stare at us, her eyes wide and reddened.

The truth unplugged a lodged, tight feeling in my chest.

John turned his chair to face me. 'You see, Fran, you've always blamed yourself for his death, but he had tried to die many years before he met you. He never knew about us. You have to stop feeling guilty. You did everything you could.'

Dilys stood up slowly and pointed her hooked forefinger at us. 'You think you two can get away with it as easily as that, do you?'

'Enough!' Camilla cried, throwing her arms into the air, stepping in between Dilys and us. 'Enough!' she cried, and then quietly, she repeated, 'Robert's death was my fault. I was his mother and I failed to protect him. I'm to blame. I'm the only one,' she sobbed, sinking to her knees and burying her face in John's lap. 'And now my other beautiful boy is like this. All of this is my fault.'

John placed a hand on his mother's head and began to cry. 'Mum, you did not do this to me. Dilys did this to me.'

Camilla's head raised itself slowly from John's lap. 'What did you do?' she spluttered at Dilys.

A sound of children's giggling rang out across the lawn behind us. 'Grandma Cam-Cam!' was called over and over again.

Dilys clutched her towel to her chest. 'I'll see to the children.'

Patrick stepped in front of Dilys. 'You will not go anywhere near those children.'

Aghast, Dilys stumbled back and fell against the chair. She then scrambled onto her knees and lunged at John's ankles, 'John, please!'

John wheeled himself back, leaving Dilys in a heap of bare limbs and wet towel on the flagstones.

'Gather your things and get off my property or I will call the police,' Patrick spat down at her, and then to me, 'Francesca, get John inside.'

Her whimpering rang in my ears as I pushed John's chair away as quickly as possible. The wind was raging around us as we made our way over the sodden grass towards the house, towards the two little girls who were running across the lawn, dressed head-to-toe in waterproofs.

'We can't let them see Dilys in that state,' Patrick said, under his breath. He looked behind him, 'Come on, Camilla!'

'We got you hot chocolates!' they cried.

'Poppets! How wonderful,' I exclaimed, pushing on forward. 'Come on, then, back to the house. We're freezing.'

'You've been ages, Mummy,' Alice said, looking up from her hood, as she jogged along beside me.

'Is Mummy coming?' Beatrice asked John.

'She'll be along in a minute,' he answered quickly.

'But her hot chocolate will get cold!' Beatrice wailed, trailing behind us.

Patrick grabbed her hand. 'Don't worry, we'll keep it warm on the Aga.'

Briefly, I looked back. Why was Camilla turning back towards the pool?

The wheelchair rumbled up the ramp to the terrace, and I slipped back a bit with the effort. The children nipped around us and ran inside.

'In we go, folks!' Patrick said, his voice breaking a little at the effort to sound cheerful. He opened the kitchen back door and let us all through it.

The heat inside hit me, sending a wave of nausea through me.

As the children peeled off their wet things, helped by Valentina, Patrick talked into my ear. 'Lock this door. I'm going to check on Camilla.'

I nodded. A frisson of fear electrified my insides.

Olivia and Harry were sitting side by side with their backs to the Aga, sipping from large blue mugs.

'Hi, guys,' Harry said.

'Come and sit next to me, Auntie Fran,' Olivia said.

'Dad, bring your chair near the Aga,' Harry said, always caring for his father.

Valentina handed me and John a mug each.

It slid in my wet hands and I almost dropped it as I crouched down to sit next to Olivia. Alice snuggled up next to us, her hair wet on my sleeve, while Beatrice climbed onto John's lap.

My back was burning with the heat of the stove and the airless room was choking me.

'Where are the others?' Harry asked.

I stared out at the rain lashing the window.

'I think they're going to walk the dogs,' John said, lamely.

'They already walked the dogs,' Valentina piped up, flicking a tea-towel at John.

'I'm sure they'll be back in a minute,' I said.

Harry glanced over at me with a frown.

I shook my head. *Please don't ask*, I was saying, and I looked away, forcing down a sip of the sickly sweet drink. The children's chatter was a background noise. The dogs began barking madly in the distance. It was the bark they used when a car arrived or left the gravel drive.

'Jump down, Bea,' John said, wheeling himself to the window. I joined him.

'That means she's gone,' he whispered.

'I'll go and check.'

Without taking my coat, I ran outside, feeling the rain dampen my clothes, not caring, too eager to follow the noise of Bracken and Holly. It was not coming from the drive. It was coming from the pool.

As I climbed the bank, their barks had become growls, frightening me. I heard Patrick's voice. 'What have you done?' he was moaning.

I rushed to the side of the pool, where Patrick was pulling at the dogs' collars, his face contorted. 'What have you done?' he kept repeating.

Camilla was half submerged, fully clothed, shuddering in the water on the steps that led into the shallow end. Her hair was flattened over her face, her lips slack and purple.

As I moved closer, I could see a dark mass floating in the pool near her.

'Get her out!' I screamed, discarding my shoes and diving in with all my clothes on. Dilys' limp, heavy body dragged me down as I swam to the side. 'Help me, someone!' I implored, gagging on the water.

Patrick let go of the dogs, who jumped into the pool and swam to Camilla, who was unresponsive to their attention.

We heaved Dilys' body out and lay her on the side. Her long limbs were limp and her head flopped to the left. I felt her wrist.

'There's no pulse. Call an ambulance, Patrick,' I said, handing him my phone.

While Patrick answered questions, with incriminating detail, about the scene in front of us, I pushed back Dilys' hair and put my lips to hers and breathed into her cold, sour mouth, before pumping at her chest. One, two, three, and on, as I had been taught to do on a first-aid course on a film once. Thirty compressions, two rescue breaths, and then again, and again, until I retched with the effort.

Camilla remained in the pool, quivering, silent, staring across the water, as the dogs licked and nudged her. Her eyes were as lifeless as Dilys' body in front of me.

She knew. She knew that there was no need for an ambulance. She knew that Dilys was dead.

CHAPTER FIFTY-SEVEN

John

John and the four children were around the table playing Snap.

'Why did Mum want to go with them on a dog walk?' Harry asked.

'SNAP!' Beatrice screamed, giggling her head off, scooping the cards across the table.

'She fancied the fresh air,' John said, trying to ignore the rain attacking the window in nasty gusts.

'Daddy, it's your turn!'

He slapped a card down, checking his watch again, wondering why Francesca was taking so long.

'And Auntie Fran joined them, too?'

'Yes, Harry. Yes. Don't worry. They'll be back soon.'

He imagined there had been some kind of trouble persuading Dilys to leave the grounds. He felt useless in his chair, and so angry that he was useless.

The sounds of the quiet slapping down of cards was interrupted by the high-pitched wail of a siren.

'Dad? What's that? What's going on?' Harry asked.

'Just stay here, okay?'

'I'm coming with you.'

'No!' Then he called out to Valentina.

She raced in, her hands over her ears. 'Wha's wrong? Wha's that noise?'

'Keep the doors locked. Do not let them outside.'

She wrung her apron in her hands. 'Okay. Okay.'

'Dad!' Harry yelled. 'Tell me what's going on! Why won't you let us outside?'

Beatrice, Olivia and Alice gaped at John. He had never seen them so still and quiet and frightened.

John rolled through the house and out of the front door. He stopped on the step. The stones of the gravel driveway prevented him from moving further.

Green and blue and yellow blurred the scene before him. Through the disorientating jumble of colours, he thought he made out a long black body bag being wheeled towards an ambulance.

The bulky, bright forms of the paramedics moved around the menacing shape slowly. There was no hurry to their destination. John could not relate to what he was seeing. Was that body a stranger? Had there been an intruder? Where were his parents? Where was Francesca?

'Francesca!' he yelled into the wind. '*Francesca!*'

His father jogged onto the driveway from around the side of the house. He was soaked through, waxen, his hair in disarray.

'DAD!' John called out, but his father couldn't hear him.

From behind John's chair, he heard the rapid tread of sneakers across the hallway.

Harry charged past him, rocking his chair. 'Harry! STOP!'

Patrick ran towards his grandson, trying to hold him back from the stretcher as the body was raised into the ambulance, but Harry was strong and pushed him away, and then shoved the paramedic, who couldn't gather himself in time to stop Harry unzipping the bag.

A tendril of wet blonde hair fell out.

'*MUM!*' Harry screamed. '*NO!*'

His anguished wail rang out through the air, stopping John's breathing like a garrotte around his throat.

He watched Harry collapse into his grandfather's arms, and then heard the sound of more sirens. A police car pulled up next to the ambulance. Two uniformed officers approached Patrick and Harry, but Harry ran from them. The officers and Patrick let him go, and walked around the side of the house, in the direction of the pool.

John was stunned, rigid, unable to move a muscle or think beyond his shock.

Harry stumbled towards John, his face pulled out of shape, white and pained. 'Daddy!' he cried, falling into John's lap, his back heaving great sobs. 'Mummy drowned!'

John could not yet grasp what had happened. He was lagging behind his son. Automatically, he put his hands out to comfort his son, but he was transfixed by the vividness of the vehicles that shot neon around his brain. Nothing in front of him made sense.

Before he had a chance to work out how to speak, how to move, the two officers appeared again, either side of his mother, who was dripping, convulsing, purpled with cold. One of the police officers was holding her by the arm: to steady her? They opened the back door of their car and seated her inside. Through the window, John could see that she was staring straight ahead.

Harry stopped crying to stare. 'Why are they taking Grandma?'

By the side of the house, Francesca appeared next to his father. They had stopped dead at the edge of the gravel. They held hands, watching on, motionless.

'Francesca! Dad!' John cried out, finding his voice.

They seemed to wake from their reverie, and they walked sombrely towards him and Harry.

Francesca spoke for his father, whose eyes were fixed into nothingness. She told John what had happened in a hoarse whisper, trembling all over, dripping, unhindered by Harry's presence, too caught up in the hellishness to be appropriate or cautious. The story reconfigured in his brain several times, but he could not find a manageable thread to process, to understand.

He watched the ambulance manoeuvre and disappear down the tree-lined driveway. In and out of the silver birch, John was sure he could see Robert as a boy, laughing, dancing around the trunks. He blinked, trying to see more clearly, but by the time he looked again, the vision was gone.

The police car followed the ambulance, respectively carrying his dead wife and guilty mother.

*

Beatrice was screaming in his lap, and John didn't know how to calm her. He wanted to call the doctor, to ask for something to sedate her, and then he realised how ironic that would be. But the noise of her was getting into his head, until he thought he might break down himself. As he withstood his daughter's anger and confusion, the void that Dilys' death left inside him was a dark mass, inexplicable and frightful.

Olivia and Harry sat at one end of the long oak table, looking small and confused, clutching each other's hands. The salted pallor of their faces was a ghastly sight to behold; one that John could never have imagined he would see. While Francesca talked quietly to them, with Alice on her lap, Patrick sat silent and stunned in the corner; disgraced by his wife, terrified for her, aging exponentially before John's eyes.

Valentina was the only person who was together enough to organise them: making pots of tea and feeding them sandwiches and spiced biscuits; leading the police in and out; entertaining the children during the informal police questioning; fielding calls from ambulance-chasing local reporters; prising the wailing Beatrice from John when he was on the phone to doctors and coroners and solicitors and more police; and helping him physically in the way that Martha would at home.

The hours rolled on at Byworth End, in a hazy, muted clump of time, gruelling and fraught. John was busy, engaged with the logistics of Dilys' dead body, and the procedures of his mother's arrest and charge. The children's strange, quiet resilience was punctured only by Beatrice's frequent tantrums, which poked at the tension in the house like a stick at a bomb.

John wanted to stay at Byworth End with his father overnight, to look after him until they knew what was going to happen to his mother.

'Are you going to be okay?' Francesca asked, before she left. 'I can stay. Honestly.'

'No, get Alice home. I'll call you tomorrow.'

'Any time, day or night, about anything, okay?'

She hugged him and he felt heady with her in his arms, and heady with shock.

Once she was gone, he gathered his three children and snuggled them into the television den to watch a film. He chose one of their favourites, *High Society*, for its innocence.

About halfway through the film, Olivia jumped down from the sofa and pressed her nose up to the window.

'Daddy! Look out there!' Olivia cried, grabbing the remote and pressing 'pause' on the film. She pointed outside, into the dusky garden.

Glinting from a clump of bushes, John spotted a large telephoto lens pointing right at his three children on the sofa. The three of them began cackling and jumping about, nervously, outrageously, inappropriately.

Beatrice cried, 'We're going to be famous!'

John drew the curtains and sought out his father, who was lying on the sofa in the sitting room, staring at the ceiling.

'Dad. There's a photographer in the garden taking photos of the kids. And I'm worried there might be more of them outside the gates,' John warned. 'Will you check? Or get Valentina to check?'

His father stirred, sitting slowly, sighing. 'I'll check.'

From the hall window, John watched the lights of his father's Jaguar swing around the drive and off past the silver birch.

His father returned with a grim face, slamming his keys into the bowl on the side-table.

'They're swarming out there. There's even a camera crew and a van. There must be twenty or so of those cretins.'

'I'll call the police. We'll have to keep the kids inside tomorrow.'

It appeared that it was not a secure house for them any more, that it was littered with insidious dangers.

'I'm going to bed,' his father said.

As he watched his father's stooped form retreat upstairs to bed, John reminded himself that they had never been secure and safe here.

He double-locked the big oak door.

His parents had kept their family secrets under lock and key for so long. But his mother's secret had destroyed Robert; and John's affair with Francesca had destroyed Dilys.

Two secrets. Two dead.

To avoid further unrest, further grief, to continue upholding some fragment of the Tennant family unit, John knew that he would have to leave his own secret – the third secret – there, within its secret passageways, behind his panels, to twist and scream with the other ghosts of their past. He wanted out.

There and then – parked alone on the antique black and white tiles, staring at a burst of his mother's blood-red tulips in a vase, eyed by the glassy black beads in the deer-head – John decided that he would take his children as far away from Byworth End as possible.

He wished, with a heavy heart, that he had done it many years before.

CHAPTER FIFTY-EIGHT

Francesca

John closed his laptop when I came in. Beyond his desk, through the bay window and across the road, sparks of sunlight shot off the sea.

'Busy?'

'No. Come in. Sit.'

A wooden-framed armchair, upholstered in blue and white linen, was placed near the large desk at the window. Across the expanse of whitewashed floorboards behind us was a double bed, covered in an array of white mohair cushions and throws. I sat down, and brought my knees up to my chest.

'What do you think of the room?'

He twisted his chair to face me.

'Perfect. I've been writing.' His eyes were bright.

'What are you writing?'

'Dunno really. A load of twisted crap, probably. But it's helping.'

'That's great, John.' I pulled out the notepad that Jo had given me. 'Numbers for a recommended physio.'

'Thanks.' He toyed with it, flicking at the pages. 'I like Jo.'

'There's such a great community down here. A proper arts scene. Painters and songwriters and novelists.'

'It suits you.' He said, looking right into my soul.

'I've been happy. Considering everything. So has Alice.'

'When do I get to see her?'

'I'll bring her round after school.' I picked at a loose thread on the chair. 'We have to tell her at some stage.'

'About me?'

'Yes.'

He scratched his fingers through his hair and inhaled sharply. 'Yes. We must.'

'She was telling me all about Mary at school. She has a new daddy. And, apparently, Mary got to be a bridesmaid at her mummy's wedding to her new daddy. She was horrified that Mary could have two daddies when she only had one. She's obsessed with other people's daddies. She wants one of her own.'

John chuckled. 'No pressure then.' And then his face darkened. 'I haven't told my lot yet, obviously.'

'How are they coping?'

He pushed his phone across the desk. 'As well as can be expected.'

'They've been very brave.'

'Harry is furious we're here.'

'What choice did you have?'

'I wish Dad had come with us.'

'Valentina will protect him from those reporters.'

He turned back to his computer. 'It feels good to hide away for a bit.'

'The interest will die down after her funeral.'

'I hope so.'

'Look. I've got some cutting-in to do upstairs. Call if you need me.'

'I'll be fine. I'm well set up here.'

'Fancy a walk at lunch?'

'A walk?'

'Oh, shut up. You know what I mean.'

He laughed. 'A walk sounds good.'

*

Alice sat on John's knee as he wheeled himself across the road to the seafront. I carried my fold-out beach chair.

Beatrice's head of blonde curls bobbed up above the pebbles and ran at us.

'Alice!' she cried, grabbing Alice's hand.

Alice jumped off John's knees. 'Can we paddle, Mummy?'

The wind whipped off the sea. 'It'll be freezing,' I warned.

'Don't care!' They cried in unison, running off.

I could see Harry and Olivia in the distance, sitting with their backs into the groyne, scowls on their faces.

'They *love* it here.' John laughed.

'Poor things.'

I opened up my chair and put it next to his on the promenade. My feet kicked at the shingle in front of us.

'We'll look after them,' I said, looking across at John.

His hair blew across his face. I reached out and pushed it back from his grey, honest eyes. 'Yes, we will,' he said.

I pulled his hand into my lap and cradled it there, looking out at the crashing waves. They were loud and aggressive and I imagined that Robert might be roiled and caught in each curl, trying to get at us but being unable to. I inhaled and exhaled. *I'm sorry, Robert, my love, I'm so sorry*, I said to him.

Robert had made his choice. And I had made mine.

EPILOGUE

Robert and Sanjeev could hear a bang on the corrugated iron shutter over the shop frontage.

'Who's that?' Sanjeev dropped the gaming remote and handed Robert the fat reefer jammed with chronic. Robert raised his head slightly from the back of the sofa to grab the roll-up and dropped his head back down again to inhale, feeling the dizzying pound of a hangover before he was even sober.

'It might be Fran,' Robert groaned.

'Do I look all right?' Sanjeev asked, standing straight.

Robert inspected his friend. His eyes were bloodshot and his stubble two days old. Robert guffawed. 'Tuck your shirt in, you reprobate.' Sanjeev tucked his buttoned-to-the-neck blue shirt into his black jeans. The gold rings shone from his hands.

He disappeared downstairs. 'Who's there?' Sanjeev shouted gruffly through the door.

Robert heard the locks being cracked open and the crash of the corrugated shutter being pulled up. Then he heard Sanjeev's tread up the stairs again.

'It's your bro. He wants a word. Looks like he's got the major hump.'

They both sniggered like a couple of teenagers.

Robert tried to focus as he walked carefully downstairs, but he stumbled on the final stair.

'Where did you go?' John asked.

His brother's handsome face was earnest and caring, and Robert wanted to punch it.

'Here?'

'We were waiting for you at the flat.'

'Sorry, *bro*,' Robert said, sounding a bit like Sanjeev, a bit like a bitter and sarcastic bastard.

John sighed. 'Fran's pissed off you didn't come back.'

'Is that any of your business?'

'Okay. I tried. See you, Robert.' John began to walk away.

Robert came after him, tugging at his shoulder aggressively.

'Make sure you head to the tube station rather than back to my wife.'

John swivelled around, surprising Robert, whose brain was slow with whisky and drugs.

'What do you mean by that?'

'I see how you look at her.'

'You're drunk,' John said, walking away again.

Robert felt a surge of pent-up rage towards his self-contained, gentle little brother. He knew how John felt about Francesca, and it threatened him. *The smug fuck will never get his hands on her*, Robert thought. Any other man could have her, but not John.

'She's not the angel you think she is, you know. You might be in with a shot,' Robert goaded.

'Jesus! That's rich, coming from you. Look at the state of you.'

'Yeah, but who is she fucking every night. Me or you?'

John's face flashed orange under the streetlight as he stormed towards Robert. Before he could run inside, Robert's feet were off the ground and he was winded as John slammed him into the side of the metal shop front.

'Don't. Talk. About. Her. Like. THAT,' John bellowed, right into his face.

Robert dropped his sneer. Suddenly, he knew.

'It was you, wasn't it?' he slurred, feeling spittle down his chin and tears pressing at his eyes. His drunken aggression flipped into self-pity.

John let him go. 'Me, what?'

'You fucked her, didn't you?'

John looked at him, square in the face. Robert knew when his little brother was about to confess to a bad thing. He knew John better than anyone.

'No.'

'You're lying!' Robert threw his head back and howled into the London streets.

John stood there, seemingly frozen to the spot.

Sanjeev appeared. 'What's going on?'

Triggered by Sanjeev's presence, Robert lunged at John, but he felt Sanjeev's arms around his waist, pulling him back.

John stepped back. 'I'm so sorry,' he said.

And Robert collapsed into Sanjeev's arms and sobbed and wailed.

Through his tears, he watched John walk away and he broke from Sanjeev and ran after John. He wanted to find him and he wanted to kill him. He ran and ran, around the streets, in a rage, in a rage so great he thought his skull would split open.

When he came to Hornsey Bridge, he saw John on the other side. The roar of traffic was below his feet. A lorry raced past his ear.

'Robert!' John cried, jogging towards him.

Robert saw distress in his little brother's face. He loved him, right down deep in his soul. The last thing he wanted to do was hurt him. He would give him what he wanted. He would give him Francesca and Alice. He deserved them more than he did.

The railings were not high enough to stop him.

There was a reason he was here, on this bridge. It was a gift. It offered respite from the agony. His tears blurred his view of John, and the spikes gouged his skin, but he clambered over the barrier and he flew. He flew away from his brother's outstretched hands, and the torment of his betrayal. He flew away from the heartache of losing his baby daughter. He flew away from the love of his life. And he flew away from his addiction. To peace. Finally. For peace.

A LETTER FROM CLARE

Dear Reader,

Thank you so much for reading my book!

The writing of this story – my second published book – has been quite a journey. Strangely, while my characters were pill-popping and being hospitalised, I, too, was in recovery from a badly broken leg, for which I needed to consume truckloads of pharmaceuticals following surgery. I don't know whether this was a bonus, in terms of authenticity, or a downfall, in terms of coherence. But I do hope the book has led you on a similar rollercoaster to the one I experienced following my accident, albeit rather more extreme! If you want to know what I'm going to be writing next, please click on the sign-up link here to stay up to date.

www.bookouture.com/clare-boyd

In this book, I wanted to write about dysfunctional families and the secrets that fester. Like the Tennants, I come from a wonderfully dysfunctional family, with many sad stories to draw from. However, unlike the Tennants, we remain very close, which I attribute to our ability to face up to the past, and to analyse the emotional impact our childhoods had on our behaviour as adults. As my friends will testify, I am a zealot about talking therapy. I believe the sharing of secrets, with the right people, in a safe environment, can profoundly heal, nourish and liberate us from the pain in our hearts. The Tennants, by burying their past, imploded. Robert self-medicated and formed addictions that exacerbated his internal turmoil. If only he had been less frightened of his mental health issues and had found the help he needed.

Many people do not find that help. I was shocked and saddened to learn recently that the biggest killer of men under 45 in the UK is suicide. This fact is deeply unsettling. I imagine that many of these men suffered in silence unnecessarily, as Robert Tennant did in my story.

Lastly, please do write a review for *Three Secrets* if you enjoyed reading it. And please email me, or follow me on Facebook or Twitter or Instagram. See below for details. I am always utterly thrilled to hear from my readers.

Thank you very much for taking the time to read my book.

With very best wishes,
Clare

 @claresboyd

@Clare Boyd

 @ClareBoydClark

ACKNOWLEDGEMENTS

I would like to thank all of those who have helped me in the writing of this book.

As ever, I would like to thank my agent, Broo Doherty, who is a continual support. Although, after reading the first draft, she told me she was scared for my husband!

Huge thanks to my wonderful editor, Jessie Botterill, who works insanely hard, and continues to remind me that my characters need a narrative! And to the amazing Bookouture team, who have somehow managed to find me so many readers.

There are some quiet and kind friends who deserve a huge, loud bear hug of thanks, for their help and expertise. In the medical profession, I would like to thank Nanci and James Doyle, and Paul Shotbolt and Lorna Richards. And thanks to my friend Alice Carey, whose knowledge of the film business never fails to astound me.

Lastly, I want to thank my family and friends, and my father, particularly, whose support and love, and interest in my career, has added greatly to the fun of this writing journey.

CPSIA information can be obtained
at www.ICGtesting.com
Printed in the USA
LVHW02s0108080818
586248LV00015B/1484/P